Penguin Books
Radcliffe

David Storey was born in 1933 and is the
third son of a mine-worker. He was educated
at the Queen Elizabeth Grammar School at
Wakefield and the Slade School of Fine Art.
He has had various jobs ranging from
professional footballer to school-teaching and
showground tent-erecting. He is now both a
novelist and dramatist.

Among his publications are *This Sporting Life*,
which won the Macmillan Fiction Award in
1960 and was also filmed; *Flight into Camden*,
which won the John Llewellyn Rhys
Memorial Prize and also the Somerset
Maugham Award; and *Pasmore*. (All three
have been published in Penguins.) These
were followed by *A Temporary Life*, *Edward*
and *Saville* which won the Booker Prize in
1976. His plays include *In Celebration*, which
has just been filmed, *Home*, *The Contractor*
and *The Changing Room*, all published in
Penguins.

David Storey lives in London. He was married
in 1956 and has four children.

D0488890

Radcliffe

David Storey

Penguin Books

Penguin Books Ltd, Harmondsworth,
Middlesex, England
Penguin Books, 625 Madison Avenue,
New York, New York 10022, U.S.A.
Penguin Books Australia Ltd, Ringwood,
Victoria, Australia
Penguin Books Canada Ltd, 2801 John Street,
Markham, Ontario, Canada L3R 1B4
Penguin Books (N.Z.) Ltd,
182–190 Wairau Road,
Auckland 10, New Zealand

First published by Longmans, Green 1963
Published in Penguin Books 1965
Reprinted 1977, 1979

Copyright © David Storey, 1963
All rights reserved

Made and printed in Great Britain by
Richard Clay (The Chaucer Press) Ltd,
Bungay, Suffolk
Set in Monotype Baskerville

THE SOUL. Seek out reality, leave things that seem.
THE HEART. What, be a singer born and lack a theme?
THE SOUL. Isaiah's coal, what more can man desire?
THE HEART. Struck dumb in the simplicity of fire!
THE SOUL. Look on that fire, salvation walks within.
THE HEART. What theme had Homer but original sin?

W. B. YEATS, Vacillation VII

I

The Headmaster brought the new boy into the classroom several weeks after the term had begun. He stood alone, the centre of the children's curiosity, as the class-teacher, a squat, kindly-faced matron, talked quietly with the Headmaster by the open door. At first he returned the solemn gaze of the children, but as the time passed he began to blush and look urgently away, the stares slowly changing to open expressions of amusement. Eventually several of the children burst out laughing at his plaintive isolation.

He was a small boy, very slight with an intense, Spanish kind of face, narrowly featured and pale, and with eyes of such a dark liquidity that they suggested an almost permanent expression of condolence. It was the kind of bland transparency seen in people of little sophistication or self-assertion, and in certain peripheral conditions of idiocy. He had thick, straight black hair and thick black eyebrows which, in private moments of despair such as this, gave his face the imitative irony of a mask. It was as if he guyed his own emotions. It amused the children intensely.

Eventually the Headmaster gave the teacher a certificate and a letter which had been flapping in his hand, and left the room. The teacher closed the door and came back to her desk. The class watched in silence as the new boy responded to her instructions, walking quickly to her chair and standing stiffly beside it while she ordered them to work. She sat down and, turning to him with a sympathetic smile, began to ask him the relevant questions.

His full name was Leonard Radcliffe, he was nine years and seven months old, and had been transferred from a private school in the centre of town. His father was a caretaker. As she copied down this final piece of information in the Register under the heading 'Father's Occupation' the teacher paused, and glanced at the boy then put down her pen and wrote the word in pencil. The gesture itself, made almost absent-mindedly, caused a

7

fresh suffusion of blood to creep up his face, and after looking hurriedly at the class he stared down at his feet in confusion.

He was given a place at the front, close to the teacher's own desk, until he should become more familiar with his surroundings. But as the weeks passed, his single desk, protruding irregularly from the set pattern behind, tended to confirm that isolation, a nervous shyness and detachment, which the children had instinctively recognized, and been amused by, when he first came into the room. Yet he was an alert boy, with an anxious alacrity, and a condoling, private kind of humour, so that when the teacher was belabouring some child at the back of the class he would twist round, his arm crooked over his chair, and watch with a slight smile of consolation. Frequently, as the teacher came to recognize his unusual if erratic intelligence, he was called upon almost as her accomplice to provide those answers which the children themselves had been unable to suggest.

One day, shortly after his arrival, the teacher had glanced meaningfully at the class then out of the large windows of the room, and pointing her broad, slightly inflamed arm, said, 'Why do you think it is that chimneys, *factory* chimneys, are so tall?' It was a question characteristic in its simplicity of her relationship with the children, as if she sought some way of antagonizing them, or of suggesting the preposterous nature of knowledge itself. She was that not unusual paradox in her profession, a sympathetic yet didactic person at heart.

Radcliffe's hand had risen immediately; but not satisfied with this response she searched round the class for others, prompting them by name and even by drawing a chimney and a factory, roughly, on the blackboard. The question defeated them: there were so many tall chimneys visible at that moment through the classroom windows, their black streamers furled over the ranked houses of the estate. Chimneys *were* tall. Eventually, as if acknowledging her oblique success, she turned to Radcliffe. 'Well, Leonard? Can you tell us?'

'They're tall so that they can carry the dirty smoke well away from the ground.'

8

Someone laughed; it was as if this simplicity confirmed the teacher's own eccentricity. She looked up amusedly.

'Well? Can anyone else think of a better reason?'

She sought a sudden and ironical confederacy in Radcliffe whenever she was opposed by the class, and as if stimulated by their amusement she turned to a large, muscular boy at the back of the room and posed a similarly disarming question: 'Why are roofs pointed and not flat like in the pictures in the Bible?' And when he could give no hope of an answer she moved towards the class, coming to a stop by Radcliffe's desk, and asked the large boy to stand up.

Tall and thickset, with dark, tightly curled hair and a frank, unwittingly surly face, he stood facing the teacher as if the question demanded some physical retaliation. His muscular figure was set in an instinctively aggressive pose. Then his eyes rolled slowly upwards in search of the answer.

Radcliffe, his head close to the teacher's thighs, had twisted round to stare almost grievedly at the boy as though his enforced furtiveness were directly his fault.

'Now, Tolson ... *Victor*,' the teacher said as if his inability served as a further illustration in her didactic pursuit of the class. 'Do you know?'

He nodded, continuing his search of the ceiling while a gradual blush lit his powerful cheekbones. And, as though disregarding his male pride, or out of some innate desire to take advantage of such an exposed muscular confusion, the teacher pressed her inquisition. 'Well, come on, then Victor. Let us all hear.' A deeper look of humiliation gave way to one of helplessness. The boy suddenly stared round guiltily at the class.

'Perhaps there's no reason for Victor to think at all. We already know where he's going to end up, don't we?' She gestured at the factory chimneys outside about which Radcliffe had already been so articulate. 'There are places waiting for him out there already. Well, never mind. Just you stand there a moment, *Vic*, and let me see you paying attention and listening.'

She left him exposed in his quaint destitution and continued her questioning further, but more superficially, round the rest of the class.

'Well, Leonard. Can you tell us?' she said eventually, almost revengefully.

'No.' He shook his head, blushing.

'Are you sure?'

He shook his head again, looking down at his desk.

'Now, you're not going to let me down?'

He looked away in confusion. Then he said hurriedly, almost inaudibly, 'So that the rain can run off.' His look continued across the room until it reached the muscular boy at the back of the class. Their eyes met. The boy's expression was one of such incoherent humiliation, half-blinded with reproach, that Radcliffe swung round to stare fixedly at his desk, his face red and peculiarly tortured.

'Roofs are pointed so that the rain can run off,' the teacher said, wiping her hands free of chalk on her smock.

It was in this way that he became associated in the class's mind with her cynical didacticism. He was, in fact, one of her instruments of instruction. In answering at all he suggested that certain naïvety and defencelessness which only knowledge and intelligence can give. Certainly it was a vulnerability in him which his white, starved face and his narrow features readily confirmed. He was a natural victim of children of this age, and always very much on his own. Occasionally, however, he was reprieved from his bullied situation, by a facility for drawing, a gift from which he appeared to derive unique pleasure and amusement, emotions that scarcely showed on his face so clearly at any other time. During art lessons, whenever the teacher was inattentive or called from the room, a small queue of frustrated and bored children would form at his desk and in a warm daze of service he would draw or outline whatever subject was required. It was only later, when he saw that his gift served no other purpose than expediency, tinged with some curiosity, and in no way brought him closer but encouraged the separation he had learned to dread, that he began to refuse to draw for other people, and would sit at his desk crying and shaking his head at the now malicious attempts to make him perform.

He became the particular victim of one group of boys who throughout each dinner hour encouraged him to carry them in turn around the playground. At first, recognizing no way of avoiding this imposition, he responded to it ambitiously, even conscientiously; bowed deeply forward, he carried each kicking and shouting burden safely round the vast perimeter of the yard. It was the deliberation and care with which he did this – a seriousness the boys interpreted as a perverse willingness – that created the demand to outrage it.

This infliction, interrupted occasionally by puzzled or amused teachers, continued for several weeks until a point was reached when he began to fall on his knees, and no amount of kicking and punching could persuade him to rise. Like any attempt to retaliate, this docility antagonized the boys, and such moments became the focus of their frustrated ambitions. They would gather round him with their curious attacks as if he were some strange creature washed up on a beach.

One particularly cold day, several months after his sudden appearance at the school, when he had lain for some time in white-faced prostration, his huge burden shouting excitedly astride his back, Tolson had come across and lifted the boy off. There was a brief argument and within a minute a fight had started.

Tolson had remarkable strength and agility; an almost adult assurance, and a kind of cool ferocity which, in its degree of control and direction, was as intimidating as his violence itself. He seemed, through his strength, deliberately to prolong the fight. When Radcliffe had dazedly risen to his feet he stood watching with a frozen expression, a clown-like impersonation of grief, which amused the boys not directly concerned with the conflict.

When it was over and, bruised and crying, the boy had gone, Tolson stood some distance away and stared sulkily at Radcliffe. His fists hung down at his sides, the knuckles crested white in his hard, chapped skin, his look at first an uncertain one of contempt; then, almost imperceptibly, growing into that same expression of bitterness and reproach which he had levelled across the classroom. Then, quite suddenly and without any sign, he began to cry.

Whether it was an accumulation of hurt and pain at the

fight, or whether some inarticulate desolation implicit in Tolson, Radcliffe at that moment appeared unable to decide. He stood watching Tolson crying for some time; then, as he began to move towards him, Tolson turned abruptly away and disappeared in the crowded yard.

The fight seemed to disturb Radcliffe far more than the persecution which had preceded it. He was absent from school for several days and when he returned it was with the remains of a slow, coughing illness. His unusual, ascetic face had a blue tinge around its temples. The bullying itself continued, but in less noticeable forms, and he managed to preserve his meagre existence by his own wiry resilience and strength.

He began to pay Tolson a solemn yet distant attention which, through a kind of surly aloofness, was obscurely returned. Relaxed, Tolson was slow and methodical, with an almost premature muscularity: already he looked a little workman. There was something intensely likeable about him, a physical assurance that, when he worked, provoked people into smiling at his sturdy, self-absorbed independence. The leader of a large gang of boys, he monopolized a corner of the playground by an ominous, though sometimes amiable, use of his strength; and with a kind of lethargy, a slowness that exaggerated his physique into an almost parental indulgence, he would watch smilingly over the territory and the friendships that his remarkable strength had secured.

It was only in the summer, when examinations were held to facilitate the division of the classes the following year, that Radcliffe made any direct approach.

It was a hot afternoon, just after the school had been dismissed for the day. Tolson was playing with several boys in the deserted playground. He was always there. Although he had several brothers and sisters at the school, he never seemed to go home, just as his thin clothes never seemed to vary from winter to summer. And after watching for some time until he was sure he had been seen, Radcliffe approached him and asked him if he'd like to go home with him. Tolson at first didn't answer. Suddenly arrested in his game, he frowned and looked away. Radcliffe was peculiarly confident, even adamant, and no longer shy. The demand was like the outcome of a long and familiar friendship.

'Don't you *want* to come?' Radcliffe said. The building where he lived was a frequent subject of the children's speculation.

'I don't know.' Tolson looked at him shrewdly, his first embarrassment giving way to curiosity, as if there were now some advantage to be gained. The boys were playing against the school wall, one line stooped down and the others running to leap on their backs. They were screaming and shouting. Tolson, red-faced and sweating, stood beside this undulating mass. He suddenly shouted at the boys, 'Are you coming?'

'Where to?' One or two stopped playing but were quickly jolted back into the game.

'They won't come,' Tolson said after a while.

'You come, then.'

'Nay, I don't know.'

Radcliffe looked at him darkly. It was like some loyalty he was being pressed into acknowledging; or a weakness.

'Come on, Vic. Come on, stay here.' The boys burst out laughing as the line of crouched figures began to break under the bucking weight of the jockeys. 'Hi-jig-a-jig, who's little pig? Hi-jig-a-jig, hi-cockalorum!' The boys collapsed on their knees, laughing and fighting.

'Come on, then,' Radcliffe said. 'We'll go.' He seemed afflicted by the noise.

Tolson looked at his face as if recognizing something that aroused his resentment as well as his curiosity. He suddenly punched Radcliffe violently on the shoulder, running past him as he cried, 'All right, then . . . I'll come for a bit.'

Radcliffe turned and, suddenly anxious, hurried after him.

The school stood at the foot of a vast escarpment crowded with the houses of a council estate. At the summit of its ridge, and raised over the symmetrical roofs like a huge and irregular extension of rock, was the black outline of the Place. One of a string of manor houses and halls which occurred every few miles in this northern part of the country, some still isolated amongst trees and pasture, others more frequently embedded in belts of factories and houses, it stood now like the detritus of a forgotten geologica cycle. The estate, its twenty thousand inhabitants a small facet of forty unbroken miles of industry absorbing over three million people, had been built on the original park and farmland of the Place itself, and had in fact taken its name – Beaumont. Once the home of a prosperous family of cloth merchants and bankers whose business had gradually been displaced by the mammoth engineering and mining interests of the area, it had survived the first twenty years of the century as a farm, its main rooms and entrances shuttered, and a small section at the rear, along with its outbuildings, converted into living and working accommodation. The war confirmed the industrial domination of this landscape, and in 1921 the last of the farmland was sold.

During the following decade the red houses of the estate crept slowly up the broad escarpment, absorbing first the stone cottages of a heathland village, then several towering oak trees and a wide avenue of elms, and finally surrounding the Place and its attendant church within a denuded perimeter of shrubbery and trees. The building had been retained by the original family under a trusteeship, and while the housing estate expanded and forced its way over the remaining green park and pasture, a caretaker was installed in the converted rooms at the rear to safeguard the structure from the curiosity of the growing army outside.

Speculation about the building's purchase, its imminent demolition, or its long-term conversion, was dispelled when the old caretaker, under whose erratic supervision the Place had been gradually despoiled, was removed and a younger person introduced who began an immediate renovation and repair. All the more obvious signs of damage disappeared and no longer were the cavernous rooms and passages accessible to any casual intruder.

It was in a solemn and speculative manner that Radcliffe now followed Tolson up the various crescents and avenues of the estate, the bigger boy rushing ahead as if it were his invitation that had inspired the visit. Then, as the chimneys of the Place came into view over the lower roofs of the houses, he began to lose his impetuosity and was soon walking quite slowly, glancing behind him occasionally with an almost disowning expression. As they passed a class-mate walking home on the opposite side of the road, Tolson suddenly called out to him and ran across. For a while they talked together confidingly, Tolson laying his arm on the boy's shoulder and resting his weight against him.

Radcliffe, walking parallel, watched them. Then seeing that the boy was to accompany them, he continued up the road alone. Tolson, his arm securely round his new companion, was content to walk some distance behind, deliberately slow. The two boys talked to one another quietly, then laughed. A moment later they began to kick stones, swinging from the single axis of their interlocked arms. Some distance down the road behind them an elderly bearded man was leading a large black dog.

When they reached the twin black columns of the gateway they stopped indecisively and stood watching while Radcliffe pushed between the metal gates. Then Tolson followed. He pressed back the gates, stooping with his back to them. But they were secured immovably, and only slightly apart, in the guttered debris from the drive, and after a moment's frustrated activity he and his companion followed Radcliffe up the heavily shadowed track.

In the treetops on either side rooks fluttered like rags, then sprang up, swaying, as the boys' feet crunched on the firmer part of the drive. As the path suddenly turned to one side, Radcliffe glanced back and, apparently reassured by the look on Tolson's face, hurried forward more expectantly. They came out into the sunshine on a gravel terrace at the front of the building.

Tolson's face turned upwards. He was sweating more heavily: perspiration streamed down his face, his eyes screwed against it and the strong light. His body had taken on a characteristically aggressive stance, his legs set firmly apart, his fists partly raised. Then his head sank back into his thick shoulders and turning slowly he gazed up at the full breadth of the crumbled façade.

A familiar look of perplexity crossed his face, and suddenly flushing he glanced behind him reassuringly at the brick houses of the estate where he lived. Then he glanced at Radcliffe.

Radcliffe was staring at him with an aloof, impassioned scrutiny, as if he'd simply brought him here to see his reaction. The other boy was forgotten. It was in that moment that Tolson's look changed. It was immediately replaced by one of threat, an instant violence and force as if he'd been secretly abused. Radcliffe, with a sudden expression of alarm, glanced away.

At the same moment the bolts shot back on the front entrance, a key turned, and the two heavy doors swung in slightly before one was pulled fully open. Radcliffe's father came out, a tall, slender man who stood frowning, his hand to his forehead, staring out into the strong light.

'Hello, Leonard. Have you brought your friends to look at the place?' He came down the steps from the deep portico, his narrow, almost military face amusedly alight. He was in rolled shirt-sleeves as if he'd just interrupted some work.

'Hello, Vic,' he said as they were introduced. 'Leonard's told me a lot about you.' He stooped slightly and held out his hand, which Tolson looked at confusedly and didn't take. 'Would you like to see around the inside of the monster?'

'No. It's all right,' Tolson said with a thick accent. He backed stubbornly away, looking up at the bruised rock of the façade. Then, blushing deeply, he picked up a stone and threw it amongst the trees. Its crashes echoed against the branches.

The other boy stood some distance away, watching. After a while Radcliffe's father went in, vanishing like a magician into his cave, the bolts and locks slamming back into place. Radcliffe watched him go. Then he turned to the drive. Tolson and the other boy had disappeared.

He hurried down the rutted track and soon saw Tolson plunging ahead, kicking at loose stones with short, powerful swings of either leg, tearing off twigs and flowers, and jumping over the low, stooped branches that encroached and almost blocked the drive. He was a small black animal leaping in the dark shadows, his arm intermittently flung up to send large stones crashing through the trees.

The other boy waited in the road. He seemed in some way embarrassed. When Tolson reached the gate, he climbed onto it and dragged it to and fro within its brief arc of suspension; as Radcliffe came up he started swaying the gate on its rusted hinges, letting the weight of his body fall from it to be retrieved by his extended arms. Then he tugged at the eroded metal with a sudden burst of laughter. Radcliffe stood watching in silence, white and exhausted by Tolson's energy.

'I'll see you tomorrow, then,' he said.

'Aye. When'll it be?'

Radcliffe stated a time, raising his hand as if precisely to indicate its significance. 'At the end of the avenue.'

Tolson dropped off the gate as though amused by the gesture itself, its minuteness. He squeezed through the narrow opening. 'All right.' He stood back a moment, watching Radcliffe through the lattice of the ironwork.

Suddenly he laughed. 'All right.' He put his arm round the other boy's shoulder, glanced at Radcliffe a moment longer then, pulling the boy slightly, ran off down the road. For a second Radcliffe could see through the bars their locked figures, running. Then they disappeared beyond the high wall.

He turned back up the drive. The boys' feet echoed under the heavy branches. 'Radcliffe! . . . Radcliffe! . . . *Radcliffe*!' His name was called several times. The rooks rose in the air, antagonized, cawing, and drifted restlessly over the heavy eaves of the house. The name crashed through the trees like a stone. When he went round the back of the Place and into the kitchen his father looked up expectantly. But Leonard had nothing to say.

2

At the age of thirty John Radcliffe had decided that his distaste for the society in which he lived was so complete that
he could no longer reconcile himself to being a member of
it. Since he observed himself to be in a minority in this
respect and since he could not be sure that this was not
merely a temperamental discontent, he saw that the most
sensible thing to do, rather than to attempt to change such
a society, was to withdraw from it altogether.

Although unmarried he was by the standards of the
world he despised a successful and resourceful man. After the
severest hardship he had emerged from the First World War
with a commissioned rank and, beginning a career in the
lowliest clerical post of a firm of textile manufacturers, had
attained after seven years a managerial position. He was
fair-minded, scrupulously conscientious, extremely hard-
working and in a situation at the age of thirty from which
professionally he could expand in almost any direction he
chose. He was also a religious man.

This was something that had matured during the war
when, in solitude, a superstitious fear of God had grown into
a profound though naïve and strangely undemonstrative
faith. He was not primarily a man who explored his own
motives or who watched very closely what was going on
in his own mind. Essentially a person who worked from an
unquestioning faith in his instincts, he liked to deal with
people and events rather than ideas; and his belief, though
obscurely confessed, was laid out in simple Christian
principles of charity, equality and good intentions. For a
time he was a Socialist.

The decision to give up his job came as a surprise, both
to himself as well as to his few friends. He experienced a
monstrous sense of helplessness that something inside him
could have acted so conclusively. It was this helplessness
that he had tried unsuccessfully to communicate to his
puzzled associates. 'I don't know what it is,' he told his

closest friend. 'I feel I need an Absolute in life, there's nowhere I can find it. Except in the decis\. That's absolute.'

For some reason, unlike his political acquaintan\. tended to see society and the human condition as sep\. things.

'But haven't you heard of that equally quaint dialectic,' his friend said, 'that the desire for an Absolute is the symptom of someone who can't tolerate relative, purely human values?'

'Whatever society we create men will consistently abuse it. To struggle after such a transitory goal only makes me despair. And it is despair. I can do nothing about it.' He watched his friend very carefully, not sure that he was not being ridiculed. 'If nothing else, politics are no longer the way for intelligent men to govern their affairs.'

Yet in the end he decided it was something deep in his nature which he could not explain. One thing was certain: the decision itself. It gave him hope.

Two events coincided with this moment of his life: he suddenly married, and the trustees of the Beaumont estate circulated amongst the members of the family their concern at the rapid deterioration of the Place. To what extent these quite independent affairs influenced his decision he had no clear idea. By that instinctive process which seemed to have taken complete possession of his life, he married a woman slightly older than himself and whom he scarcely knew. She worked as a supervisor in one of the mills with which he had dealings, and ostensibly they had nothing in common except their single state and a practical experience of the manufacture of wool. Yet, almost complacently, he felt the same reassurance about his marriage as he did about the decision to abandon his career.

On a not dissimilar impulse he had written to the trustees of the estate offering his services as a resident caretaker, and after some further correspondence he had been granted the position. Beaumont had until then played no part in his life whatsoever. He had been there only once when, sometime after its conversion to a farm, his father had taken the entire family to see the place of his birth. John's father had been one of three sons who had all spent their earliest years at the Place and who, long before its conversion, had left to live in considerably reduced circumstances and subsequently to enter the wool trade, with which the family had strong historical connexions. The two brothers of John's father had died childless but he himself had produced a family of ten children, one of whom had died very early of diphtheria and three of whom were killed almost within the same month in the First World War. He was, as John remembered him, a modest yet passionate man, reticent about his background of a decayed landed family, an amateur painter and antiquarian, and for a short period a J.P. Despite the number of his children, he had married late in life and had died at what appeared to be the height of his powers. Each one of his surviving children had gone quite separate ways, finding what livelihoods they could, and with only two had John maintained any sort of connexion: with Austen, the next surviving eldest, and with the 'baby', Isabel.

It was only on the morning that he and Stella travelled to Beaumont by train that the full strangeness of this venture occurred to him for the first time. He still retained his childhood memory of the Place seen through a long avenue of elms, a late autumn sunlight reflected in its numerous windows, something dark and even frightening against a pale and luminous sky. There had been a vast moorland crowded with sheep and, beyond, a park across which were scattered great trees. The Place had seemed like an animal crouched at the summit of the hill. Scarcely that: something he could not describe. There was the black stonework, the smell of damp stone, and the walls that had seemed so tall that they must fall down. And somewhere, whether a statue or a carved relief, a large and fragmentary stone figure. It was as if he had sensed his father's own disappointment with such a deserted monument, as if there were something obscene in its desolation. As he sat in the train and tried to recollect this impression, he realized that in all his thinking about the Place the building itself had never developed for him beyond an abstraction: one which fitted exactly, however, into some central vortex of his mind.

He recalled the moment of his life when, after four years in the war and the death of his three elder brothers, he had met his mother again for the first time. On a heavy, clouded morning he had hurried towards her familiar figure where it waited in the shadows of a station only to discover a face he scarcely recognized. It was as if the skin had been torn away to leave a bare and lifeless armature of bone; something to remind him derisively of what he had once known and loved. He had never forgiven her her suffering, that vulnerability which deprived him of consolation and of pride. He had wished then that he had died with his brothers. In a peculiar way, he had never forgiven himself for his survival.

Yet, rather than the Place itself, it was the houses so closely surrounding it that sent a preliminary pulse through his body, like the confirmation of an indistinct yet grotesque premonition. As the taxi slowly climbed the crescents of the estate, passing over what he still vaguely recognized as undulating moorland, a remote sense of desolation stirred in him. At the summit of the first rise he had seen, stretching across what had once been the tree-strewn park, an endless vista of houses crushed so closely together in this steepening perspective that their walls appeared to merge into one another, overlapping, compressed so intensely that nowhere was the ground itself visible. Here and there above the matted roofs rose the broken heads of a few remnant trees. It had a bewildering and ominous familiarity.

Only as the taxi moved over the last rise and the Place came into view did this sense of recognition merge into the transparent image of something he had witnessed before. It had been at the beginning of the war when, arriving at the Front, the truck he was travelling in had breasted a steep rise and for the first time he saw below him the trampled plain of a battlefield. It had been a bright morning after a night of heavy rain, there was no one else in sight. Numerous crescents of earth flowed into one another, interlocked; craters erupted within craters, the swollen volutes of clay frozen in restlessness. This turgid convolution of blackened earth was interspersed with the white fragments of trees, giant splinters that traced the percussive ghosts of in-numerable explosions. A thin wreath of smoke rose in the centre, straight and unwavering in the still air. Beyond, on the opposite ridge, the rock had burst through this ruptured skin and lay like a dark bone glistening in the sun. Everything was moist and translucent. Now, as they approached the Place, he saw this bony structure protruding from the bricky confusion of the houses.

Beaumont had been a large building. At one time three wings had extended from its rear, its northern side; but with the renovation of this section to suit first the functions of a farm then of a caretaker, they had been removed. The Place was now rather like a body deprived of its limbs, the scars of amputation still visible but shielded by thick and extensive vegetation. There was an air of concealment about its mutilated frame, a giant hiding in a forest with his head still projecting aggressively above the trees. It had long since lost any architectural significance it might have once possessed; it was a simple if enigmatic protrusion from the houses of the estate, an incongruous secretion of rock, forced up, the volcanic apex to the restless escarpment.

It was the black cliff of the main, southern façade that first confronted them. Here the long rows of shuttered windows were relieved by a massive pediment set asymmetrically from the centre and running to the ground in four heavy pilasters. To the left of the pediment the flank was extended by an older building, the uniformity interrupted by a large oriel window which grew like a blister on the fabric of the house. It was surrounded at irregular intervals by several heavily eroded mullion windows. Here a balustrade replaced the cornice of the principal part of the house. The entire stonework was blackened, flaking yellow in parts, as if it had been subjected to long and immense heat. It seemed burned, like some strangely resistant ash.

Afterwards John quickly forgot the nervous desolation of the first weeks. What remained fixedly within his memory was the remarkable way in which his wife had adapted herself to the bare rooms, to the cold, to the smell of damp and decay. The agent, spending the first day showing them over the building, scarcely concealed beneath his gloomy assessment of its condition his profounder distrust of their presence. Their rooms were at the rear where a wing of dilapidated farm buildings projected from the main body of the Place, enclosing a muddy, deeply-rutted yard flanked on its only exposed side by a row of trees. Several of the ground and first floor windows which overlooked this area had been painted, and a door of incongruously recent design stood at the kitchen entrance. It was through this that, as they arrived, their furniture was about to be carried. In the upper stories, and further along the façade, innumerable broken windows exaggerated the context of decay.

Their rooms comprised a large kitchen on the ground floor, lit by three square windows and adjoined by a much smaller room which the previous occupant had used for storage. Miscellaneous tools and cleaning equipment and several large and irregular sections of panelling lay on the floor. From the kitchen, which had apparently served the full requirements of the Place during its occupation, rose a narrow winding staircase leading to the first floor. Here a tall sash window at the side of the building illuminated a broad landing from which opened out eight rooms, four overlooking the yard and four, securely fastened, over-looking the front. The landing terminated in a wooden partition that occupied the whole width from floor to ceiling. In the centre was a door secured by a multitude of locks and bolts. This led into the main body of the building beyond.

Gradually John had set about the work of restoration, employing builders to repair the broken sections of the high wall surrounding the denuded grounds, and a watch-man to discourage the intrusion of children. Eventually he secured all the possible entrances to the building itself, repairing the windows and protecting them with new, white-painted shutters. He threw himself into the work unthinkingly, thankful that the sense of desolation could be alleviated by physical activity. Then, when the last of the builders and the last joiners had gone, and when a kind of security had been achieved, he began to look inwards on his predicament.

His sense of disenchantment, aroused initially by the question, 'What am I working for: why isn't there a unity between what I feel and what I do?' tended to be stimulated by things which he didn't really believe. His emotions were aroused very easily by generalities: by the Church, by newspapers, by politics and crowds, so that whenever he was confronted by any aspect of these he could never prevent an almost hysterical desire to escape from springing up inside him. He began to see himself as a synthesis of negative assertions, too fair-minded to be partisan, too sensitive to be political, too intelligent to subject the variety of life to a dogma. Yet from none of these sentiments could he extract any sense of reassurance. Newspapers were puerile, the Church was impotent, politics were corrupt, people were bestial: but how could any of these things matter? The greatest enemy was oneself.

It was into this void that the Place had seemed to fit. It was as if the building itself represented a complete abdication; and to the extent that he struggled now to preserve and secure it from outside interference. During this period, now almost a year since his arrival, he had begun to see an increasing amount of his brother.

Austen lived just across the valley in town. Unmarried, the manager of a furniture shop which divided its wares tactfully between antiquarian and contemporary extremes, he was a man of some fashion and taste, a virginal dandy with a parochial wit. From Austen he received a kind of help which, though nothing practical, consisted of something more than advice and criticism: an almost mordant, self-amused complicity.

'Are you content with all this?' Austen had asked him one day as he watched his brother working on the floor of one of the larger rooms.

'No.'

'But you do justify it.'

'I suppose so. But perhaps I won't stay here long. In another year I might well go back to industry.'

'I don't think so.'

'Oh?' John stood up, laying the hammer down and going to the window of the room. It overlooked the vast sweep of the estate. 'And why not?'

'Well, for one thing . . .' Austen began to smile as though, in this instance, he were concerned more with his own feelings than those of John. 'You're such a Cromwell. Well, no. Perhaps that is ambitious. But do you know what I mean? Giants of self-restraint and melancholy strength.'

'Is that how you see me? Some sort of majestic puritan.'

'I think so.' Austen looked round at the empty room with a vaguely arrogant expression, yet still furtively amused.

'Perhaps it might mean something in one sense,' John said after a while. 'I mean, at the back of my mind there's always lurking this ambition for some sort of complete action. One that exists simultaneously in both worlds. Someone who acts politically and religiously in the same event.'

'And where does one collect such a convenient double harness?'

'Nowhere. The world's grown empty of such men. And such opportunities.' He suddenly looked up at Austen in surprise. 'Why! Are you looking for some such militancy in me?'

'No. But there have been evangelists before, despairing of their vision. Singers without a song.' And when John did not answer he added, 'Cromwell, however, could *act*. He was the complete puritan. The one whose guilt matched his ambitions.'

John suddenly returned to his work, retrieving his hammer and stooping down as though unsure now whether he was being provoked or merely ridiculed.

At about this time Leonard was born.

At first John had thought that he had married Stella to appease, if only in his own mind, that class by whom he felt opposed but for whom he had a strong and even passionate sympathy. As an officer, and later as a manager, he had looked upon the difference between himself and the men he controlled as a class difference. Yet he felt instinctively apart from them, isolated. Only gradually did it occur to him that this difference was more one of temperament than of social instinct.

During the war he had been responsible for a grotesque accident. One night a large group of women and children and several old men had stumbled into an ambush he had carefully prepared, and they had immediately come under heavy and prolonged fire. The following morning, when the slaughter was revealed, he had been alarmed not so much by the spectacle itself as by the nature of his own feelings. There seemed to be no sense of shock at all, but rather a profound irritation at his men's dejection and bitterness. That they could view such a terrible event as an accident enraged him. If in his own mind he discovered in it the dignity of a judgement, they themselves saw it simply as a confirmation of their own destitution, the meaninglessness not only of war but of life itself. He hated their despair; he loathed their suffering. They graced nothing with divine intention. He pitied them. In the end, from this pity grew his affection for them.

At first, then, he thought that he had been drawn to Stella through a similar sympathy, as though to be reprieved from the loneliness of his own faith by one of 'them'. But as they worked together in the Place he discovered that what he had first taken to be her 'working-classness' – her narrow-mindedness, even snobbishness, the way she saw people condemned by their behaviour – was in fact her religious judgement of people. She was as much at home in the austere atmosphere of this manor house as he was himself – even more so: her asceticism was expressed more directly in physical things, in work, in cleanliness, in the management of their day to day affairs. He found some peace in this revelation. Then, when Leonard was born, he was filled with dismay as though, through having a son, he realized that none of this could be true.

He was thrown into confusion. Was all this, then, an elaborate charade? For a reason he couldn't understand, he felt that Leonard was less the outcome than the purpose of his retreat.

'What do you mean when you describe people . . . me, for example, as a puritan?' he had asked Austen.

'It's really the description of a kind of temperament, a *basic* temperament,' Austen stressed, watching his brother very carefully. 'I mean that kind which is always concerned with a particular sort of guilt.'

'Guilt? What guilt?'

'To have to stoop to something so physical in order to propagate oneself in God's likeness, or any likeness at all, is the one indignity a puritan can scarcely tolerate. That they are *physically* vulnerable – that's what puritans hate. Their self-effacement, their stoicism come from that, a contempt of the physical. No!' he insisted as John tried to interrupt. 'They despise their bodies. Their temporality.'

'Where then does your promiscuity come from?' John said angrily since his brother, a confirmed bachelor, had a reputation as a seducer. 'How can you cut yourself off so completely from me?'

'The only difference between us is that you submit to it whereas I choose to deride it,' Austen said slowly. 'My promiscuity, as you call it, is still a pathetic thing. Its little nucleus, its energy still springs from the same guilt. To that extent I might just as well be celibate as deny it. Or like you. Coming here not because the world smells, but because your own flesh stinks. To propagate. To propagate yourself in private. Poor Leonard. He's your confession.'

Although John never believed this – there was after all, he thought, not only a mischievous superficiality in Austen's dandyism but an unrecognized envy and resentment – it did affect his attitude towards his son. In fact, now having a child, he felt very much like returning to his old job and to a more normal way of life. But something held him back. It might have been Leonard himself. He was a tiny child and, despite his mother's robust health, his birth had been a complicated and tedious affair. For a year his life was in doubt. It was like someone resenting an intrusion: there seemed to be a resistance to life in that slight, straggly and perpetually flushed body, a tenacity almost greater than the will to breathe. For days he would vomit his food, crying whenever he was touched as though refusing to accept any sustenance or reassurance.

Yet, from within this prolonged and endless agitation, his eyes peered out with a curious, almost calm expression. In their large, withdrawn darknesses John often thought he had identified some incoherent and inexplicable reproach, and occasionally almost something that could be a sense of condolence. It was as though something separate, profounder and more intimidating was contained within that nervous and resentful body. Then, when Leonard was about a year old – as though it were the final exasperated residue of this struggle – he was afflicted by slight convulsions. Almost like fits of anger and frustration – a deep flushing of his face and trembling of his limbs – they gradually became more violent, making him gasp breathlessly and provoking swollen rashes on his skin. John and Stella became more desperate. It was at this point that the three of them underwent a disturbing experience.

John had just become used to the enigmatic sounds of the building, the distant, anonymous movements in the empty rooms, the perpetual creaking of the woodwork, and often at night he lay awake listening to the throbbing of steam engines in the tunnel that ran beneath the escarpment. He had gone out one morning, soon after their arrival at Beaumont, and walked over the estate to where the escarpment terminated in a sudden cliff face. It dropped down from a row of back gardens in a series of huge orange and black wedges of rock. It was here that the stone for the Place had been quarried. At its foot a broad railway track curved into the cliff, the tunnel-mouth almost a natural feature of that stony face, the rails like slender strands of nerve. The soft pounding of the engines at night had a heart-like beat which, as he listened, united stone and rock within a single, recurring pulse.

One night they were awakened by a huge and reverberating crash. It was as if a blow had been struck massively against the outside wall of the house, yet muffled, like a stone buried in cloth. It shook the entire structure. For a moment neither of them knew what to do. They listened to the sound of the flaked plaster falling around them. Then the building was struck again, a heavy, booming vibration. It was as if a part of the house had collapsed. The baby cried out from its cot at the foot of the bed. As John sprang up a third and more violent crash shook the room and they heard somewhere the thud of falling masonry. Leaving Stella to soothe the child, John took a lamp, unlocked the partition and went into the Place. The air was cold from a heavy frost and there was a smell slightly more pungent and more stifling than that of dust. Yet apart from a broken frieze of plaster, there was no further sign of damage. He returned to their room to find Leonard in the throes of a violent fit. It was only several hours later, after John had hurried out to fetch a doctor, that his tiny body was finally calmed.

The following morning the agent provided an explanation of the occurrence. A series of minor faults ran through the escarpment and had been disturbed by the construction of the railway tunnel and later by the mining in the area. They had a common focus in the strata immediately beneath the Place. Whenever a shift of rock occurred, the building absorbed the sound and gave it a peculiar resonance within its own eccentric structure. Although John was somewhat reassured by this explanation, he nevertheless soon found that he was relating the event portentously to Leonard's birth. He despised such a mystical interpretation, yet knew that Stella also saw in it a superstitious significance which she would never admit to him. The need in him to interpret this as an omen, however, gradually disappeared, to be replaced by the recognition that he still retained a desire that Leonard should *be* portentous. He even began to look on his son with an almost evangelical zeal, as though in his tiny body and withdrawn eyes he might discover a significance and a meaning which had so far eluded him.

Leonard's fits never re-occurred. He developed a calm and rather passive nature. The consoling expression of the eyes remained, a kind of simplicity, as did the slightness of physique, but they never again appeared to be in opposition to one another. It was as if he had accepted the intrusion of life and given it reluctant accommodation.

3

The decision that Leonard should go to a council school had been his father's. The original decision taken four years earlier, that he should have a private education, had been his uncle's.

Austen appeared to Leonard as a man both of importance and distinction. From him he learned the circumstances of his situation, for even at that age he was made aware that his family as well as he himself were somehow different from other people. During the four years that he attended the private school Austen dominated his life. Afterwards he realized that the location of the school in the street next to where his uncle managed his furniture shop had been as important a factor in the choice of his education as the more ostensible one so frequently put forward: namely, that Leonard's was an exceptional temperament and should be treated in an appropriate way. He perceived that Austen had a great influence upon his father.

Those four years were the happiest he could recollect. His clearest memories of this school were of those moments when he came out of the stuccoed Georgian entrance and saw his uncle waiting there, leaning on his cane, his face and smile as reassuring as the light itself which, in retrospect, always had a peculiar radiance and warmth. It was in this role of a man of fashion that Leonard knew his uncle best, rather than in his later guise of a dandy, when his tolerance and sympathy had given way to a strained, epigrammatic indulgence.

Austen's shop was in one of the central thoroughfares of the town. Later, Leonard discovered how genuinely perceptive were his uncle's tastes: at the time it was simply furniture that he never saw used – except in his Aunt Isabel's house. He learned to look upon the individual pieces with that sense of affinity which he felt afterwards other children of his age discovered through their friends. His relationships with children were practically nonexistent; it was for the simple, sculptured shapes in his uncle's shop that he felt the closest sympathy: with those and with his uncle himself.

In a corner of the shop, which ran back deeply from its narrow street frontage, were several mounds of carpets. Frequently, when he saw his uncle engaged with his assistants or a customer, he would crawl across these soft piles, exploring their alarming colours and swirling shapes with his body; or, waiting impatiently until his uncle peeled back the next layer, he would run his hand through the short, tufted texture, peering intently at the incoherent designs as if in them he discovered a significance which had eluded him in the chaos outside. These expanses of colour, the chairs and tables of such rigid and precise construction, possessed a reality, even a friendliness which later he thought he might have found in people. But outside, the street, the passing crowds, the bruised and sooted surface of the buildings were of a hardness which not only confused him but which he knew quite simply to be *wrong*. The rhythmical colours and the devised structures, all unused, were the good things: outside everything was grey, and used, and even painful.

Although he soon realized that his Uncle Austen and his Aunt Isabel weren't husband and wife but brother and sister, the one unmarried and the other disastrously married and separated from her husband, he still tended to see them as one person. That is, as one unit. He scarcely saw people as people, but more simply and certainly as states of feeling and association, so that his sense of a piece of distinctively designed furniture and his sense of a particular person weren't to that extent separable. The thing which for him animated human beings also animated colours and shapes.

His aunt was a beautiful woman in much the same way as his uncle was distinguished looking, and her house, a tall, rambling Georgian one in a large square, held the same significance and reassurance for him as the shop: it was furnished with similar objects. Here, stimulated by his aunt's ferocious bursts of emotion, and by her numerous adult visitors and friends, he found an added confirmation of his eccentric perception of things. He was 'that extraordinary and unique little boy', and his adult admirers provided a court to his absorbed contemplation of the world. He was treated as a 'prince'. It was for this reason that he loved to see his aunt and his uncle at the Place, to see them in the building itself, for they brought out not only a sense of assurance in him but an admission of humour in his father, an emotion which, apart from these occasions, he scarcely saw. The cold and desperate building was somehow restored by their arguments and laughter.

Only with his mother did his feeling of unease merge into hostility. Partly in this he reflected Austen's own unspoken antipathy. Within his protected world Leonard acquired a precocious instinct for atmosphere and feeling, more than for the objects which later, in isolation, came to represent them. When at last he could distinguish between feelings and objects, that is, when he no longer invested his own life with whatever things appealed to him, he recognized the dislike he had of his mother. Superficially, he was physically docile and acquiescent; mentally he was quick and alert. He could never commit any of his feelings to action. With his mother, however, these characteristics were reversed. In her presence he became physically active, almost militantly decisive, yet slow in understanding. Strangely, his mother seemed to welcome this reversal as though within it she recognized the unmistakable evidence of his affection for her. She treated him kindly, yet strictly; the only real moments of wildness came on very rare, frustrated occasions, from his milder and more tolerant father.

His mother was broad-set, with light brown, fluffy hair and a round phlegmatic face. Physically she gave the impression of being much stronger than his father, and Leonard sensed from the beginning that this dominance in some solemn and perhaps benevolent way extended into their emotional relationship as well. His father was deeply yet never overtly dependent upon his mother. It was, however, her appearance that divided Leonard's life. Her oval, coarsely serious face, her greyish, bland eyes, separated her so distinctly from the dark, intenser look that united his father, Austen and Isabel and himself in such a remarkable similarity of expression, that he looked on her as an intruder into their private family world. In some important and inexplicable way, when he first saw Tolson he immediately confused him with his mother. It might have explained why, later, whenever he had been distressed by Tolson it was to his mother that he suddenly ran, clasping his arms round her thighs in a blind sense of submission which afterwards he always intensely regretted.

Yet on one occasion, much later, with Austen when he had been particularly articulate about this division of his world, his uncle had answered facetiously, 'Yes, your father married a peasant and he can never bring himself to believe we've forgiven him.' Although he didn't then understand the simple allusion, it seemed to touch in him much deeper implications, and so decisively that the innocent course of his relationship with Austen was immediately changed. For no reason at all he began to sense a restlessness in Austen which transformed his entire view of his character.

These, however, were intuitions about an incoherent yet relatively peaceful world. It was his father, as if in despair both of such an enclosed environment, as well as of Leonard's delicate physical health, who suddenly flung open the door and let in the robust thunder of the council school and of Tolson himself.

Almost at the same time Leonard's sister Elizabeth was born, her Radcliffe features unmistakably stamped in the delicacy of her face.

For Leonard, however, there were certain strange impressions that continued to grow and even to become persistent. At times, in his dreams, he would see the dark landscape around the Place stripped of its buildings and streets; and across it, like projections of the rock itself, strode giants – black and massive creatures who, as they approached the Place, would rear up and by some monstrous articulation of their limbs leap high into the air. Here, against the bulwark of clouds, they would fling themselves in contortions that shuddered the land, a reverberation that echoed in the sky itself; claps of thunder and prickled sheets of lightning that for a moment would thrust across the sweeping hills and valley, across the rock buttresses, crowns and pillars; a glare that made the stone itself glow, an illumination beaming from the earth itself.

And occasionally, as though he too were poised on some upper pinnacle of the Place, he would see dimly across the valley, standing on the jagged summit of the ridge opposite, the tallest and most massive giant of all, a tower rearing to the sky with a head set like a sun against the cloud, radiant and luminous and almost young. Dark wedges of hair sprouted like forests around its planetary skull.

Once he saw this figure stooping a moment as though to take a burden, then springing up, hands and arms outstretched like immense peninsulas of the earth to tear its passage through the clouds and disappear amongst cascading figures and stars. More usually, however, it stood aloof and still, gazing sometimes into the sky and at other times, it seemed, directly at him. Sometimes he would try and hide, crouch down, or hurry through the corridors of the Place itself, only to gaze up and see above him the poised face peering ferociously down.

At times it seemed that he recognized a look of despair on this giant face when it would stand like a frozen tower on the valley's edge, peering out through the misty apertures about its head, and so still that if it moved it seemed as though the earth itself would crack. At other times he would see its arms stretched out towards him, thick arcs of flesh and bone flung like bridges across the valley, the fingers each like trunks never quite reaching him. He would back away and stand trembling, his body burning at the notion of its touch.

Often on moonlit nights he flew over the dark land, saw below like a luminous thread the river coiled between its pennine ridges; and heard, as each city of white towers passed below, its name whispered in the air, and the names too of giants and kings he had never known before. The names, repeated and confirmed, grew into the private mythology of his dreams, neither confided to nor shared with anyone.

Yet these had only been dreams. It was, in fact, through Tolson that he discovered a day-time context for his existence, and for the Place; that is, it was through Tolson's sudden and violent intrusion that he learned to identify feelings with people, although he still tended to invest with feelings certain inanimate objects which instinctively he sensed should possess them: certain trees and stones, the Place itself, certain remarkable undulations of the land. If much later he took a delight, and even found a particular refuge, in abstracting his relationship with Tolson, at the time itself, as Tolson became a frequent visitor to the Place, their friendship was expressed in a vigorous physical delight and in Tolson's sudden outbursts of curiosity about the building and his family. He even began to forget at times about his dreams.

Occasionally, like a dark shadow on this brightening cloud of interest and achievement – since Tolson was the first direct human contact Leonard had made in his life – he would notice on Tolson's face as they emerged from some game, or inspection of the large and dusty rooms, a blunt, cautious reflectiveness, the look of someone scouting an enemy camp before an attack. It had the same disturbing effect as those other, equally infrequent moments when, explaining some historical aspect of the Place, Leonard would catch a glimpse of a vaguely familiar reproach: that same reproach which drew up Tolson's figure in an instinctive gesture of aggression and pride. Leonard always felt that in some way the Place existed to the detriment of Tolson.

Nevertheless their relationship became the vehicle of his first excursion into that new and intimidating world outside. And as if to secure his position there, his curiosity about the building and the family was aroused to a pitch which only once, much later, was ever repeated. It was Austen rather than his father, Isabel rather than his mother, who provided the answers to his innumerable questions. His parents appeared to know little, and attach even less importance to the history of the Place. He passed on his information directly to Tolson as if to inflame him with the wonder implicit in this ancient house and, more indirectly yet importantly, in their friendship.

It was a promontory into his expanding world. He began

to visit Tolson's home, crowded with the muscular intentness of his numerous brothers and sisters, a pleasure as significant now as his previous visits to Austen's shop and Isabel's house. Leonard's sombre and reflective face, his shy, startled humour, amused those impetuous half-adults of Tolson's family, and they produced in him a spontaneity and directness which he had never experienced before.

Tolson had no father; he had been killed within the first few months of the Second World War – at about the time, Leonard afterwards decided, when he had first seen Tolson fight. Now Tolson presided over these visits to his house with a moody seriousness. He never joined in his brothers' rough play with Leonard but stood watching it with a slow, jealous regard as though it were something he controlled with a precise power. Leonard recognized a certain strangeness in this as in the fact that, although invited, Tolson never brought his brothers and sisters to the Place. Yet it was something which he dismissed as easily as his mother's resentment of Tolson. At this time she was giving all her attention to her daughter, Elizabeth, and it was his father who encouraged his friendship with Tolson as if it were the one thing he looked for in his son's life. He had said to Leonard after meeting Tolson for the second time, 'Victor's very unsure of himself. Do you know what I mean? Let him know he can *trust* you.' It had appealed intensely to a sense of loyalty deep in Leonard's nature. His friendship was like a service he willingly and even passionately performed.

This apparent closeness and amicability lasted for two years. During that time Leonard was frequently reminded not only of Tolson's remarkable physical strength – often he lay helpless beneath that giant body in some apparently friendly yet vaguely purposeful game – but also of a kind of frustration, a scarcely suppressed antagonism which resulted in sudden and irrational bursts of violence. These bouts grew to be a familiar part of Tolson's behaviour, so that Leonard would watch with a shy smile whenever his friend relentlessly and mercilessly pursued a moth or butterfly, swatting it cleanly out of the air and beating it vigorously until it was an indistinguishable part of the leaves and debris on the ground. On other occasions he would suddenly throw stones up at the Place, narrowly missing the windows with an uncanny and malicious skill. Leonard never completely rid himself of this sense of a huge and pernicious energy hanging above his head: it came from the feeling in him that he was unworthily privileged to know such a complete person as Tolson. He increased his efforts to consolidate their friendship.

It became Austen's habit, now that Leonard's visits to the shop were comparatively rare, to visit the Place each week, and, whenever he could, to use the opportunity to show Leonard and Tolson some feature of the building that he imagined might interest them. More, however, he seemed interested in the relationship between the two boys themselves, to the extent that after a while Leonard began to recognize these apparent lectures as intrusions on his own informative role: rather than supplementing they began to detract from his means of maintaining Tolson's interest. Whereas Tolson was frequently amused by Austen, by his appearance and manner rather than the content of what he said, Leonard began to look upon his uncle with increasing irritation. Austen revealed something absurd in his situation which Tolson only too quickly appreciated.

One hot day in summer Austen called the boys in through the open front doors of the Place and led them into the 'Braganza Room'. This was the largest room on the ground floor, to the left of the main hall, and took its name from a florid and spectacular ceiling. Its central motif was an Indian corn plant, its cob partially shelled to reveal the grain, and symbolizing, according to Austen, the acquisition of India by Charles II as the dowry of Catherine of Braganza. It was Austen's favourite room and, as Leonard already knew, he spent a great deal of his time there alone either admiring its features or, more frequently, gazing abstractedly out of its windows. At the end opposite the door was the 'Jezebel Mantelpiece', a large slab of Caen stone carved in a Flemish style of the sixteenth century and set in an elaborate mantel of columns and decorative friezes.

Tolson was bored; he stood fidgeting, glancing up at the

swirling relief of the ceiling, then out at the bright sunshine at the front of the house. At the same time as Leonard was aware of this, his irritated attention was drawn to Austen's description of the stone as if in some way it represented the exact nature of his uncle's personality. The meticulous shapes and incisions, the smoothed protrusions of the stone seemed to fit his 'sense' of Austen to a remarkable degree.

At the foot of the narrow tower, the summit of which was surmounted by a decorative pinnacle, lay Jezebel herself. Around her prostrate body were gathered several dogs and snakes, their legs and bodies delicately interlaced, and a toad and a lion, apparently intending to devour her. It was only as Austen described these extraordinary animals that Tolson actually looked at the carving. Jehu, in a Roman helmet, sat astride a magnificent horse surrounded by a group of heavily moustached soldiers, thick matchlocks on their shoulders: they all stared down impassively at the broken figure of the woman. It was at her that Tolson finally looked too, blushing. Then quite suddenly he laughed. She was naked.

Leonard felt stifled by the incident. As they came out of the room he suddenly experienced a moment of complete terror. It was as if Austen's meticulous description of these carved figures and Tolson's final snigger were outcomes of the same event: one that had just taken place and from which he had been strangely excluded. In some way they had formed an alliance that derided him. This disturbing sense of conspiracy accompanied him as he followed them to the first floor.

Tolson watched Austen now with the friendly expectancy he might have afforded a clown. He walked alertly beside him as they mounted the broad central staircase, glancing back to grin mischievously at Leonard, then finally running ahead into the York Room.

This was the largest and most important room in the house. Its five tall windows, rising from floor to ceiling, overlooked the huge sweep of the estate as it fell, first gradually then with increasing abruptness into the valley. The crenellated silhouette of the city faced it on the opposite ridge. The room's high, sculptured ceiling had disintegrated in several places and fragments had recently been removed: it was a surging and senseless mass of broken figures and plaster volutes that hung over the airless space.

At one end was a mantelpiece similar to that in the Braganza Room below but cruder and larger, occupying almost the entire width of the room. Over the fireplace itself, and set between pairs of thick columns, was a carved and apparently incomplete figure, half-crouched, with the equally incomplete outline of a massive architectural structure beyond, of columns mounting like rocks to a thick, overhanging entablature above. That had been how Austen had described it; but to Leonard, who had often wondered about such a monstrous piece of stone, the incompleteness of the carving had never occurred to him. Still slow and in fact reluctant to recognize objects in the disassociated way peculiar to Austen and most adults, he saw the incoherence of the carving as part of the violence of the figure itself.

Tolson stood gazing at its jagged texture for some time, obviously unable to recognize any shape at all. Then, as Austen's slim hand traced out the contour of the bowed figure, Tolson's mouth dropped open in a grimace of recognition and almost at the same moment he turned round and went to the opposite end of the room. There he skulked in silence until Austen, looking up from his absorption in the panel, saw Leonard's glowering expression and Tolson's apparent indifference. Perhaps sensing at last that there might have been an intrusion on his part, he made some sort of excuse and a few moments later left the room.

Hearing a movement behind him Leonard turned to see a remarkable sight. Already half way across the floor and running at full speed was Tolson, his face lit in an excited and triumphant expression. It was a private look of exultation. A burst of terror seized him in the moment before Tolson struck him and sent him crashing into the fireplace. Before he could struggle up Tolson leapt upon him and, sitting astride his chest, caught his head between his hands and forced open his mouth.

Immediately above his head Leonard could see a bright

circular disc. It seemed a long time later before he recognized it as the inside of the chimney silhouetted against the sky. Numerous shelves and crevices were outlined along its interior. Still in his ears was the crashing of Tolson's running feet, while Tolson's fingers were like a clamp around his jaw. The impression he had of Tolson's face was vaguely that of someone surprised and even embarrassed by his own violence. The next moment Tolson suddenly laughed down at him and said through clenched teeth, as though mocking his peculiar action, 'I could kill you now if I wanted.' It was an almost childish assertion yet expressed with an adult, physical conviction. Tolson had in fact become completely unrecognizable to Leonard; it was as if the stone relief itself or some impersonal weight had fallen on him. The most bewildering moment of all, however, was when, after Tolson had suddenly, almost shyly released him and he had struggled to his feet, he saw standing in the doorway Austen himself, watching the incident in silence. As Leonard recognized him he turned away and vanished.

By the time Leonard had come to his senses Tolson had run out of the room and disappeared. The building was completely silent. Leonard was left standing in front of the fireplace with the impression of the chimney's cavernous interior still in his mind and yet as if nothing had actually occurred. When he went back down the broad staircase and out of the still open door, he found Tolson waiting for him in the sunshine, kicking his feet in the gravel and looking about him with a bored and disinterested expression.

They walked down the curving roads of the estate, to Tolson's house, in silence. Then, as they neared his home, Tolson suddenly fell. He blundered slightly against Leonard and deliberately collapsed onto his hands and knees. Almost as a reconciliatory gesture he lowered himself onto his stomach.

'You tripped me!' he said in a startling, babyish voice which Leonard had never heard before; and looking up with an embarrassed anger. 'You tripped me up!'

Leonard shook his head, surprised and denying. He was shocked, overwhelmed by the accusation.

'You tripped me,' Tolson said. He had burst into tears and now lay crying on the ground in an attitude of complete despair, his face buried in his arms, his hands protecting his head.

He lay there for some time completely forgetful of Leonard, it seemed, and crying heartfully. But as an elderly man came along the road leading a dog he hurriedly stood up. Leonard saw with a renewed sense of alarm that there was in fact a large bruise on Tolson's forehead. It was from beneath this self-inflicted wound that Tolson looked at him, passionately and full of reproach.

After the old man had passed them, trailing the large black dog, and nodding at Tolson in some vague, absent-minded gesture of commiseration or perhaps abuse, he said, 'You *did* trip me, didn't you?' His tears streaked his face like a ferocious mask.

'No.'

'You *did* trip me.' Tolson looked at him aggrievedly. Then suddenly he seized his arm. 'You did trip me. Didn't you?'

Leonard wilted, appalled at his wilful desperation.

'You tripped me, then?' Tolson insisted.

'Yes.'

Tolson stood gripping his arm and nodding, peering into Leonard's face. Then as tears slowly came back into his eyes and his body began to be shaken by heavy, violent sobs, he released him uncertainly; when Leonard reached the scullery door at the back of the house, he found Tolson showing his wound to his mother and describing to her how it had been caused. When, later, his brothers started to play on the lawn, Tolson joined in for the first time, yet playing with a deliberate restraint as if determined that his excessive strength should not be asserted. His mother, a small, silent and tenacious woman, stood at one side of the lawn watching him intently. The sun lit up her face in a fixed, obsessive frown.

Moments like these, violent and inexplicable, and burned into Leonard's memory, were nevertheless embedded in long periods of amicability and genuine, conciliatory friendship. Times when to rush from the restrained atmosphere of the Place to that of Tolson's small and crowded home became a regular and compulsive feature of his life. Even his mother succumbed to Tolson's heavy, self-amused charm, as when he would laugh at his own clumsiness or, leaning over the pram where Leonard's sister lay sleeping, he would stare intently at her calm face with a monstrous look, then turn towards them smiling unself-consciously, half-confused. He frequently watched the baby with shy consternation as if in its peculiar stillness and the delicacy of its features he traced the antithesis of his own impetuous life.

Certainly Leonard, seeing the effect that his sister had on Tolson, felt that here his powerful friend was truly admonished. It was these moments of confusion that Leonard longed to see, when he felt that everything in Tolson was accessible to him and the frenzied rivalry forgotten. It was moments such as these that Tolson himself came to recognize and promote, a sort of innocence to which he surrendered helplessly whenever he recognized the look of delight on his audience's face. As if cautiously excited by the humour he could arouse, he struggled to promote it: there was deep in Tolson the ferocious anxiety of the professional clown.

4

After almost three years at the council school, when their friendship had reached its most intriguing stage, Leonard gained a scholarship to the grammar school. It happened almost without his knowing it so that he felt in some way that he'd been deceived. When his name was read out in the short list of successful candidates and he suddenly realized that he was to be uprooted again, he felt himself the victim of a conspiracy. Partly out of anger and partly out of his own sense of deception he avoided Tolson throughout the morning of the announcement, and at dinner-time he stayed in the lavatories until the playground was deserted. Only then did he venture out to take the news home. He was half way across the asphalt arena when he heard someone running quickly and lightly behind him and, before he could turn, he was knocked to the ground by an indescribable strength. The next thing he knew he was lying on his back looking up at his class-teacher's face. She was the only person in sight. He was taken home in her car and he never discovered whether she had seen what had happened or not.

Afterwards it seemed strange to him that he had never objected; that he never in fact refused to accept the scholarship. It was as if he acceded to events in this way because they came from some vague source of authority he knew had to be obeyed. It was this, rather than the assault itself, which finally determined him that he would never see Tolson again. And as if to test out the strength of his determination, once he had recovered from the attack he went to Tolson's house for the last time. Getting no answer to his knocking he realized that the entire family were somehow involved in his betrayal. Several weeks later, when he arrived at the grammar school, he felt a great sense of relief, as if in some way he'd been released.

Yet, strangely, the grammar school broke him in two. Without the compensation and protection of Tolson he found himself even more isolated than in his first year at the elementary school. The physical health and assurance which he'd acquired were rapidly displaced by that white-faced recluseness which he had considered to be a forgotten part of his life. Now he became the victim of a persecution more subtle and intense than that of mere physical assault, and since he never tried to appease his new tormentors it seemed to them that he secretly invited it. It was as if he recognized within himself the working of a virtually implacable pessimism, for he neither opposed these assaults nor felt the least inclination to deplore his situation. His despair, however acute, never drove him to action, and he began to suspect – and with the slowest yet profoundest shock of his life – that what in fact so hugely dominated his existence, to the extent that he could scarcely recognize it, was an inscrutable sense of guilt.

This suspicion, prompted quite suddenly by a conversation with Austen, came at the moment when he realized he had survived the more vigorous attacks on his nature. During the six years he spent at the grammar school he re-discovered the anomaly of his intelligence and his continued facility for drawing. There was an abnormality about his gifts. That this wretched figure should possess an intelligence and a talent which people of a healthier and more sociable disposition had to do without, bred a sort of incoherent resentment which even the masters themselves did not trouble to hide. The opposition to Leonard was complete, and varied only in subtlety and direction according to his detractor's age. It was as if, both by his indifference to his gifts and to the animosity they aroused, he were commenting not so much on his own deficiencies as on those of the people around him. The instinct to disown everything within him which he felt to be unusual made him an ideal target for persecution.

It was because of this that he turned to drawing, as if to detach himself from something he could not understand. All he was aware of was a morbid self-preoccupation, something to which he was helplessly bound, and yet which he despised. Closeting himself in some distant room of the Place, he would spend hours gazing at fragments of paper, the minute size of which seemed an indication of his resentment. At times he found his pencil moving ferociously over a fragment no larger than a stamp: yet it seemed in this way that the absurdity of his situation was expressed to his own satisfaction. The tiny rectangles answered a solemn and anonymous reproach, and the minute figures and landscapes tempered his unease. He derived an obscure satisfaction from the drawings; he threw none of them away, but pinned them to the wall of his room much as a grocer might affix bills due to him at some indeterminate time in the future. Austen vociferously approved of them; his father was sceptical. His mother hated them.

Certain childhood illnesses began to re-occur. These were brief fits, similar to fits of anger in naturally volatile people: a sudden flushing of his face, a slight protrusion of his eyes and a trembling of his limbs. But the emotion which

44

normally might have accompanied such symptoms was completely absent in him.

None of these disturbances ever amounted to the full, rampaging disorder of a fit; there was even a certain calmness and restraint about them which, as they recurred, persuaded his father that they might be wilfully induced. It was his father who, strangely, was the more disturbed by them. These moments of rageless anger, however, distracted his mother from her absorbed attention in her daughter, and she turned now to Leonard with anxious, maternal indulgence, stroking his arms and legs and his face with a kind of solemn tenderness which soon allayed the more distressing symptoms.

If these illnesses never seriously alarmed his parents – they seemed, after all, almost natural expressions of his sensitive nature – what did disturb them was his growing self-absorption. Although his mother hated his drawings, as though they were almost evidence of demoniac possession, his father never displayed anything more than an irritable suspicion; what antagonized him so fiercely was Leonard's self-preoccupation and the recluseness that produced them. Whenever he was on one of his constant journeys of repair around the Place and found Leonard drawing in some distant room, his anger would break out violently. As at school, Leonard's reaction to these outbursts was only a slight tensing of his figure and a sudden flushing of his cheeks. No one could tolerate such abject humility.

Gradually he took to being absent from school. After a while it seemed he had never been there. All the evidence of his six years' attendance was contained in several drawings and paintings hoarded amongst numerous others by a sympathetic though incredulous art master. The intermittent absences occasioned by his slight fits developed into more prolonged periods when he began to suffer from mild yet lingering asthmatic attacks. It seemed as though he were physically disintegrating and that his sporadic attendances were belated and futile attempts to satisfy some vague, lost ambition. For a while he was too ill to do anything. Until he was twenty he was virtually confined to the Place by alternate bouts of depression and nervous, convulsive elation, venturing out only occasionally to visit Austen's shop, where he would sit moodily watching the customers coming and going and discussing their purchases; or to Isabel's house where, in the same attitude of dejected aloofness, he would listen to the earnest debates of her numerous visitors and to his aunt's highly emotional charges. As if his detachment were contagious, his father succumbed to a similar aloofness, becoming increasingly absorbed in the maintenance of the Place to the exclusion of everything else.

In his early twenties Leonard began to get jobs. Physically if not temperamentally unsuited to the kind of work he found for himself, his absences were as frequent as they had been from school, and he seldom retained his employment long. There was now an undeniable wilfulness in his behaviour, as if he sought some way of evading his difference from other people and taking upon himself the conventional identity of a workman. If he was trying sincerely to touch on those ordinary experiences of life from which he felt excluded, it seemed to those people who superficially observed him that he was assuming the guise of an idiot. For several years he drifted aimlessly from job to job and brought upon himself an increasing reputation for idiocy. By children, who continued to exert their unique and primitive instincts, he was openly abused; he was often followed or pursued down the roads and crescents of the estate by a chanting host who had no cause for fear, since he still preserved a remarkable opacity, and reluctance for action.

Austen occasionally reproved John now for his lack of interest and indifference towards his son. But never with any great force: more, he seemed curious about his own loss of conviction in Leonard, though he still encouraged him in his drawing.

'But what can I do?' John said on what proved to be the last occasion that Austen so reproached him. 'He's a man now. I give him all the affection he appears to need. There's no real necessity for him to work. I'd even be some sort of friend to him if he ever showed any inclination for friendship.'

'Do you think he needs treatment? I mean, attention of a different sort.'

'I don't know.'

'Don't you feel anything real for him?'

'Not what I imagine one should for a son. He seems to be beyond help.'

'Or even sympathy?'

'Or sympathy. He carries his disillusionment around with him, it seems to me. It's as if all the time he's reproving you for showing any interest. Worse. It's as if he reproves himself for arousing people's interest. He seems determined not to exist. He's like a person of no importance, interest or significance whatsoever. He's nothing at all like Elizabeth. I used to think it was something in me. But she – she's got such a happy temperament.' He looked at Austen sharply. 'Well, and where does guilt enter into all this?'

Austen shrugged and didn't answer.

'I thought Leonard was your hero. Your guilty man of action. Your *Cromwell*.' John laughed ferociously at the allusion.

'This is the chrysalis,' Austen said eventually. 'We've yet to see whether it's to be an ugly or a beautiful moth that emerges.'

'At times you appal me – more than any other person I know. You, with your talk of repressions and guilt. It's terrifying.'

'Why, don't you believe in psychoanalysis?'

'This fashionable and frivolous self-exposure. What is there beneath that elegant suit, Austen? Just an equally elegant and fashionable soul? A *psychological* soul?' John turned abruptly away from Austen: 'You patronize other people's experience as well as your own. It's obscene!'

John had, in fact, reached a stage which, at some earlier point in his life, might have made him more adaptable. He was now able to externalize the disabilities of his own temperament and to attach them securely to the society around him. He brooded much more on his situation as if, still walking determinedly in a circle, he were deliberating in which direction he would finally decide to move.

If Leonard noticed the disruption he had created between

his father and his uncle he showed no awareness of it. As if to break the aloofness that existed between the three of them, Austen now began to encourage Leonard's other uncles to visit the Place; one of them, Thomas, more than the other two.

Thomas was a small man, unusually small for a Radcliffe, with a gaunt face and large, staring eyes, like two brutally exposed nerves; in his youth he had suffered from a tubercular complaint. Quiet, and with a kind of modest intensity, he seemed after his first visit to be as much a part of the Place as either Leonard or his father. He was a clerk in a local government department, yet never mentioned his work other than to point out how ill-health had continually jeopardized his chances of promotion and how he was continually under the supervision of inferior men. His wife, a large, cheerful woman, seemed always apprehensively on the verge of some delightful experience.

They had two children who had died early in life, and in face of this tragedy Thomas himself had quietly withdrawn from events and now pursued, not so much his own existence as that of his fellows with a relentless and unabating sympathy. It had a frightening tenacity. For a while he and John discovered some sort of mutual attraction in one another; and although they had scarcely known each other since they were boys, when Thomas was a mischievous younger brother, they now walked about the Place and the grounds wrapped in conversation as though since their youth no moment of privacy had gone unrevealed.

Yet simply because he provided such a patient and sympathetic audience John soon began to tire of and then, even, to avoid him. Nodding his head slowly and continuously as each fact or opinion was revealed, his hands held appreciatively together in slow gestures of condolence, Thomas suggested a kind of faceless commiseration behind which John began to suspect a parasitic attitude that fed on adversity as instinctively as a leech on blood. After a while, no longer provided with sustenance from John, and discovering no such source in Leonard, Thomas's visits to the Place became less frequent and subsequently stopped altogether. His wife continued to come, and with an increasing frequency. As if encouraged by the dissolution of their husbands' relationship, she and Stella formed a securer and more intimate one of their own.

Matthew, the next to the youngest of Leonard's uncles, made regular, well-spaced visits to the Place, usually with his wife, a blonde, smartly-dressed woman who was a celebrated hostess in the rural region to the east. By profession an accountant, and therefore morbidly addicted, Thomas had earnestly stated, to the assessing of other people's incomes, Matthew had recently been appointed to a directorship in an important firm of mining engineers. Usually his visits occurred while he was on his way to or from some more important business, and invariably ended with a heated discussion with John over his ideas of leasing, converting or of selling the Place altogether. Tall, elegantly dressed, with a bony face and rather large, importuning eyes, he presented the kind of functional exterior which, John discovered, had earned him the title of 'The Fridge' amongst his colleagues. His visits left John with a feeling of total helplessness, a satellite ineffectually circling its parent body.

If Austen had any particular motive in introducing Leonard's uncles to the Place, it was most clearly realized in the infrequent though boisterous visits of the youngest, Alex. The Radcliffes varied curiously in height. John, Austen and Matthew were all tall; Thomas, Isabel and Alex were small. Alex lived some distance away to the south and his visits usually lasted two or more days. Crew-cut, dogmatic, extremely energetic, so that his body was continually occupied in unnecessary action, he always seemed like some critical though well-intentioned intruder in the passive household. He was in charge of industrial relations in a giant corporation of motor manufacturers, and appeared to be a man who in the service of some higher ideal rode over his own feelings as much as those of others with a nerveless energy which caused Leonard, whenever he came into contact with him, to shy away as though he had been confronted with a wild beast.

For a while Austen appeared to satisfy himself by

arranging these visits of his brothers to the Place; they were like carefully planned assaults which he directed on some stubbornly resisting citadel. Then, as a kind of mutual incomprehension settled on both sides, blunting even Alex's insistent demands that Leonard should get a job, that they should move out of the Place, that even John himself should look for some more worthwhile employment, he began to grow increasingly frustrated, so that occasionally he would flare up in strident and uncharacteristic arguments, railing against John, and against Leonard. His behaviour was as incomprehensible to himself as it was to John; and for a while he stayed away from the Place altogether and the only news they ever had of him was through Isabel.

For a time he formed a friendship with a man whom he had first seen singing in a club in town. He was a coal-miner who now made his living exclusively from performing in various halls and institutions and it was as if in the man's oddly ravaged features Austen recognized something of his own unspoken distress. What oblique need for companionship drove him into this relationship he had no idea.

'Men undergo a change of life in the same way as women,' he had told Isabel, who in turn had told John – 'except in men it's less physical and therefore perhaps more subtle and devastating in its effects.'

'But what can you have in common with a miner?' Isabel had said, antagonized by what she interpreted as a reference to her own increasing years.

'I've no idea. Though he's not a miner. He sees himself as some sort of artist. Perhaps it's because I see him as a man trying to escape his predicament. You see, he's completely self-educated.'

Yet in Austen himself, although this relationship was confined to endless arguments, not dissimilar to those he held with John, but conducted, strangely, with the energy of a much younger man, he felt that beneath the surface there was a desire to know this tortured man so completely that in the end it would have to include some sort of physical embrace. It was this that apparently led him on.

There was in this new acquaintance a gauche and passionate sense of inquiry and speculation, a wilfulness and abandonment, that attracted him considerably. They were both quite elderly men.

One day when his friend failed to turn up at an appointed time Austen went in search of him with a recklessness that not only surprised but profoundly excited him, visiting pubs and institutions where in the previous few weeks he had watched him singing, enquiring for his address. When, some time later, he heard that the man had been arrested and subsequently imprisoned for a kind of behaviour which, tormentedly, had been at the back of his own mind, he felt that a part of his body had been torn away.

His immediate reaction had been drastic: he decided to sell his business and to leave the district. At first, undecided where to go, he had visited his brothers, finally arriving at Alex's. He was more than ordinarily frustrated. If at first Austen had found Alex's energy and nervelessness exciting, he was now completely intimidated by it. If this was at last his 'guilty man of action' then it was one whose purpose and intentions he could neither condone nor appreciate. After a while, growing more and more restless, he went abroad.

For two years he travelled aimlessly across Europe, visiting the northern fringes of Africa and the Middle East, but always returning to some centre close to the main capitals. Invariably alone, the solitary occupant of rooms and restaurant tables, there were in all this time scarcely a dozen people whom he could later with any clarity recollect having met. His mind was in an extraordinary state. It was as if it were a vessel gradually being emptied. Slowly it poured itself away in these unknown, unfelt places until, when it seemed that the last drop had gone, he rose early one morning and took the most direct passage home. He had only one thought, a quiet determination and sense of purpose regarding his nephew, Leonard.

Almost at the same time as Austen's departure Isabel had begun to interest herself in religious activities. Belief had always been latent in her energetic character, and for a while she had attended a spiritualist church before embracing the more orthodox Anglican faith. At first Leonard had played something of the role of catalyst in the initial alarming process of her conversion, but as she subsided into a less fervent and more practical acceptance of her new faith, Leonard found himself discarded, first as an encumbrance, then as an embarrassment in the company which now frequented his aunt's drawing-room. 'The Prince' had now become a silent Jester, and eventually he was discouraged from attending court altogether.

He continued to produce his strange miniatures, some so small that they were indecipherable to his father who occasionally brought himself to examine them. Afterwards, looking back on these years of isolation, Leonard himself was surprised by their purposelessness. He had no recollection of them other than of vague, ominous dreams induced largely by his aunt's religious fanaticism. They seemed an increasingly misty void marked only by a bewildering debris of drawings. He was now the most familiar person on the estate. Whether followed by a jeering band of school-children or walking alone in some stooped attitude of self-absorption, his slim, raincoated figure attracted the immediate attention of every passer-by.

Whether despite Austen's absence or because of it, he began to discover certain things about himself. His mind, for example, worked in a rather extraordinary way. He was strangely pleased by the discovery: it seemed that he tended to see things in separate camera-like impressions. He had never appreciated this before. The difference was, however, that whereas a film ran at a predetermined speed, animating each individual picture by its sustained momentum, in him the feelings that normally might have provided this motor-force, uniting several separate sensations in a single image, were frequently absent or functioned only intermittently. If he saw himself as such a projector and the life he absorbed as a film, then the screen of his consciousness was interspersed with long periods of flickering, incoherent light, alternating with sudden, extremely vivid impressions. It was the disconnectedness that made these intermittent pictures so alarming and gave him a feverish anxiety to know exactly what had occurred in between to cause them. It was this, he decided, which gave rise to his alternate bouts of elation and depression.

He was very absent-minded. He had a memory which his parents found both bewildering and irritating. Many apparently obvious events he would completely forget or, it seemed, show no awareness of their having occurred. Others, which to his parents might have appeared more obscure or elusive, he could recall with a remarkable clarity and precision. If this were some form of unconscious censorship, it had a persistence which not only bewildered his parents but appeared also to distress Leonard himself. The excisions were prompted so obscurely that his state of mind began to assume the dignity of a mystical condition.

Frequently he discovered a discrepancy between the images and the sensations that accompanied them, as if the sound-track and the film were running at different speeds. Yet, because he could recognize this inconsistency so clearly, he assumed it was not so much a disorder as a heightening of his perceptiveness which, until he should grow more familiar with it, would remain unintelligible. He began to look upon this strange phenomenon with the interest of a spectator. His life was a series of enigmatic fragments, a roomful of discarded and arbitrary drawings. Soon they would be arranged to some purpose.

When Austen suddenly returned Leonard wondered for the first time about his absence, yet his curiosity was never sufficiently aroused either by this or by other slightly unusual circumstances to question it. There was some change in Austen which he couldn't explain: a purpose-fulness and energy, a certain intensity which he could not be sure had existed before. The immediate effect of his arrival was a renewal of affability in his father, and a slight sharpening of animosity in Isabel. It was as if she were resisting something.

For a while Austen lived at the Place, and during this time Leonard became aware of the hardening in his uncle's temperament, an urgent sort of militancy and anxiety. Then Austen found a flat in town and a job similar, though inferior, to his previous occupation; the original shop had quietly closed shortly after his disappearance. For several weeks, in fact, Leonard worked as his uncle's assistant in the shop – the branch of a large national retailer of furniture – and appeared to be very much at the centre of Austen's concern until, at the end of this period, Austen declared that he would have to find him a more suitable occupation. His inquiries amongst his numerous acquaintances in the town absorbed him completely. Then, after three weeks of exploration, Austen suddenly announced that he had found Leonard a job.

5

When he first saw the tent contractor's yard Leonard was immediately struck by its similarity to that at the rear of the Place. A low-lying block of offices and workshops represented the main building, and from it an L-shaped wing of sheds and storerooms enclosed a large rectangular area of red ash opening on its only exposed side into a larger paddock formed by the intersection of two high railway embankments. Here several derelict lorries slumped wheel-less in the thick grass and huge expanses of greying canvas hung drying on a network of poles. It was a bay of sinking ships, their masts and sails arrested above the confused surface.

Forty or fifty men were crouched down in a narrow shaft of sunlight that came over the long row of sheds. Their backs resting against the dark woodwork, they leaned forward waiting silently like men around a fire. Under the overhanging eaves of the main shed stood five red-painted lorries and two 15 cwt trucks: all were converted army vehicles brutally stripped down to their minimum weight. The name 'EWBANK' was painted in dark blue on a shield mounted above each of the cabs.

The men looked up as the contractor came into the yard from the central doors of the office block. He was a tall, thin man, dressed in a black suit, his red, sunburnt face overshadowed by the broad brim of a black shallow-crowned hat: his tiny eyes were virtually concealed, yet they glistened like decorative buttons pinned either side of his long and slender nose. He walked with sharp, hurried strides, his short arms moving busily either side of his stubborn projecting chest. His feet seemed to crunch excessively loudly in the morning air. There was something about him, whether deliberately implanted there or not, which suggested the conventional image of the solitary cowboy.

Leonard, dressed in work clothes, the strap of a haversack containing his lunch slung across his narrow body, walked slightly behind Ewbank and to one side. The men watched him in silence; then, smiling slowly, several stood up. They began to light cigarettes and to talk.

The contractor pinned up a list on the wall of the shed nearest the lorries and the men gradually moved over towards it. Their names were divided into five columns at the head of each of which were typed their place of destination and, in capital letters, the name of their foreman. The first two columns were linked by a bracket to indicate a common destination. At the bottom of the fifth list 'Radcliffe' was written in pencil. At the top of the column was typed the name 'TOLSON'.

Ewbank directed the new man to one of the lorries where, taking off his bag and his coat, he began to help in the loading of the canvas. He worked quickly, urgently following each instruction given him by the men, and hurrying with short, stumbling strides under the heavy loads. Soon he was breathless, his pale face deeply flushed; yet at the same time he laughed and smiled at the inquisitive remarks of the men. As he dropped each load on the back of the truck he scarcely looked up at the tall, darkly-burned figure who stood there directing and arranging the loading. Only at a sharp and irritated command did he glance up and with a sudden, repeated backward look see a face which gradually grew into certain memorable and familiar features. The moment of recognition was like a heat pressing over his nervous body, a fur-like warmth that spread over his back and across his neck. It absorbed his shoulders and his head. His body fell into the warmth and disappeared. Tolson watched him shyly. He was confused.

To Leonard, his figure seemed to grow larger, suddenly huge and overwhelming, suffocatingly warm.

They acknowledged each other briefly. During the next few days they scarcely spoke or even confirmed their recognition. Each morning they drove to a showground several miles from the town where they were erecting a large number of marquees; several times they found themselves working alongside one another yet treating each other with the deference of men newly acquainted. They were cautious and deliberate; it gave them the appearance of a clumsy amicability. They spoke formally and within the restricted reference of their work. To begin with, Ewbank drove Leonard to the site each morning in his car, apparently glad of someone reputedly educated to talk to. But gradually these lifts became more infrequent and eventually Leonard was making the daily journeys with the rest of the men in the back of the truck.

Over the summer a restrained friendship developed between Leonard and Tolson which the men watched with half-concealed amusement; their curiosity was never openly revealed. And a change had come over Leonard himself. His narrow, whitish face filled out, his cheeks reddened in the sun, and his eyes were suddenly warm and nervously alight. His movements took on a spontaneity which, though familiar to his mother, came as a reassuring revelation to his father. Neither of them had known of the renewal with Tolson, and when Austen eventually confided it to them their immediate sense of unease scarcely diminished their general relief.

In fact, when John witnessed the change that had come over Leonard, and when he discovered its cause, it gave him a peculiar sensation, a mixture of elation and alarm; as though somehow everything had been taken out of his hands. He went out of his way to walk through those parts of the estate where he now knew Tolson to live, recognizing him easily enough one evening when he rode past on his motor-bike and dismounted at a gate some distance ahead.

When John reached the spot and looked down the gap between the houses he saw Tolson stooping over his machine in the garden at the back. There was about him the muscular confidence and assurance that had distinguished him as a boy. It was an aggressive and powerful head that hung down over the machine, dark, thick-necked, with a kind of unknowledgeable assertiveness. That his own incoherent and almost meaningless hopes should rest upon such a person, one whom he scarcely knew and of whom for some reason he felt instinctively afraid, filled him with renewed alarm. But whatever his feeling then, the change in Leonard himself was unmistakable: out of that dull opacity of character he saw his son come suddenly alive. Even his drawing had ceased, as though in some way his self-absorption had been averted and broken at last.

The two men continued to maintain the formality of their relationship with a shy, probing uncertainty, carefully pacing out the area in which they could manoeuvre, as though reluctant to relinquish the sense of accident and coincidence in their meeting. Leonard heard briefly of Tolson's marriage, his conscription into the army, the several jobs he had tried since coming out, a restlessness similar to, if more determinate than, his own. There was in this casual exchange of information a bated, suppressed sense of relief.

One Sunday three lorries were loaded in the yard and the following morning, arriving an hour earlier than usual, twenty of the men, including Leonard and Tolson, crowded into the back of the truck and the various cabs and, followed by Ewbank's car, set off in convoy through the town.

They travelled westward for several hours, gradually leaving behind the immediate signs of industry and habitation as they climbed steadily up a narrow winding valley. Broad escarpments of white rock and heavy moorland replaced the close embankments of houses and factories, and the dull swirl of the river that ran through the region gave way to a clear, sparkling luminescence occasionally visible through narrow belts of trees at one side of the road.

Later in the morning they arrived at a village in the upper reaches of the valley close to the summit of the upland. The lorries turned off the road and bounced down into a large field that sloped towards the river. Above this section of the valley, and perched on a darkening outcrop of rock, was the broken stump of a small castle. It was at this, rather than at the village beyond the trees, that the men gazed as they stiffly climbed out and lit cigarettes.

It was very hot. For the next hour they unloaded the vehicles, then broke off to eat their sandwiches, resuming work when the sun was almost vertically over the highest peak of rock. By late afternoon the majority of the tents had been marked out, their stakes driven in, and the principal marquee erected. It was inside this that the equipment was stacked, along with the sacks of tenting and the poles. As the men climbed back into the truck and the cabs, Ewbank took Tolson on one side.

For a while they stood talking in the shadow of the truck. Then Tolson suddenly looked up and crossed over to Leonard. He asked him a question, stubbing his boot toe into the earth.

'But why? What for?' Leonard said.

'To look after the tents till the Show starts at the end of the week.'

Tolson watched him closely, bending forward slightly, his hands splayed on his hips. He was burned dark from the sun. 'We'd have five days here, not much work to do, and we'd be on double time. I'll bring the motor-bike, and a gramophone.' He looked away, momentarily listless, then added, 'We should have a good time.' He glanced back at Leonard shyly. 'What do you think?'

After a while Leonard nodded, murmuring his assent. That night he met Tolson's wife and his two children.

The following morning Tolson's motor-bike was loaded onto the back of one of the lorries, along with a portable gramophone and his luggage as well as Leonard's. With a smaller number of men they returned to the site to complete the erection of the tents.

It was another hot day. People came down from the village to watch the men working. Amongst them was a girl of about fifteen, small and heavily built, with long dark hair that curled over her shoulders, her alert, ruggedly animated face exaggerated by heavy lines of make-up. A woman's deliberation intensified her doll-like hardness. The men watched her impassively at first. As they hauled up the heavy sheets of canvas, laced them and secured the long ropes, they paused to stare at her kicking against the stone wall. Then they turned to smile at one another nervously.

Ewbank appeared to ignore her as he walked to and fro in the centre of the field, and when he told the men to break off for lunch they quickly dispersed in the fields and meadows around the site. The girl meantime had disappeared. It wasn't until the men re-started work that they noticed her absence at all. A short while later they saw her drop down from the back of the 15 cwt Ford and run off, with crab-like movements, towards the village. Pilkington, a squat, red-haired workman, climbed out of the truck wiping down his trousers with a rag. He was a stocky, bow-legged man of forty, and he walked past the men with a lurching of his bowed limbs, smiling. They laughed awkwardly, half-shocked, and glanced across at Ewbank; the tall figure of the contractor shouted across at the men working on the farthest tents. Then he eased his hands in the small of his back and stretched.

By mid-afternoon the girl had re-appeared, standing by the wall with her arms folded and staring at the men with an authoritative look. She wandered slowly from group to group in the heat of the afternoon, confident, taunting.

The two teams of men worked slowly towards one another from opposite sides of the field, talking in tight, half-humorous voices, tense, watching her, then Pilkington, and calling out every now and then, 'What's your name, young'un?'

'Enid.'

'How old are you?'

She laughed back, not answering.

'What d'you think to Walter, then?'

She shook her head, frowning.

'What about old Shaw, then?' They indicated an older man who laughed exaggeratedly at the suggestion: he was the usual butt of the men. She shook her head again, but laughing with them. They all stood back, amused by certain gestures of the old man as he thrust out his hips towards her.

'Is he fitted out all right, then?'

She nodded, though pouting her lips dubiously.

'How many of us could you take on, love? Do you think you could manage two of us side by side together?'

The men laughed, though they watched the girl shyly.

Ewbank, smoking a cheroot, sauntered about the field bending occasionally to roll up a guy-line or to retrieve a loose stake, but watching the men whenever they spoke and turning away to smile, then glancing back at the girl, his small red eyes tired yet furtively alert.

Leonard suddenly went across to her and told her to go. And in such a way that she stumbled back, then went, looking over her shoulder, murderous and hungry. He walked back silently past the men.

'Why d'you tell her to go? Why did you do that?'

He said nothing, going back to his work. The men drew away. Tolson had blushed but said nothing, as though he'd scarcely noticed.

Ewbank watched Leonard intently, yet still cautious in the way he turned his head and smiled at the empty fields, the acute distance he kept between himself and his men. When they had walled and secured the marquees, hauled and pushed the lorries out of the dry slough of the field, the men sat in the back of the truck and watched Enid standing in the dusk by the stone wall, her sombre face full of contempt. She waved as the truck load of men swayed and jarred over the ruts and mounted onto the road. They lurched and jolted like a single body, silent and suddenly aloof.

Leonard stood by the small blackened tent at the top of the field watching her. He was perfectly still. Then he turned to gaze up at the castle, the stump of which protruded redly against the evening sky. A moment later Tolson came out of the tent and together they walked slowly down to the river. The girl stood watching them. The trucks had disappeared down the valley. For a while there was the distant murmur of their engines, then simply the stillness of the evening air. Leonard had reached the river. He gazed down into the water. When Tolson reached him he put his arm round Leonard's shoulder, leaning on him slightly.

Later, there was a faint glow of a lamp in the tent and the distorted shadow of the motor-bike inside stretched hugely on the canvas. The soft sound of a gramophone whined in the night air.

Leonard woke to a strange sight. Moonlight filtered through the canvas above his head. The lamp had gone out. Tolson was kneeling beside him, stooped forward and apparently gazing at his body moulded in the thick texture of the blankets. Leonard closed his eyes. He lay perfectly still. It seemed only a few seconds, yet when he looked again he saw that Tolson was in fact lying in his bed on the other side of the bike. No longer frightened but considerably bewildered, he lay awake for some time. Then, lulled by the rhythmical breathing of Tolson, he slowly fell asleep.

The next two days and night passed without incident. An elderly night-watchman was installed in a small caravan at the opposite end of the field to guard the trade equipment which was daily brought into the ground. They finished the small amount of necessary work on the tents and rode up onto the moorland, where Tolson swam in the river. He seemed, if anything, bored. On the Friday, the day before the Show, it rained. They stayed in the tent most of the day, lying on the beds, and only venturing out to wander aimlessly through the empty marquees. In the evening it rained even harder and, unable to sleep, they lay listening to the heavy drumming on the tight canvas. Flashes of lightning produced brief, startling images on the stained fabric of the tent. Then the rain suddenly lightened and, some time later, Leonard fell asleep.

6

Leonard woke early. Turning on his side, he saw in the pale light Tolson's face latticed by the spokes and frame of his bike; the smell was of some fetid monster that had stabled with them all night.

Tolson didn't move. Even so, there seemed a certain awareness under the shut eyes, the black fans of the lashes alive as if concealing laughter. There was something stunning, deliberately ugly about the face, split into sections between the ribs of the bike, each part sullen and heavily relaxed. Tolson didn't seem to sleep; he seemed fully awake, as though aware that Leonard was watching him.

Leonard stood up over the joist of his bed, his head stooped under the roof of the tent, bowed forward. At the end of the bed was Tolson's suitcase, torn apart at the seams, his clothes spilt out like entrails. His footmarks were all over the tent, and on the roof which he'd been kicking, imprisoned by the rain the previous afternoon. Between the two beds were empty beer bottles, a guttered oil lamp and, spreading across the muddy wheel tracks, violet stains that had dripped steadily from the bike during the previous four nights. Tolson's bed was surrounded by balls of paper which he'd crumpled up before going to sleep and, all over the ground, cigarette butts. It was as if he were just a piece of his own debris, his great steel bike as strong as eight horses skulking in the shadows of the tent like an intense part of him, waiting for him, watching for him, another segment of his huge body. Leonard lifted his clothes from the line by his head and pulled them on.

He slid his feet into his boots and crawled under Tolson's hanging clothes to the flap. Crouching down he wound up the small portable gramophone. The handle creaked loudly in the tent. He moved the needle to the edge of the record and for a moment longer watched Tolson's heavy face. Then, as it started to play '*What do you want if you don't want money?*' he squeezed out under the brailing.

The dawn air was live. The heavy rain of the night had left the air clean and the limestone hills on either side of the valley were shrouded in deep white mists, reddening and yellowing already where the sun splattered over the escarpment bank. The stump of the castle tower was now indistinguishable from the rock scars overlooking the dale.

The square of marquees surrounding the field were stiff and white. Like whales cast up on a beach, they lay about the field empty and disused, the carcases taut with rain and dew, the guy-lines strained at their moorings. Stakes had been torn out with the contraction of the canvas. He picked up a sledge-hammer from a row standing by the blackened tent and, his slight figure curved to the weight, walked across the glistening field.

He slackened the guys and knocked the aluminium rods back in, his hands clenched round the hammer neck until the points were bedded firmly in the ground. His arms trembled with the weight.

He stood back and paused, his hands wrapped round the hammer-shaft. Then he swayed, half-folded, and swung the stone weight over his head and down on the penny-size top of the stakes. He worked slowly, the hammer swung over not by strength but by a nervous litheness that seemed to spring from his hips. It seemed an inner convulsion that manoeuvred the heaviness through the air.

Beyond a row of lime-trees a dog was barking, in the village, and on the moors curlews called with a strangled cry. Then the music stopped.

Leonard stood up, resting the hammer. For a second the needle wailed over the record, then silence. A minute later 'Mack the Knife' started. Leonard gazed up at the tent. He waited a moment. Then, hurriedly, he turned and walked down to the river at the opposite end of the field.

It rushed down from its mountain coldness, clear and hard, folding over and round the torn rocks. It had a quiet ferocity. He picked up a stone, clenched it briefly in his hand, then threw it in, almost lunging at the water which burst and sprang apart, the ripples arcing over the smooth surface, breaking against the rocks before they were absorbed in the deepening currents by the far bank. The river surged morosely between the grey rocks. Nothing moved but the water.

He lifted the hammer and swung it down on a boulder. He glanced up once more at the tent. He brought the hammer down again, more fiercely. The grey skin split to a yellow-brown core. The hammer cracked bleakly in the still air, the steel echoing off the stone surface, then crushing, slurring, as it bit between the fragments. The splinters flicked into the surface of the river. The boulder was crushed.

63

Then just as suddenly he bent forward. He coughed, then knelt down casually and half-supported himself with one arm. His breathlessness contracted his whole figure. He coughed heartfully into the grass, heaving forward so violently that eventually he lay down. His forehead rested against the wet grass. Again the music suddenly stopped. He hurriedly pushed himself to his feet and, without glancing up, scrambled to the edge of the river. He stretched his head out over the water, his hands thrust down into the pebbly bed. Then he drank with short, rapid breaths. When he climbed back up the bank the coughing had almost stopped. The air rasped in his throat and he spat out the phlegm awkwardly. He seemed angry.

He'd almost reached the tent when the motor-bike started and blue exhaust fumes drifted under the brailing. The engine revved explosively. Leonard immediately dropped the hammer and unlaced the flap.

Tolson sat astride the bike, his broad back curving, suddenly relaxed as he sensed Leonard's entry. He exploded the machine in the tent, the metallic apparatus shuddering within its rubber frame. Its fumes shrouded the place. He throttled back the engine and, without looking up, began to heave himself and the machine out backwards.

His bare toes curled under the gear. The bike turned. For a moment his foot held the lever, trembling with the bike, his head twisted away from the acrid fumes, then he lurched forward. The rear wheel spun out a cord of mud.

The engine screamed as the bike disappeared amongst the empty tents, then moaned, fell back, as Tolson came up between the marquees and the stone wall. Suddenly the sound was muffled, swallowed up as the bike ran inside the large beer tent. An intent insect, it shot out roaring, and made straight for Leonard. The engine opened up, the bike spinning over the mounds. Tolson's face was concealed by the deep stoop of his body. He lay on the machine. The tyres seized. They skidded, ripping the grass, suddenly immobile. His foot came down, sliding in the mud, his body wrenched forward, the bike hurrying towards the tent with an impersonal momentum. It stopped within touch of Leonard. Tolson glanced up at him. Then he smiled, throttling the engine. His eyes were screwed up from the smoke of a cigarette.

'How about a ride round the showground, Len?'

He looked down at the engine, fingering it as he tilted the machine between his thighs.

'How about it, then? I see you've been round resetting the stakes.'

'What about some breakfast?' Leonard hadn't moved.

'We'll get that. The Show won't start for a couple of hours.' Tolson shook the bike from side to side, swirling the fuel in the tank. 'It won't kill you. Least, it's evens it won't.' He waited, twisting the throttle grip, booming the engine, and shivering slightly now as the early morning penetrated his thin clothes.

Leonard climbed on behind.

Tolson waited a second while he slotted his hands round the strut, then they were flung forward.

The machine sprang forward. It sprayed through the muddy earth towards the river. Tolson saw an avenue under a row of guy-lines and, ducking low, took the bike underneath.

Leonard crouched against his massive back, his mouth pulled open. The ropes clipped his hair. As they came out onto open ground Tolson's shoulders expanded, the bike bursting forward, drumming over the tight grassy mounds and bouncing hugely under their weight. His body had relaxed, holding the machine beneath him, its rigidity vibrating into his body and into the limbs gripping his sides. They were one piece. The wheels bucked and twisted as they slid between the rows of stakes, then leaned over, the tyres driving, compressed, into the mud tracks, up and over the thick clay ridges and ruts, swinging from side to side, Tolson's foot groping out like a discarded limb. The bike moaned into its madness, crazed by its own scream. It raced by the high stone wall, the buttress catching Tolson's arm, glancing, and the frozen assemblage sliding and the engine wailing before the bike came round, thundered, splaying mud in wide screes, fanned out. Beneath him, Leonard felt the savage rip of the tyres burning against the wet grass.

They rose, curled over, shuddering on the even mounds of the lower field, then dipping. The bike turned, dropping, stooped over the slipping grass and braking into the broad front of the beer tent. Their bodies were crushed together, bent down, turning across the length of the trestled bar. Tolson edged the bike round with his bare feet and in the gloomy interior revved the engine. It shuddered a moment in the clutch, then drove them past the tent poles and screening. Leonard closed his eyes: he clung to the figure between his legs, the crescendo of metal throbbing on the canvas behind him. Then they were in the daylight again, and the cold air.

Tolson cut the engine and the bike moaned to itself, softly; it jolted and slowed towards their tent. He braked quickly and Leonard's head creased against his back. He got off and went into the tent. A moment later he came out with the Primus stove and the fuel can and started to fill it. He was breathing heavily, almost panting, his crouched legs trembling as he stooped forward.

Tolson watched him a while. Then he pulled the bike onto its stand and took the stove from him and lit it. His pyjamas and feet were spattered with mud, his right foot bloodied from fumbling with the gears. He squatted down leisurely and pumped the stove. The bike moved slightly on its stand, its front forks turning a moment like a limb at rest.

Tolson's thick hands waved over the flame, and his face, reddened now under tight, black curls, turned up to Leonard. His eyes had a curious, half-startled look; then he stood up. His stare was suddenly diffident, pointedly casual, and he glanced back at the stove.

'Did you bring the bacon?'

'I couldn't find it. It's somewhere in your mess.'

'Oh, yes?' He held his hands together for warmth. 'I'll have a look, then. It can't be far.' He stated it quietly. 'You can fetch some water if you like.' He went into the tent and started searching amongst the debris of his belongings.

Leonard picked up the pan and walked down to the river. He was trembling. Out of the hill-mist taut sails of pink cloud bulged into the overhead blueness. On the road

66

down the valley a man cycled slowly, looking over the stone wall at the showground.

In the grass by the river was the shape of his body pressed out in the short, broad blades. He stopped, gazing down at it for some time: it was narrow and small, crumpled. Then he stepped in the centre of it and dug in his boots, tearing them across it. He worked intently. In a short while the grass was squashed and torn, the pressed shape quickly trampled out of all recognition.

Tolson was hunched over the stove as he came back with the water. From half way down the field he could smell the bacon frying and see Tolson sawing the bread into large, square blocks and laying them out on a newspaper. Tolson picked up one of the wedges in his thick fingers and dipped it into the sweet-smelling fat, chewing it while he worked. The muscle was taut and mobile in his face. Leonard let his shadow lie across him.

'Your bike's sinking in the mud,' he said after a while.

'It's all right.' Tolson gave it a quick look as though he knew it would never betray him. He turned the sizzling bacon over.

Then he glanced up at Leonard shyly. He'd flushed. He stared round at the deserted hills and the moor, then he stood up. 'Shall we leave this, then?' He leaned forward slightly, his eyes intent. 'Shall we?'

Leonard didn't answer. He frowned, and glanced down at the fire. As he turned to the tent, however, he saw Tolson stoop swiftly and remove the pan from the flame. Then he felt his hands across his shoulders.

'We better get undressed,' Tolson said. He secured the tent flap and turned quickly, staring at Leonard in the faint interior. 'If we take everything off we'll be as warm as anything under the blankets. Shall we do that?' He began to take off his thin, mud-stained pyjamas, watching Leonard closely, almost threateningly. Slowly Leonard began to remove his jacket, still gazing down at the ground.

A moment later, naked, Tolson came and touched him. 'Hold me. Hold me!' he said, his lips buried in the hair behind Leonard's ear.

7

Wetherby was early, it being the day of the Show. Leonard, working near their tent, didn't hear his car drive up but was suddenly aware of the lean, well-dressed figure in the middle of the field stooped on its shooting-stick, its black eye-patch turned towards the sun. For a while the Colonel watched the showground people coming out of their caravans in the next field then, as he drew up his stick and walked across the central arena, he noticed the bike tracks that ran in and around the marquees and across the reserved area of the show-ring. He glanced in the direction of the contractor's tent and saw Leonard watching him. He walked briskly across and, noticing the ugly pile of clothes and belongings laid in the mouth of the tent, stopped a short distance away and called out, 'Is that your motor bike there?'

'No.'

'Oh? Whose is it?' He waited. 'Somebody's been riding through the bloody tents . . . and across the show-ring. Do you know anything about it?'

Leonard didn't answer. Wetherby stared across at him uneasily. 'I hope you'll have your tackle here tidied up before the Show starts. It's frightfully scruffy . . . There'll be a lorry along any time now to fill up these ruts with ash. I'd be obliged if you'd tell your work-mate not to ride his bike across here. It's not a public thoroughfare.' He waited to examine the effect of his words, and when Leonard turned away it was several seconds before he heard the Colonel's feet slur through the hardening mud, picking their way back to the firmer part of the field.

Leonard watched Wetherby go round the marquees, unlacing the smaller trade tents to peer in at the equipment, and occasionally lifting his head to glance back at him. As he went out of the gate he met Tolson, half-stripped, coming up from washing in the river. They stood close together, Tolson listening and staring soberly at the Colonel as he gestured at the bike tracks; then, in response to something that Tolson demanded, the Colonel appeared to forget his complaint and talked animatedly about the tents, pointing out two in illustration. Then he shook his stick free of mud and nodding agreeably got into his small saloon car by the gate and drove off.

'Nay, you don't want to get him riled,' Tolson said when he came up. He rubbed his chest and back vigorously with his stained towel, staring at Leonard.

'No . . . I know.' Leonard glanced away.

'The poor sod only wants you to call him "sir", then you can burn them down for all he cares.' He looked at Leonard more purposefully.

Leonard stared back. Slowly Tolson's face relaxed into a smile. He wiped his hands concealingly over his reddening cheeks. Then suddenly, together, they burst out laughing.

The day brightened. People had begun to flood into the field, unloading farm machinery and industrial samples, assembling hoardings and trade stands. Wetherby, in jodhpurs and a hacking jacket, returned an hour later with four workmen in his car. He supervised the erection of white posts round the show-ring and the threading of a long white rope, held preciously away from the ground by a line of men. In the next field herdsmen and labourers were bringing in cattle and sheep from the surrounding farms; the road along the dale held a regular line of trucks, vans and the first cars; the track winding down from the moors was marked now by odd, silhouetted figures and, in the distance, a tractor pulling a loaded trailer. Behind the larger marquees caterers were setting up a field kitchen, and steam already rose from its tall rusty funnel. A brewer's lorry had bounced its way across the showground to the beer tent, and barrels were thumped down into the soft earth and rolled under the canvas. The marquees and the lanes between them gradually took on the appearance of a busy city.

Leonard and Tolson moved leisurely round the show-ground and, as the tent contractor's men, re-arranged doorways and walling, checked the guy-lines and stakes, and erected a small twelve-by-twelve tent for the St John

Ambulance. People from the village had come to watch the growing activity. Amongst them Leonard recognized Enid, familiar from five days before.

She'd come into the field with several boys, and he watched for a while as she moved amongst the tents and trade stands, the men turning to stare at her noisy procession. Then she disappeared amongst the larger marquees and he could only hear the occasional cries of the accompanying boys marking her progress round the field.

He turned away. Tolson was working beside him, securing the stakes down one side of the largest tent. Stripped to the waist and sweating in the sun, he swung the sledge-hammer above his head like a stick, drawing his body sharply away from the descending weight as it struck the stake, forcing all his pulled strength into the stroke. The men had stopped in their work to watch him: the steel swinging over his head and flashing onto the slim necks of the stakes. He never missed. He rested the hammer a moment on each stake to judge its distance, set his feet, and swung with a supple undulation of his back and shoulders. He scarcely paused.

In the centre of the show-ring Wetherby had leaned casually back on his stick. For a while he'd been shouting orders to the men who were lifting jumping gates and hurdles onto the unmarked grass, but now they worked under the impetus of his directions and he watched with some detachment as the final details of the showground fell into place around him.

Enid had suddenly re-appeared alone and stepped into the arena. She stood a short distance behind Wetherby, watching several men arrange a red and white jumping gate. Wetherby, his eye-patch turning slowly from the sun in a casual inspection, momentarily noticed the girl with a slight upwards movement of his head. For a while the circular motion of his head continued then, briefly, he glanced back at her and a moment later drew up his stick and moved slowly away. Just as it seemed he would walk past Tolson, he stopped and watched the regular rotation of the hammer head as if he were consulting a clock. He seemed lost for several moments as he followed the powerful oscillation of the steel and the odd suction of the earth as the rods were driven in. Round each stake was a ring of liquid, forced up as the metal burst into the ground.

He reached out his stick and arrested the hammer at the summit of its swing. He pointed down towards the river where the latrines stood and, giving some instructions which he made Tolson repeat, left the showground for the second time that morning and drove off in his small car.

Leonard and Tolson had gone down to the latrines and, removing one side of the screening, had begun to extend the structure. A few moments later Enid entered the gap in the screening and stood watching them work. She stayed by the entrance, motionless, her hands clenched together and hanging in front of her, watching Tolson hammering up the screen. She was deeply tanned, her mouth lined with pale lipstick. Black lines exaggerated inaccurately the contours of her eyes; they seemed to be set disjointedly in her head.

'If you want to use it you'll have to wait,' Tolson said.

'Why did you shout at me last Tuesday?' she said to Leonard, yet not looking at him, rather regarding her hand, the fingers of which she laid across the 'Ladies' sign by her head.

Tolson worked indifferently to her, standing on one of the cans and banging in the tacks with a hammer head clenched in his hand. He carefully measured out the laths and planned their intersections, Leonard handing up the pieces for him to assemble. He worked with a great dexterity and precision.

'You! Why did you shout?' she said, suddenly turning to Leonard.

Tolson looked down; Leonard didn't answer. He was white. Tolson said, 'Go on – you better run off before you get hurt.'

'What's up with that man with the black patch, then? What's the matter with his eye?' She diverted Tolson's interest, watching Leonard now through cautious, narrowed eyes.

'I've told you, love. You better go,' Tolson said.

'I'll stay if I want to.'

Tolson climbed down. It seemed it was her clown-like intentness that incensed him. As he caught her she grasped the nearest lath, and when he tried to tear her away the whole structure of the latrines shook.

'You better get off me, mate,' she warned him.

Leonard watched them in silence. Tolson started to break the girl's hold as he might have stripped a tree, ripping down her arms; but before he could drag her out, Wetherby came round the screening.

'How near are you to being finished?' he said. He was irritated. He stared directly into the faces of the two men as though the girl were not there. In the doorway behind him were four latrine cans which he had just put down.

'Can you ask this girl to go, sir?' Tolson said, flushed and dark now that his violence had been interrupted. 'She won't leave us alone.'

Wetherby glanced at the girl briefly with his clear eye. It was several seconds before he spoke. 'Get out!' he said. It was virtually a cry.

The girl winced slightly. The single eye was quite still. 'Get out! And don't let me find you in here again.'

She seemed about to slip past him. But in the same movement she stepped inside the nearest cubicle and, lifting her skirt and lowering her knickers, placed herself securely on the can. She paused there a moment to an accompanying sound of jetted liquid, then re-arranging her clothes and without a glance at either of the three men, except for a brief frenzied smile at Leonard, she squeezed out between the four cans standing in the doorway.

For a moment Wetherby didn't move. Then, as though he had mistaken the incident completely, he smiled at the two men, and taking the shooting stick from under his arm pushed back the canvas doors of the completed cubicles. 'You seem to have done a good job, men.' He glanced at them separately and unsmilingly, then shook the structure with his foot. 'It's firm.' He nodded and went out.

Tolson had burst out laughing. 'Well, I'll go fuck a duck,' he said, bending forward, then straightening suddenly as Wetherby returned.

'By the way, I've four what-have-you's outside. Borrowed them. Put them in the end there, the east wing, then I'll know exactly which ones they are.'

The sun had flooded into the dale, and the whitened rock and hedged fields trembled and pounded upwards. The ground ate up the heat, and the river was the only live thing, boiling and frothing through its grey-rocked bed and past the bare scars on the hillside.

The castle above the village was now part of the rock; its stone rubble melted into the hill, and green and brown and grey had filtered into a hazy glare. The ridge had drawn away and the valley grew out of the rock embrace.

Along the road running like a nerve through the centre of the dale cars were parked two deep, trucks and farm vehicles sidling between them; and in the fields on either side of the showground the cattle stalls were surrounded by neat rows of vehicles. All morning smartly-dressed men and women had crowded into the site, the flowered dresses moving restlessly between the white flanks of the canvas until, as the heat and density increased, the women, illuminated by their bright colours, appeared to seethe and drone in the packed lanes. Tolson, his hammer draped over his naked shoulder, moved amongst the glowing fabrics and polished leathers, accepting drinks at the stalls and watching the neatly jodhpured figures mounting horses and trotting into the show-ring, his muscled figure growing familiar to the crowds as the day wore on.

8

Leonard had climbed the limestone scar to the castle. It was a small ruin, its one original tower now broken. He found a crevice on the front wall and, crouched there, stared down into the valley. Almost motionless from this distance and height, the river flashed intermittently between the smooth fields, the light glinting remotely from the baler parked at the Fordson tent, its forked elevators turning slowly in the sun. The riders were no more than targets now, moving round and round, occasionally dropping down or stopping.

Behind him a small apron of grass lined the yard of the castle, the soft velvet stretching up to the grey wall from which fierce tufts of longer grass escaped. A net of ivy had grown over the stone, scrambling up the crumbled surface of the square building to its jagged summit. The rutted socket of the tower had, like its clinging plants, grown out of the rock.

These impressions enfolded Leonard as he crouched there, a pebble in its worn façade, a part of its slow erosion. Beyond the smooth grass and the tower stump, thorn trees leaned from the prevailing wind and thrust out branches like hands plucked from the south. Frozen in their long siege, they fought the building's aggressive immobility, their structures withered like bone. Over the moor, and over the twisted rocks to the broken lip of the valley, shapes grew and writhed until they reached the stone of the castle. And within the coils of bracken and bramble, and the ragged belt of rock scar, was laid the square patch of grass, even, short and delicately trimmed.

A broad shadow had begun to move, the blackness creeping out from the tower and turning the green into a deep blue mould. The heaviness moved slowly across the lawn, absorbing the blades, the specks of wind-blown debris; then a moth, yellow and russet brown. Its pale meandering towards the stone of the tower burned for a moment, then faltered, and was extinguished like a flame.

Tolson burst out of the shadow.

'What're you doing up here, then? I saw you from down yonder.' He put his foot on the parapet and looked down at the tents. 'I thought we could get some of the smaller ones down tonight, then we won't be hanging around so much with all the others tomorrow.'

The arena was emptying, the last knots of people round the marquees breaking up. The trade tents were deserted, and already the machinery and displays were being removed. Creeping down the valley was a steady stream of single line traffic; and from the village vans and trucks had begun to edge amongst the stalls for loading up. On the track over the moors small groups of figures were moving slowly against the sky, balloons and kites floating like bright leaves in their wake. Climbing up the track out of the valley rode a thin line of mounted figures, disappearing round the rock scar, then emerging close to the castle.

'A couple of hours and they'll have all the cars and stuff out,' Tolson said. 'I'm surprised you coming up here. I've enjoyed myself down yonder.' His face was flushed under his deep sunburn, his thick chest and arms burned by the heat. A singlet hung loosely over his trousers, and its whiteness gave his skin and his features, his black hair, a negroid look.

Leonard stood up, half-smiling. 'You won't let me down?' he said. 'Will you?'

'What do you mean?' Tolson had already backed slightly away.

'You know well enough.'

'Why should I let you down?'

The blood had rushed to Leonard's face. He put his hands on Tolson's shoulders, and for a moment stood quite still feeling the hot skin beneath his fingers, and staring into his face. Then he leaned forward and kissed his arm, opening his mouth over Tolson's biceps. With an almost ferocious energy, he pulled Tolson against him, running his hands over his body. 'Let me feel you,' he said, half laughing, pulling Tolson against him. He pressed his hand between Tolson's legs, and the larger man stumbled back, catching his heels against the rock. But Leonard pursued him.

'Come on,' said Tolson, 'We'll go down and see about the tents.'

But, laughing, Leonard ran at him, throwing himself forward and clutching Tolson's legs so that they both fell on the grass. For a moment, pinioned by Tolson's arms, Leonard didn't move. Then twisting to free his arm he ran his hand up again between Tolson's thighs, pressing himself forward as Tolson tried to drag himself away. Almost simultaneously he was flung back with great violence and Tolson stood up.

'Leave me alone!' he shouted.

The line of horsemen was now quite near, and there was the sound of a child talking anxiously and soothingly to an animal.

Tolson had turned away. He walked into the shadow, then paused for Leonard to catch him up. He was laughing still, and breathless, but Tolson only glanced at him and strode down the slope more rapidly, so that Leonard had to run to keep up.

Along the crescent of the hills shallow arcs of plumed cloud burned round the sun, crimson and yellow, sealing the dale with shadows, and a great keel of shadow crept along the river. Shooting up into the deep overhead blueness red fangs of cloud broke from the horizon, the sharp, slow loops fading and reappearing, vicious and searing over the fused purple of the moor. They groped ferociously eastwards where the sky darkened and melted into the seeping hollow-mist down the valley. The castle was broken now by shadow.

The land had begun to eat into the sun; the showfield was darkening and almost deserted. A few people loitered between the mounds of paper and refuse, and dogs from the village hurried from place to place followed by boys searching amongst the rubbish. A lone woman took her horse over the jumps in the arena, reining it in at the far end and leaping her way back, the leather creaking in the still air with the animal's panting. A thin breeze dragged straw and paper over the ground, releasing them to flap against the hardened mud. By his tent Wetherby was talking to three women in head-scarves and jodhpurs who, as they listened, tapped the backs of their thighs with leather whips.

The two men worked hard, taking down all the small trade tents and pulling up the stakes with a chain. By the time they had lowered Wetherby's office-tent he had disappeared, driving off in his car with two of the women.

Tolson stooped down to the stakes of the next tent. A coolness had drifted up from the river. The slopes above the valley turned black, a hard blue-black that brought them tumbling into the dale, each weight of shadow crumbling on the next, fold after fold from the sombre ridge. Above it settled the sun, a half-drugged eye over the moor, as if with its own weight it might push the earth down. The blackness swayed a moment, the land shuddered with its colour and haze, and the crimson bulb sank. Red flanges of mist and cloud studded the falling sky. The ground suddenly darkened.

Tolson looked up, poised, then rubbed his shoulders at the quick chilling of the air. A moment later he said, 'We'll leave the latrines. I reckon they'll stand till tomorrow.' He hooked down the canvas like toy balloons.

At the gate Enid stood and watched them.

She walked closer. The two men worked in rhythm, folding the tent walling.

'Aren't you taking all those big tents down as well?' she said.

Tolson looked up at her. For a while he didn't answer. Then he said, 'It'll take five or six men to get them down.' He stared up at the looming canvas.

'When will they fetch them down, then?'

'Tomorrow. They'll all be here tomorrow.'

'Are you looking forward to going back?' She glanced from Tolson to Leonard, as though pleased at her reception. 'I don't think your friend is.'

Tolson smiled at Leonard's faintly tensed figure.

'What's your name, then?' she asked.

'Vic,' Tolson said when it seemed Leonard might answer. He held out the canvas to Leonard, nodding at the girl, then bending down.

They worked instinctively together, folding the length of tent wall on the ground, drawing it up and laying it neatly seam on seam.

For a while the girl watched, then she bent down to collect the stakes, and after they'd packed the walling and the roof in the hessian bags, Tolson showed her how to lay the stakes and rolled guy-lines on top.

They laced up the heavy bags, and she walked and ran behind them as they hurried with the heavy, bulging sacks to the large marquee to stack. She tried to lift one, planting her feet astride it, her arms dragged down by the weight.

'You'll do yourself an hurt,' Tolson said. 'They weigh more than ninety pounds.' He put one on his shoulder to laugh at her.

'Where did you get your muscles from?' she asked him.

77

'Bread and fat. Isn't that right?' He looked at Leonard a moment, then back at the girl. 'Though thy's got a couple of muscles that can beat any two of mine.'

Engines roared in the next field as the last machines were drawn out. A few people stood talking among the cattle-pens and in the lane. But in the showground the three of them were alone.

Tolson rubbed his hands on his thighs and shivered with the chill in the air. 'There's not much else we can do,' he said, scarcely glancing at Leonard. 'I reckon we can call it a day and see if we can find ought.'

He picked up his hammer and walked across to the beer tent. The girl ran after him. When Leonard reached the door Tolson was cracking the hammer head against the empty barrels. The tent was dark, the canvas old and heavily stained. He knocked through the refuse and crates, suddenly impatient, pushing them over. He made a path through to the opposite entrance. All round the bar were pools of metal caps.

Tolson walked frustratedly through this deserted palace, from one debris-filled hall to another, each with its separate smell of oil, of food, of animals and birds, of people. Everything had gone.

His hand was clutched round the neck of the hammer, the steel head gleaming like an irregular extension of his arm. The girl trailed behind him, running to keep up, darting about the gloom of the interiors.

Leonard followed more slowly, occasionally glimpsing through some gap in the canvas the flickering shape of the girl, then the heavier, impetuous shadow of Tolson. When he eventually found them the girl was soberly watching Tolson as he turned over the tables in the Domestic tent, swinging his hammer down on piles of cracked plates. The pot shrapnel shot against the tent wall, dull and searing the canvas.

'Shall we go round smashing them all down?' she said.

'No.' The idea surprised him. He glanced round at the litter of tables and trestles and folding chairs, then began to stack them neatly against the tent-poles.

He seemed quite numb. His hammer stood upright

beside him. The girl had planted her feet on the hammer head and, her hands gripping the shaft between her legs, she swayed backwards and forwards, rocking on the wooden pendulum. Leonard watched her in silence, his mouth slightly parted, as though with the first impact of shock.

'Are you going anywhere on your bike tonight?' she said to Tolson. 'Give us a ride on it.'

Tolson suddenly pulled the hammer from under her feet. She fell back laughing against the wall of the tent and for a moment sprawled there, upright, struggling to regain her balance. Then she darted out after Tolson, running after him, thrusting her arm in his and skipping along beside him. Her hair suddenly fell down over her shoulders.

'Take care. Now just be careful,' he said, holding her off his sunburned skin.

'Will you take us a ride?'

'I'll think about it.' He glanced awkwardly at Leonard who followed slowly behind. 'We're going to get something to eat.'

'I'll cook for you, if you like. If you'll give us a ride. I'm good at cooking. I am, honest.'

'Ah . . . I'll see about that.'

Tolson started the Primus. Leonard stood beside him as though drained of all strength and interest. The girl prepared the meal.

Later, while they ate, she went down to the river with the pan. They said nothing as she walked away across the deserted showground. They were crouched quite close together, silent, Tolson occasionally eating. She returned slowly up the field, walking stiffly, with the pan held carefully before her in both hands, and stopping inter-mittently, laughing, as it splashed her legs. She put the pan on the stove and stooped down, waiting for it to boil. She seemed lost in her task, oblivious. Tolson stood up. He rubbed his shoulders. 'It's getting cold.' He looked round for something to put on.

The girl poured out the tea, stirred it, and stood back. 'There, will you take us a ride now?' She stood licking the spoon, watching Tolson.

'It's too dark.'

'It'll be all right. It will.'

'How am I going to see?'

'You've got lights on your bike.' She was looking at it inside the gloom of the tent. Tolson watched her as he drank his tea. His look followed her carefully in anticipation as she moved about in front of the tent.

'Go on. Just a short ride.'

'I'll take you just round the field,' he told her.

'Shall I pull it out for you, Vic?'

He moved forward. 'No. Tha'll never.' He went across to the tent-flap but she was already inside.

'Get on outside,' Leonard heard him say. 'I'll fetch it out.'

She was holding onto the bike as he wheeled it out. He leaned over the machine possessively, feeling the engine. He switched on the petrol and stepped over the bike, shaking it violently from side to side. Leonard held his cup in both hands, watching.

The engine roar sprang into the valley, louder now in the stillness, crisp and staccato. The thudding boomed in the place. As the bike shuddered the girl climbed on, her legs white against his dark mass and her thin arms like rods of the machine itself. She sat clutched to him while he beamed the headlight.

They moved away towards the tents and the noise became a continuous echo. The beam of light, stiff and angular, trembled and jarred in the dimness, splaying out then exploding in a wide ring on the canvas. It disappeared, then suddenly burst out between the blankness of the marquees.

In the small square caravan near the trade tents the old watchman had come to the top of his steps: Leonard could see his silhouette bowed against the cream paint and the lamplit interior. It was darkening, the sky had lost its colour and a white tongue of moon probed the cloud mists. At the fringe of the sky the light drew out clouds, hanging now like phosphorescent dew, fat globules, round and bursting in the distance with an orange sheen. Under the dying sky and the murderous line of rocks the engine slowly circled the field. They swept past, a sudden huge and swift shape, the engine stuttering over the ruts and the headlamp shuddering, both of them pressed together.

The shape reached the flat stretch at the side of the field and the light suddenly moved in a fast stream: it ran smoothly and quickly. On the level platform down to the river it all came quick to life. For a moment. Then it suddenly jolted, the beam writhed and twisted as if caught in a snare, shuddered, and the engine cut back quickly and stopped.

The beam of light stood silent by the river. Tolson's voice came distantly in the still air. Then the headlight was swung from side to side, loosely, as the bike was pulled backwards, edging it out of the mud. It stood still. For a while Leonard heard nothing.

The engine was re-started quietly, muffled and oddly subdued. The dark shape circuited the field. Tolson held the bike preciously as it ran up to the tent, the chain purring over the cogs. He stood up, rigid, as the girl climbed off. The light from the lamp exaggerated the texture of the grass: it grew like shining metal nails.

'We were nearly in the river,' Tolson said. His voice was quiet in the silence after the engine, vaguely disappointed. They seemed tired and past talking.

'Can you drive it?' the girl asked Leonard.

'No.'

She fingered the handlebar and the instruments mounted round the lamp. Tolson turned the bike away from her. Footsteps crunched in the lane from the village. A voice shouted her name, thick and demanding.

'Enid! Are ye there?'

'Who is it?' Tolson asked her. 'Is it your father?'

The man shouted again.

'It's our Alan.'

They listened to the silence in the lane, staring at the pale outline of each other's face.

'I better go,' she said.

'I'll go with you,' Leonard suddenly told her. 'To the gate. You'll find your way from there.'

They both looked at him.

The man's voice shouted from somewhere at the side of the field, from the low shadows of the trees. He waited. Then his steps sounded as though they were coming into the showground. Yet they crunched persistently in the road and slowly faded towards the houses.

'Come on,' Leonard said.

The girl glanced at Tolson. He didn't move. She turned towards the gate and Leonard began to walk beside her. She called back to Tolson softly. He stood silently by the bike. The dew struck their faces as they walked. The air was filled with the dank evening smell of grasses. She moved slowly beside Leonard, then stood in the ruts at the entrance to the field, waiting.

'What will your father say?' he asked her.

She rubbed her feet in the ashes and glanced into the darkness of the lane. 'He's dead. That's our Alan. My brother.'

'Do you want me to come any further with you?'

'No.'

'Good night, then.'

She stood looking into his face a moment. Then she ran off quickly up the lane.

'We'll go up to the pub,' Tolson said when Leonard got back. He had already wheeled the bike into the tent, and he scarcely looked up. He seemed stooped slightly, pained.

The pub was almost empty. They didn't talk. Leonard stood under a pale, orange light: it was like a weight on his slim figure, heavy and distorting. It was late. They scarcely drank. The night-watchman sat by himself, an old bearded figure, stooped over a table. His fingers were splayed out anciently either side on the bare wooden surface. Tolson bought him a drink, and after a while they walked back to the field together. The old man invited them into his small caravan and, at Tolson's insistence, they began to play cards. In the corner of the van was chained a large black dog.

They crouched closely round the table, an oil lamp burning over their heads. The old man was in shadow, only his curled thumbs and the arthritic bulbs of his knuckles visible as he flicked out the cards. A bird screeched over the moorland. The sound throbbed in the hut. The pool of light laid itself carefully over their three figures, the old man's eyes staring out like coals from the shadow, his hands fidgeting. The cards, dropping crisply, clicked on the plain deal table.

Tolson played on restlessly, smoking. The old man hardly looked up, watching Tolson's fingers, each like a muscle, laying the cards down thin as wafers. He gazed at their casual strength and then, at the last moment, glanced up at Tolson's face. He stared back at the cards, suddenly blind to them.

Eventually he stood up, unhooked another lamp out of the darkness and lit it. The new light doubled on his cracked features and laid back the shadows to the corner of the van, illuminating the huge dog. Its teeth were like white rivets set in its metal head. It didn't move. Their figures trailed giant shadows.

They went out. The old man leashed the dog and followed them. Leonard coughed, clutching his chest a second, as he climbed down the steps. The air was ragingly fresh. It was dark, the moon hidden. Far away on one of the ridges was a single speck of light; and the screaming, still, of a bird up on the moor.

The old man walked behind them, his lamp swinging low, throwing the weight of their shadows forward, lighting up the hardened ruts and the quilting of the ground. Once he tripped over a guy and stumbled. He said nothing. The lamp rattled, then he came on. The dog itself made no sound.

The tents were luminous, pale cliffs around the field, glowing as the light fell on them as if the canvas absorbed it, contained it. Stars glistened in the torn patches between the clouds. When they got nearer the tent Leonard called to the old man and they left him. He gave no answer. His lamp swung away slowly towards his van, outlining the moving shape of the dog. In the sudden blackness Leonard walked close to Tolson. He walked softly, tensed to the coldness, and touching Tolson with his arm, his shoulder, and then his hand. Their feet crunched in the ash ruts.

Tolson unfastened the tent-flap and held it up as Leonard pushed his way in.

It smelt of oil. He squeezed past the bike, crawling along

83

his bed and feeling for the lamp. The wire handle caught against his hand; he pulled the globe up and struck a match and lit it. Tolson scraped his boots at the door.

The yellow flame gradually raised itself inside the glass sheath, tapering like a spear, then wavering. A thin jet of black smoke fled from its tip. Then the light steadied and spread around the tent. The place glowed.

Enid was sitting opposite him, crouched at the end of Tolson's bed. For a second Leonard wasn't sure that it was he himself who had let out a cry. It was so quickly muffled by the tent.

'I guessed it wa're her,' Tolson said.

Her face was white, peeled back, featureless in the lamplight, no more than that of a doll. Leonard sat on the edge of the bed staring numbly at her, frozen, then up at Tolson by the door. He was lighting a cigarette, his eyes momentarily distorted over the brief glow.

'What've you been stealing, then?' he said.

'Nothing. I just came.'

Tolson nodded his head at her heavily, unsurprised. 'Ah, well. You better go now, then.'

She shook her head determinedly and glanced at Leonard. His mouth trembled with the cold and his body shook, held rigidly between his elbows. He might have been crying. The shadow of the bike was flung up against the roof, stretched and poised and animated by every quiver of the flame.

'I better find her father in the village,' Tolson said.

'I only came to have a talk. There's never anybody to talk to round here.' Her face fell into the shadow of the bike. The spokes sent long lines curling across her mouth. She looked crabbed and ancient.

'Why should I give a sod?' Tolson pulled the flaps down and came in. He felt the bike a moment then warmed his hands round the lamp, sitting on his bed next to the girl. 'How long are you planning on staying? We've had a long day today.'

The shadow fell on them both, uniting them in a frantic pattern of cuts and slashes. The girl hardly moved in the bizarre web of shadow.

84

Tolson leaned past her and wound up the portable and put the needle on the record he had played that morning. Leonard suddenly got under his blankets, lay down and covered himself. His face was almost concealed.

The girl asked Tolson for a cigarette. She lit it in the broad flame cupped in Tolson's hands. They listened to the music a moment, then she said, 'Can't you play it softer?' She smoked inexpertly, her mouth full of smoke.

'It won't go any softer, mate. Put a coat over it if it annoys you.'

'No. It doesn't annoy me.' She poured smoke from her mouth. 'It's cold.'

Tolson lay down. 'Come under the blankets,' he said.

'No.' She stood up suddenly. 'I'll go with your friend.'

She didn't look at Leonard. She sat quite casually on his bed and carefully pushed her legs down. At first he made some resistance to her intrusion, then she slid down quite easily beside him.

Tolson turned over the record, replaced the needle, and wrapped himself in his blanket. He hooded it over his head. The girl was looking across at him, holding her cigarette away from the blankets. 'Are you married?' she said.

'I am.'

'Is your friend? . . . Are *you* married?'

Tolson laughed. She turned to look at Leonard's head beside her. It was scarcely visible within the shadow of the blanket.

'What's up with that?' she asked. 'Is he divorced or something?'

'No. I was just laughing. He lives at home does Len.'

'Do you, Len?' she asked.

She moved her face against his cheek. 'Don't you like me?' When he didn't reply she added, 'If you talk and I press me head against yours like this I can hear it inside your head. Have you ever tried it? You listen as I talk,' she went on as Tolson laughed again.

Leonard didn't move. She put her arm across him, moving it down beneath the blankets.

Suddenly the tent-flap moved, and the next moment it was clumsily flung back.

The girl cried out. She screamed. A figure stood there, leaning in. Strangely, Leonard hadn't moved.

It was the old man. 'Can you put your wireless down?' he said bitterly. 'I can't get to sleep because of it.'

'Sorry, love.' Tolson leaned out of the blanket and lifted the needle off the record.

They were silent. They could see the man's face now, old, like a rock. He stood in the darkness outside the tent for some time, and for a moment they heard the dog scenting the canvas somewhere close to their heads.

Tolson said, 'Do you want to come in?'

'No. No. It's all right. I'm just off to bed.' It was as if he'd forgotten his complaint.

They could see him for a moment beyond the tent flap as he moved away. The girl was sobbing.

'It's all right,' Leonard said. His voice was distant and calm.

'It's the old lad from across the field,' Tolson said. 'He died last week but nobody bothered to tell him.'

'Oh, I don't know.' She was breathless. 'Just coming like that.'

'She thought it was her brother,' said Leonard quietly.

'Is it late?' the girl said.

'Nay, but you'll stay the night now,' Tolson told her.

'But I *can't*.'

'It's all right. We'll look after you.'

'I can't. I can't.' She didn't recognize his humour.

'Len won't mind. He'll put you up.'

'No. I'll have to go. I've been sitting here an hour for you already.' She drew up her legs in the bed, full of some private misery. 'Do you want me to stay?' She looked at Tolson.

Suddenly he stood up. 'I'll see you back,' he said, then added to Leonard when it seemed he might get up, 'No. You stay here. No good two of us getting cold. . . . Come on, I'll see you to the gate, then you can run up from there.'

She climbed out from beside Leonard and smoothed down her skirt.

'Good night, then, Len,' she said from the door. Her voice was light, relieved.

Leonard lay back. He listened to the soft thud of their feet in the grass, the occasional slur as they walked through the ashes, then the quiet murmur of their fading voices.

The night was completely still. A soft illumination from outside flowed over the tent, draining the heavy shadow of the bike on the roof. The light on the tent paused, faded, and the roof sagged a moment in shadow. The canvas lightened as the cloud drew off the moon.

The bed creaked as he stood up. He listened, his hands clenched and his arms held stiffly by his sides. He moved to the door, paused, then hurriedly pushed his way out.

The field was vast in moonlight. He ran a few steps then spun round and stared at the tent as if it were an animal he'd flung from his back. The place was still and deserted. He walked up and down a few moments. All round him was a frozen sea, glowing with the soft light. The waves of the tents splayed up luminously and smoothly to the curving swell of the moors, looming and lined by the dark, ragged edges of the rock. The gigantic sea was drawn up to the sky, pinned by the moon, large and pallid. Nothing broke the stillness. It was a room.

The gate leading to the lane was open. White, and silvered with lime dust, the lane curved into the pitched shadows of the trees. It was deserted. He walked up towards the houses, his boots crunching like a giant, far off, walking on the moors.

Two strands of light glowed above his head. Long threads, they stretched delicately between and through the leaves, piercing the branches. Somewhere down the valley a vehicle had turned. Its lights caught the wires. The filaments burned in the darkness, quivering, then slowly disappeared. He stopped, and turned back.

The tents and the rocks crouched like monuments in the crook of the valley. He stood at the gate.

''Vic!'

The sound burst and broke on the walls of the valley. Above the trees rose the stump of the castle, sharp and isolated on the shoulder of rock. Its broken pinnacle grazed the sky. Shadows poured across its buttressed wall as a cloud slid from the moon.

'Vic!'

The sound rose like a scream. Out of the valley side, by the castle, a shape floated. Soundless, without a movement, it glided out and up, over the field, larger and blacker, formless in the faint light. It rustled over his head, a thin wafting sound, like wood pounding the air.

'Vic!'

He ran back to the tent. The lamp smelt acrid, at the end of its fuel. He pulled the flap down, pegged it securely, and got into bed, covering himself with the blankets. The redness suddenly faded and the shadow of the bike, spreadeagled on the roof, wavered. The lamp went out. He closed his eyes and curled into himself, and after a while he no longer moved at all.

Yet he was not asleep when, some time later, Tolson pushed his way through the flap, tearing it. He swore.

'What've you pegged the bloody thing for?'

'Where have you been?'

Tolson groped about exaggeratedly in the dark, swearing to himself. He made a great deal of noise.

'Where's the bloody lamp gone?' He was deliberately aggrieved.

'It went out. Some time ago.'

Tolson pushed past his bike and reached his bed. His foot crunched on the gramophone. 'Have you been asleep?' he said, suddenly indulgent. 'I took a stroll round after I left her.'

'Didn't you see her home?'

'Just to the gate. Then she ran off like the wind.'

Tolson's smell filled the tent. He lay down quickly, covering himself. The bike leaned between them.

Leonard, trembling and in tears, pulled the blanket over his head and turned to sleep.

9

The bell from the church was ringing for morning service as the three red lorries and the 15 cwt truck, preceded by

Ewbank's Armstrong Siddeley, dipped into the field. They parked in a loose line across the centre of the arena. The men began to climb out and stare confusedly at the flattened field. The doors on Ewbank's car, however, remained firmly closed.

The showground had been destroyed. Canvas, poles, screening, ropes and stakes were scattered over the grass and the beaten earth as though from some giant disembowelling. The men stood by their vehicles too astonished, it seemed, to approach.

From the single surviving tent at the top of the field Leonard suddenly emerged. For a moment he stood quite still, gazing round at the scene. Then, only gradually, did he seem to become aware of the vehicles and the silent crowd of men. The door on Ewbank's car was slowly pushed open. A moment later the contractor's tall, black figure uncoiled from the opening.

He looked up towards Leonard, waiting. The men had turned in his direction too. Leonard approached them very slowly.

'Well?' Ewbank said.

'Tolson's gone.'

Ewbank watched him. He made no attempt to examine the tents. The sheets of canvas flapped loosely in a light breeze, stirring against the ground.

'He must have done this,' Leonard added.

For a while Ewbank didn't answer. He stared intently at Leonard. Then he glanced up swiftly, almost blindly, at the men.

'You mean Tolson took all these down by himself?' he said. 'I don't believe it. Not for a minute.'

The expression in his reddened eyes expanded. He gazed at Leonard a moment longer, struggling to interpret the feeling in that intensely pale face, then he looked away at the tents. The smoke from his cheroot curled idly round his eyes. The men began to gather more closely about their employer.

He felt in his top suit pocket and brought out his glasses, putting them on to regard each detail freshly through the frameless lenses.

'And where's Victor God Almighty Tolson now?'

'I don't know.'

He glanced sharply to the top of the field. Their small blackened tent billowed slightly in the wind. He took off his glasses.

'How do you mean, you don't know?'

'I haven't seen him at all this morning.'

'But what the bloody hell. I mean, what've you been doing all the time? What's been happening?' He shouted now the thing took possession of him.

'The Show went off all right. But it was like this when I got up just now. When I heard the lorries.'

The men had drawn up in a half-circle. Some of them started to smoke.

'He must have done it very early. I never heard him. He's taken his bike and gone.'

Ewbank's small hands unfastened the buttons of his suit jacket. He seemed imprisoned by his inability to understand.

'And gone where?'

'Home. Back to town. I don't know.'

'And what were you doing all this time?'

'We'd a heavy day yesterday. We took down all the small tents last night.'

It seemed that Ewbank grew smaller, diminished by his rage. Desperate to take some sort of advantage he stood with his long legs firmly astride and his fist clenched round his glasses in some vague gesture of threat. Yet Leonard regarded him almost calmly, with a dark, blank look.

'You expect me to believe that one man took all this down? God in heaven, what do you think I am, for Christ's sake?'

'Whatever's happened I don't see how all your shouting can help.' There was now a torn grievance in Leonard's voice.

'You don't!' Ewbank's figure sprang apart, his arms flung out at the tents, as though he had been plucked from the air. 'I've got five ... six thousand poundsworth of tenting laid up in this field and if there's as much as a footprint laid on it I'll make sure ... you and Tolson.' He stared desperately at Leonard, demandingly, unable to express the extent of his feelings.

'I feel bad enough about it myself.'

'*You* do. . . .' Ewbank turned away. 'I just don't understand this. Nobody could sleep through a thing like this. Nobody!' He stared at the fawn brilliance of his car with stifled rage.

'We didn't get to sleep until late.'

'Till late. I see . . . I just don't understand, that's all. I employ a mindless bloody gorilla on the one hand and a mental defective on the other. And nobody tells *me*. How the bloody hell am I supposed to know? Why on God's earth. . . .' He put away his glasses, then took the cheroot from his mouth and dropped it in the mud. He examined it for a while, then closed his small shoe over it and spread it evenly over the ground. 'Wait here.'

He began to walk over to the nearest stretch of canvas. He turned round.

'That means all of you standing there. Every single one of you. Look where you're standing, where your fucking feet are – now *look*! And bloody well stay there.'

He strode over to the canvas and lifted the nearest edge. He examined it carefully, peering round at the deflated surface of the tent then passing on, lifting and examining each section.

Leonard followed him at a distance, looking at the canvas. A gust of wind swept under the tenting and it throbbed into smooth, uneven waves, a flapping corrugation. Ewbank watched it come to life with the same impotent expression. He wiped his face and his neck with a white handkerchief, crisp and unstained. All this evidence of fantastic industry had to mean something.

Leonard passed each of the corpses and saw that there was no mutilation, no deliberate damage at all. Despite the impression of destruction, it was obvious that the tents had not been wildly collapsed but brought down methodically and with prodigious industry. Tolson must have worked with maniacal speed to lower each marquee uniformly, rushing from pole to pole to regulate the weight of descent evenly on the pulleys, unlacing the sheets of canvas and disengaging the guys so that nothing would be torn; the intensity and ferocity of his work lay everywhere, giant-like, purposeless, impossible. It was too huge, too carefully done.

'It's obvious enough,' Ewbank said more calmly. He recognized the skill in the work. 'This is the work of a madman.'

'I don't think so.'

'You admit you helped him, then?'

'No. I only got up a few minutes ago. When I heard the lorries.'

'All right, then.' Ewbank took out a cheroot and lit it carefully, his eyes intent on the flame. He threw the match away with the same care. 'If I believe that, then this *is* insanity.' He stared at him demandingly, almost curious now. 'You can't tell me that that's normal. Not any of it. It's done by someone who's insane, is that.' He gestured aggrievedly at the sprawled mass of the beer marquee. The men had come up to examine the tents for themselves; they watched Leonard and Ewbank suspiciously. 'Come on, then, I want an explanation.'

'I haven't got one.'

'No. And I'm not surprised. I know what's behind all this.' He fed the men's looks; they watched Leonard aloofly.

'There's no damage,' Leonard said slowly. 'The tents haven't been harmed.' His dark eyes had widened with reproach.

'No.' Ewbank stressed his leniency. Smoke drifted from his mouth. 'And who do I have to thank for that?' He waited some time for Leonard to answer. The men moved uneasily, glancing at the tents with new suspicion. 'Come on. What have you and Tolson been up to here together?'

A man laughed and for a second Ewbank's face relaxed, his eyes narrowing as though unknown to him they were smiling. He almost physically projected his distaste. Leonard's face had taken on a claustrophobic expression. He seemed stifled, turning away.

Ewbank watched him walk back to the tent. He blew his nose, dabbing it cautiously with his crisp handkerchief. Then, turning briskly, he set the men to work packing the marquees and loading the trucks. They were on double time and half the day's work had already been done.

'Radcliffe. . . .' Ewbank went over to the tent. He glanced in a moment, then stepped back alertly. 'You better leave off packing your things and go down to the latrines. I see he didn't bother to take them down. And no wonder.' As Leonard emerged he lowered his voice and added, 'Since you put them up you'll know how they come down. I'll send Shaw down to give you a hand.' He had intended to sound lenient, but Leonard was already walking away.

For a while Leonard worked alone. He took down the screening round the Men's and rolled it up. Then he sat under the hedge and waited.

Shaw was slow. When he came he glanced at the hessian screening the Ladies, and sat down under the hedge a short distance away and rolled a cigarette. He was old, and disinterested. His thick, square hands folded the cigarette and his tongue crept out from his angular face to lick the gum; the edge was pressed down, secured, and stroked flat by heavy thumbs. Then he lit the loose strands carelessly, the narrow cigarette flaming, and from his boiler suit pockets he brought a small piece of metal and a file. He worked with a peculiar delicacy at the metal, shaping it to some design embedded deeply within his broad skull.

Once, he glanced up the field to where Ewbank supervised the loading. Then he continued his filing. The smoke streamed past his eyes. After a while he said, 'Thy mate's pissed it up this time all right. We had a good twelve hours today and now we'll be back before three o'clock.' He put his file down and re-lit his cigarette. 'Then he sends me down on this job.' His fingers held the stub tightly to his mouth while he smoked it fiercely to a rind, worrying it with his lips, then throwing it away with a gasp as the heat touched his fingers. He spat out the shreds in the front of his mouth, and filed more carefully along the sharp edge of the metal.

Leonard stood up and went over to the latrines. Shaw

glanced up the field once more towards Ewbank, saw the contractor gazing in his direction, and got up. He slid the file and metal into separate pockets, buttoned up his overalls completely, blew his nose through his fingers, stooped forward, and after a while followed Leonard to the screening.

The latrines seethed with flies. In the cubicles clouds hovered and droned over each zinc can: the air was solid, the liquid surface separate, composite nests of insects.

Shaw stopped in the muddy entrance, taken by surprise at the mechanical droning, his face screwed up, his hands rising to the sides of his head. He twisted round as if caught by his feet. Flies detached themselves to muzzle his face, settling on his shoulders and covering his hands. He pushed against the screening, mistaking the door, then fell back to the entrance and ran towards the hedge. He bent over and spat. Insects mounted like a curtain over his head. He doubled up and retched, then pulled a rag from his overalls and wiped his burning face. He sat down, drawing himself into the shadow of the hedge and wiping his eyes and his mouth. His hand was held against his stomach and he belched with a deep, stricken rasp. He shook his head and was sick between his legs.

Leonard sat by the hedge and waited. Unaffected by the insects he sat watching the older man, a hardness and resignation about him which, for that moment, made his figure seem in some way much bigger.

Shaw had pushed himself backwards, feeling in his pocket at the same time and bringing out another rag. He wiped his face then tried to clean his overalls.

'Do you want any help?' Leonard said. Shaw sucked hard at the air then held his arm coolly to his forehead and shook his head. He knelt silently for a while, self-absorbed, alternately wiping his eyes and his mouth. When he stood up he stared round unseeingly at the field and the valley with a perplexed look, coughing and pulling out his tobacco. He rolled a cigarette, then lit it, smoking quickly and fiercely. After a while he bent down and snatched handfuls of grass and wiped down his boiler suit. The stooping was too much; he sat down and did it more slowly.

Leonard went back to the latrine and unhooked the canvas doors from the cubicles, flinging them out over the screening. He worked his way back along the row, ripping the hessian from the tacks and bundling it in his arms until he could force it out between the laths. Soon there was just the bare scaffolding standing, held together by binding and stakes. Each can was full, spilled over, droning with insects. They hung in an unsettled cloud, black and pulsating in their murmurous rise and fall. The ground had been pulped into a brown grassless mud as if within the tiny space an hysterical herd had been endlessly confined. Leonard worked with quick, efficient movements, aided by a peculiar resignation to the place.

Shaw still sat under the hedge smoking, crouched forward in a forgetful, absent way.

'You'd better move,' Leonard said. 'I'm going to pitch the cans in there.'

Shaw stood up and walked down the field towards the river; then he stopped, reminded of something, and turned to watch as Leonard picked up the buckets. He walked quickly, stiff-legged, staggering with the weight of the two cans and, flinging them forward, sprang back as the liquid splashed into the ditch. He pulled his boots through the grass, coughing, and wiped his face.

'Come on, Shaw. You've to give me a hand.'

'I'm not going near.'

'I better tell Ewbank that, then,' and he started up the field.

'It's my belly,' Shaw called. 'I can't stand the smell.'

'Are you going to help me?'

'Oh, God.' Shaw turned round and kicked the ground. 'God blind these bleeding, dirty, sodding, stinking *women*!' He fingered the metal parts in his pocket and with his free arm brushed the flies from his head.

'I'm not doing it on my own.'

'Aye, well.' Shaw narrowed his eyes, drawing up emotion. Both hands now rested in his pockets. 'That's just like you. And don't give me that. I know your sort. Soft-arsing it around to everybody who's got a bit and when it comes to somebody like me – *that*!' He spat out sideways and unintentionally it went a long way. 'You and that Tolson pillock. He never took them tents down by himself – you're nothing but a bloody liar, man.'

'I'll give you a minute to get the cans in your hand.'

'I'm not frightened of work. Don't worry. I'm a *workman*.' He went over to them and tried to lift one in each hand. But feeling the weight of the first he contented himself with that, grasping the handle in his left hand while his right groped at the air. He stopped half way to the hedge, his face turned from the pollution. He changed hands, then tried to carry the can in both. When he tipped it into the ditch he kicked it savagely, pulling his feet wildly through the grass before he ran backwards.

Leonard returned, lifted two more cans and gasping with their weight walked stiffly to the ditch and plunged them in. He wiped his boots and sat down, nervously exhausted.

'Come on, Shaw.'

'You know what you can do, bloody hell.' He felt round in his pockets but found nothing. 'I'll tell you how to get shut of these.'

He strode over to the cans, put his foot against the rim of the nearest and pushed it over. The flies roared up like a black flame. Before Leonard could move he'd done the same to the remainder, crashing them in all directions despite their weight.

The liquid spread in a slow pool round the posts and stakes, flooding the shallow declivities. Shaw had started to run back, but he stopped to watch it.

'I don't know why you didn't do it with all of them,' he said. He fingered the shapes in his pocket and stared at the expanding pool with blank fascination. Leonard had crouched forward over his knees: he stared at the fresh grass by his feet.

When Ewbank came, he stood gazing at the patch for some time, his black neatly dressed figure standing by it as if unaware of the cloud that throbbed round his head and threatened to envelop him. Then he said, 'Who's responsible for this?'

'Shaw.' Leonard had stood up; he had rolled the hessian into tight piles and now he watched Ewbank listlessly.

'Where is he?'

'He's down by the river. He says he feels sick.'

'Sick . . . Christ. What an absolute lousy stinking bloody sodding *shit*.' He seemed unable to drag his eyes from the odorous ground. 'Why for Christ's sake . . . God in heaven.'

'He kicked them over before I could move. I tried to get him to help me.'

Ewbank glanced away over the fields to the line of hills. A saloon car rocked its way through the gate and into the field, accelerating alertly until it pulled up alongside Ewbank's Armstrong Siddeley. Wetherby got out with the two women who had accompanied him the day before. He was dressed in a dark lounge suit and the two women wore pale, flower-patterned frocks and silk scarves. It was a warm day. They had probably just come from church and were chatting amicably.

Ewbank went to meet them, turning away abruptly and calling back, 'Radcliffe, get as much down as you can . . . Shaw. . . .' He added something which Leonard couldn't hear.

Ewbank met the party half way down the field and led them back up to where the trucks were loading. They stood talking and laughing, watching the men work.

Leonard dragged the upturned cans to the ditch and left them to drain. The scaffolding was difficult to dislodge; the knots and binding were so tightly pulled together that his knife wouldn't sink through them. For a while he sawed at the lashings, then he stepped back, uprooted a guy-line and hauled the assemblage down.

It creaked, two wooden limbs cracked and the white splintered wood was left upright in the dark pool. The ropes groaned as the long wooden legs fell over, splayed out on their side, pointing gawkily into the air. The flies drove upwards in wild spirals. The structure lay in the pool, its long, stiffened limbs drooping slowly to the ground. Leonard tried to drag it from the pool, but under the surface of the liquid it was still secured. It wouldn't move.

He went down to the river and washed his hands and arms, then his face. He rinsed his boots. Further along he could see the top of Shaw's head as he sat in the long grass. He'd rolled another cigarette, and from the silent movements of his head he was working at the piece of metal with his file. Shaw had a hobby of making model railway engines.

Wetherby was standing by the site of the latrines when Leonard got back. The two women stood with him and from their attitude it was obvious that they'd come upon the pollution by accident. Ewbank stood away from it as if his distance served as apology. None of them moved as they stared at the wooden framework in the pool. Beyond, the men had started to drift towards them, drawn by the stillness of the four people and by the stench that had begun to spread across the field. No one spoke. No one looked at the spot directly but gave it sharp hurried glances, identifying the mounds of solid floating in the liquid, the stained pieces of cloth, and half sunken sheets of paper.

Soon they had all drifted to this part of the field. The flies were denser, gyrating over the expanding sludge with a drone that could be heard through the entire field. Wetherby had averted his eyes as if by his look alone he could escape from the scene. The men had begun to glance uneasily at the women, their looks moving from the pool to their two figures. One of the women smoothed down her flowered frock, paused as if she would go on standing there, then walked back up the field. Her companion returned the looks of the men. They peered at her heavily. For a moment she stroked her bare arm, then she turned too and suddenly walked away with particularly clumsy movements.

Ewbank strode across to Leonard. 'This gentleman here tells me that Tolson was riding his motor-bike through the tents. . . .' Wetherby had turned at the voice. His single eye looked out of focus, deranged.

'There's some ash,' he said to Ewbank. 'You can scrape it out of the ruts and spread it over.' He started to walk lifelessly up the field. 'Oh, and four of those cans are mine,' he added. The two women stood waiting for him by the car.

Ewbank shouted at the men: he set two of them with shovels to cover the area and to dig out the broken scaffolding. Leonard went to the tent and started taking it down and packing his and Tolson's things. Wetherby held the door of his car for the women to climb in. The door banged and the car jolted its way to the gate, a cork bouncing on the waves. In the middle of the field Ewbank was supervising the loading by signs rather than shouting, occasionally looking up without expression at the tent where Leonard worked.

When he called for lunch the men left the lorries quickly, jumping down and running to the 15 cwt truck and taking their bags. They climbed over into the next field and bedded themselves down in the straw.

Leonard had gone into the long grass under the hedge by the road and lain down. He hadn't any food. He closed his eyes and tried to sleep. A shadow fell over him, and he found Enid standing there dressed in a suit slightly too large for her.

'Where's Vic?' She held several flowers separately in her hand from which she plucked petals. 'I had to go to church this morning. I came on as soon as I could.'

She stared down at him with the same curiosity as the night before; then she glanced at the lorries, deserted and strung across the field like animals grazing. 'Where's Vic, Len?'

She said it so emptily that it appeared to echo his own feelings and he sat up.

'I think you'd better go,' he said. 'The men are here today. Vic's gone.'

'On his bike? . . . I got into a row with our Alan. But he didn't know. Where I'd been, I mean.'

'I think you'd better go.'

She stared down at him reproachfully, moving forward slightly as if she might step on his narrow body. 'Why's Vic gone?'

'I don't know.'

'How d'you mean? Where's he gone, Len?'

'Look – go away!'

She stood watching him. Then she kicked him, but lightly as if in the middle of the blow she'd been suppressed. 'It's right what he said about you last night.'

He didn't move, and she started walking slowly away. The smell from the lower end of the field had strengthened.

It pervaded the whole of the showground. The girl's head lifted.

'Will you give him a message when you see him?' she called back. 'That I love him.' She waited. 'Will you tell him?'

Leonard lay back in the grass. Through the long blades he could see Ewbank in the front seat of his car, having his lunch. The white mask turned as the girl went to the gate. Another patch of white moved as he brought a sandwich up to his face, then the red of his Thermos.

Enid had reached the edge of the field. She looked back and saw Leonard still lying in the grass. She stood gazing in at the men in the next field, then walked on up the lane as a man called from the houses.

Shaw had come up from the river and taken his bag out of the truck. He sat in its shade, his back against the rear wheel. The sun was now very hot; flights of midges hovered round the edges of the field and in the shadows. As he ate his sandwiches he stroked his file over the pointed strip of steel.

'What did I tell you?' he said to Leonard who'd suddenly come down to stand near him. 'Nobody puts one over me.'

'I'll have to try it myself next time.'

'You?' He ate his sandwich and from a lemonade bottle swallowed cold tea. He picked up his file. 'I've watched you. You'll get nowhere in life. You're like an open book to me. So's Tolson, the big ape. And that Jewish pillock over there.'

'Who's that?'

'They're all bleeding Jews. And don't come with that. You're an open book. You're after one of these sandwiches, aren't you?' He laughed genially and pleasantly. 'Well . . . how about this one?' He held out an egg and tomato sandwich in the flat of his hand, and when Leonard moved to take it he screwed it up like paper. Tomato seeds and a yellow pulp seeped between his large fingers. 'You can't have it!' He laughed. His teeth were set widely apart in his mouth.

'I wouldn't want it,' Leonard said. 'You've got that filth all over your hands.'

Shaw glanced at them briefly, then put down his file and the strip of metal and held out his hands. 'I've washed them in the river, so that's a lie for a start.' He gazed up at him triumphantly. 'They're cleaner than yours, so you can't catch me with that. God Christ, Radcliffe, you're as thick as they come. What was that Ewbank said . . . .?' He laughed genially and casually, looking down for his file. 'What've you been doing the last few days, then? Stuffing it into old Tolson's chocolate box? Rooting it about amongst the raspberry creams?'

As he half turned away Leonard suddenly kicked the strip of metal under the rear of the Struck. haw, turning back, felt for it. His fingers groped in the grass.

'Where's it gone? That bit of linking?'

'It's under the truck.'

Shaw bent down and reached for it quickly, with a surprising energy, his legs kicking out. Leonard picked up the packet of sandwiches and put them inside his shirt. As Shaw's head came up Leonard said, 'I'm going down to the river. Are you coming?'

Shaw shook his head smilingly at him. 'Not likely. Not with all that mess down there. . . . Go on. You go. You'll feel more at home with all that.'

When Leonard reached the site of the latrines he looked back. Shaw was standing by the truck, searching for his lunch. Leonard held the packet up for him to see.

Shaw started forward, shouting, then paused as Leonard went to one of the cans and with his foot tipped it upright from the ditch. He held up the sandwiches, picked out the first and dropped it in. Shaw didn't move. The file and metal part were still in his hand. Leonard dropped in the sandwiches one by one, the slices of egg and tomato falling in separately as the bread came apart in the air. There was a small bun with currants in, and he dropped that in last.

Shaw walked slowly down the field. He went to the can and looked in at his sandwiches and the bun. He examined them in silence, his eyes moving slightly. Then he turned round and walked across to Leonard. He stepped through the pool of sewage, the flies rising lethargically round his head. His large boots collected wedges of black mud.

'You shouldn't have done that,' he said, so quietly that at first Leonard didn't hear. Shaw peered at him fixedly with strangely narrowed eyes. 'You shouldn't have done that.' His head shook from side to side. 'It'll bring more trouble down on you than ever you realized. I'm sorry for you now.' A heavy smell rose from him; it encased his words and breath. 'You'll be sorry. I've warned you.' His face relaxed as if assuaged by violence.

'Are you going to eat them now,' Leonard said, 'or later?'

Shaw gazed at him a moment longer. The skin crept like insects round his eyes; the black pupils vanished. His eyes closed. He gazed at Leonard blindly for several seconds, then swung round and walked away through the sludge. The flies roared at his intrusion, settling on his head and feet, and on his hands which he held peculiarly flattened and stretched out by his sides. He didn't look back.

Leonard went down to the river. The water crashed loudly over the exposed rocks: the level had sunk from the day before. Leonard was in tears. Hearing feet behind him and thinking it was Shaw, he turned round.

'I saw all that,' Ewbank said. 'Why did you have to do it?'

Leonard didn't answer. The contractor took out a cheroot from a tin and belched as he lit it. He threw the match into the river and tried to follow its passage in the turbulent water.

'What's happened then between you and Tolson?' he said calmly, looking slightly to one side of Leonard's eyes.

Leonard walked away. Ewbank watched him, his head nodding. Then he sauntered towards the centre of the field, his hands in the small of his back, looking up at the hills and the moor side. He picked up a loose stake and a guy-line and flung them into the back of the truck, walked on a few paces then stopped to gaze up at the green fields and the rocks, softened by the bright sunlight. He took off his black hat and stroked his head gently. He was bald. He glanced at his watch, replaced his hat and went across to the men, chatting with them a few minutes.

Within an hour the three lorries were parked in a line across the field, their tall loads roped up and tarpaulined.

The men stood about silently, smoking, while Ewbank walked round the worn showground minutely inspecting it for equipment. He picked up several fragments of pegs, a strand of rope, a twisted metal stake, and threw them in the back of the truck. He shouted across to the drivers and the lorries began to move off. They swayed over the field like stricken beasts, their backs burdened with long poles and banks of canvas, sagging from side to side as they sank into ruts and groaned over the low hummocks.

The men hardly spoke. They watched as Leonard put Tolson's gramophone and battered suitcase, his own suitcase and the two camp beds into the back of the truck. He lifted up the tent and pushed it in himself.

Ewbank stood at the gate, by his car, and watched the first lorry through. Its rear wheels slid into the gate-post, drove hard against it and drew it under its tyres. The following lorry rode over the gate as it dropped into its path. The wood splintered into fragments. Ewbank stepped back. He stopped the third lorry and the vehicle was immediately bogged down in the deep ruts.

He secured the tow rope himself, leaning awkwardly over it then standing hurriedly back with the men as the two heavy vehicles fought one another, their engines tearing, the huge apparatus shuddering and vibrating, burning the ground. The loads swayed, jarred, and the tyres crunched against the lips of the ruts. The thick treads broke open the hard clay, and slowly the blunt noses rose and screamed over the banking onto the road. The men climbed into the cabs and into the back of the 15 cwt, still parked in the middle of the field. The small vehicle bumped its way to the broken gate, trundled over the remnants and ran up onto the road behind the line of trucks.

In the corner of the field was the watchman's caravan. Apart from an occasional trail of thin smoke from its slender chimney there'd been no sign of life from the old man at all. Now, however, the narrow door opened and he appeared, gazing round at the deserted arena.

Towards the far end of the field and growing steadily towards the middle, a dark stain of earth had spread out in an irregular shape. In the centre two broken laths stood upright, bedded firmly in the ground. It was towards these that, the moment it was released from the caravan, the watchman's black dog bolted. It was a large animal; running swiftly, it darted excitedly about the pool, its curiosity aroused simultaneously in several directions. Only when it reached the two posts did it momentarily pause. It raised its hind leg and, thrusting forward slightly, urinated on them both.

'Have you got your own and Tolson's luggage?' Ewbank called into the back of the truck. Leonard nodded. The contractor stared in at him, then at the men. Someone offered him a cigarette. He slid it into his top pocket and returned to the gate.

'We must have lost two or three pounds apiece today,' a man said.

A voice called outside, 'There's that young tart yonder, the one Pilkington nobbled.'

Enid had come down the lane from the village. She watched Ewbank and the two men at the gate.

'I bet Tolson's shot his load with her,' Pilkington said. 'Isn't that right, Radcliffe?'

Leonard didn't answer.

Pilkington pushed past Leonard and leaned out of the back of the truck.

'Go on, Sammy,' someone said. 'We've got five minutes to spare.'

Ewbank shouted down to the first lorry. Its engine roared and it began to move off. The two men at the gate hurried to the truck and scrambled in. Shaw, in the corner, had begun to laugh quietly as the convoy rolled slowly forward.

Enid stood by the broken gate. Behind her the field smouldered in the heat. The showground was empty. Bare patches of earth, areas of yellowed grass and mounds of refuse marked the site of the previous day's activity. Wetherby's four cans stood alone in the centre. She walked across it, inspecting the outlines of the marquees. The dog had turned, and begun to run towards her.

The field disappeared through the fringe of trees. Leonard

sat stiffly, swaying with the truck, his gaze fixed on the scene behind. For a while he could see the castle silhouetted several miles away, marking the spot; then the heavier, smoother shoulders of the lower valley rose up. The road dropped suddenly and they ran between the first bands of stone terraces. The green and white strands vanished, and the brown shadow of the valley bottom closed over the line of speeding trucks.

Houses, perched on the rocky outcrops, clung to the terraced edge of the moors. Somewhere, running among them, was the river; its smell came into the truck as they followed its hidden course. Then they rose into the sun again, the valley cleared below and the river flowed through a narrow strip of woods and over a ridge of shallow falls. They rode with it for some time, then swept down again, the country levelling out. The strings of houses enveloped the valley, first one side then the other, growing into a broader elongation of brick and stone, thickening, deepening, then darkening.

Ewbank stopped twice to pick up wooden pegs which, unknown to him, had been purposely dropped from the truck. Then his car caught up with them again, and cruised behind.

The lorries slowed. Familiar structures filled the scene from the back of the truck. Leonard, leaning forward over his case, seemed morose, nervously resigned. Buildings of black stone were massed on a steep hill thrust up from the northern side of the valley. Old, built in bursts of a forgotten energy, they rose against the sky like fortresses; their silhouettes varied, alternately breaking then confirming the steep contours of the hill, a citadel of dark and eroded stone that loomed above the valley. The whole landscape had been gathered into the silhouette of the central hill: spires and towers, squat domes and high, pointed roofs thrust up anciently above the close horizons, breaking the stranglehold of rock.

They moved below it, amongst the long, low structures by the river. Like shapes spun out from the central vortex of stone, estates of houses flanked the valley, rising up the slopes in vast screes of dull red rock. They groped out from the core of the city, enclosing between them an outcrop of older buildings, a small heathland village of weathered stone, surrounding it, pulling it into their embrace and breaking it down within their own fabric of brick and slate. Beyond them, further south, like waves pushed out by their encroachment, the ground rose awkwardly and abruptly to a mass of chimneys and colliery headgears, ranges of slag mounted like black froth on their summits.

The tyres whined on the smooth road. As they passed the Beaumont estate, Leonard saw the black roof of the Place rising steadily above the narrow shapes of the brick houses. The lines and apexes of the surrounding roofs formed a moving pattern of curves and figures with the droning vehicle, so that only the Place itself seemed constant. He was relieved: it pleased him that the familiar point of his own home should be the only constant, the only absolute in that vast geometric confusion of other people's houses.

10

In the afternoon heat the estate was quiet, its empty, lime-planted roads curled like tired limbs over the slopes. As Leonard walked up between the houses, rooks drifted over the roofs, swaying in the wind, their fierce shapes like torn segments of cloud. Driven up by the wind, they swept in its eddy; then shuddering, stiffened by the stream of air, they glided smoothly over the symmetrical roofs. The estate was covered by the broken cloud, the birds flung like debris over the carefully planted houses.

Leonard walked quickly beneath the flowing flocks of birds. They drove ceaselessly over his head, wave after wave, as he climbed up the steepening crescents and roads. A clock boomed from the crown of the city across the valley. At this altitude he could hear the wind as it pressed among the leaves on either side, a body bending and folding to an unrhythmical pressure. He was sweating, carrying his suitcase; the weight, pulling at his arms, made him walk with a slight limp.

He tugged the case through the gap between the gates and hurried up the heavily-shadowed drive. At the point where it broadened onto the terrace at the front of the Place he turned off along a path that ran round the side of the building. From the jungle of fruit trees, rhododendrons and elders rose the encrusted trunks of oak trees, stunted, bent down as if oppressed invisibly from above. The air was cool and heavy with the scent of wet stone. Cries of children and the thudding of a ball rose from between the estate houses. A car engine started. The sounds reached all round the house from beyond the wall of trees.

At the back it was quieter. The projecting wing of dilapidated outbuildings enclosed a lawn and garden which was flanked on its only exposed side by a row of walnut trees. In incongruous contrast to the decaying stone, the lawn had recently been cut. It was smooth and clean. In the centre was a blackbird. It was nervously tearing out a worm, poised back, tugging at the stretched tendon. A swarm of sparrows chattered wildly across the far side of the outbuildings. They flew up, tiny blown shadows, as Leonard came round the side of the house. The blackbird sprang along the ground, leapt up and darted forward, swaying low between the trees with its warning chatter. An old mowing machine, its blades still damp with grass, stood on the part of the lawn shadowed by the building.

The sounds of the estate were filtered now: voices calling and screaming, and the distant roar of engines. The yard was secluded, even the light itself, for the shadow of the house angled over the low roofs of the outbuildings and the lawn. Under the row of walnut trees hollyhocks had flowered, pointing up narrowly into the whitish-green leaves.

The gravel path had been raked and weeded, the pebbles still wet with disturbance. As if this evidence of recent energy disturbed him, Leonard hurried over to the kitchen entrance, glancing back once at the tall columns of flowers before pushing open the door.

His father stood up quickly as Leonard entered, as if he had been disturbed in the middle of his thoughts or at the climax of a conversation.

'Why, Leonard!' John said, his tall figure pushing slowly from the table where he'd been sitting.

Leonard put down his case and felt his hand taken between his father's strong, nervous fingers.

'Your mother said you wouldn't be back until late today. And here *I* am. I've just been gardening.' He indicated his old clothes with a helpless gesture. 'You're looking a deal browner. You haven't carried that all the way up, have you?'

John studied him cautiously before releasing his hand, then watched with a sudden smile as Leonard offered some brief explanation of his early arrival.

'You've just got back, then? Now come on, sit down. I thought I saw Vic this morning on the estate. On his bike.'

'He came back earlier, on his own.'

'Ah, yes. I see. . . .'

As though vaguely aware of someone else in the room, Leonard had turned around. A figure stepped from the shadows beyond the large range.

'And what's Austen doing up here, father? Has he been tormenting you again?' His humour, like a wounded bird, never quite cleared the ground. The two older men laughed.

As if to confirm his presence Austen laid his yellow woollen gloves on the table. Already lying there were his walking stick, a well-brushed though faded Homburg hat and a newspaper. A thin black overcoat lay carefully folded over the back of a chair.

'As a matter of fact I've only just arrived myself, Leonard.'

He nodded slightly, an odd, genteel parody of politeness. 'He still refuses to buy a single newspaper and I have to keep him informed of the goings-on of our diminutive world.' As if at this touch of sympathy, and in deprecation, Leonard smiled at his uncle.

'Ah, now . . .' his father said.

'And I arrived, of course, to find him cutting the lawn.' Austen sat down at the long plainwood table. He laughed. His hands for a moment rose to his hair, then, as if wounded, collapsed into his lap. With a reflective, slightly affected grace, his head tilted to one side, he stared speculatively at his nephew.

'Have you had anything to eat, Leonard?' John asked. His hands rested anxiously on his thighs. 'Elizabeth and your mother are out at the church, but I can get you something easily enough.' His concern was betrayed by a slight formality of manner.

'It's all right. I'll wait till we eat. How's the furniture shop, Austen?'

Austen moved slowly, crossing his legs and allowing one hand to play idly on the table. He seemed amused, yet uncertain whether he was being provoked into defending his job or whether the question came purely from Leonard's obvious unease.

'Oh, well enough. And how's your work? How did you get on?'

He didn't look at Leonard but at John, and with a gesture of his slim hand he added lightly, 'Six days in the wilderness don't seem to have changed his impervious temperament.'

Leonard, still smiling, gazed intensely at Austen's expression: in the muted light of the room each feature of his uncle's face seemed deliberately moulded to the skull and not merely formed there by the incidence of nature. There was in Austen, unlike his father, a superficial sense of ease bordering, at times, on indifference. Nevertheless both now looked at him with concern.

'Have you been trying to make too much of it again?' John said.

An exhausted expression had crept over Leonard's face since his entry, one that seemed more than the result of carrying his heavy case and the long walk through the estate.

'No.' He made no concealment of his tiredness. 'Vic did most of the work.'

'And how is Vic?'

'He's fine.' Leonard turned listlessly away: he was suddenly absorbed by the shadows of the room. 'It's very fine countryside.'

'I thought I'd noticed a certain farmyard redolence since you came in,' Austen said, then stood up immediately as Leonard suddenly went out. 'You'll come down, Leonard, before I go?'

'Yes, I'll come down.'

Austen watched him with an almost frantic look of grievance. But Leonard climbed quickly up the narrow stairs and didn't look back.

A tall side window which illuminated the landing was shaded from the late afternoon light. The broad passage was deep in shadow, its several dressers and wardrobes looming forward like protrusions of the building itself. The partition door at the opposite end of the landing, which separated the renovated section from the principal part of the Place, was completely obscured. He gazed round at the several doors as if the significance of their entry into his, Elizabeth's and his parents' rooms had eluded him. He seemed uncertain towards which to move when suddenly he hurried to the one furthest from the window and, overcome by a fit of coughing, closed the door behind him.

He secured it firmly and dropped onto his bed. The light, reflected from the trees and the outbuildings, glided into the tall room. He stared up at its cracked, moulded ceiling for some time, then turned sharply on his side to gaze at the innumerable drawings pinned to the wall.

Yellowing, they were held together like remnants of wallpaper, their intermittent production marked distinctly in their varied discolouring. They were landscapes, but of a scale disproportionate to their minute size, and animated by small, fragile figures, tiny creatures overwhelmed by huge surfaces of rock. No sooner had he seen them than he turned awkwardly onto his back and stared up again at the distant ceiling. His coughing had ceased.

Flies droned in the room. Birds chattered under the broken eaves of the outbuildings, and from above came the faint, anonymous sounds of the empty rooms. His father's voice murmured from the kitchen below.

He lay on the bed calmly. Apart from turning occasionally from side to side, as if unconsciously he were enjoying the softness of the bed, there was no outward indication of his struggle to contain his feelings. This divorce of his body from his thoughts was something which he seldom noticed, but on this occasion it intensified his senses to such an extent that he felt as if he were looking down on an empty shell or the lifeless branch of a tree. Then it seemed that out of this exhaustion he began to sense the Place as an extension of his own mind.

It was as if he, lying in this room, were one central component. The faint voice of his father now represented the working of some distant cell, and the broad window through which flowed that even light was the opening to some incoherent brightness which only within the context of the room could be defined and given meaning. His habitation of the Place was like his habitation of his own brain, its cellular structure disposed around him as the endless ramifications of his thoughts. The identity of the building itself, its size and the scale of its architecture, its sense of duration, seemed to be that exact image he now possessed of his own mind. As he took on the identity of the Place, and became the building in the sense that all his feelings were invested in it, the aristocratic form of its dark shape became that essence which occupied every cell and atom of his brain.

For some time this massive projection was more real and frightening than any of his experiences of that day; so that whereas, at some distant level of his mind, he was aware of his mother and sister entering the room below, and the faint voices of Austen and his father, they seemed only the peripheral accommodation of his mind to some new and uncertain experience. When, a few moments later, the door of his room opened and his mother dutifully stood there, the fact seemed simply the mechanical confirmation of his previous sensations. She turned away, evidently thinking him asleep, glancing back to allay some brief anxiety, then quietly shut the door. Her footsteps sounded briskly along the landing to the stairs.

His senses radiated from him with a compressed uninter-rupted energy. The birds chattering shrilly across the lawn were swiftly absorbed in his mental abstraction. He felt an acute reluctance to extend his mind further than the Place, so that the faint cries of the children playing on the estate were suddenly rejected and he heard them no more.

It was the sound of the door shutting and of his mother's footsteps, the note of deference, that sent a preliminary pulse through his body. For a second that enigmatic energy faltered and, like some formidable contour torn across a beach by a storm, he saw his mind once more confined to the narrow structure of his body but shaped now by the force of his recent experience.

His awareness of the room grew, and a shocked tiredness overwhelmed him. For a while he struggled to keep himself awake. He stared at the drawings pinned on the wall as though to recall their faded enthusiasms. But tiredness weighed him down, enclosing him more tightly until, at the point when it seemed he must fall asleep, he got up stubbornly from the bed.

He went to the door and out onto the landing. The voices of the family rose in mild argument from below. He turned to the partition that occupied the whole width of the landing and stood for some time at the door on the point of grasping the handle and pulling it open. But with a final gesture of despair he swung round and went back to his room. Within a few minutes of lying on his bed he had fallen into a deep sleep. Only some hours later, in the early evening, was he woken by his mother. She came into the room and stood there as if she sensed his need for re-assurance.

He opened his eyes to see her beside his bed. At that moment her coarseness and simplicity of expression were no more than an extension of that figure which had dominated his dreams; her affinity to Tolson seemed stronger than his own less discernible bond of flesh and blood.

'How are you feeling, then? Goodness, you're looking browner. I've brought you up some tea. Your uncle said you'd promised to come down and see him before he left.'

It was only at that moment that he woke. He sat up, coughing, and felt the mug guided into his hand.

'Well, how are you feeling? You look fitter. . . .'

He answered her mechanically and drank mechanically, his body stiff and awkward. She watched him almost morosely, a weary and familiar sympathy verging on indulgence.

'I'll start your meal,' she said as she went to the door. 'You better get washed and changed before you come down, and leave those clothes up here for me to wash.'

He scarcely heard her instructions and she was about to repeat them when he was suddenly overcome with confusion and, blushing violently, got up quickly from his bed.

For a while she stood watching him, her own face slightly flushed. Then she slowly came from the door and stood over him.

He had sat down on the edge of the bed, stooping forward, his arms resting on his thighs. She put her hands on his narrow shoulders, feeling them at first gently, then gripping them almost ferociously.

'Now . . . come on,' she said slowly.

He didn't move, but appeared to stiffen under her fingers. His head touched her stomach.

'Your father said Tolson came back this morning,' she said.

'Yes.'

'By himself?'

'Yes. I came back with the men.'

She waited, staring down at the straight black hair.

'Did you have an argument?'

'No.'

But he moved against her vaguely. His arms had risen now; for a moment they were folded round her thighs. She bent down and kissed his head. He stood up.

'I'll get washed then.'

'Yes. . . .'

She watched his strange confusion. Then she picked up the empty mug from beside the bed. 'Now you hurry up,' she said suddenly and without any recrimination in her voice. She closed the door quietly, as though from an habitual deference.

Leonard stood at the window and undressed. It was early evening. The row of walnut trees was eroded with shadow, dissolving the leaves and dispersing the branches against a descending sky. The rooks were gliding back now towards the outskirts of the city, silent, blackly poised. Insects floated like dust in the space between the outbuildings.

In the bathroom he was able to watch himself in the

mirror. His face was tanned brown, reddening over the high cheekbones. His whitened body intersected the large blank wall behind, and confirmed the tall outline of the sash window. The panes were shrouded outside by leaves.

On one side, a fireplace had been sealed off and bulges in the plaster traced the contours and directions of an eccentric maze of plumbing. The basin stood on a narrow pedestal set slightly away from the wall. The floorboards were bare except for a small mat at the side of the bath which itself lay against the wall like the defunct cylinder of a vanished machine. The dim interior was reflected in the mirror. It was against this variegated texture, as though so many things presented an unfelt touch to his skin, that the room was composed and re-composed, accommodating its scale to every movement of his body.

As he crossed the landing again to his room he heard Austen's voice in the kitchen below say, 'If it seems so, then forgive me. At least it wasn't done with that intention.'

Leonard closed his door and returned to the window to dress. The narrow towers of hollyhocks were thrust up into the darkness of the trees in pink and purple wedges. The long stems swayed slightly with their ungainly weight, the lower, crumpled leaves drooping on white, fibrous stalks. They were torn slivers of colour in the darkness.

Watching them, his head pressed against the window, the flowers congealed in the growing dusk until, gradually, they floated out like live crests from the shadows. He suddenly turned from the window and, dressed in clean shirt and trousers, went out onto the landing. The smell of cooking meat rose from the kitchen below.

He went to the partition door, turned the key, and pulled it open. The landing continued as a long broad passage to the opposite end of the building. Here it was illuminated by a tall window, partly shuttered on the inside, but admitting sufficient light to indicate the numerous doorways and the main staircase opening off the corridor. Cold air moved in where he was standing, and, having opened the door, he seemed undecided whether to go any further. Faint sounds came from the dark interior: the intermittent creaking of wood, the movement of water in pipes, and a low murmur that emerged from the heavy stillness of the deserted rooms themselves.

Any decision he might have made was interrupted by a voice behind him. 'Have you heard something?'

Elizabeth stood in the faint light of the passage, a slim girl of eighteen.

'Did you hear something?' She glanced at him expectantly, then beyond at the interior. They were silent, standing side by side.

He watched her expression a moment, then said, 'No,' and closed the door. He bolted it. 'Which of them sent you up?' His voice was suddenly indulgent, as though some familiar ritual were to be performed.

'Guess.' She turned her face shyly towards him as though to penetrate his reserve. She was very slender. Her black hair was parted and drawn back smoothly and tightly, like a close-fitting cap to her small and peculiarly delicate features. It was a child-like face, excessively alert.

'You wouldn't have come up on your own, since you have no affection, interest or respect for me. It must have been Austen sent you.'

'No. But then do you think he has all those admirable things?'

'Wouldn't you say so?'

'It was my mother. How's Vic?' She turned, her yellow frock flaring out.

'You don't know him. Why should you ask?'

She swung away as though in one movement she were abbreviating several steps of a dance.

Leonard said very suddenly, 'See if you notice any change.'

She followed him into his room. He put on the light and she stood frowning in the door. Then she stepped in. 'You look browner.'

'Do you think I look healthier?'

'No. But certainly browner.'

He watched her a moment as she moved elusively round the room. She had a strange restlessness, almost ritualistic, as though each movement were pre-determined and conformed to some eccentric pattern in her mind.

'Do you think I look like a workman?'

'No.'

'Do you notice *any* change?' he said, very intently.

'Yes.'

'Well? What is it?'

'Not in you.'

He was suddenly bewildered, frowning. 'What?'

'Not in you. In my father.'

Leonard began to tidy his discarded clothes, picking them up carefully, folding them, then flinging them loosely beneath the bed.

'What a smell,' Elizabeth said. 'My father was very happy this morning. He was down at dawn, gardening. You can tell. Now he's sitting down there as though he's been hit on the head.'

Leonard said nothing. He went to the door and waited with his hand on the switch.

Elizabeth stooped and began to examine the drawings. 'Did you have a good time while you were away?'

'Yes.' He put out the light. She stood quite still in the darkening room. Then Leonard added, 'The other night I had a dream about my mother where I slit open her belly, stuffed it with apricots and peaches, and braised her in the oven for three hours. I invited all the family to dinner and they commented on the unusual delicacy of the meat.'

He started down the landing. She followed him, walking on her toes and swaying to some silent rhythm as though mockingly she were stalking him.

'I had a letter while you were away,' she said. 'I can go to college next year. They've given me a place.'

He reached the top of the stairs and paused. Then he went to the single window at the end of the landing and looked down. She waited for him, moving still on her toes as if to indicate certain divisions of the carpeted floor. 'I have to wait the one year, though,' she added.

He stood with his back to her, gazing out of the window. The silhouettes of the trees grew from his head; they were like huge antlers; he was lit by the red evening light. Massive horns reared up in profile from his head. When he turned round he said, 'You look like a flower, standing there.'

'Oh? And which one?'

'A hollyhock.'

'God. How ugly. That's not very complimentary, is it? Why did you say that, Leonard?'

'Are they ugly?' He looked at her with an almost private alarm.

'Well. Not if you don't think so.'

She waited on the top step for him to lead the way. Then, when he didn't move, she started down. He immediately followed her.

'Perhaps it's just the name that's ugly,' he said.

'No. It's the plant. It's hard and fibrous.'

'But the flower . . .'

She burst out laughing, her face turning up to his, half-lit from the kitchen below. 'Why, what is the matter?' she said.

'Nothing. I don't know.' He seemed distressed and suddenly restless. Then he started to cough.

She was about to ask him something when her mother called from the kitchen, 'Oh, for goodness sake, Elizabeth, let him come. . . .'

As Leonard entered the kitchen he saw Austen sitting with John at the opposite end by the open door. They were gazing out into the yard. The evening light and the electric light mingled on their figures so that it seemed they had been revealed through an invisible wall: the easy chairs, the long, central table, the sofa, were like boulders reflected in the dull reddish glow of the three windows. Between them moved the melting shapes of his mother and Elizabeth.

Austen stood up. By his feet were his hat and gloves, and his coat was laid ready over a chair.

'Come and look at this, Leonard,' he said.

Leonard crossed the room and stared out into the darkened yard. Several bats flickered against the pale sky.

'What is it?'

'Can't you see?'

Leonard glanced down at his father. John was leaning

back, gazing abstractly into the faint light. The roof of the outbuildings was a simple orange sheen.

'In the middle of the lawn,' Austen said.

'What is it?'

'A cat.'

Leonard could just distinguish the animal; then more clearly as it moved, apparently tugging at the ground. It was a stiff, ferocious action, vibrating and tense. Austen, his eyes still on the animal, had sat down again.

'They've been sitting there for hours just watching it,' Stella said. She worked at the gas stove beside the large polished range.

'But what is it?' Leonard seemed stifled by the attention they gave the cat.

'Can't you see what it's doing?' Austen said. 'It's caught something.'

'Oh, no. ...' Elizabeth had come to the door. 'What is it?'

She ran out and stamped her feet in the gravel and shouted. The animal scurried away. A moment later it crashed through the shrubberies. Austen began to laugh.

'It was a blackbird,' John said. 'The grounds are full of them.'

Both men stood up. Austen stretched.

'It stalked it across the whole width of the lawn and caught it,' John added.

Elizabeth came in again, flushed. 'It was a bird. It's awful.'

'It's true,' Austen said. 'Life's very ugly. But then death's not so pleasant either.' He glanced at Leonard and picked up his coat, automatically handing it to John to hold up.

'You see what your absences do, Leonard,' his father said, shuddering slightly as Austen forced his arms down the tight sleeves. 'They simply make Austen mischievous.'

He tugged the collar of the coat up to the back of Austen's slender neck.

'The greatest peace of all,' Austen stated, 'is that of other people's misunderstanding.' He buttoned his coat carefully, sliding the buttons through the holes with his thumb and forefinger, then pulling at the lapels. 'Well, I must be off. You are what your absences say you are. I came up today to make a suggestion to your father, amongst other things, Leonard. No, *he* can tell you. When I've gone. I'm not arguing tonight. . . . It's a beautiful evening. I think I shall walk back to town.'

He picked up his hat and gloves, and his stick, nodding at the two women. 'Good night, Stella, good night, Elizabeth. I'll see you again soon, Leonard. Whenever you have any time free, come to the shop, won't you? I'll be glad to see you.'

He stooped slightly as he went through the door, then paused to place his hat carefully on his head. John followed him, waiting a moment like a shadow behind him, then their feet crunched on the gravel.

In the kitchen they could hear Austen saying, 'You see, even if I wanted to ring for a taxi I'd still have to walk down to the end of the estate.' Their voices faded round the side of the Place. Then they heard John laugh. It was a wounded sound.

'Do you mean they both just sat here watching it?' Elizabeth said.

Neither her mother nor Leonard replied, and when John came in a short while later he said, 'It's not until one hasn't seen Austen for a while that you realize what an aphoristic machine he really is. . . . He came to see you, Leonard, of course.'

Leonard sat at the table staring down at the white wood. His finger followed the grain minutely, his head moving as though acknowledging his father. Then he suddenly stood up and without a word went out into the yard.

Austen had gone. For a moment it seemed that it was his uncle whom he'd rushed out to see. He stood on the gravel path a while, then walked across the lawn and stood gazing at the tall columns of hollyhocks.

A pool of orange light was reflected under the trees from an upper window of the Place. It glowed beneath the dark foliage, holding the tall stems of the flowers. The cups trembled in the breeze. They were smooth: a light pinkish white drawn in and veined round the yellow stamens.

The veins spread from the stamens, yellow and light green threads splayed minutely through the pink flesh. They grew, startled, caught in a tiny web of veins, a smooth, greased texture like porcelain. The veins sprang along the petals from the roots of the stamens. The centre of the flower was raw. It was huge. Round the root of the stamens, deep in the cup of the flower, the tissue was red.

He had swung round in sudden agitation and walked back through the deepening shadow. Then he stopped, so violently that it was as if he had been physically arrested. His shoulders shook and his eyes closed.

For several seconds he stood, frozen in mid-stride, his feet awkwardly apart and his body recoiling. Then, just as suddenly, he continued walking. He went to the stone doorway, stepped inside, and in an unusually loud voice said that he was going to see Tolson.

I I

In the upper windows of the house no shadows moved at all; the thick, unpatterned curtains were a dull yellow. The lower windows were unlit, their darkness anchoring the building to the uninterrupted row of houses on either side.

Leonard had stopped within the shadow of a large beech tree opposite Tolson's house at the corner of the main avenue. Noises came from the low buildings, a child crying, a piano playing; and someone was hammering a wooden shed.

He waited for two men to pass. They came down the road talking, their bodies pushing urgently against one another. They shouldered into the privet hedges lining the gardens. One of them lay back, couched and swaying in the leaves. He laughed, his hands held up helplessly as he drowned. His friend pulled him up, bending to exaggerate his effort. They giggled together and punched each other's shoulders. One of them laughed again and said, 'Ah, she'll never forget.'

Leonard crossed the road quietly and pushed open the thick wooden gate with his toe. The concrete path he followed went round the side of the house, passing the entrance to the lower flat, and continuing to the back. The motor-bike stood on a narrow strip of lawn, a toy. Beneath it the grass was matted with a long accumulation of oil; all round the machine stretched a black pond of earth. Beyond, as far as the railings that backed onto the gardens of the opposite houses, the ground had been massively dug. Nothing grew there.

The machine leaned slightly on its stand, its rear wheel missing. The chain hung down through the forks in a loose coil.

He climbed the steps to the back door with a sudden weariness, virtually exhausted. When he knocked footsteps immediately ran down the stairs and the door was pulled open as if he were expected. Yet Tolson's wife stared at him in surprise.

'Oh . . . Len!' Her full, matronly figure stood hesitantly in the doorway.

'Audrey. Is Vic in?'

'Yes.' She stood to one side, holding the door. It was someone else she'd expected. She watched him as he strangely lowered his head, stooped, and entered. He went through the small kitchen and up the stairs as though in fear of the ceiling.

Tolson was crouched forward on an easy chair with his eldest son, Peter, naked between his thighs. The boy stood in a bowl of hot water and a thin steam rose round their two figures. Tolson, washing him, looked up at Leonard without surprise.

'Hallo, mate. What time did you get back, then?'

'This afternoon.'

'Have a seat. I'll just finish the little lad first.' Peter was seven, a muscular, dark-haired boy.

Audrey came into the room. A second boy had just been bathed and stood behind a large chair in a corner of the room. Audrey lifted him, a sturdy child of four years, and nodding to Leonard carried the struggling boy into their bedroom to be dressed.

Tolson silently bathed the elder boy. He did it with a strange lightness of his thick arms, turning him round in his large hands, washing his back and shoulders, squeezing the water over his neck. The boy watched Leonard gravely, twisting his head quickly whenever he was moved so that he could gaze uninterruptedly at the visitor. Beyond Tolson, leaning against the wall, was the rear wheel of the motor-bike.

'Why, you've seen Len before,' Tolson said. He washed the boy carefully and thoroughly, glancing up at Leonard to smile, then stooping forward and rubbing the boy's legs, holding him as he lifted first one foot out of the water then the other. From the next room came the inquiring voice of the younger child, almost complaining, 'When's Uncle Denis coming?', then Audrey's deeper answering tone.

Tolson ran his hand roughly through the boy's hair as Peter stepped out of the bath. His father pushed it aside with one foot and wrapped a towel tightly round him. He rubbed the boy through the towel, then gave him it to dry himself. He watched him smilingly, nodding his head with some knowledge of his son's nature. When he was dry he helped him dress in a short vest and his pyjamas, taking the clothes from in front of the coal fire and feeling them on his cheek.

Tolson lifted the bowl and carried it out. The boy, standing by the empty chair, watched Leonard a moment. Then, when it seemed Leonard was about to speak, he suddenly ran out into the next room. Leonard could hear him crying and Audrey irritatedly reassuring him.

He sat alone. Tolson was talking to the boy in the next room, threatening then suddenly angry, his voice calling out. The child was quiet. No sound came from the house. Opposite Leonard was the bike wheel standing on a newspaper gritted and stained with oil. A rag hung through the spokes. The furniture rested like huge rocks in the room.

When Tolson came in he picked up the wheel and sat down in the easy chair. He balanced the wheel under one hand while he pushed newspaper beneath it. He started to clean the shining metal round the hub. 'They're going off to bed soon,' he said. 'They're a bit late but I hadn't seen them for a few days. I've been giving them one or two games.' He cleaned the wheel with delicacy, an adroitness and quickness of his large hands. Leonard watched them, his lips parted.

'What happened to you this morning, Vic?' he said.

Tolson glanced up at him casually and recognizing Leonard's intense expression said, 'I couldn't sleep at nights in that tent. I don't know what it was.'

Audrey had come in. After putting toys into a cardboard box and folding the boys' clothes she sat down facing Leonard. She was several years older than Tolson, a large-featured woman, almost forty. Her tawny hair was luminous in the electric light; it swirled, loosely coiled, round her head and the heavy features of her face, the stubby nose and the blue, fleshy eyes. Her arms were folded determinedly under her large breasts.

'I got up early,' Tolson said, glancing at her. 'I felt that bit restless. I took the tents down and came on home on the bike ... I thought you'd heard me. You rolled over a couple of times when I pulled the bike out.' He seemed wearied by it and gave all his attention to the wheel.

'I didn't wake up until Ewbank came with the men.'

'Ewbank.' Tolson laughed without looking up. 'I can just imagine what he said.'

Leonard watched him calmly. A boy's voice had called from the next room and after a moment's hesitation Audrey got up. 'They'll have finished their prayers,' she said and went out.

They could hear her talking quietly next door, the creaking of the bed, then the door closing.

'Don't worry,' Tolson said, 'I'll let Ewbank know about it all when we go in tomorrow.'

'Are you going to work tomorrow?'

'Why not? There was nothing wrong with the tents. I took them all down properly. I worked like a pig, I did. There wasn't a mark on them.' He looked concernedly at Leonard, aggrieved.

'Why did you go without telling me?'

'I've told you. I got browned off stuck out in that tent. I didn't mean to drive all the way back home. Isn't that right, love?' he said as Audrey came back in, closing the door. 'I just went to drive round a bit and before I knew where I was ... That's right, Audrey, isn't it? I've told you.'

'I wouldn't let it upset you so much,' she said to Leonard. She looked at him indulgently. 'What did Ewbank say?'

Leonard shook his head. 'He was annoyed.'

'Annoyed? Why annoyed? I worked like a bloody nigger on those tents. He can thank me for all the double-time he's saved. You watch, when I go back in that yard tomorrow he won't say a word. He'll just look at me over that bleeding cheroot and say nothing.' He bounced the wheel under his hand, shaking the room, then rolled it over and propped it against the wall.

Leonard sat silently staring at the floor.

'Do you want some tea, we're just making some?' Tolson said. 'We can't go out, or we could go to the pub. They're out downstairs, Sugdeons, and we're keeping an eye on their kids in bed.'

'*You* could go out,' Leonard said.

Tolson didn't answer. Then Audrey said, 'Will you have some tea, Len?' She waited until he'd answered her, then went downstairs to the kitchen they shared.

They listened to her moving below. Tolson picked mud from the tyre with a screwdriver. 'Where did you leave my case and the portable?' he asked.

'At the yard.'

He looked at Leonard. The light fell coarsely on his features. He bent down and collected the greased newspapers and screwed them together. He pushed them into the fireplace and they flared up.

'Why did you go without me?' Leonard said.

'Are you upset about it?'

Leonard didn't move.

'Ewbank couldn't blame you for aught. I did whatever there was done and he'll say nothing to me.'

Leonard looked slowly round the room. The bulbous suite and square table filled it. Large rose patterns pressed the walls inwards, reducing the room. The ceiling was low. From it hung a broad yellow lampshade. Everything was as if inflated to fill a space several times this size.

'What do you want me to do, then?' Tolson said. 'Fall on my knees and say I'm sorry? What's all the can about?'

'The girl came back to the field this morning, looking for you.'

'Forget it.' He went to the bike wheel and lifted it, about to take it down to the yard. Then he dropped it back on the floor. The room shook.

'What's the matter with me going?' he said. 'If you don't like it you know what you can do.'

'Don't you think it's strange you rushing off like that? I wouldn't have minded if you'd told me you were going. Did you feel guilty or ashamed about something?'

Tolson didn't answer.

'Are you frightened of me?' Leonard said.

'I don't give a sod about you.'

'No . . .' Leonard looked away, blushing. 'Do you care about anything really, anything at all?' He gestured round at the room. 'Except this and the few sticks and stones you've collected together.'

'It's a family and a home. I've got two kids in there. I care about them. Nobody else does. What have you got?'

'I've got my family and home.'

Tolson laughed. 'Yeh. Well, that's true.'

'Why are you frightened of me?'

'I'm not frightened.'

'Ashamed, then. I'm not ashamed of knowing you.'

'I'm not frightened and I'm not ashamed.'

'Why did you run away, then?'

'Who ran away? I didn't run away. If I want to do *anything* why should I have to ask you all the time?'

'You know why.'

Tolson flushed and turned away. He seemed huge and desperate, towering in the room.

'And it isn't *ask*,' Leonard said. 'If you'd just told me. That girl . . . I wouldn't have minded, if you hadn't been so underhand about it. Why do you do things like that? Why? You make everything obscene and grotesque just to get some sort of revenge. But revenge for what?'

'The girl – she was nothing.'

'I don't care! I don't care!' Leonard cried, standing up. 'If you'd only been open about it. I don't care what you do like that, honestly I don't care, if you'd only be honest and open about it. Don't you understand?'

'You're soft. You're just too soft. You don't take these things as you should. You should laugh at it.'

'No. You didn't laugh at it when it was something you wanted.'

'I don't want to be owned by anybody, that's all!'

'I don't own you.'

'No. You don't. And doesn't that just make you mad?'

'Vic! You just make it like this. You know it's not true.'

'How do I know?'

'I only want one thing. For everything to be completely *honest*. Not playing with people, then running away. You — you make everything into some sort of battle.'

'Well that's how things are.'

'It isn't!'

'Look. I'm getting tired. I just got fed up of that place and came away.'

'You didn't. It was meant to mean something. I understand why you went away.' Leonard turned aside, his hands clenched tightly together.

'You're insane coming here,' Tolson said suddenly and in despair. 'What're you trying to do. Tell *her*?'

The back door had slammed downstairs and there was the sound of Audrey's and a man's voice.

Someone was already mounting the stairs. A man called out, 'Vic. . . .?' His feet sounded irregularly as if he climbed with difficulty.

'You see! You see!' Tolson whispered. 'What kind of trouble are you trying to cause?'

Leonard suddenly made an incoherent sound. He hurried out of the room onto the darkened landing. Behind him the children's door was slightly open and the crying of the youngest boy broke out as the man, now almost at the top of the stairs, called, 'Come on, Vic. It's no good your hiding yourself up here.'

It wasn't Sugdeon, the man who lived below. The visitor climbing the stairs was limping, one hand held out from his raincoat and clutching the banister.

Tolson stood in the door of the living room looking at Leonard in the darkness.

'I'll see you at work,' Leonard said.

'Why, who's this here?' The visitor jumped aside as Leonard started past him.

Leonard dropped down the stairs, past Audrey, and reached the back door.

'What was that, then? The cat?' he heard the man say.

But whatever Tolson's reply, it wasn't in answer to the question. He heard them laughing as he stepped into the fresh air.

At the gate he paused and looked up at the lighted windows. The yellow curtains hadn't moved. He walked across the road to the tree. As he did so he counted the number of steps he was taking as if deep within him he were making an important calculation.

He waited in the shadow. The road now was lit solely by the lamps and was unaffected by the light still glowing faintly in the distant parts of the sky. After a while a van drew up at the gate. The Sugdeons got out: a stubby middle-aged couple. The wife went down the path and her white dress disappeared at the side entrance of the house. Sugdeon himself, dressed in a suit, locked up the doors of the van, his small stocky figure slowly circling the vehicle, coughing over a cigarette. Leonard could see the dark patch of his moustache over the glow of it. The lights went on in the lower half of the house. The faint crying of a child started, then as suddenly stopped. Sugdeon's feet crunched across the pavement, he pushed open the heavy wooden gate and walked down to the side entrance. The door closed and the road was silent.

Lights glowed from the mass of houses either side. Leonard stared up at the curtains across which shadows occasionally moved: Audrey's or the visitor's, too small for Tolson's. Stray thoughts moved through his mind. Beneath them he was aware of an obscure but relentless kind of calculation. Three windows of the neighbouring house overlooked the footpath down the side of Tolson's house; the privet hedge on that side of the road hid anyone arriving or leaving. By the gate was a lilac tree that had spread into a broad, thick bush growing over the lawn at the front of the house and concealing anyone from the house who opened or closed the gate. They would have to walk three paces before they came briefly into view of the lower windows.

Normally provided for one family, the house had been divided into two flats: this thought persisted irrelevantly as he glanced from the overlooking windows of the next house to the bush by the gate, and from the tall, ranging line of privet to the yellow curtains at the plain lighted windows below. After a while he seemed so confused by these rootless observations that he turned away, pushed his hands into his pockets and began to walk up and down in the limited space of the tree's shadow. He was sweating, yet glancing up at those yellow windows coolly, almost impersonally, as if he looked up at one which he'd chosen quite arbitrarily for some definite purpose.

The houses now were so dark that they formed a single line like a long cliff curving away from the corner where he stood, the lamps laid as separate pools along the foot of the rock. Then, as he was on the point of breaking his meaningless vigil, he heard several voices opposite, and standing in mid-stride he eventually recognized Tolson and the visitor as they came up the side of the house. They stood a moment at the gate murmuring together and concealed by the van. Then Tolson called out, 'Good night . . . good night, Denis. Sorry I can't give you a lift.'

'Good night, Vic. . . . I'll be round next week.'

The gate squealed then softly thudded as it met the post. The visitor limped off down the road. As he passed through the lamplight Leonard had the impression of a tall, bony man in a raincoat who walked as if one leg were artificial or completely paralysed.

He'd been staring at the man so intensely that he didn't see Tolson until he was half way across the road. It was the vague silhouette of his massive figure suddenly standing there that caught his attention. It seemed several moments before he realized that Tolson wasn't in fact moving, but simply standing in the middle of the road staring in at the shadows. Yet it was as if he *had* discovered him: the tight grip on his arm and the triumphant voice: 'What are you doing here?'

The sweat burst from his face. Tolson looked directly at him as if simply waiting for him to step out of the shadows and make some confession. Leonard stood rigidly, his feet astride, with no sound or movement.

Tolson turned away. His feet grated on the road, were silent for two paces on the grass verge, then grated again as he banged through the gate and down the side of the house.

Leonard hadn't moved. He heard the back door shut. Down the road he could still see the lame man arcing his body through the distant pools of light. He seemed to have been there for hours, pinioned by the light.

He stepped onto the footpath and set off home. He glanced back at the yellow curtains but they were still undisturbed, and with the sweat drying coldly on his face he strode quickly, almost triumphantly, through the darkness, his mind suddenly indifferent to whether Tolson had seen him or not, and locked even further inside certain meaningless observations which he felt were somehow involved with something he'd already decided to do.

12

His father was sitting in a tall, upholstered chair, his features sheathed in the red light of a reading lamp. The narrow ligaments of the ancient chair framed his erect body. He'd been reading as Leonard came into his bedroom.

The book lay in his lap, his long fingers caught round its edges and the sleeves of his woollen jacket rolled back as if the task of reading were in itself a physical effort. As the door closed he turned towards Leonard with the gleam of the lamp fully in his eyes, the skin corrugated into minute ripples by the intense shadow.

'What time is it?' he asked.

'Nearly eleven . . . I saw your light under the door.'

'Your mother's been waiting up for you.'

'I've just seen her. She's coming up to bed.'

John rubbed his narrow thighs, displacing the book. It turned sideways on his knees, released from his hands. The light exposed the bony structure of his face.

'Did you see Tolson?'

'Yes.'

'Why don't you sit down?'

The room was sparsely furnished with lean, simple furniture, old and well-kept. Leonard moved familiarly about its shadowed spaces. As he sat down his father's head was silhouetted against one of the two paintings in the room; a pale shape of water cascaded between dark rocks, like a tongue springing from his narrow skull.

Leonard's mother and Elizabeth moved in their separate rooms. The timber creaked perpetually through the building. Then faintly came a regular, mounting beat. It thudded hollowly in the rock beneath them, growing steadily and sending a dull vibration through the room like a lifeless pulse: fractured sounds came from the stone walls and the intervening wooden frames. It was huge and intrusive, muffled by the rock, and pounding: a train in the tunnel beneath the Place.

The engine passed slowly beneath them, a heavy rhythmic shudder. Then the sound decreased and the clacking of metal echoed and faded through the rock.

They looked at one another in silence. His father's hands, holding one another, showed whitely against his tall figure, and his head, turned towards Leonard, was flushed with the light glowing through the thin fringe of hair.

'Have you quarrelled with him, then?' John said almost inaudibly.

'I don't know.' Leonard looked away into the darker spaces of the room. His father's book had dropped; out of the corner of his eye Leonard saw the awkward movement of his legs as he tried to arrest it, then his clumsy stoop to retrieve it.

'Do you *want* to talk about it?' his father asked.

'I don't mind.'

Then John said frustratedly, 'Isn't it something that you can talk about?'

'I don't know.' Leonard suddenly added, 'It's just that I expect too much. . . .'

'Too much of whom?'

'Of *them! Them!*'

John's head turned slowly from side to side as if he were searching the room, forgetful.

'All along I've tortured myself thinking it was *me* who was at fault. That it was *me*. That somehow I had to blunt my senses, disregard my better feelings. But Tolson . . .'

'Whatever thing it is that's upset you, you shouldn't let it overwhelm you like this,' John said, still looking about the room as though refusing to accept Leonard at all.

'But don't you see? Tolson, all the time, has to try and belittle me.'

'But why?'

'Not because of *himself*. But because of what he is. A workman. He has to bring me down to that before he'll accept me.'

Leonard got up and began to walk the room, almost distractedly, his hand touching each piece of furniture as he passed. 'And the worst thing is, half of me wants it. To be like that. But the other . . . there's a part of me that won't be reduced.'

'Perhaps you should leave him,' John said, looking down at his book. He turned a page, then ran his hand over the print as if it were set in relief.

'But I can't. I don't know what it is. But with him I have a hold on things I'd never have otherwise. You just don't know . . . you don't know how ugly and spiritless he is. Working . . .' He suddenly stopped to gaze in tears at his father. 'Working men are the most thoughtless and lifeless people that have ever lived. And not because they are workmen, but because of what they are themselves. They become workmen because of what they *are*. Caterpillars. Caterpillars!'

His father looked up at him lifelessly. 'There's nothing I can say, really, is there? I hoped that with Tolson, well . . . that you'd begin to look out at things a bit. Not that you'd just stay with him, but that he might lead you to other things and people. You see, I'm not so sure that you're not condemning Tolson, not because of some deficiency in him, but because of something in yourself. That you're rationalizing something. When you talk about "workmen" . . .'

'No. No! You don't understand what it is.'

'It's *rationalizing*! Believe me. *I* know how things can be reduced in this way.'

'Then why did you encourage me? If it wasn't that you saw in Tolson exactly that touch of the commonplace which you always insinuate is the one quality I lack.' He suddenly strode across to the wall and switched on the main light. 'I'm not frightened of Tolson. And I'm not frightened of how people regard me. Elizabeth . . . Elizabeth treats me as a madman to be humoured. Austen as though I'm something to be provoked inside a cage. And you. God alone knows how you see me. But all this. All this . . .' He swung his arm round at the room, then stood gazing emptily at his father as though he had forgotten completely what it was he'd intended to say.

John, blinded by the glare, stood up. His hand moved up to shield his eyes. Leonard continued to stare at him without any expression at all, except perhaps one of mild consternation. Then he said quietly, 'Don't you see? Vic's the only real touch I have on things.'

John didn't answer. He turned away, with a negligent movement, as if he'd suddenly been reminded of something more important. When he turned back Leonard was staring at him with a half-broken, demanding expression.

'You can't really help me, can you?' he said. 'You've made me, but you can't really help me. For you can't really help yourself.'

John didn't answer. The book was still in his hand. He heard Leonard go to the door, and thought he heard it close. When he looked up, however, his son was still gazing in at him.

'What was it that Austen wanted?' Leonard said.

'Austen?'

'He came to see you about something. Or so he said.'

'Oh. It's just an idea he has. Of inviting the family back here for a day.'

'Why?'

'You'd better ask him. I believe he has some vague idea.'

'Of what?'

'That the family should ask the trustees to sell the house. But really, that's just his excuse for inviting them here. For his *party*.'

'Doesn't anything ever strike you as strange about Austen?'

His father didn't answer. He seemed suddenly impatient for Leonard to leave.

'Have you noticed the *intentness* with which Austen does everything now? The way he got me a job at Ewbank's. And now his "idea".' He watched his father a moment longer, then added, 'Will you agree to his so-called party?'

'I don't know . . . Perhaps now I will.'

Leonard turned to go. His father stood in the middle of the room. The light was directly above his head. He stooped slightly as though bored, absent-minded. His eyes were concealed by shadow.

'With Vic, it's not something I can let go. Not until it's finished and at an *absolute* end.' His father nodded. His head seemed broken by the light. 'Do you understand?'

'I don't know.' John looked up at him. 'Perhaps he'll just debase you. Destroy you.'

'No. You're wrong. Because he cares as well. If he didn't, then perhaps it wouldn't be so bad. But he does. And the thing's very simple. Either to be loved or to be destroyed.'

'Or to be loved *and* destroyed.' His father sank down in the chair.

'That's *their* decision, isn't it?' Leonard said. ' *Them.*'

He watched his father a moment. Then he closed the door. A thin strip of red light glowed from beneath it. He stood on the landing for a while uncertainly, as though hopelessly undecided what exactly he had intended to do. Then, swinging clumsily around, he went to his room.

He lay down on the bed, restless, his head flung from side to side. A small reading lamp was alight, and within this pool of illumination his head shone. In the tunnel beneath the house a train rumbled again. It hauled along, pounding in the rock. The noise mounted, pulsing and vibrating, a rhythmic thunder. Long after the sound had disappeared it echoed through the place. It beat in his ears, the sunken percussion of his blood.

He lay, quite still now, with his eyes open, the faint night glow of the estate reflected on the ceiling and meeting the glare from his own lamp. It seemed to him that his senses gradually extended from him until he experienced once again that strange projection of his body. The building was like the vast instrument of his thoughts. It mounted in him until, by some deeper extension, he was absorbed by the vast flange of rock itself, that eroded escarpment upon which both the estate and the Place rested. He sprawled across the land like a giant, his limbs and body colossal ligaments of the earth. It seemed he lay there not asleep but waiting.

Yet, the next moment, his head was raised up, hoisted by some monumental articulation of his neck, like a hill rising from the ground. Beneath the blackened sky appeared the dark sweep of the valley and, above, the furnace of the sun. It jettisoned colossal wreaths across the sky beneath which, along the upper ridges of the valley on either side, smoked the stacks and heaps of innumerable collieries, transfused by the light itself, and from which were torn vast, curling sheets of steam and smoke. Fluorescent yellow flares glowed through the misty apertures illuminating pitty fields of waste, pocked craters torn out flank by flank, the swirls of coaly clay spun out by the light on endless spirals into the night.

In the valley, like a silver mesh across the swinging contour of the land, stretched rows of armoured men, the light glinting fiercely on the white metal of limbs and the cylinders of strange and innumerable weapons. They curled across the valley like the strata of rock itself, bared luminous nerves splattered from the earth. Row after row of giant men encased in multiple sheaths of steel, heads like metal foliage on metal trunks, rose one by one and advanced, twin columns face to face, the ground spewed up in the wake of metal feet, growing and mounting towards each other like opposing breakers in a sea.

And as they met the sky divided at the metallic clash, the rasp and screech of metal man on man, and he heard his own voice cry out. In the sky, above the roaring band, appeared a figure, springing down, alighting and, from across the valley, pausing with outstretched hands to survey the scene.

It rose, poised, a limb of the earth itself, and above the roaring of the armies and the cries he heard a voice boom out, the echoed fall of metal flange on flange, 'Radcliffe! Radcliffe! Radcliffe!' and, feeling the heat flash through his giant limbs, he too rose, springing up, and across the screaming chasm faced the giant that had called his name.

He looked up. Out of the red glow of his room his father's face peered down, huge and, it seemed, surrounded by knots of flaming hair. Then, more clearly, he recognized him concernedly leaning down.

'Are you all right? I heard you calling out.'

'Yes.'

'Are you sure?'

Leonard rose from the bed to reassure him and, after a certain hesitation, his father went out.

He lay back. Through the window the sky was pale with a hidden moon and full of the rush of bulbous clouds.

13

The road swung from side to side, narrowly accommodating the truck in its lean width and crushing the howling tyres against the roots of hawthorn-scrub and the white, clayey fringes of the tarmac. The men swayed, the loose equipment thudding against their backs and legs and the worn planks, without any of them speaking. Leonard had watched the road unfolding behind for some time: the factories and houses on either side had disappeared, and the shape of the countryside grown unfamiliar. He felt himself relaxing; seeing it expanding rearward, he could greet it fatalistically like a traveller watching an unknown but predestined landscape appear. If nothing else now, this line of unfolding hills expressed his determination to be with these men and to be undefeated by them.

The truck swung off the road and entered a deep valley, a gulch of green, close-cropped grass. It narrowed abruptly, one wall brushing the side of the vehicle and the engine growling with a penned-in wildness. It darkened, the rock mounting over them: its creviced surface filled the back of the truck. They were climbing. For a moment they clung to the rock face, then the road suddenly left them, swinging behind in an arc, and they were running on straight, smooth tarmac.

It darkened; they shot under an archway, then between low barbed-wire fences. The arch stood behind them, isolated, something surprised, a huge circular eye blank against the sky.

'What's this, then?' Shaw said. 'What's this?' He leaned over, gripping the tailboard and staring out at the flocks of white sheep. They were laid like models in the mounded fields. Long, dark banks of woods were fastened up against the sky.

'It's Meerstone Park,' Pilkington said, and began taking off his neatly polished shoes and pulling on his cut-down Wellington boots. Shaw fell back, felt round for his bag and unwrapped his sandwiches, examining them carefully before replacing them in their greaseproof paper. He glanced quickly at Leonard and smiled.

The road ran straight and flat from the distant eye of the arch, the woods dropping down to the road in swinging curves. The truck rose suddenly, slowing abruptly and jarring with the pressure of a slope, and for the first time they heard the whine of the loaded lorry in front. The trees clipped the canvas hood. Then came the heavy scent of pines.

The sound of the two vehicles grew to a steady scream, the track winding steeply, and for a second the men caught sight of Ewbank's car leading the small convoy. Suddenly the sounds were obliterated by an onslaught of branches and leaves torn off by the heavy load in front. The scent of pines was drowned in a deeper smell of fern. They squeezed between sharp, precipitous hills, a wake of crushed branches and leaves strewn behind them, then slowed onto loose gravel between two broad smooth lawns. The grass lay like a lake at the bottom of a large hollow. They stopped and for some time there was absolute silence.

The door banged on Ewbank's car. His tiny feet crunched over the gravel. The men began to climb stiffly down. The lorries were parked in front of a large stone building, ivy-covered, and completely surrounded by steep, wooded hills rising from the edge of the lawns and garden.

The building's mellowed stone grew out of the bare rock, a natural protrusion of the sharp, conical hills, its thin coils of smoke curling up like an airy vegetation. The men scarcely moved, standing round the vehicles their bags dangling from their hands, staring up at the tall windows set crisply with white paint in the eroded skin of the house. Ewbank had disappeared round a path at the side, and a bell rang faintly in some deep recess.

At a french window, surrounded by roses, a young man was standing with his hands in his pockets looking out at the men and the two battered vehicles. His mouth moved slightly as if he were talking to someone who preferred to remain out of sight. Shaw stared in at the window with an amicable grin as he ate his sandwiches, his eyes occasionally moving sideways as though furtively to convey a message. The young man moved further back into the room's shadow, bent down and picked up a newspaper; then glanced out of the window once again to find Shaw still gazing in at him. Yet Shaw was seeing nothing; he always appeared preoccupied in this strange way whenever he had food in his mouth.

Pilkington, his trousers tucked in his Wellington boots, had taken off his shirt, his red, hirsute chest inflamed as he leaned against the back wheel of the truck relieving himself. He gazed up hopefully at the sky.

Somewhere in the house a dog barked, then several others. The men wandered about the drive, starting to eat. A middle-aged man came round the corner of the building with Ewbank. He was in flannels and a check sports coat, a yellow scarf tucked in the open collar of his red shirt. Three whippets darted round his legs, racing off across the lawn towards Leonard, who had crossed to the opposite side, and sweeping back in swift, dancing leaps.

'Come on,' Ewbank shouted. 'Get that cover off. Get them onto it, Tolson.'

He added something to the middle-aged man and they both stood smiling, watching the men laying down their food and starting to work.

The sun shone directly into the hollow. Throughout the morning the house itself was silent, the windows deserted.

The barking of dogs soon died down. The men were the only moving things, trampling the neat lawns and the small shrubberies and borders to squeeze in the white mushroom of new canvas. Inside they raised a lining of pink and white striped muslin and, before they broke off for lunch, laid out the battens inside the marquee as the foundation of a dance floor.

Occasionally Shaw had wandered off to the truck to inspect or to consume his remaining sandwiches. He was just completing his lunch as the men filed past him to collect their bags, and he followed them with his empty sandwich papers as they sat down in the shade of the tent awning.

'Nay, you can't expect any of mine if you've eaten your dinner already,' Pilkington said to him.

Ewbank had gone to his car; he slid in behind the wheel and lowered the window, to which he clipped a plastic tray. He unwrapped his lunch, laying it out in separate sections neatly divided by a knife, his Thermos and a small ivory toothpick he kept in his wallet. He ate thoughtfully, gazing ahead through the windscreen at the blank wall of trees, and occasionally twisting round to unscrew his Thermos and pour himself a cupful of tea.

Leonard sat down amongst the men. They turned to watch him take off the elastic bands from his lunch packet and unravel two sheets of tissue paper. Pilkington had started to laugh and Leonard looked up. He took out his sandwiches and glanced round at the men. They gazed up at the house unconcernedly. Tolson crouched against a tent-pole slashing the ground with a pen knife.

Leonard folded the paper back from the sandwiches and picked up the top one. He bit it, and chewed.

Then he spat it out and stood up. He spat again. Rubbing his sleeve across his mouth he spat again. The men burst out laughing, one of them rolling on the lawn. The sandwich had fallen open by his feet. Pressed into the buttered bread were two pieces of excrement, one bitten off at the corner.

'What is it, Radcliffe?' Pilkington said.

The men, laughing helplessly, gazed tearfully up at his figure.

'God, it's a pair of Shaw specials.' They pressed forward

to look at the object. Leonard had turned white and his lips, smeared with the sandwich, had coloured a peculiar blue, so intense that the men began to look at him rather than at the broken bread. They quietened, staring up at his frozen figure. Then as Leonard moved towards Shaw Tolson, a few feet away, stood up, grasped him by the shoulders and almost dragged him off the ground.

'Leave him alone.'

Leonard stared down at Shaw who had turned only now. Then he pulled himself free of Tolson's grip.

'Leave the poor bugger alone,' Tolson said.

'What's the matter?' Shaw gazed round in surprise. The men had stood up. Ewbank had stepped from his car, his glasses pushed up on his forehead and a newspaper folded in his hand. He stood by the open door looking across. His toothpick hung limply from his mouth.

The men stood around Leonard. He seemed scarcely to be breathing. A slight flush tinged his high cheekbones. His eyes were peculiarly clear and transparent, almost as if he were sleeping.

'Did Shaw do it then?' he said suddenly and in a strangely reasonable voice.

Tolson didn't answer.

'Ah, you want to leave Shaw alone,' one of the men said.

They began to move back listlessly. Shaw stood up and walked away, glancing back at the two men, then breaking into high, almost soundless laughter. He leaned against the truck, his head resting against his hand.

Tolson watched Shaw a moment then smiled, turning to look at Leonard with an almost apologetic stare. Several of the men started to laugh again and Tolson went back to his food, crouching down by the tent-pole and digging his knife in the grass as he ate. The men returned to their places, sitting down under the rich lining of the tent. One of them kicked the dirtied sandwich away and in doing so caught the remainder with his foot, scattering the small pile across the width of the drive. One piece flew under the truck. He looked at Leonard apologetically and, blushing, sat down again by his own food. Shaw stooped to peer under the truck.

Leonard walked clumsily through the tent, his foot jarring

against the laid joists; then he tripped and fell on his hands. He picked himself up and walked on with stiff angular movements. Shaw, bending down by the truck, had burst into hysterical giggling. The men laughed helplessly at him. In the house the young man had reappeared at the french window. He stood wiping his mouth on a napkin, then turned back. Several figures could be dimly seen seated round a table, eating.

Leonard came out on a rocky ridge a few yards in width, the summit of one of the hills overlooking the house. As he crossed the ridge he saw that the house stood just above an even deeper hollow, a broadening valley in which were set small stone cottages almost concealed beneath the canopies of beech trees. A policeman on a bike rode down a steep, sunken lane, rose briefly into sight and disappeared. At the same moment a man came from a side entrance of the house and crunched down the drive. Three dogs ran after him, barking and leaping. He strode below the hill and down towards the village.

Two broad wings were set back from the central front of the house, almost penetrating the steep, rocky flank of the opposite hill. In an upstairs window on the side away from the lawn a young woman was half visible. She was taking off her dress. It swirled round her head, a faint pinkness in the shadow of the room; then she stood watching herself in a mirror. She disappeared, passed two intervening windows and reappeared at a third. She put on a blue and white frock, slipping it over her shoulders, her hands clutching above her. She fastened the neck and sat down, her head and shoulders just visible. Then she let down her hair and brushed it. It fell in a sudden shock, draining over her shoulders. She drew the brush through it with slight backward motions of her head, and fastened it with a ribbon. She came to stare out of the window at the trees which grew in an arc along that side of the house; then with a sudden, almost violent movement, she disappeared.

On the lawn the men lay eating. Tolson was swinging a hammer rhythmically over a stake. When Leonard went down the men looked past him as if they scarcely noticed his return.

He worked on his own, hooking up the walling in one corner of the tent, yet continuously looking round as if searching for something. His head twisted anxiously about, at the narrow drive which coiled into the hollow, and at the thin strands of smoke that drifted upwards from the chimneys. The house was like a heart buried in the flesh of the hills; the pines curved to its quiet pounding. He hadn't looked at Tolson.

In the french window, laid now as if within a second pane of shadow, the young man watched him working, a newspaper in his hand. Beside him several points of silver glowed on a laden tray. He shook the paper out, stretched out his arms and carefully folded it. The man in the check sports coat came out to watch for a while, standing with his feet astride, the three dogs twining themselves round his legs on thin leads. He lit a cigarette then went away.

The hollow contained the heat: the men were red and sweating, grimed, crashing the long wooden tables onto the battening and levelling them with chocks of wood as the base to the dance floor. They worked silently, periodically breaking off to stoop over a garden tap and fill their mouths with water.

Tolson worked in the centre of the men, guiding the tables into position on the narrow battens and nailing them down with a hammer which he rested in his belt. He worked absorbedly and intently, ordering the men with quick movements of his hands and with brief, violent exclamations. They responded to him alertly. At the one point when he did look up, it was to see Leonard gazing, not at him directly, but at the hammer he held in his fist. A long claw curved back from its narrow head. Tolson held it up, nodding, then prised out a nail between the sharp forks. Leonard smiled as if he recognized the friendly significance of the gesture.

From time to time the young man came to the window, the newspaper held loosely in his hand. He watched for a while, stretched, and then returned to his chair. A thick dust rose in the heavy air from the old, over-used timber as Tolson crawled across the flooring banging in the long nails. It mixed with the sweat and the men turned grey-faced working under the shadow of the tent. When the rough, wooden flooring was completed they pulled flat, square cases from the back of the lorry and, unfastening the clasps, slid out the shining oak panels of the dance floor.

Tolson moved the heavy shapes into position, crouching to the ground so that he could gauge the level of the wood, his head bowed to it; then he slid strips of aluminium into the grooves alongside each panel, binding them together. He worked swiftly and agilely, grooving the hard shapes together, running his hand smoothly over the joints, then springing along the floor to direct the next assembling. Above his crouched figure the canvas billowed in a light breeze, rising and falling in slow waves. The guy-lines tensed, then relaxed in slack loops.

The luminous sheen of the floor slowly spread across the interior of the tent. Tolson worked with a hurried accuracy, self-absorbed, the men responding to every swinging gesture of his arm. The polished wood stretched round him like silk, its ochre gleam reflecting the pink and white muslin lining of the roof. Ewbank, perfectly and blackly mirrored, walked up and down the assembled surface smoking a cheroot, pausing occasionally to watch Tolson's directions, and pointing his foot to test his weight on each section before him.

By mid-afternoon the floor was nearly laid: a canvas-lidded lake on the lawn filling out to the bursting shrub-beries and flower-beds. Tolson worked alone now in the centre of the electric surface. Leonard had joined the rest of the men to clear up the boxes and hessian bags and the litter of unused materials. Shaw stood by the truck rolling a cigarette and watching the men as they passed him with their loads. He giggled whenever Leonard came near, watching him with a helpless expression, shaking his head and clicking his tongue as Leonard went by. Now that the work was almost done the men began to call and shout at one another more loudly. They looked up at the house quite confidently.

Tolson, alone in the tent, had stopped working. He crouched down to the luminous floor. A girl had come into the tent. Tall and slender, her stiffened blue and white striped frock was reflected like a stain in the polished wood. Her face glowed with the sunny luminosity. The men looked in at her in silence.

A second woman came to the edge of the floor, middle-aged, with grey hair. She watched the girl intently. 'Do you like it, darling?' she said.

The girl swung round to her; shadows ran up through her frock to her bare shoulders. 'Oh, mummy! It's wonderful . . . simply wonderful.'

'What do you think, Steven?' The mother turned as the young man appeared beside her, his hands in his pockets.

'It's splendid,' he said, testing his foot lightly on the dance floor.

The girl watched her mother and the young man, waiting for them to share her enthusiasm. Then she cried out, 'Oh, it's absolutely marvellous! Don't you think so, Steven?' She swung round, splaying her skirt, her feet sliding in simple steps across the polished wood.

'Bleeding hell,' Pilkington said. He crouched down by the side of the truck to watch. 'I bet that puts some lead in your pencil, Shaw.' The old man looked up absent-mindedly from filing his strip of metal.

Tolson hadn't moved. The girl stopped as she saw his crouched figure. His hands were held over the fine joint of a panel. The colour swayed in her, the blueness shadowed by her sudden stillness. The mother and the young man looked in from the fringe of the tent. The girl and Tolson were alone on the floor.

A strange noise filled the tent; a soft moaning which steadily grew wilder, mounting to a grinding whine. For a moment it seemed that the noise came from the two frozen figures, the beginning of some terrible event. Standing alone at the end of the tent, silhouetted against the bright light, Leonard was gazing in at Tolson. Beyond him, through the trees moved the red legend of one of Ewbank's lorries. It climbed cautiously up the hill, loaded to a high peak with folding chairs, tearing through the lower branches. As it swayed round the lower edge of the lawn and came to a halt, the men moved towards it.

Ewbank removed his hat and stepped cautiously across

the polished floor to the girl's mother, his face twisted into a smile. Tolson had stood up.

The girl watched the lorry with an angered, half-shocked expression, then glanced at Tolson before looking up at the pink and white muslin, draped in a luminous film from the ridge of the tent. She walked back to her mother and stood listening to Ewbank, her back to the glowing interior. Whenever she glanced up she gazed blankly at the front of the house and its rows of dark windows. Presently she, her mother, and her fiancé went in.

The sun lit up the front of the house piercing the tops of the firs with forked rays so that the ochre stone glowed dully and warmly. The walls of the tent were laced up and the chairs set round the perimeter of the dance floor. The interior was suffused like the inside of a giant bulb, lit up by contrary gleams and reflections. Two gardeners brought in trays of plants and arranged them on rugs round the bases of the three main poles. A large chandelier had been hauled above the dance floor. Beneath it Tolson worked alone, moving cautiously on his bare feet as he tested his weight on the joints of each panel.

One end of the tent was still open. Outside, and standing between the flower-beds, the girl had returned to gaze in at the glowing interior. The men worked round her packing the last of the equipment. Tolson had stopped to stare across at her slight figure. The hammer hung from his hand.

Then he looked round at the tent. A moment later he put the hammer down on the floor and walked slowly across to the girl.

Leonard, watching the movement, saw the girl's eyes turning slowly to Tolson as she flushed about her brow and cheeks. Tolson stood listening with a frozen grim shyness as the girl spoke; then he turned towards the tent to smile in some slight confusion. The girl looked at his cheek and neck.

A few moments later Leonard realized that, as Tolson spoke to the girl, he was staring in through the shadows of the tent directly at him; it was almost as if he were speaking to him. He saw the girl looking round as if she sensed the presence of some third person, and for a second her eyes rested perplexedly on his before moving on. He turned

144

away to his work. Tolson's claw hammer was still lying in the gleaming centre of the floor.

He looked up again as a woman's voice called from the house. The girl glanced up sharply at the windows, with the same angered, half-shocked expression; then the woman's voice called again. She turned towards Tolson as he stood watching her aloofly, then bent down to a dog that had come rushing out and was jumping round her. The next moment the young man came round the corner of the house.

'Katherine?'

The girl's head swung angrily; she glared in at the tent. Then she began to move away with the dog. The young man waited. Tolson hadn't moved. She glanced back at him, frowning, and with a heavy, upraised gesture of her bare shoulders went towards the house. Tolson walked back into the tent. His hammer had gone. When he looked back the girl and the young man had disappeared round the corner of the house.

The men loaded the empty floor boxes onto the truck, pulled on their coats and waited, smoking, while Ewbank and Tolson walked round the tent, inspecting the ropes and searching.

'Have any of you seen a claw hammer?' Ewbank said when he came back. He looked sharply at the men over his cheroot, his hands in the coat-pockets of his black suit. 'The one that Tolson had,' he said, gazing into their faces.

'It's probably under the floor,' Pilkington said. 'We'll get it when we take it up.'

Ewbank nodded disbelievingly and went back to the tent. He searched it thoroughly, disappearing for some time behind the walling. But when he emerged it was with several potted plants which he carefully placed in the boot of his car.

The firs, silhouetted at the summit of the hill, were single, hair-like lashes against the red sun. The house had sunk into the rock, melting within a deep, misty shadow that crept slowly upwards from the root of the hollow. The tent glowed now, white and new.

Just before the vehicles drew out Tolson got down from

the cab of the lorry and climbed into the back of the truck. Leonard was there with Pilkington and Shaw.

They sat in silence until the engines started. Then Tolson said, 'I've been meaning to ask you. Do you want to come out with us tonight? With Audrey and me, I mean.'

Leonard was crouched to one side, his bag held tightly between his knees. For a while he didn't answer. He stared at Tolson, almost as if he were a stranger. Then he said in a surprised, half-startled voice, 'Yes, all right.'

Tolson laughed. 'Ewbank was really annoyed at losing that hammer,' he said.

'He never loses aught that he doesn't make up,' Pilkington said.

Shaw, filing his strip of metal, began to laugh quietly, a contained sound so that none of the men looked up.

'Who was that young girl, then?' Pilkington asked.

Tolson shrugged. He turned to Leonard again. 'It's somebody I want you to meet . . . tonight, I mean. Somebody who's asked to meet you.' He looked at Leonard concernedly. 'You'll be able to come, then, will you?'

'Yes. I'll come.'

Yet Tolson still seemed unsatisfied. He continued to glance at Leonard suspiciously, then at the bag he clutched so tightly between his knees. Clearly outlined there by the sweat from his hands was the hard shape of the hammer. Its claws had even penetrated the fabric of the bag.

Shaw rubbed briskly at the metal, pursing his lips over it to blow gently, then holding it to one eye and gazing along its surface. He glanced up at Tolson, then at Leonard, who was staring out at the retreating crest of the trees. He began to laugh more loudly until suddenly the sound was swamped by Ewbank's car drawing up behind.

Tolson had turned away, his eyes glazed as though he were moodily excited.

14

The tall, thin figure on the stage was the same man that Leonard had last seen limping away through pools of lamplight from Tolson's house. Now he was dressed in large trousers that drooped from his waist on a child's elastic braces. A collarless flannel shirt and a school jacket covered his angular body. Sweat ran in thin streams through the white powder on his face: only his eyes were alive, large and black, and the red thickness of his mouth. He stared round apprehensively waiting for the crowded room to quieten.

Tolson, his bare arms laid on the table, leant past Audrey and said to Leonard, 'He'll come down afterwards. You'll like him. No, I mean that. You will.' He turned to Audrey, smiling, but she was looking towards the back of the hall where an extremely tall man was shouting, 'Fifteen. Sixty-two. Thirty-nine. . . . Twenty. . . . Number eleven.'

An equally tall man, with a long, dark moustache that curled round his mouth and a vaguely consumptive face, was sitting at a large table under the stage. 'Yes . . . yes . . . yes,' he said into a microphone held close to one cheek. 'What was that? What was *that*?'

'Eighty! *Eighty!*' the winner shouted. He was crimson, holding onto two men beside him. 'Don't worry. I've *won*, all right,' he shouted aside to someone. 'I've won, I tell you.' He started calling his numbers again.

Apparently satisfied, the secretary took his card, then pushed his long body upwards to reach a battery of switches above his head. The lights dimmed. 'I've told you before,' he called through the microphone. 'If you want to talk you can go into the billiard room. The rule in here's silence for the artists.'

People turned their chairs to face the lighted stage, crushing against one another in the heavy atmosphere and tearing up their uncompleted housey-housey forms.

'And now, Ladies and Gentlemen. . . .' The secretary reached up again to the switches, the microphone still pressed to his cheek. 'We have your favourite and mine, the one and only Gormless Gordon the gump from Gorseforth.'

A spotlight lit the stage to one side of the white figure: he stepped hurriedly into it. A burst of laughter ran through the hall: he'd pulled his trousers down to his groin and they sprang up to his armpits on the thin elastic braces. 'A've come . . . and to prove it I'm here!' He made a shy undulation of his body within the tight jacket and large trousers. 'I know you wouldn't think it, love, would you.' He laughed, opening wide an empty mouth. 'I don't look as though I'm all here, do I love?' He leaned down as if he spoke privately to Audrey. They laughed up at him.

A large, fat woman sat at the piano at the side of the stage out of range of the spotlight. She turned and smiled down at the audience, then nodded her head at the comedian.

'You think I'm bloody simple, don't you?' he said, waiting for the response to die down. An anxious expression gave his face an almost feminine concern. He was looking down at Tolson, then nodding, and glancing at Leonard, who stared up at him with a sombre intentness. 'I'm not simple, you know. I'm not.' He said it with a fierce, mocking exasperation. 'As a matter of fact, I was up at the nut-house only the other day . . . sorry, the mental horse-pital. No. And it wasn't for that. I'm not daft, you know. No, it was just that we were thinking of sending our Sally there. She's so fat. She's alus eating. She never stops. . . . Only the other day she had an argument about it with her boy friend and he hit her under the left breast and shattered her knee cap.'

The audience was laughing, distracted, and staring up at the swaying painted figure with expressions of half-resentment. Tolson leaned on the table and on Audrey's chair, nodding his head for her to look at Leonard: he was gazing at the performer with an intense, frozen embarrassment, a cautious look of hatred.

'Anyway, like, I went up to the mental insti . . . insti . . . to the rat kennel, and I saw this chap who's supposed to be in charge. I could tell he was in charge because he shook hands. Well . . . he didn't shake hands exactly. He got hold of my left hand, and got hold of my right hand, put them together and said, "How d'you do." . . . I said to him, "Why d'you do that – put my left hand into my right hand and say, 'How d'you do?'" He said, "Don't you always shake hands when you meet strangers?" . . . No, though. I said to him, "I can see you've got two heads but I didn't bang 'em together when I came in, did I?" . . . "You can see I've got two heads?" "Yes, I can see you've got two heads.". . .'

Leonard had turned away, staring round at the attentive, grimacing faces. He was surrounded by a wall of bodies. He half stood, then sank down as Tolson turned towards him laughing.

'Double vision!' Tolson said.

Leonard rubbed his glass between his hands.

'. . . Half way across this hall and I saw this other chap hanging on a chandelier. *Hanging on a chandelier!* And I sort of noticed him, then I looked again, and I caught hold of this doctor's arm and I whispered to him, quietly like, "There's a man up there, hanging on the chandelier." And he just looked up and said, "Oh, that's all right my man." "How d'you mean, that's all right?" I said. "Oh, it's perfectly all right. He thinks he's an electric wire, that's all." "An electric wire?" I said. "Yes. It's perfectly all right." "But why don't you tell him he's not?" "What," he said, "and put all the bleeding lights out?"'

The men laughed thickly, sullenly, watching now as the comedian opened his painted mouth, then pursed it, whistling and beating himself violently with his small fists, thumping his thighs to encourage the sounds around him. The woman at the piano had played a few bars of introductory music.

'I've come, you know! And to prove it I'm here!' He laughed soundlessly, his face split by his featureless mouth. 'But our Sally. You should see her, you know. She's so fat. When she gets on a bus the driver rises to the top deck. . . . And she's always buying clothes. Always those biblical gowns . . . you know the kind: low and *behold*.'

Tolson had lain his head on his arms, bending over the

table; he looked up sideways at the stage, his shoulders shaking silently with laughter. Leonard watched him acutely.

'And it's not as if the wife's responsible . . . she's as thin as a rail. In fact she's so thin that when I had her tattooed on her chest the colours came out on her back. . . . Mind you, she's not as young as she was. Not by a long way. She isn't. I was only thinking yesterday, she's got so many wrinkles on her face that if you put a cord through her ears you could run it up like a venetian blind.'

'Oh, bloody hell,' Tolson said. 'Have you ever seen such a pissed-up wreck?' He laughed into his bare arms, glancing up for Audrey to share his amusement. The crowd was leaning forward to laugh as the emaciated figure tapped the ash of his cigarette down the front of his trousers. Leonard was staring up at him now, blushing and confused, his hands gripping the edge of the table, then turning to gaze at Tolson. He watched Tolson with a wild, almost frantic expression.

'I can't look through the knot-hole in her leg any more it's bunged so tight with dry rot. . . .' His voice was lost in the dull surge of amusement. 'I'm to give you a little dirty . . . I mean, a little ditty, entitled, "You have worked for me a long time, mother, now go and work for yourself" . . . Hickory, dickory, dock, two mice ran up her frock. One reached her garter, the other was smarter. . . . No, no. I don't think I'll give you that one. Instead I would like to render that song well loved by the patrons of this establishment, "Don't cry in the beer, old man, it's three parts water already".'

The pianist began slowly to play the tune, 'Somewhere Over the Rainbow.'

'Seriously, though . . . . No, seriously, Ladies and Gentlemen, I would like to give you a song of my own choosing to which I'm very attached, called "Please take back your heart, my dear, I only ordered liver", or, as it's entitled in Russia, "When the sheets are short then the bed seems longer". When we reach the line, "Father, cut your toenails, they're tearing mother's hair," I want you all to join in the chorus, which is . . .'

He began to sing, 'Some . . . where under the bedclothes, here with you, I find two little so-and-so's, and one little what-not too. . . .'

The secretary was fastening up the housey-housey forms in a large cardboard box. Then soundlessly, only his lips trembling beneath his moustache, he began to count the money, sliding it across the table under a particularly slender hand.

'I undid that and loosened this, I gave her just a little kiss, I burrowed here and hurried there, soon had her little what-not bare, I wandered high, I wandered low. . . .'

'What's his name?' a man said, leaning over Tolson. 'Gormless what?'

'Gordon.'

'Aye. Gormless Gordon. Have you ever seen such a shit!' He laughed pleasurably at the lighted stage. Applause had broken out as he came to the end of the song, and with a final tug of his trousers, holding them down to his groin then allowing them to spring up, he turned to leave the stage. The trousers fell from his armpits to the floor, dragging round his ankles. With a mock gesture of embarrassment, his arms flung up in the air, he scurried to the back of the stage and disappeared through a small door marked 'Artists'.

15

'I wouldn't say he enjoyed it, Denis,' Tolson said. He pressed Audrey's back to draw her more closely into the group: the asphalt yard was crowded with the members leaving the club. 'Len. This is Denis Blakeley.'

The comedian turned from talking to Audrey to look at Leonard, who stood with his arms held stiffly to his sides. Blakeley was dressed in a raincoat, his face only half-illuminated by the gas flares over the yard. He had thin, sharp features, his hair brushed smoothly back over his scalp. He smiled at Leonard and said, 'If not, why not?'

'It's not important,' Leonard said, getting ready to go.

'Oh, but it is.' Blakeley caught his arm and limped a step nearer. For a moment Leonard had the clear recollection that on the stage Blakeley hadn't limped at all. Then he was suddenly confused as he saw Blakeley's face close to his and the anxious, vaguely feminine look, inquisitive and almost sensitive, exaggerated by the faint patches of white powder still adhering to his skin. 'I think it's important or I wouldn't do it.'

Leonard didn't reply: he gazed slowly at Tolson.

'Come on. What didn't you like?' Blakeley said. He was friendly, even courteous in a slightly absurd way, waiting patiently yet still gripping Leonard's arm. 'What didn't you like about it? I don't mind what you say, but for God's sake just *say* it.'

'It's the way you pandered down to them,' Leonard said. He seemed cold, his face frozen by the orange light. 'You don't have to feed yourself to them.'

'Oh, now. . . .' Blakeley shuffled closer as if he had been encouraged. 'Are you sure that's what I do?'

Leonard moved away, but as Tolson said, 'Come on, leave him, Denis, he takes all this stuff too seriously,' Blakeley called over his shoulder, 'No, you get off on your bike. . . . Me and Radcliffe here have something to talk about.' He looked at Leonard confidingly, pressing his hand firmly against his back.

'Ah, now leave him,' Tolson said. He sounded strangely concerned.

But Blakeley was already guiding Leonard towards the brick pillars of the gateway. 'Now, Vic, there's no need to worry. I shall look after him. I'll take every care. Good night, Audrey. . . . Good night, love. Night, Vic. And don't worry, I'll take care of him.' He called once more over his back. Then they were in the comparative darkness of the street. 'Vic'll be all right,' Blakeley said, winking and glancing back.

They walked in silence for some time. Leonard felt the man as some impediment of his own as he limped beside him. He glanced at his eroded face only once, then felt himself walking along as if that stiff, exaggerated articulation were a feature of his own mind.

'How long have you known Tolson ... Vic, then?'
Blakeley said.

'Not long.'

'Who was it before that?'

'How do you mean?'

'Oh, never mind. From the way he talks about you,
you'd think he'd known you a lifetime. He's always been
threatening he'd let me meet you. He met you at Ewbank's
apparently? How long have you worked there, then?'

'Only this summer.'

'What did you do before?'

Leonard didn't answer, but Blakeley said, 'No, I'm
asking you.'

'I sometimes work in an office. Sometimes not at all.' But
when Blakeley questioned him further he wouldn't reply.
When they reached the road up to the estate Leonard
stopped.

'Oh, you go that way, then?' Blakeley said.

'It's the quickest from here.'

'What you were saying back there,' Blakeley began
difficultly. 'I know exactly what you mean. But it's not ...
how can I put it?'

Leonard had a brief suspicion he was being derided. He
couldn't be sure that Blakeley by his expression and gestures
wasn't mocking him. Yet he stood gazing at him aloofly.

'What I'm trying to say is that I take it seriously. I take it
more seriously perhaps than you imagine – performing.
Being an artist as I look upon it.' He moved round Leonard,
drawing his leg in a stiff, angular arc, and looking away
into the looming darkness of the estate. 'Back there, I could
see what you mean. Pandering down to them. Yes, I can
see that. But then, that's not the way I look at it. I know
these things are difficult to talk about. But I feel you'd
understand if I can explain. ... It's important to me, you
see.' He smiled and caught hold of Leonard's arm. 'No. I
can see you think I'm that bit pretentious.' He stated it
hurriedly as if by self-criticism he could secure Leonard's
real attention. 'What I'm trying to say is that I have several
theories about art ... about being an artist, what I do.
Look!' He suddenly laughed, catching Leonard's sleeve

more sharply. 'Why don't you come home with me? Just for a few minutes. Have a cup of tea or a drop of something. I only live a few houses away.' As he saw the tortured look of indecision on Leonard's face he added more confidently, 'I must stress that I'm a family man. I wouldn't say that they're my *entire* life. . . .' He laughed again, holding Leonard's arm more tightly and beginning to walk him up the nearest avenue. 'That would be fatal wouldn't it? But without them, the family, I just don't know what I should do. . . . The amusing thing is that I like to think that without me they'd be in a similar plight. Do you know what I mean? We're completely together. We stick together. You must *see* them. . . . You don't mind me talking like this, do you? But I'm afraid I've no patience with politeness and all that *shit*. I like to talk straight away, straight off about the important things. And to me what I *do* and my family are the important things. . . . I know a man hates to meet another man's family like that. But if you don't meet *my* family I can't honestly say that you've really met *me*.' He laughed again, enjoyably. The road wound steeply up between the darkened houses.

Leonard, though alarmed, appeared to follow the man simply at his insistence. When they reached the gate to the council house and he glanced back he was almost relieved to see that in fact Tolson had been following them. He was some distance lower down the dimly-lit road, sitting on his silent machine after free-wheeling down the opposite incline. There was no sign, however, of Audrey.

Although it was late there were three children playing in the small living-room. One of them was completely naked and the other two only half-dressed; they looked up at Leonard without curiosity and went on shouting as they threw themselves aimlessly over the furniture in some strenuous game. The walls of the room were covered in photographs of Blakeley in different costumes and parts.

'So you've managed to catch him after all. Well, you were quick.' A woman of about thirty sat in the corner of the room sewing one of the children's clothes. Leonard, confused by the sudden brilliance of light and the shouting stared sullenly, almost aggressively, at her. She smiled at him directly as if she recognized something familiar in his response. Not unlike Blakeley in looks, she had a more confident, trusting face, and a decisive, undismayed expression, vaguely self-amused.

'Oh, now. . . .' Blakeley said, but the woman went on, 'He said he was going to get hold of you on your own, Tolson or no Tolson.' She continued sewing, yet looking up at him undemandingly, vaguely contemptuous.

'I thought all these'd be in bed by now,' Blakeley said, so disappointed that he appeared to forget Leonard completely and went to sit by the stove that dominated the small room. He gazed at the low fire, leaning forward, his elbows on his knees.

'My mother's upstairs,' the woman said to him. 'We're trying to find them all something to sleep in. Now stop it!' She stood up and caught hold of the two noisiest, half-clad children and flung them down on a large settee, hitting the legs of the oldest so hard that all three were immediately silent. They became aware of Leonard standing palely in the door.

'Won't you sit down?' she said. 'We're not very straight but we've left things a bit late tonight.' She pulled a stack of ironed clothes from an easy chair and he took off his raincoat and sat down.

'Oh, I'm sorry,' Blakeley said, watching him fold his coat over the arm of the chair. 'This is my eldest daughter, Kathleen.'

She seemed about to add something to her father's introduction, but her expression suddenly lightened and she said, 'What do I call you? Leonard . . . or Mr Radcliffe?'

'Oh . . . Leonard.' He nodded his head, smiling. She seemed pleased that her abruptness should confuse him.

'Come on,' she said to the children. 'Upstairs. We'll finish you off up there. And if you make any noise you know what to expect.'

They responded eagerly. They pushed each other out of the room and ran noisily up the narrow stairs.

'She's very good with the kids,' Blakeley said. 'She treats them like pigs and they'll do anything for her. It's very strange is that. I'm sorry about all this. As you can see, I've got a fair whack of a family. And I can tell you – we only meant to have the one. Kathleen. But these last few years they've been tumbling out. 'Course, it gives Kathleen a good laugh, seeing her mother stuffed up so late in life. The wife's over fifty, you know.'

'Were you intending, then, to bring me back here?' Leonard looked at him with the same shyness, an expectancy that drew a heavy blush down his face. He seemed disconcerted by what had happened.

'Well, there you are again. I told them I might. Tolson said he'd bring you along . . . and introduce us. I can tell you, I was more nervous than I've ever been tonight, knowing you were there.'

'Why?'

Blakeley laughed and glanced casually at him. 'Ah, well. . . . Perhaps you don't know what a pride Tolson takes in you.'

'What does that mean?'

'Oh. You must know him as well as I do by now. Vic has a great lust for power. Unconditional power. . . . He has this lust to possess people.' He stated it awkwardly and provocatively, but Leonard remained silent. The ceiling groaned with the children overhead. 'I suppose with not knowing him long you don't realize. And then again, it might be a part of everybody, and I haven't noticed.' He laughed slightly though, it seemed, without any change of expression. 'But with Vic it's built up into something that dominates all the rest of his life. I mean, although he's never told you about me – and I've known him now for seven or eight years, since before he was married – *he's* told me all about you right from the beginning. You see, when you said you hadn't known him long, as a matter of fact it's nine weeks and four days, to the nearest day. He came here the evening of your very first day at Ewbank's.' He brushed his hand against his face, then laughed; it was almost a gesture from his performance. 'Do you know how he described you? Can you guess?' He watched Leonard's expression with some satisfaction. 'He came bursting in here and said, "Do you know, I've met a prince today." That's how he described you. And when I said, "How d'you mean, a *prince*?" he said, "Oh, I don't know. It's just how I've always imagined a prince was".' Blakeley laughed, knocking his fist slightly against his thigh. 'Then he started to tell me about a prince he'd read about as a boy. At school ... there you are. You fulfilling some childhood fantasy of Tolson's. And he's kept you to himself ever since.'

Leonard had blushed and seemed about to get up when Kathleen came back into the room. It was as if all Blakeley's vaguely feminine characteristics had been suddenly projected and clearly defined in her; he gazed up at her as if it were she who had been speaking.

'My mother'll be down in a few minutes. What's he been telling you?' She looked from Leonard to her father and back with the same antagonistic expression.

'You mind your own business,' Blakeley said. 'Is there anything in to drink?'

'I'll put the kettle on for some tea, if that's what you mean. There's nothing else.' She turned directly to Leonard, standing over him. 'I want to hear what you thought of his act first, though.'

'I didn't like it at all,' Leonard said with such evident simplicity that she started smiling, then suddenly giggled, glancing at her father and turning away.

'Why not?' she said.

'He thinks I'm obscene. I belittle myself,' Blakeley said. 'And it's quite true, I do. What was it you said? I pander to them. Stoop down to them. Perhaps he thinks I should be satirical and witty, and sing folk songs with a guitar.' Apparently recognizing himself in this role, Blakeley burst out laughing. 'I've come, and to prove it I'm here!' he said.

Kathleen laughed with her father; they were curiously alike, except that the woman was harder and firmer, even physically stronger than her father.

'Perhaps you're a bit above it all,' she said to Leonard. Then added, with her father's deprecating gesture, 'No, I'm wrong. It is sickening, isn't it? I can never watch it. I don't know why he goes on doing it, feeding himself to them, and they sit there like fat ducks in the pond. If it wasn't him, it'd be someone else. There's no point to it. But you'll be surprised,' she said, looking at her father, who was smiling at her with some sort of enjoyment, 'surprised how much pleasure he gets out of it. He can even make it all look fine and noble if you let him talk long enough about it. And there's only one thing you can really say for him. And that's that he can sing. He's got a lovely tenor voice. But he's just given in. . . .'

'Given in, she calls it,' Blakeley cried.

'Well, I'm glad Leonard's told you.'

Blakeley laughed more loudly genuinely pleased with his daughter, and glancing at Leonard now with relief. 'What do you think to her? Don't you think she should go up instead of me?'

'A woman would never do what you do. Stoop . . . *grovel.*'

'Ah, don't you be too sure,' Blakeley said, some scarcely concealed feeling suddenly passing between them. 'My own flesh and blood,' he added indulgently. 'What do you think they'll invent next after children?' His hand beat unconsciously against his side as he laughed. Kathleen looked away as someone else came into the room. Leonard stood up.

'Nay, don't get up for me, love,' Blakeley's wife said. A heavily-built woman, red-faced with greyed, almost white hair, she pushed indifferently between the furniture as if by disregarding Leonard she could make him feel at home.

'I've put the kettle on. Kathleen can make it when it boils. We've got all the pyjamas in the wash. They're wrapped up in all sorts of stuff.' She laughed at her husband but her eyes, small and tired, had an undiminished look of anxiety, as if some deep and early concern about him had never been arrested. The real child of the family was Blakeley.

'You see,' he said, 'she never asks me how I got on.'

'I don't need to, love. I can always tell,' she said, not looking at him and sinking into a chair. But a moment later she pulled her heavy frame up and started to tidy the room. She picked up several fragments of food and numerous small, broken toys.

'Nothing stays in one piece for long in this house,' Blakeley said, watching her. 'Not even the people. We get broken up amongst one another. Don't you think that . . .'

'So you work with Tolson, then,' Kathleen said with the aggressiveness that accompanied even her slightest gestures.

'Why do you say it in that tone?' Leonard said.

'What tone? Was there a tone? I thought if there's one person I'm detached about it's Vic.'

'You see, like the rest of us,' her father said, 'she's also had some experience of Victor.' He held his hand to the side of his face as if simulating concern.

'I was asking for his opinion not yours,' she said harshly, almost childishly.

Leonard had put on an oppressed, stifled expression as if now he were completely bewildered. Kathleen seemed to take it as a look of shyness or embarrassment: provocatively she added, 'I suppose my father's told you what sort of regard . . . what sort of *pernicious* regard Tolson holds you in.'

'No. . . . No, I don't think . . .'

'Perhaps you don't realize just how destructive Tolson is? No, I can see in your face that you know well enough. After all, why would he *choose* you if he didn't see that you were so vulnerable?'

'No, you're wrong!' Leonard said angrily. 'I don't know why you should be so malicious. If you understand *why* he behaves in the way he does then you'll find that . . .' He shook his head, stammering slightly as if he'd suddenly lost his train of thought altogether. 'You'll see that there are ways of *directing* him.'

'And what sort of understanding is it then that's required?' Kathleen said, but with such a wildness that he only stared at her in silence. 'Go on, I'm listening. What sort of understanding is required?'

'You've got to see that he's a big person, and intensely lonely,' Leonard said, but so subduedly that is seemed only Kathleen, leaning accusingly towards him, actually heard.

'What was that? He's a what person. . . ?' Blakeley said.

Kathleen had turned away. 'Oh, so that's how it's done,' she said quietly, but it was a tone of disappointment rather than contempt.

'Ah, now.' Blakeley had stood up as if only now realizing

that some quarrel had to be mended. 'Perhaps Leonard's experience of Tolson isn't quite ours. As I've said to Kathleen before we ever met you, perhaps you're a stronger character than any of us imagine.'

But Kathleen hadn't stayed to listen; she'd gone into the scullery, and a few moments later her mother followed her, her apron scooped up to contain the large amount of debris she'd collected.

Blakeley sat down again, but more alertly. They could hear the two women talking rapidly and intensely in the next room.

'You see, I don't know how well you know Tolson, Leonard. But in our experience, well, his influence has always been destructive. And there are lots of people with much the *same* sort of experience. He's such a strong sort of person. He doesn't see perhaps how he knocks other people over. But you: you think there are ways of handling him, then?'

Leonard couldn't be certain that Blakeley wasn't looking at him mischievously or whether it were simply a more genuine expression of concern than he'd seen before.

'I don't know,' he said.

'You see,' Blakeley went on, 'Vic sees everything in terms of *victories*, of his assimilation of other people. He consumes people.'

'I don't see why you should be so malicious about him,' Leonard said, his body twisting narrowly. He rubbed his face tormentedly. 'I don't know. I feel that you've got me here just to . . .' He shook his head.

'Perhaps it's simply that you're a bony piece that won't digest,' Blakeley said, as if recognizing and encouraging Leonard's bewilderment.

'What is it? Do you feel that *you've* been destroyed by Tolson or something? I don't see anything extraordinary in him at all.'

Blakeley, as if both alarmed yet intrigued that he had attracted Leonard's attention in this way, waved his hand across his face as if brushing, almost pushing, some obstruction away. 'As you say, perhaps the best thing is to give in to him straight away and let him use you. After all his only real pleasure comes from overpowering people, swamping them, and after that he can just patronize them. Perhaps it's best then simply to be patronized.'

'But I never said that!'

'I thought that's what you meant when you said there are ways of directing him. I mean, why do you think he introduced us? He knew I'd take you off for a long talk. He worked up my interest in you, talking of you as some sort of artist, a *prince*! all that sort of nonsense. Why, us talking here, us reacting here is all the result of a deliberate plan of Tolson's. ... Not deliberate in the way you're thinking. That's the worst part about it. He doesn't plan it on paper or anything like that. No, it's all intuition. He's hardly aware of it himself, although *he* does it. That's the really monstrous, the *really* destructive part of it! Intuition!'

Leonard had stood up and began to glance round the room. His face had hardened as if having recognized this nightmare he were prepared to accommodate it if only it would allow him to move his body casually round the room. He went across to the table just as Kathleen came in carrying a large, steaming tea-pot and a bottle of milk. As he moved several things aside, she glanced at him bitterly and said, 'Has my father told you about what he calls "our Spanish Heritage"?'

She laughed, but Blakeley himself added, 'Oh, now, we can leave that alone for once.'

'Why should we? It was the real reason you asked Leonard back here tonight.' She turned to Leonard accusingly. 'You see, it was about the first thing that he told Tolson and we've never heard the last of it since.'

Blakeley's wife came in and put down several cups and saucers.

'That's enough, Kathleen,' he said. 'It's going to your head.'

'You'll know, of course, about the Peninsular War and how the Duke of Wellington went out there with an English army.' She nodded reprovingly at her mother, then turned all her attention on Leonard. 'How he went out to fight Napoleon. Such big names! Well, one of the officers, believe it or not, was called *Blakeley*. And he married a

Spanish lady. A princess related to the Spanish royal family. Now can you see how it all ties up? This talk of princes. He thinks we're related to Spanish aristocracy, and that you, being a *Radcliffe* ... a Radcliffe, that you both have something in common. . . . And we live like *this*! He's spent nearly all his life down the pit and so did his father before him, and he only came out because of his lungs. Yet he insists that we're aristocrats! You ask him! You ask him! He knows your family's entire history, the whole history of the Place. Down to what year? 1470 and the Wars of the Roses! Do you see how Tolson must be laughing. Two aristocrats meeting for the first time!' She broke into a breathless sort of laughter, while she tried to set out the tea things on the table.

'That's why he calls himself an artist – to impress himself that he's got better feelings, that he's more sensitive. That he's *elevated* above the rest of the herd. Even the doctor, when he was pensioned off from the pit, even the doctor said the trouble with his lungs was largely self-induced.'

'He didn't. That's wrong,' Blakeley said very formally. 'He said it was aggravated by a nervous temperament.'

'No such bloody thing! Rubbish!' Kathleen was now giggling helplessly, both hands laid on the table.

'Well, you'll be able to understand one thing,' Blakeley said. He was still sitting by the fire. His wife poured out the tea as if nothing had happened. 'We educated Kathleen thinking she'd be the only child we'd have. She didn't leave school till she was eighteen.' He had leaned back in his chair and suddenly started to cry, his mouth dropping open in a huge, maundering leer and his eyes closing with tears. Yet the tone of his voice was peculiarly calm, as if he were unaware that he was crying at all. Only a kind of whine at the back of his throat had made his wife look up and go across to him. 'As you can see,' he went on, 'she can express herself quite clearly. She's an intelligent girl. An intellectual, you know. The only trouble is she doesn't see that she only gets worked up about these things out of an affection for me. She just doesn't see that.'

'Oh, now you'll get the complete performance,' Kathleen said wildly as though this were quite simply a private remark directed solely at her. 'This's what usually happens. He's such a sensitive soul.' She stood watching the large figure of her mother stooping silently over her father with a strange look of envy. 'I'm sorry. But why did he have to bring Radcliffe back here? He should have known.' She shook her head angrily and turned back to the table. But she finished the pouring out of the tea which her mother had left uncompleted.

'I think I'd better go,' Leonard said. He had stood back in the corner of the room while the argument flared, but now he moved towards the chair where his coat lay.

'No ... no, you must stay,' Blakeley said, getting up urgently from beneath the figure of his wife. 'You see how it is. One thing leads to another. We're just that bit excited. Nervous at you being here.' He'd come to hold Leonard's arm.

'Yes,' Kathleen said, 'I don't blame you. It's that my father makes himself so vulnerable. He's no protection against somebody like Tolson.'

'But *why* do you let Tolson tyrannize you?' Leonard said despairingly. 'I don't understand it. . . .'

'Ah, but then you don't know the half of it,' Blakeley said, sounding disappointed that Leonard hadn't understood. 'Do you realize, for example, that it's *spiritual* things Tolson seeks to possess most of all. Things he can't acquire through his own temperament. He's bound to attack, to *consume* people in whom he recognizes some sort of spiritual quality. And naturally, they're the ones who are most vulnerable to his physical sort of energy.'

'I'll have to go,' Leonard said and immediately went to the door, pushing it open and groping around in the darkened hall. He found the handle of the front door and pulled it open. A stream of cold air rushed into the over-heated room.

'Now wait! I'll come with you,' Blakeley called. 'To the end of the avenue.' He pulled on his jacket as he hurried after him.

They walked in silence. Leonard felt himself drinking in the cold air, clearing the confusion in his mind. Somewhere he had the impression that Blakeley was no longer limping, that he walked beside him quite naturally, but the idea never penetrated sufficiently to cause him to look. After glancing round to see if anyone were waiting in the street, he allowed himself to be lulled by the cold air and the rhythm of his walk and to become completely absorbed by his own thoughts.

'What I really wanted to say,' Blakeley said as they reached the road junction, 'was that ... the sort of performance I gave tonight, it wasn't so much me as a *person*, but me reflecting *them* – the audience. Do you know what I mean? It's important to me, is this. It's my job to reflect what *they* are. That's the theory I wanted to ask you about. After all, this is how I see it: I *am* them. If I wasn't they wouldn't have me there. I'm there by their permission.'

He was clinging to Leonard's sleeve and trying to turn him so that he could see into his face. No lamp stood directly at the corner and in the faint light he could only recognize Leonard's face as a pale mask. 'Don't you see? It's *their* humour, not mine. But I'm not apologizing for them. Nor for myself. At some other club I do something entirely different. Just singing straight ballads. But I want you to understand: *this is all they've got.*'

He wasn't sure that Leonard had even heard him, but he went on explaining more earnestly until Leonard suddenly turned round to him and said quietly, 'There's one thing I realize. That there are certain people ... certain families who invite people to their homes simply so that they can become a vehicle, a sort of catalyst for all that family's troubles and quarrels. They're of no account themselves. It's simply that they become a receptacle. . . .'

'Do you think I've done that?' Blakeley said in a strange voice.

'Oh, I'm not blaming you,' Leonard added. 'It's entirely my own fault. I'm very slow at understanding certain things ... situations. It's entirely my fault. I should have seen. I seem to go into things with my eyes completely shut.' And when Blakeley seemed about to interrupt he went on more excitedly, 'I mean, the absurd thing is that although I don't know what Tolson's told you about me, the fact is that we knew each other as boys. We were very good friends for two or three years even.'

'But is that true? Are you sure? But of course you must be sure or you wouldn't say it like that. And in that tone of voice. It must be true.' Blakeley appeared to walk off by himself, moving several paces in one direction, then another, until he returned to his original position. 'That's very strange,' he said, looking carefully at Leonard's faintly illuminated face. 'I wonder *why* he never told me. For he knew I was bound to find out when we met. Do you notice any change? Any change in him, I mean, between then and now.'

'I shall have to go now,' Leonard said. 'It's just that I wanted you to realize how absurd the situation is.'

'Yes, yes, of course. I realize that now. I see that. We've both been deceived. But why?'

Leonard had turned to go, but with a sudden movement Blakeley took hold of his arm and pulled it against him.

'Has Tolson told you anything about us? About me, I mean. Or Kathleen?' he said. Then before Leonard could answer he added in an extremely pleased and relaxed voice, 'What do you think to Kathleen? She's a great admiration for you, you know. That's to say, she's intimidated by you. Don't be put off by that aggressiveness. She's always like that when she feels drawn to a person. I'm afraid it's the unfortunate result of her past experience.' He now gripped Leonard's arm and shoulder in both his hands, and for a moment held him in silence. 'I'm sorry if I disappoint you,' he said quietly.

There was something so familiar in the sudden tone and accent that Leonard turned to stare at him in astonishment. It was a voice he had known and heard so many times before that he could only shake his head in bewilderment. Despite its familiarity, its identity eluded him.

'You've got to understand,' Blakeley said. 'All this . . . I've never had an education. I don't really know how to express these things. Not in a way that you'd understand and sympathize with, I mean.'

'You'd better let me go,' Leonard said almost inaudibly.

'You see. You think it's an *act*, don't you? That I'm trying to mislead you. Isn't that it? You think it's some peculiar game of deception.'

'No, it doesn't matter,' Leonard said, pulling more

fiercely now and grasping Blakeley's fingers to prise them from his arm. He stared at the older man in complete confusion. A motor-bike had started somewhere down the road. Leonard stiffened, his head twisting violently round.

Blakeley suddenly released him and stood dejectedly aside. 'Ah well. Perhaps it's just as Tolson intended it should be.'

'Did you know that he'd followed us? To your house. And now here.'

'No. But then what does it matter?' He didn't even look round.

'I don't understand. I don't understand any of this,' Leonard said, still staring at Blakeley intensely as though he expected the shape of another person entirely to appear there. The motor-bike engine was being revved, heavily and slowly.

'I think you do,' Blakeley said. 'But you're just refusing to see. This is Vic's attempt to say to *me*, "Keep off!"'

'Keep off? Keep off what?'

'Him. For me to keep off him.' Blakeley appeared to turn away slightly with a vague gesture of despair. 'Well, that *and* showing you off. Both things together.'

'I shall have to go.' Leonard shook his head wildly. 'This . . . it's just some sort of impersonation. I shall have to go.'

He immediately hurried away. He didn't look round. He heard no other sound from Blakeley and assumed that the older man was watching him out of sight. He walked more quickly. As he passed a side road he heard a motor-bike retreating from the opposite end. It sounded lighter than Tolson's. He couldn't be sure that it wasn't the effect of the steep rise of the estate. He broke into a run. It was only as he pushed his way round the darkened Place that he let out a cry of frustration as he realized that he had left his raincoat at Blakeley's house.

16

With his handkerchief Shaw wiped the metal dust from his file and put the thin slip of metal back into his boiler suit pocket. As he blew his nose he was flung to one side, the truck swinging abruptly round the sharply curved drive. He crouched down against the tailboard, gripping it tightly in square, chapped hands, and stared out at the fir trees rising stiffly from the mist.

As the hills split apart and they drew into the hollow Leonard pulled himself up and was the first man to drop down onto the gravel. The tent sagged with the dampness, the ropes slack from a week's neglect. The canvas itself was darker. The stone house, merging into the mist and the darker shape of the trees, was larger and silent. The house dominated the hollow. The marquee seemed shrivelled and sunken.

Shaw climbed slowly down and stood by the truck rolling a cigarette while he watched Ewbank back out of the driving seat and walk alertly across to the tent. The contractor looked in. Then he took off his shallow trilby and stroked his thin remnant of hair, running the exhausted strands slowly between finger and thumb. Shaw scarcely noticed his change of mood: he glanced uneasily at Leonard. Tolson hadn't arrived at the yard that morning.

The men went to look at the tent. The muslin lining had been ripped down: it lay like a torn film over the upturned chairs and debris. Round the perimeter lay empty bottles glowing like fragments of ice, broken, split, some half full of liquid. At the door Ewbank was standing with his arm raised as if both to acknowledge the event that had taken place inside and to prevent anyone from entering.

'It's all right,' he said and stepped forward. Glass crunched beneath his feet. 'It's all right. Just nobody come in.' His tall, black figure stood for several minutes gazing vacantly, almost disinterestedly, at the wrecked interior.

The men stood at the entrance in silence. They started smoking. The hollow was very quiet. A bird sang from the summit of one of the conical hills. Ewbank emerged from the tent, put on his hat and disappeared round the corner of the house.

Shaw hadn't moved from the side of the truck. He stood watching Leonard, a strange, half-apologetic smile contorting his face. He looked as if he were in the middle of a conversation. Three dogs suddenly ran round the corner of the house.

Ewbank reappeared with the middle-aged gentleman in the check coat. He had a yellow scarf tucked inside his collar. Three leads hung from the fingers of his left hand. His right was thrust into his trouser pocket. It was he rather than Ewbank who led the way to the door. They both looked inside in silence.

'Take a look for yourself,' Ewbank said eventually. The man nodded, gazing reflectively at the interior. 'When we left it, sir, it was laid out well ... beautifully. It was extremely beautiful.'

'I know,' the man said. He watched the dogs running inside the tent, plunging through the muslin as though it were waves. 'But you know how these things are. We had nearly four hundred people here. It was a wedding.' He smiled at Ewbank as though this were an explanation they both could appreciate.

'Did you say four hundred people or four hundred pigs?' the contractor said. He stammered slightly, flushing.

The man turned to him again, half-smiling. 'Ah, yes. . . . It looks that way, doesn't it? Drake! . . . *Drake*!'

Ewbank jumped, trembling slightly. But the man was calling the dog. It stood, one leg uplifted, in the opposite corner of the tent.

'You'll let me know what the damage amounts to,' the man said.

'It's not that,' Ewbank almost cried out. 'I mean, I don't know. It looked so lovely.'

'It did. That's true.'

'And just look at the place, sir. You can't think that a human being could have stepped inside it.' Ewbank seemed bewildered, betrayed; this was the kind of man he could have respected and trusted above all others. 'Why, even if my own men had the use of tent they could never have done this to it,' he said, trying to find words for his disappointment.

The man whistled at the dogs and they ran to him immediately, scattering the muslin and several soiled napkins as they sprang for the opening.

'I hope they haven't cut their feet, there's a lot of broken glass about,' he said. 'I ought to have thought.' He touched Ewbank's shoulder genially as the dogs tugged at his legs. 'If you want me, I'll be available most of the day.' He seemed genuinely surprised when Ewbank swung round without answering. Then he moved off with the dogs towards the house.

'The man's mad. He's fucking insane. He never heard a word I said,' Ewbank told the men nearest him. He was flushed, his hands pushed down in the pockets of his coat. He gazed bitterly at the ground, then up at the men as silently they began to drift into the work.

At first Leonard worked slowly. Beside him, Shaw strained to reach the hooks, lifting them off the roof and dropping the canvas round his feet where it was trampled as he struggled with the next piece. Gradually Leonard increased his pace. The canvas dropped like a serpent on the grass outside the tent, Shaw panting at its restless head. Beyond them the men had lifted the torn skin of muslin and laid bare the dislocated structure of the dance floor: sections of it had been dislodged and upturned. Ewbank watched as though it were a body borne up from an accident.

Shaw trembled with his work, reaching up on the toes of his stubby boots to unhook the heavy canvas. He tugged, almost dragged it down with the descending weight of his body. At his shoulder Leonard pressed him on faster. The old man's face grew tense, with a redness tinged by the white glow from the canvas itself. His breathing drummed in the hollow eaves of the tent. Yet he worked for a while with an unnatural persistence, deliberately resisting the pressure beside him.

Then he moaned quietly and leaned forward. He held himself up, his hands spread like claws on the canvas.

The men crashed the chairs into a loose pile outside the tent. Ewbank, seeing Shaw collapse and Leonard bending over him, went across.

'Is he all right?' he said.

Shaw was coughing, but he stood up at the sound of Ewbank's voice. It was a vaguely military gesture, his fists thrust down at his sides. His eyes were closed and watering.

'Go and sit down, Shaw,' Ewbank said. 'Go on. Get a chair off the pile.'

'Yes, *sir*.'

Shaw stood stiffly at attention for a moment, then, his eyes opening slightly, he walked slowly across the tent. Without looking at Leonard, Ewbank returned to his position in the centre of the tent.

Leonard worked alone. The walling was heavy. Occasionally he glanced up to where Shaw was sitting. He had opened a chair only a few feet from where Ewbank was standing, and was leaning forward, his elbows on his knees, rolling a cigarette.

When he looked up again Ewbank was only a few yards away. He was stooping down at the edge of the flooring and, glancing round to see if he was observed, he began to conceal something under several pieces of paper. When, sometime later, Leonard stood over the place taking down the walling he moved the paper to one side with his foot. Beneath were four unopened bottles of champagne, side by side.

The debris inside the tent was cleared, the walling folded and bagged, and the first line of flooring lifted. At lunch time Ewbank sat in the cab of the truck by himself, but once the men had settled down on chairs in the drive he got out again and wandered absent-mindedly through the tent. The men watched him in silence. He reached his hiding place, casually bent down and lifted the paper aside. He felt more determinedly between the battens. Then he pulled out an empty bottle, then a second, broken one. He kicked them away with a private sort of savagery.

The men had burst out laughing. Ewbank stared down the length of the tent to where they sprawled in the drive.

'Ay up, Sammy,' Pilkington called. 'Have you lost something?'

Ewbank turned away and continued his indifferent progress through the tent.

'Are you looking for these?' Pilkington called.

Ewbank looked up again to see Pilkington holding a champagne bottle in one hand and indicating three more by his feet.

Ewbank walked slowly over to the men. 'Why, what have you got there?' he said.

'Ah, now. What would you think it is?' Pilkington said. 'Go on. Have a guess. It begins with s-h.'

'Oh, I see.'

'Radcliffe here saw you hiding them away.'

'Oh.' Ewbank glanced round at the smiling men. 'And who moved them?'

'Old Radcliffe. He knew you'd want to share it all round. Share and share alike, the Ewbank motto. Come on, Sammy, a fair cop.'

'Ah, well.' Ewbank stared at Leonard. He was sitting to one side, blushing slightly, his face peculiarly open and vulnerable. 'The famous Radcliffe humour, then.' He continued staring at the younger man until Leonard turned away.

'He's off his leash now Tolson's away,' Pilkington said.

'I'll get my cup,' Ewbank said.

The men watched Pilkington pull out the cork with his teeth. He struggled with it for a while, then Ewbank, returning with his china cup, said, 'There's a wire catch at the side that'll release the cork.' But it suddenly came away in Pilkington's grimacing mouth.

'Christ,' Pilkington said. He blew out his cheeks. The neck of the bottle smoked between his thick hands.

'They were all four just laid there,' Ewbank said. 'They must have been hidden by one of his so-called guests.'

'That'll be it,' one of the men said. 'These rich pricks aren't above snaffling a bit when it comes their way.'

'Christ.' Pilkington stroked his mouth. A trickle of blood had appeared at one corner. Ewbank took the bottle from him and poured out the first cupful, raising it slowly to his mouth and sipping. His trilby was tipped to the back of his head as if recently he had been travelling at high speed; his small, reddened eyes were furtively self-absorbed.

'Well, Sammy?' Pilkington said. 'It's not vinegar after

all, is it?' He held his hands now either side of his mouth.

The contractor smiled leniently, then replenished his cup. The men suddenly laughed and held out a row of broken mugs. Ewbank went slowly along, filling them. Shaw raised his cup immediately and swallowed it like water.

'Aren't you having any, Radcliffe?' Ewbank said.

Leonard shook his head. He'd begun to eat his sandwiches and they lay in a neat pile in his lap.

'Do you mean you don't wish to take advantage of your own generosity?' Ewbank said. He glanced at the men: the bottle was raised towards Leonard as if the contractor intended pouring it whether there were a cup there or not. Several drops fell onto Leonard's sandwiches. 'Come on. Have some. There's plenty.'

Leonard moved his legs aside. 'It's all right. I don't want any.'

'I don't mind a bit of humour at my expense,' Ewbank said.

'Ah, leave him, Sammy,' one of the men said. Ewbank had become threatening, the bottle thrust out before him.

'I think he should have a share,' Ewbank insisted. 'After all, he found it, as it were.'

'Ah, come off him,' Pilkington said. He started opening the second bottle, twisting the wire this time.

'Why did you go to the trouble of finding the bottles, then, if you didn't want a share?' Ewbank said. Leonard had blushed more deeply, rubbing his hand briefly against his forehead.

'He thought it was a joke, that's all, Sammy,' Pilkington said. 'It was just his bit of fun. Leave the sod alone and get some of this down you.'

'Oh, so that was it.' Ewbank laughed. 'A bit of fun.' He laughed again. The trilby fell from the back of his head. He appeared not to notice. 'Oh, I thought it was something personal at first.' He looked at Pilkington and the two men suddenly laughed together.

'Come on, Sammy. Let's get this bubbly down before the old lad comes out of the house.'

They turned away, Ewbank stepping on his hat, then stooping down, still laughing, to pick it up. Yet a moment later he glanced back at Leonard, apparently dissatisfied and with a wilder look of frustration.

The men grew noisier. As they started eating their dinners, and Shaw searched for his bag, one of them called out, 'By the way, Shaw, I didn't think you'd need your sandwiches today. What with the drink and one thing and another. So I threw them in the bushes yonder. I hope you don't mind.'

Someone had started laughing.

'Oh, for Christ's sake not again,' Pilkington said. 'Here – have one of mine, Shaw, till these buggers grow up.'

Shaw sat holding his cup tightly against his chest.

'I hope you don't mind, Shaw,' the man said again.

'No. Why should I?'

Shaw had stood up. Then he suddenly threw his mug away. It clattered bouncing over the gravel of the drive; then, just as it came to rest, it broke. The men laughed again, diverted from the overlooking presence of the house. Pilkington also stood up. He twisted the wire cap off the last bottle and the cork exploded. The wine flowed down his hands as the men hurried towards him. Shaw walked away, into the tent.

'Oh, now, not too much in my cup,' Ewbank said, his hand on the bottle as Pilkington poured it out. 'Just fill it to the brim and no further.'

He sat down on the nearest chair, holding the cup unsteadily in both hands. He sipped clumsily from the flooded lip, glancing up at the house. Leonard, seated some distance away, intercepted his look. Beyond him an elderly woman was standing at a tall ground floor window. She looked out at the men, then upwards. It had suddenly begun to rain.

It took the men some time to pull one another over the tailboard. They staggered from their chairs laughing, their mouths hanging open to the sky as the rain increased. For a while Ewbank helped them to climb into the back of the truck, then he went round unsteadily to the cab and climbed in. The four bottles lay discarded amongst the tumbled chairs.

'I'm sorry,' Pilkington said as Leonard climbed in. 'I'll have to get out again and get shut of some.'

He fell out of the back. For a time he lay on the gravel moaning quietly. When Leonard dropped down to help him, he suddenly stood up with a loud burst of laughter. 'I knew you'd give us a hand in the end!' He staggered away and crashed into the bushes. 'I knew you were a good sort. That you'd get down and give us a hand. A good sort. A really good sort is Leonard.'

Yet he was only gone several seconds: he suddenly reappeared from amongst the shrubberies, walking with unusually long strides as if he were just completing a march. His red hair was plastered like a wound to the broad width of his scalp.

'Radcliffe! There's old Shaw out there. The other side of the tent. Crying.' He stared in at the dazed faces of the men. They began to laugh again, stubbornly. 'No, though, he's bent down on his knees, crying like a baby. You have a look.' A man put his head out from the truck, felt the weight of rain, and withdrew.

Leonard stared out at the rain. He was cold: it gave his face a pinched, apprehensive look. His body was jarred as Pilkington thrust his way in past him.

'You have a look at Shaw,' Pilkington said. 'Just have a look.'

The men laughed more deeply, falling further back into the truck to accommodate Pilkington's huge body. The vehicle swayed clumsily on its springs, squeaking. From the house a dog had suddenly started barking.

Leonard climbed down onto the drive. The ground was unusually wet, as if it had been raining for hours. In the cab Ewbank sat with his hat pushed to the back of his head. He gazed fixedly ahead through the windscreen to where a figure was humped just inside the tent.

It looked as though Shaw were praying. He was crouched down on the wrecked dance floor, the rain thundering on the canvas over his head. As he stood over him Leonard could hear Shaw's broken voice, singing. Only then did he gradually decipher a single repetitive phrase: 'What've *I* done?' Shaw moaned. 'What've *I* done?'

Leonard stood watching him for some time. His crouched

back heaved intermittently as if his chest revolted at the bony pressure of his knees.

The rain slackened. A wind swept it up from the hollow, shaking it free of the pines. The canvas swayed, billowing on the poles, and water cascaded over the eaves of the drooped tent. The wind surged under the roof and inflated the canvas body until the stakes tore the ground and the ropes rose vertically in the air. Leaves and paper were sucked into the tent .

Leonard touched the crouched figure with his foot. It was shuddering slightly now, chilled by the sudden upsurge of air. The canvas groaned, then cracked in vicious waves from the rising wind. Inside the tent the air was bitterly cold.

'Come on, Shaw. Get up.'

He touched the huddled figure again with his foot and it drew itself in closer, in a sly movement of protection. Leonard kicked him gently.

'Come on. Get up.'

Shaw buried his skull under his large, square hands. His back had suddenly stiffened, arching up, no longer shuddering.

Leonard gazed down at the tensed shape with growing exasperation.

'Come on, Shaw. Get up!' He seemed almost in tears, stooping slightly as if his words could prise open the clenched figure. 'For Christ's sake get up, Shaw!' He kicked him again, gently; then, when he didn't move, more wildly.

Shaw's body seemed to settle more comfortably between its broad arms. They were like a single protective claw to the shell of his body. Leonard began thrusting his foot against Shaw's body, rapidly at first, then more slowly as each blow took on greater weight and intention. His foot thudded again and again into the body. 'For Christ's sake, Shaw! *Get up*!'

It was the lack of movement, the passivity, that incensed him.

At about three o'clock in the afternoon Ewbank pushed

open the door of the cab and climbed stiffly down. He winced as each foot touched the ground. It was still raining. He pulled a macintosh and a sou'wester from under the seat and put them on; then, holding to the side of the truck, walked round the back and ordered the men out. Pilkington and a second man were asleep and couldn't be wakened. The rest eventually scrambled down and stumbled across to the shelter of the tent.

Leonard was stooping down at the far end. He was working rapidly, taking up the square sections of the dance floor and stacking them wildly on either side. Almost the entire dance floor had been lifted and laid out in this way.

'Ah, well, at least somebody's working,' Ewbank said, frowning. He rubbed his temples and stared across at the active figure. 'The rest of you, get on with the battening and the tables. I want it all up in an hour.'

Suddenly he laughed, rubbing his head more vigorously and, going over to the nearest of the three poles that supported the tent, he unfastened the thin rope that secured the remnants of the muslin lining. The pink and white cloth floated down like a ragged mist. It fell over Shaw who was still crouched motionless on the floor of the tent.

'Shaw?' Ewbank glaced across at the mounded figure as he loosely wrapped the torn lining. 'Shaw?'

Mummified by the thin cloth the old man seemed one more part of the detritus. As they lifted it from him the men were laughing, holding their heads painfully and kneeling down as they tried ineffectually to uproot the floor. 'Bloody Shaw!'

Ewbank packed the muslin into a large hessian bag, looking back at the old figure now and shaking his head. A lorry had begun to whine up the narrow drive between the trees. As it emerged from under the wet foliage the men stood up cheering.

Tolson leapt down from the cab. He was in shirt sleeves and dungarees, and darted through the rain to the tent where he stood shaking himself.

'What's been happening here?' he said slowly.

Ewbank had come to stand in the middle of the half-uprooted floor, gazing at the lorry as if disappointed in some way by its arrival.

'We've had a right pissing time,' a man said. 'You should've been here. They buggered up the tent and left four bottles of stuff lying around. . . .'

Tolson seemed scarcely to listen: he was looking up at the far end of the tent where Leonard stood with the last unassembled sections of the dance floor. Half way between them lay the buried figure of Shaw.

'And where have you been all day?' Ewbank said, adding as if Tolson had answered, 'Well just get these chairs loaded up, then. And you, Tolson, had better help this lot with the floor. They've been on with it all day. Just pulling out two nails.'

Tolson had gone across to Shaw. He spoke quietly to him a moment, then bent down.

The men had started laughing again, kneeling once more by the half-uprooted floor.

'What's happened to him? Has he fallen?' Tolson called out. And as Ewbank turned towards him he asked, 'What's this blood on him?'

'Ah, it's old Radcliffe,' a man said. 'He's been giving the lad some boot.'

Tolson stared at a stain on his hand. He glanced up at Leonard, but so swiftly that it was like a meaningless flick of his head. He plunged his hands under Shaw's arms and seemed to fling him to his feet. The old man groaned, then cried out. Tolson carried him out and sat him on a chair. He bent over him as if searching him, the rain falling steadily on their two figures. Then he lifted him into the back of the truck.

They both stayed there for some time, hidden from the men. When Tolson reappeared he went straight into the tent, calling briskly to the men, and began to lift up the floor in large sections, tearing its nailed members apart with a hammer. He worked silently, ruthlessly dismembering the work which a few days before he'd so patiently assembled. He ignored Leonard completely.

Throughout the remainder of the afternoon the men worked intently. The stained site of yellowed grass was gradually revealed as the floor was taken up and stacked on the lorry. The tables, the flooring, the walling and the muslin bags were loaded on top and the long battens laid in the crevice between the evenly distributed sides. Eventually only the roof remained, tightened by the rain and swaying in the wind; and soon that too succumbed to Tolson's restless energy: it was lowered, unlaced and packed into its separate bags, bulky and soggy with rain.

Leonard now worked slowly at the fringe of this hurried activity. He helped to rope the lorry's high load, tugging lifelessly at each slip knot. The vehicle swayed and creaked as the net of ropes compressed the irregular and stubborn shape. Leonard seemed forgetful.

It was almost dark by the time the lorry was driven away, boring two tracks through the flooded gravel. The men waited by the small truck while Ewbank walked slowly round the lawn, stooping, occasionally retrieving a stake or a piece of rope. Several lights had come on in the house throwing confused beams onto the lawn; it now looked like the drained bed of a lake.

Ewbank glanced up at the house, then went to the edge of the lawn. He uprooted several plants from the flower-bed, wrapped them in loose pieces of paper and brought them back to the truck. He laid them carefully in the cab.

In the back, Shaw was crying as the men climbed in beside him.

When Leonard started to follow, Tolson, who was standing in the drive, laid a hand on his arm. 'Those sandwiches with the shit inside,' he said, waiting, closely watching Leonard's recollection of the event. 'The sandwiches you thought Shaw had done. *I* did it. I shoved that crap inside. It was *my* shit.' He continued to watch Leonard with an almost appealing stare, half-enraptured, dazed. 'It was my shit you ate! *Mine!*'

There was a stiffening of Leonard's body, scarcely perceptible, a slight discarding movement, negligible as he pulled gently away from his grasp.

'I thought I better tell you. It wasn't Shaw, then. It was me.'

Leonard stood by the tailboard, quite still but for an odd,

slight swaying of his arms. Tolson lifted up the last of the equipment into the truck, several loose pieces of walling, a few stakes and four hammers. He lifted the hammers in last, swinging them up by their heads so the men could grab the handles and pull them inside. The last hammer he swung by the handle itself, forcefully. He swung it up to his shoulder. The steel head rammed up sharply from the gravel and drove directly into Leonard's face. It crunched against his cheekbone.

His face split open. He swung round carelessly as his body fell against the tailboard. Blood sprang out in a large rose on his cheek.

Tolson tossed the hammer into the truck. The men had scarcely moved. Then the engine started, and Ewbank was banging on the door of the cab.

'Are you ready?' he called back. The truck's lights sprang out across the drive. 'Are you ready in there?'

Someone banged in answer and the engine revved. Tolson half-dragged, half-lifted Leonard into the back. The truck reversed across the lawn and flower-beds, then swung round through the ploughed earth and accelerated erratically down the drive.

Leonard no longer heard the vehicle's roar. He clutched the metal struts on either side as if determined that neither of his hands should acknowledge the source of pain. Blood oozed like grease along his face. But he was invisible; he could see neither the men nor the vehicle as he swayed with its motion.

Then, as his eyes grew accustomed to the dark, he gradually distinguished the large, bowed shape opposite. Lying on the floor between them Shaw's flung figure rolled with the truck's momentum. Faintly the vehicle's sounds returned, a distant echo, and someone crying still.

He seemed to see Tolson rear up towards him, enveloping him like a shadow, something springing out of the vehicle's motion, rising and curling over like a wave. Then he realized it was some eccentricity of his sight accompanying the sudden restoration of his hearing.

Now he could see Tolson clearly, and hear Shaw's endless and peculiarly inexhaustible wailing.

17

He thought he saw a figure, even several figures, that he vaguely recognized. It was just a moment of recognition, interrupted by the trees and shrubbery that characterized this part of the park. It was a bright, luminous day with a thin ceiling of cloud, low down, that magnified the light. The smoothly eroded hills of the park and the undulating grass seemed to glow. From the craggy outcrop of buildings the park spread like a surface of green stone, the trees the remnant of a deliberate and cultured wildness.

As he passed each isolated trunk, its shadow – or simply some trick of its formal spacing – clicked in his mind like a ratchet. Something seemed to fall as each wooden column passed on his left-hand side. He was now walking up the central hill and, as if his own physical momentum corresponded to some clock-like insistence of mood, he began to feel alternately alert and bemused.

Between each tree he endured a curious sensation of deafness. The blood pounded in his ears. His body swayed with a peculiar heaviness. These bouts were interspersed with moments of extraordinary alertness when even the distant noises of the city, of individual vehicles and engines, were as clear as the nearer sounds of children running and shouting, and the single, calling voice of a woman, half-protesting, half-laughing. As he approached the summit of the hill and the last of the trees he began to sense a further and corresponding alternation of the light itself. It seemed to darken and grow misty as his deafness increased. Then it expanded with an almost explosive radiance as the city and the park became audible again.

He was just beginning to wonder whether this was a subjective distortion, or whether it was simply the effect of exhaustion, or even a complete illusion altogether when, half way between two trees, he heard a voice say, 'I can imagine why you've come up here today ... they're working just over the other side of the hill.'

At first he thought he recognized Enid: a distant,

cauterized memory, so that his mind tumbled back in a hazy confusion of marquees, a burning lamp, the bed breaking under his and Tolson's weight. The torn fringe of rock scar. Then he recognized the sharp, questioning features of Blakeley, of Kathleen. Beyond her were the three running figures of the children. They seemed to spin round a large bush.

'I've been watching you come up the hill,' she said. She was laughing, glancing across at the children, then looking into his face with puzzled amusement. 'What an *aloof* sort of look you have. What an air of detachment.' She leaned towards him with a mixture of irritation and reproach, a scarcely suppressed frustration. 'You look exhausted. Are you always so *tired*?'

'No.' He shook his head confusedly at her.

'I know your sort. Trying to look interesting all the time, making people think you possess some huge *secret*. I'm very familiar with that sort of game.' She watched his expression with a private amusement of her own.

'What are you doing up here?' he said. It was like a long conversation that had been resumed.

'Oh, just giving them a run. We'll be going down there soon.' She pointed to the foot of the hill which Leonard had just climbed. A vast, asphalted recreation ground was animated by numerous scurrying figures. Yet no sound of the playing children reached the top of the hill. It seemed very far away.

She said nothing for a while, staring across to the opposite crown of the city and the encroaching flank of the estate. It was as if she had been produced by the extraordinary effort of his climb.

'Well, have you recovered?' she said eventually.

'It's a steep climb.' It was almost a tone of complaint.

'No. I mean your accident.' She looked directly at him, vaguely angered. 'I heard all about it.'

'I've been ill for the past few days. I still feel a bit strange.'

'Oh?' She suddenly called to the children. 'Colin! Colin! We're going this way now.'

She didn't wait for him, but started moving slowly along a path that circuited the top of the hill. The summit itself was a concentric series of ridges rising to a point of dense shrubbery. It was through this that the children crashed, shouting confusedly from separate places. The mound was the site of a Norman fort. Nothing remained but these symmetrical swellings of the grass.

'I heard about your accident. How is your face?'

Leonard turned his cheek towards her. A green and purple bruise surrounded a large scab on his right cheekbone. His eye was also discoloured.

'It's better now. The swelling's gone down.' He laughed. 'My face was like a balloon.'

'Did it do any actual damage?'

'No.' He glanced reassuringly at her, as if she were seeking consolation. 'The bone was bruised, but apparently nothing's broken. I had some terrible headaches. But they've gone now as well.'

She walked on in silence. They were circuiting the summit of the hill. Below them appeared the fringe of an arena.

'How did it happen?'

'It was an accident.'

'Ah, yes. . . . And when are you going back to Ewbank's then?'

'I don't know. I think I've finished there for good. I don't think I'll go back.' He spoke out of some deep preoccupation, staring at the ground just in front of his moving feet.

She said, 'You haven't been there long,' then laughed. 'No.'

'And Tolson? What will he do?' He didn't answer, and she added, 'He was a drifter until he got that job. Then he settled down. He seems to like it for some reason. Putting up then taking down those elephantine things.' She looked at him acutely. He seemed to be walking along oblivious of her. 'Is that why you came up here today?' She said it with a skilful note of irritation.

Leonard blushed slightly and shrugged his shoulders.

'I've been expecting to see you up here,' she said. 'I've been bringing the kids here for the past three days. Watching *them*.'

She indicated the arena which was now coming into full view below. On a broad circle of smooth grass was set out a familiar flotilla of marquees: they ran in an arc round one side of the arena and onto the slope itself above the terrace. Here, on the side of the hill, people were standing watching the men working. The steady and rhythmic crackling of hammers on steel stakes reached the top of the hill; a group of five men stood in a circle, their hammers rising in a staggered and regular wave.

'He'll be down there,' Kathleen said, watching Leonard now as a certain anxiety came into his face. Then she added, 'Probably with the same hammer.'

Leonard suddenly smiled. 'It's strange. You always make me feel I owe you something. Do you always put people under an obligation to you when you first meet them?' He took her look of surprise with a shy smile; and with a slow forgetful gesture of his hand added, 'I realize it's your defensiveness . . . your way of resisting people. But do you do it irrespective of, well, your real feeling for someone?' He laughed. 'You seem too embittered to be true. Do you think I'm being unfair?'

'No.'

'This sort of aggressiveness you have – behind it, there's a morbid, inward-looking thing.'

'And you don't have it?'

He laughed again, with a peculiar simplicity. 'Ah, yes. But not so completely. You see. I'm not aggressive.'

He had turned away now to look down at the tents with an expression almost of arrogance, an assured look of satisfaction. She saw that he'd suddenly identified Tolson's figure below. He looked almost prim.

She glanced round and called to the children; the only evidence of their presence was the occasional movement of the leaves. She called again, then stared down at the arena. Several figures were moving quickly round a white shroud of canvas. Slowly it was lifted into the air, like an animal rising, first on its knees, then its rear legs, then swaying and eventually standing. Two tents were being raised simultaneously; the second opened with a uniform and corresponding growth.

'I was sure I wasn't going to see you again,' Leonard suddenly stated.

'Why?'

'Your father – I think he frightens me. It's not his manner. It's a kind of tenacity, the *hold* he takes on things.'

Leonard started walking. At last the sound of the men's voices reached the top of the hill.

'And why have you? Seen me, I mean?'

'Oh, this is an accident,' he said quickly.

'I don't think so. There's no accidents in your life.'

'Aren't there?' He ignored her tone. 'I've been in bed nearly a week. I see things differently now.' He stated it almost inconsequentially, yet began to walk more quickly. They were gradually returning to the point where they'd first met.

'Apparently you told my father that you knew Tolson when you were boys.'

'Yes.'

'It's strange *he's* never mentioned it. Tolson. He's usually so full of it when he's talking about you.' Then she added immediately, 'I'm not going on walking at this pace even if you are. So we'd better say good-bye.'

'Oh, I'm sorry. . . .' He seemed genuinely apologetic, even alarmed. 'I get carried away.' He looked about him suddenly as if surprised to discover where he was.

'It must have been a shock. To meet him again so suddenly,' she said, as though taking advantage of his vague mood. He was frowning and looking up at the trees in confusion.

'Yes. . . . But it was all arranged.'

'How d'you mean?'

'It doesn't matter.' He brushed his hand against his face.

'How long was it since you'd last seen him, though?'

'I don't know. I knew him when I was ten or twelve.'

'You must have had a lot to talk about.'

'No.'

'Weren't you interested in what he'd been doing all that time?'

'No.'

'You met his wife, though, I gather. What did you think to her?'

'She's the kind of woman I imagined.'

'Don't you think she's rather old for him? I mean, she's nearly forty. Ten years older. It's rather strange. Such an older woman. And you never talked about the past? Even when you went camping?'

Leonard had blushed again and turned away from her questioning. His moods and feelings changed quickly. They were almost as subtly irregular as the light itself.

'You met each other again after all this time, worked together without hardly speaking, then suddenly went camping together. And you didn't talk about the past?' Leonard didn't answer. 'Vic's wife was married before, you know. Her husband left her. Then she met Vic. Both the children are Vic's. It's very strange. I wonder he never mentioned it.'

Leonard had started to move away. At the same moment the three children came crashing through the bushes by his side and cascaded round him. He staggered and almost fell. Strangely, the accident seemed to cheer him. He looked back at Kathleen and smiled.

'Come on, we're going down to the Rec now,' she called to them, and immediately they began running down the hill, screaming, their feet pounding heavily on the steep slope. They ran in long jarring strides. 'Are you coming with us? Or are you going over to watch *them*?' she said.

Leonard thrust his hands into his pockets and after standing indecisively a second started down the slope, walking at an angle in order to negotiate the steepness. One of the children had fallen. He rolled some distance before springing up and running after the others.

'What do you think of them?' Kathleen said, following just behind him. 'The children, I mean. My father probably told you otherwise, but all three are mine.'

Leonard had already stopped by the nearest tree, his hand raised to the bark. Now he looked up at her with a startled, frozen look. The children still plunged down the slope in hugely unnatural strides.

'I suppose he told you my mother . . . that I was their sister, in fact.'

'Yes.'

'You can't blame him. Though he knew that you'd find

out soon enough. I shall have to go down. They can't go far without one of them falling or crying.'

She started down the hill and a moment later he followed. Half way down she stopped and waited for him and they continued to the foot of the hill together.

In the playground several women were supervising the children. They looked up at Leonard with curiosity but he scarcely appeared to notice them. He sat on a bench and, after playing with the children for a while, Kathleen came to join him.

'Don't be frightened of my father,' she said as she sat down. 'I mean, don't look down on him. He's a strange sort of man. But he's not trying to mislead you.' He smiled and shook his head. The skin over his cheek bones had reddened slightly which, with the wound, gave him an expression of a private, bewildered self-absorption. 'He just fights out these huge fictional battles with himself,' Kathleen said, as though thoroughly roused by Leonard's solemnity. 'I know it's a bit bewildering if you're just looking on. But if you saw more of him I think you'd understand.'

She wasn't sure, then, that he had heard her. He was gazing down at the asphalt close to his feet.

Then he said, 'All that he says about Tolson, then – all that about being persecuted – is that fiction as well?'

Kathleen didn't answer for a while. Then she said, 'Don't you realize what Tolson is?' She watched him minutely: he was still gazing at the asphalt as though making important calculations about its composition. 'He collects "afflicted" people. What he thinks are afflicted people. Like my father. Like *you*.' When she saw that, curiously, his expression hadn't changed, she added, 'How long have you known him? Scarcely three months. Don't tell me he hasn't played any of his famous *tricks* on you.'

'But then, I think you're the same,' Leonard said quietly, out of the same mood of absorption. 'Collecting "afflicted" people, I mean.' His face had a shy, pursed look of cunning. 'Are they really your children?' he said.

For a moment he wasn't sure what emotion was about to explode on her face. Then she burst out laughing. 'Yes, but I don't expect you to believe it!' It was an exaggerated, slightly indulgent humour.

'I'm sorry,' he said quietly.

'Why?' She looked at him with the same, exaggerated surprise.

'I *do* believe they're yours.'

'It's all right. You don't have to.'

'Don't I? I know now why you're so aggressive.'

She looked away at the angular skeletons that inhabited the playground. The metal armatures were swollen into life by the crowded bodies of children.

'I don't know what you're getting at,' she said tonelessly. 'But they are mine, and I don't want to talk about it any more.'

She leaned forward suddenly. Then he saw that she was crying to herself, quietly and moodily, and almost without tears. It was like the sudden maundering crying of her father.

'This's what comes of talking to an idiot,' she said bitterly. 'A fool, a defective, a *madman*.'

Leonard, it seemed, had not penetrated her feelings at all, but simply her method of feeling. It was alarming. As if *he*, at the centre, felt nothing.

'I've always had a very excitable sort of nature,' he said, as though this were a completely different conversation. 'Very inconsistent, that is. Sometimes scarcely controllable and at other times so inert as to be almost depressing.' He laughed at his own peculiarity; it was as if he were now trying to amuse and cheer her. 'And yet not at all demonstrative. Sort of inside. Well, you'll know what I mean. None of it ever shows.' He laughed again with a fresh sort of bewilderment. 'It makes it all sound a bit strange. But there's never been any real need for me to work.'

She looked at him with a sudden slyness. Then she stood up and went across the playground. It was now almost deserted. The three children were playing on a roundabout, two hanging precariously to the metal struts and the third sitting clutching the wooden seat, crying. She brought this youngest child back with her, standing it between her knees and wiping its face.

After a while she said, 'Do you know the *real* way Tolson afflicts people?' She held the child now with a remote kind of strength, gripping it impersonally between her thighs. She stared across the yard at the two laughing children. 'He makes them humourless.'

When Leonard didn't answer she looked at him quickly and said, 'That's another way, of course, of saying that he sucks people dry. He exhausts them. Do you know the kind of person who takes that sort of strength away from people? Isn't that what he does to you?'

Leonard showed no sign that he'd even heard. He gazed abstractly at the barricade of trees which separated the park from the street beyond. His expression had the same seriousness as before, an aged look of intentness. Then he said, 'He doesn't have the same effect on everybody. With the men, at Ewbank's, he's very popular.'

'But aren't they a bit frightened of him?' She said it as if she were talking to the child, and looked anxiously into his face.

'Yes. But then he doesn't *oppress* them. Not directly, that is.'

'No. Not directly. He doesn't need to. . . . Those he oppresses directly are only afflicted people. Like my father said, those people afflicted by a "spiritual temperament".'

Leonard sat watching the boy between her knees. The child stood perfectly still, yet relaxed, looking across at the other two children still playing on the roundabout. Its arms hung over Kathleen's thighs. In appearance, and in that particular resigned pose, he looked astoundingly like Blakeley himself.

'Perhaps you don't really understand the *intensity* with which Tolson chooses his victims,' she went on. 'When he senses, when he finds – whatever process he goes through in discovering such a person – he pursues them until they *are* finished. Until they're completely destroyed. He has this passion to do things *absolutely*. . . . And the amazing thing is, he does it with a kind of dignity. The most *peculiar* dignity you can imagine. . . . So that dignity itself becomes an obnoxious thing. And the only thing you have left is a belief in your own nothingness. That you are nothing. That you're nothing at all. And you're satisfied with that.'

'But why did he do this to you?' Leonard said quietly.

'To me?' She turned to him in genuine surprise. Then she went on more hurriedly, 'And the really amazing thing is that the victim is always the last person to realize. Don't you think that that's incredible? However many people tell her, however much she sees and experiences, the really terrible thing is the victim never knows she's a victim until it's too late. The reason being, of course, that they think all Tolson's actions are governed by some sort of affection he has for them, which . . . and I hope you can understand this . . . which *he really has*!' She burst out laughing, profoundly amused by this ironical analysis. 'He really has an affection for them. It's as if he massacres them just to spite himself. There, what a monster you've tangled yourself up with. A man who destroys things out of his affection for them.'

She glanced at Leonard now with a hardened reproach, as if he were directly responsible for what she had been saying. But he was gazing fixedly towards the trees. At the opposite side, on the path that skirted the playground, stood Tolson himself. He had evidently been coming away from work with several of the men, and now he stood peering across at them with what appeared, at this distance, to be a sombre smile of surprise. The men, after seeing Leonard and making some joke about his companion, were walking on towards the gates, glancing back now and again as if to re-animate their laughter.

Tolson stubbed his boots against the low metal fence that circuited that half of the playground. For a moment he seemed completely preoccupied, as if methodically cleaning off the mud. When he looked up again it was with a grimace so intense that neither of them spoke. Leonard noticed that Kathleen had blushed deeply: she was unable to turn her eyes away from the heavy figure, who now appeared to be about to move towards them. Yet Tolson did not move. Only when the two children playing on the roundabout let out a cry and ran towards him, familiarly, did he suddenly turn round and walk hurriedly away. He seemed to exaggerate his actions, so that to Leonard he appeared to be neither running nor walking, but simply moving with an authoritative and compulsive gesture towards the gates.

The two children were now running towards them. 'It was Uncle Vic! Uncle Vic!'

'You see,' Kathleen said, still flushed. 'It's not something that children recognize. To him innocence is just another utensil.'

Yet Leonard seemed unsurprised, as if reassured by Tolson's sudden appearance, something he'd anticipated and hoped for. He even seemed pleased and excited. After a while they themselves started off towards the gates.

'What happened to their father, then?' Leonard said, nodding at the children.

'He left me. Went away,' she answered immediately.

'Just like that?'

'I've just said it. He went away.' She was suddenly brusque and angry.

'Because of Vic?'

'Yes. Yes, if you like.'

'Do you love him, then?' he said casually, and as if it were of no importance, nor even of any interest to him. And when she didn't answer he walked on, following the children, as though he hadn't asked the question or as if, if he had, he had forgotten about it completely.

In fact, for no reason at all, he had started thinking in his usual disturbed vein. Quite suddenly he felt strangely exultant. He hardly even heard Kathleen when she said, 'I forgot. You left your raincoat at our house. Perhaps some evening or afternoon you'd like to collect it.'

18

'Thomas,' Austen said, 'is like the little man you used to see following the horses up and down the streets with a bucket and a shovel.'

John laughed, yet as though in some way the remark had hurt him.

'Well, almost. Except that he only collects emotional

droppings,' Austen added, seeing his brother's pained expression with surprise.

John immediately stepped in front of him and opened the double doors of the York Room. A thin cone of yellow light came through a gap in one of the shutters and faintly illuminated the large interior. They waited a moment while Leonard came along the passage, then entered together.

'Matthew, on the other hand,' Austen went on, speaking into the darkness, 'is altogether different. It isn't so much that you can scarcely distinguish between what part of him is *him*, and what part is the computer, but that he is quite content that you shouldn't separate the two.'

The cone of light was broken in two. It stretched across the bare floorboards, then snapped against the wall, rising vertically as a triangle, leaning slightly to one side. Its apex rested just beneath the decorative frieze which, interrupted only by the five tall windows, circled the entire room.

'And Alex?' John said.

'Alex moves through things so rapidly . . . well, things and people, that if he ever stopped you'd feel that his arms, his legs and finally his head would slowly drop off and roll away. And even then, roll away with a gradually increasing acceleration.' He paused to look at Leonard. 'I suppose Alex is the last flame of the Radcliffe fire.'

Leonard had in fact come to stand in the middle of the room and was staring up at the ceiling. Its interlocking figures surged in a formless complexity, colourless and crude; they hung like giants in an obtuse perspective. He gazed up, as though awaiting the climax of a huge event. Then suddenly he stood revealed in a pool of light. The two men were pulling back the shutters.

'And Leonard?' Austen said. 'What about you? I suppose you are the thing that appears after the fire has gone out.'

'And what's that?' John asked.

'The vision, the blurring, whatever it is that overcomes the senses immediately a light has disappeared.' Austen crashed back the shutters into their recesses, then coughed and dusted down his suit. He looked up at Leonard. 'No? You don't think it's true?'

Leonard turned to the windows. The estate stretched below in a large and ordered pattern, slow arcs intersecting the receding ground. The houses spiked the smooth contour of the hill. Beyond the final ridge of houses was the undulating level of the valley, its long rows of buildings splayed like ribs across the slopes. And facing them on the opposing ridge was the black crown of the city's central hill, its old buildings groping up from the hard outline of rock, fingers clutched above the skyline, trailing at their summits a thin and ebbing wreath of mist. Low clouds hung over the land.

'I think this room will suit us splendidly,' Austen said.

'It needs cleaning.'

'Of course. I don't mind that. But the whole thing. It'll be quite impressive.'

Leonard was very pale, the large, matted bruise at the side of his head giving his face the broken appearance of a mask, disused, almost forgotten, only the eyes piercing through. He moved past the windows, the third and the fourth, and paused at the one nearest the fireplace. It was streaked on the outside with dried courses of rain. The hard, red knots of the houses were clenched now like fists beneath the bony shield of the sky. The landscape was heavy, reddened.

'Don't let Austen rush you into something you don't want, father,' he said quite suddenly.

'No. Of course not. Why should he?'

'I don't know. Except that I feel he's not the person to plan such a family party without having something in mind.'

'Something?'

'Some purpose.'

John glanced at Austen apologetically.

'And what purpose would that be?' Austen said.

'I don't know.'

'Perhaps it's something I want too,' John said. 'An event. To see people in the Place after all these years. If you feel it's something surreptitiously designed – to what end, I don't know – then no doubt you'll find greater satisfaction in staying away.'

John stared at Leonard a moment as though expecting some sort of answer, then went to the door. He paused there, waiting, then hurried out into the passage. They could hear his feet moving down to the stairs.

'What is it that he wants after all this time?' Leonard said. 'A crusade?'

'Perhaps it is. Perhaps it is,' Austen answered, smiling at his nephew.

'And what do *you* hope to gain by it?'

'Oh, now, Leonard.' Austen laughed. He closed the shutters on the second window, looking down from the darkened end of the room to where Leonard was standing beneath the fireplace examining the carving. 'Do you know what that figure is?' he asked. It projected heavily into the room, into the oblique angle of the light. 'The one downstairs, if you remember, is Jehu. This, this one, is supposed to be Samson.'

He slammed the final shutter into place. The room was suddenly in complete darkness. Austen stood still, as though in some way confused by his own action and trying to locate Leonard across the room.

'Have you noticed,' he said after a moment, 'as your eyes grow accustomed to the dark you begin to feel that this is the natural light and that those tiny bright cracks round the shutters are unnatural? You feel this is the natural light, yet it's almost completely dark in here.'

Leonard was indiscernible against the staggered shadows and crevices of the huge fireplace. Austen waited a moment, then said, 'You see, Leonard, there are two kinds of puritan temperament. The liberal and the coercive. After spending nearly the whole of his life as the one, your father's decided that all along he really intended to be the other. The evangelical, I mean.' Austen paused. 'Can you see me from where you're standing?' he said.

'No.'

He listened to the tone of Leonard's voice. 'But you are looking in my direction?'

'Yes.'

Suddenly Leonard's voice asked with a kind of ludicrous anxiety, 'Austen, have you any idea of the time?'

Austen paused again. Then he said, 'It must be somewhere between two and three.'

They stood in silence for a while. Then Austen went on

slowly, 'Your father's predicament is not so unusual, you know. He's got to solve a problem which he knows to be insoluble. Not only won't the first line of the equation work, but the factors themselves are almost unrecognizable. He begins to doubt, not whether the problem exists – his despair and misery more than confirm that – but whether his will to discover a solution is right. Who willed us? Who instructed us? His intelligence provides him with no escape from this extraordinary predicament. In fact, only one thing ever will. His intuition. And it is specifically this that his puritan temperament denies. This is his real conflict. The thing he's never realized until now, is that his puritanism is that of a practical ascetic, one whose battles take place in public, not here in this cloister. That's why he's throwing open the door. Now he's waiting, almost insisting even, that something should happen, that something should arrive.'

Austen stood listening for a while. He had thought in fact that he heard Leonard moving, but all was now completely silent and still. He began to move forward, identifying in several places the possible silhouette of his nephew.

'Do you understand that?' he said into the silence. 'It means that *you* are his image, and he's searching round now for a suitable setting in which to present it. Otherwise . . . otherwise he's reduced to a very simple thing. To seeing his misery and his despair as in some way his only achievement.'

Austen had now almost reached the fireplace. It rose massively before him in the faint light. Then he realized quite suddenly that Leonard was no longer there. That in fact, as his search quickly revealed, he was not even in the room.

As he turned to the door he gave a loud sob, but whether of frustration, or anger, or grief, it was impossible, even for him, to tell.

19

That same morning Leonard had come down rather late to find his mother waiting for him in the kitchen. Looking up from the table where she was working she had smiled at him and handed him a thick blue envelope.

Though unstamped, his name and address had been written across it, the letters large and shaped with unusual care. It was this, he assumed, that had amused his mother, and after examining it a moment, turning it over several times as though uncertain whether to accept it, he had glanced at her severely and taken it with him back to his room.

The letter had been unsigned, and composed in the same laborious handwriting. It alluded in detail to his conversation in the park with Kathleen, even to the encounter with Tolson, yet was written with a rhetorical affectation he associated more with Blakeley than with anything that he knew of his daughter. Its general tone of apology was abruptly terminated by a demand that he should call at the house at a specific time in the afternoon. No mention was made of the coat.

When, some time later, he returned to the kitchen it was to discover Austen already there; and although his mother made no direct reference to 'the little messenger', as she'd called the boy who had delivered the letter, it was clear that the subject had been more than thoroughly discussed. It was a relief when Austen had begun to announce his arrangements for the party and it was only after lunch, when he and Austen and his father had gone up to the York Room to assess its possibilities, that he remembered the letter again. Without thinking, he hurried out of the room and was already well on his way to Blakeley's house before he even realized the circumstances in which he had left his uncle.

He reached the end of the road where Blakeley lived at what he judged to be several minutes before three o'clock, the hour stated in the letter, and taking another turning that led more circuitously to his destination, he walked up and round a crescent and down a second avenue to arrive at the opposite end of the same road. He walked slowly along to the house and arrived there, he surmised, several minutes late.

For a while there was no answer to his knocking. He waited indecisively on the top step, glancing up to reassure himself of the number. The road, in mid-afternoon, was completely silent and deserted. Then from the rear of the house he thought he detected whispered voices and a hurried, hastily-suppressed shuffling of feet. A moment later the door was pulled open and Kathleen stood looking down at him, her face slightly flushed and creased in that now familiar sardonic smile.

'So you decided to come twenty minutes early,' she said. 'And confound us all.'

'Early?'

'It's only twenty minutes to three. But then, perhaps you didn't read the letter very closely.'

'I was just guessing the time,' he said as though he were about to go. 'I'd no real idea.'

Suddenly she laughed. 'Come in. Come in. You don't think I'll make you walk up and down outside until the proper moment arrives do you? . . . Come in. There's no need to look so guilty. I've got your coat waiting already.'

She had to take his arm before he actually entered the hallway, and then push him forward slightly in order to close the door. As she did so he had the impression of voices and feet on the path outside hurrying round from the rear of the house.

'I suppose, really, I'm surprised you *have* come,' she said once they were in the living-room and the door finally shut. His coat lay folded neatly over the arm of a chair. He went to stand by it, uncertainly. 'And now you have come I suppose you'll take it, say thank you, and leave straight away.'

'There was no mention of the coat in the letter,' he said blankly, staring down at it as if so patent a device for their meeting could now only embarrass him.

'The letter? No.' She came purposely to stand quite close

196

to him. 'What did you think to the letter? Didn't you think it was cleverly composed?'

He suddenly turned away from the coat, and rather confidently went to the wall and began to examine the numerous photographs pinned there. They were all of Blakeley caught in some amusing climax to one of his acts; in each the costume and expression were different. In only one had he been pictured with someone else.

'Why did you come?' she added. And when he gave her no answer she hastily went on, 'I suppose you heard all the discreet sounds of departure when you came in. Enter Radcliffe, the hero of forlorn aspect; exit family of the opposite disposition. I must say you were very clever. You caught us very nicely. Denis mustering them all through the back door with stifled expletives while you stood gazing innocently around on the front step.'

He'd looked up at her. It was the first time he recollected hearing her refer to her father by his first name. The tone of familiarity surprised him.

She glanced away. Then suddenly sat down.

He looked back at the photographs. The central one was of Kathleen and Blakeley, staring solemnly before them. Their hands rested on the shoulders of the three young children. They too shared the same expression of solemnity. The camera, presumably, had been held by Blakeley's wife.

'You're always revealing things,' he said suddenly. 'Particularly those things which most people would take every trouble to conceal. In fact, things which your *father* obviously does go to a great deal of trouble to conceal. And all the time you're pulling the curtain aside to reveal him in his little act.' He swung round hastily, and abruptly went to sit in a chair. It was a particularly clumsy action. 'Yet I feel the whole time that these endless revelations are only to conceal something much huger.'

'You're very clever. And what huge thing can it be?'

'I don't know.'

'Well. You better take your coat, then, I suppose. That's what you came for, isn't it?' When he didn't answer, but merely looked uncomfortably around him, she began to fumble with her skirt, an absent-minded and vaguely absurd gesture, for she added, 'What did you think to the letter?' and before he could answer went on, 'I suppose you realized by its tone and its quaint omission of a signature that it wasn't in fact composed by me at all but by my well-intentioned father.'

'I did think it was.'

'Oh, you *did* think it was,' she said. 'Then the fact that you have come after all must surely mean something. Well? . . . Was it to spite Tolson? To *show* him?'

He looked at her with a blank, undisturbed stare.

They sat in silence for a while.

Then Kathleen added viciously, 'You'll laugh at this. No. Perhaps you won't. Most likely it'll frighten you. But can't you guess why *he* wrote it?' She stared at him with a triumphant expression, her hands pressed forward on her knees. 'Why, it's the traditional tactics of the father in marrying off his daughter. Didn't you guess? But you must have done, of course. All his furtive attempts to have the house empty when you arrived you must have found particularly encouraging. Why, he's created what he believes are the "ideal circumstances" for a proposal of marriage! *He* wants *you* to marry *me*!'

If this revelation itself confused him, what was more intimidating was the tone in which it was expressed, one both of despair and outrage. It was as if she taunted him with something of his own pessimism. He stood up and in a very unnatural voice shouted absurdly, 'What! Are you determined never to be saved!'

'From what?' she said, smiling slightly.

'I don't know. I don't know. . . . Your only real contact with people comes from intimidating them.'

'Does it embarrass you? I mean the real reason for you being asked here. My father's reason.'

'I don't understand you. Not at all.'

'No. But then I doubt if you understand women at all, do you? Or men, for that matter. Do you *honestly* see anything of what goes on around you?' She watched him with the same frozen smile, as though the expression were bitterly imposed on her face.

They were silent for a moment. Then she said, 'What would you do if I suddenly started showing my legs to you?

Or taking off my blouse?' She watched him acutely, for she was already drawing her skirt over her knees. 'No, you needn't be frightened,' she said. 'I'm not going to give you a peep show. I've no doubt at all what you'd do. Run for the door and I'd never see you again.'

'Why do you abase yourself in this way?' he said, rigid in his chair. They were still sitting facing one another, Leonard's terrified eyes glancing from her to the photographs on the wall. 'It's as if you and your father were rotten with the same disease.'

She sat watching him without expression; with a seriousness that for the first time left a peculiar calmness on her face. She slowly pulled her skirt down. Then she began to smile, half-ugly, derisive.

Leonard sat still, his hands clenched over the arms of the chair. The next moment, however, he stood up and with extraordinary slowness, as though his actions imitated those of a much larger man, he crossed the room and bent over her. He stooped down and kissed her lightly on the mouth. He was awkwardly supported by one hand. Her face was quite aged, with numerous small lines springing outwards from the corners of her eyes. He kissed her again. Then he stood up. He was extremely pale, ashen.

'You better take your raincoat,' Kathleen said, tonelessly and unmoving. Leonard stood gazing down at her.

'You accuse me of aloofness,' he said. 'But look at this! Look at you now!' He seemed in absolute despair at her passivity.

'Now you know why my father thought we'd be suitable for one another. Two equally resistant people. You internally, me . . . well, something a bit different.' And when he didn't answer, but stood there watching her with aimless violence, she added, 'Doesn't it offend you? Knowing why you were sent for?'

'No.'

'What? Are you so desperate?' She looked up at him swiftly, but no longer with contempt or amusement. More, it was a look of challenge.

'If we've nothing but deprivation in common, why did you see me? You could have left with the rest of them. In five minutes I'd have gone away. Why are you like this?

The whole time. Why have me here if it's only to take something out of me? You can do that anywhere, anytime. Ask anyone and they'll tell you.' He had returned to the same wildness of manner and voice, his hands shaking helplessly at his sides. 'When I first met you I thought all this was deliberate. That it was a deliberate insult. But now. It just seems pathetic. That's all it is.'

Kathleen stood up. 'You better go,' she said quietly. 'It was a mistake you coming. I can't apologize. I know I should. But I can't. You've been taken advantage of, that's all.'

'But why did you agree? The letter – it mentioned everything we'd talked about yesterday. You must have told him everything. Why?'

'Yes. Yes. But then you shouldn't have tried to spite Tolson. And I shouldn't have told *him*. He was just trying to do his best for me. Do you understand?'

Leonard didn't answer. He gazed at her as though this were yet another attempt to ridicule him.

'It's as simple as that. He just happens to think that you'd make me the ideal husband.' Suddenly she began to laugh, almost the same maundering cry Leonard had witnessed before, an hysterical confusion of relief and distress. 'That's how simple, how elemental he is.'

Leonard stared once more at the numerous images of Blakeley on the wall. Then he said despairingly, 'You might as well have been Tolson for all the mindlessness you have at your disposal.'

'No. No! It's not that! Don't you see? It's *he* who is in love with Tolson and wants you out of the way!'

He had begun to move towards the door.

Immediately she stepped forward and put her arms across his shoulders, tentatively at first but as he paused gripping him with a kind of ferocity. It was as if she had physically encountered him in the darkness of a room, unexpected, half-frightened. She buried her face against his with such a wildness that he cried out, more in shock than alarm, for the next moment she wrenched him against her in a sudden gesture of despair.

Her mouth hurried over his face until, with an extension

of the same compulsive movement, she pulled down at his shoulders; they subsided first against a chair, then more slowly to the floor. Her hands struggled with his clothes. Then, as her fingers closed over his nakedness, she lay back thrusting her legs apart. It was almost a swimming-like motion of her body as she worked him against her, drawing him down more forcefully, insensibly against her hips. Finally she pulled him in against her with both her hands and very slowly began to arch her back up from the floor.

Looking up through half-blinded eyes, Leonard saw directly above him a window in the centre of which, looking in, was the face of Tolson. It hung there like a painted cloth, an hallucinatory pattern vaguely composed in the features of a grinning man.

Leonard buried his head in the shoulder beneath him, his body curving as though in this act alone he could gain concealment. The movement of his hips became more sporadic, erratic shudders that passed into the tormented figure below.

When she eventually turned her head aside, lying back, Kathleen said, 'You look lost. Like somebody lost on a journey.'

She was breathless, distraught, her head twisted to one side in some strange detachment. Then suddenly she thrust her hand down between them. 'Why! Didn't you feel anything?' she said. 'Why. You didn't do anything!'

'Tolson. Tolson was here.' He buried his head again in her shoulder.

'You didn't do anything!'

'Tolson's here!'

Her hand still feverishly gripped him. She seemed scarcely to hear, was scarcely even concerned.

'He was there.'

Leonard had begun to draw himself up on his hands, raising himself, but she still gripped him.

'Look,' she said, 'Look. You never did anything!'

He flung himself away, fumbling at his clothes as she released him, and struggled to his feet.

Kathleen still lay on the floor, her head averted as though driven back by force.

'It was Tolson. He was at the window,' Leonard said, sobbing.

Kathleen suddenly stood up. She tried to loosen her skirt which was twisted tightly around her waist.

'Tolson where? You imagined it.'

At that moment Tolson reappeared at the window, smoking and gazing in at them, a thoughtful expression turning to a shy smile. He nodded at them briefly, then glanced down at Kathleen.

For a moment he continued to look at them, slowly removing the cigarette from his lips. Only half-revealed through the window, he appeared like some imaginary embodiment, fixed there. When suddenly he moved away it was without apparent effort, so that he seemed to be propelled by some impersonal force.

Leonard, his shoulders shuddering, had sat down. Intermittently a more violent spasm swept through his body, so that his head was flung from side to side.

'It doesn't matter,' Kathleen said. 'What does it matter? He only saw that. Why, it's an everyday occurrence.'

Her bitterness had returned with greater stridency. She strode over to the window and looked out. 'It's just a thing men and women do, unimaginative, tedious. Any fool can do it. Why should it be so important? Now we're rid of it, what does it matter? What does it matter if he saw? Why, in a minute I expect he'll be striding in here and waiting for me to flop down again on my back.' She laughed, looking round at Leonard. 'And the amusing thing is that I would. I think I would. If he strides in this next minute I'll entertain you with exactly the same display. Perhaps you'll be able to pick up a few tips.'

Leonard, his hands clenched between his knees, gazed down at the floor, shivering.

'Where's your brave talk of yesterday?' She went and stood beside him. 'Didn't you feel anything?' she asked quietly. 'I mean, can't you do anything in that way?'

'It was Tolson.'

'But what does that matter? In any case. . . . It's done. I only wanted to show you.'

'Show me what?' he said without raising his head.

'No. No, of course. It was nothing. Perhaps you didn't realize how crude, how much cruder in fact I am than my father. At least, he and I are *matched* in that respect.' She watched him intently, as though for some sign. 'But that little *act* we've just committed, it was merely to indicate to you how destitute I am. What would you want from me now?'

He didn't answer. For a moment she stared down at his bowed head with increasing wildness. Then suddenly she knelt down and pressed her face feverishly between his thighs.

Leonard sprang up. He seemed flung apart. He leaned against the wall and fastened his clothes.

Kathleen crouched forward over the chair where Leonard had been sitting and cradled her head in her arms. 'It's quite true. My father arranged this meeting with the best intentions. Hoping that it might achieve something. Yet, despite that, he couldn't help himself telling Tolson. And telling him knowingly. *Knowing* that he'd come here. Don't you think that's very strange? Perhaps he wanted it to be a disaster from the start. He wanted to be rid of you yet couldn't bear to rid himself of *me*!'

'I don't understand. I don't understand.'

She raised her head and looked directly at Leonard. 'Can't you explain that? Why he should want both things?' And when he simply shook his head she added, 'I could tell you, of course. But I shan't. The only thing is, I'm exactly the same. I would have married you. I would. Yet somehow, I'd have made sure I didn't. You see, we're bound together like steel. And not one of us will split. You'll see. You'll see. One day you'll see. And now you must go.'

She stood up and went straight to the door, tugging at her skirt irritatedly as she did so. She hurried out of the room into the kitchen and a moment later reappeared. In her hand was a small knife. She picked up his raincoat, thrust it into his hands and half-led, half-pulled him to the door. In the hallway she stopped and pulled open the front door.

'You must never see me again. Do you understand?'

When he didn't reply she caught his arms and shook him. 'Do you understand! You mustn't see me again!'

Suddenly she raised her hand, and lifting the knife slit open the ball of her thumb. A stream of blood sprang out. '*Do you understand*! You mustn't see me again!'

Leonard stood gazing at her without moving. Then, with a stiffened gesture, almost a caricature of obeisance, he leaned forward and kissed the furled ridge of the wound. The hand was lowered beneath the weight of his head. Then it was pressed against his mouth.

They stood, caught in the action, without moving. Then Leonard slowly raised his face. He frowned slightly. Kathleen started laughing.

'Oh, God. You fool. You poor fool!' She held her hands to her cheeks as she laughed.

His mouth was enlarged by a crimson stain, clown-like, oddly disjointed. He swung round and stumbled down the steps. When he reached the road he heard the sound of her laughter joined by several others. He saw Tolson, and then Blakeley, standing in the road laughing. Though not, it seemed, so much at him as at some allusion that had passed privately between them. They stood quite close together, looking into each other's faces.

Yet, as he hurried up the road, they began to follow him. And at such a pace that Tolson, who had easily outstripped the limping Blakeley, soon caught him up. For a while he walked closely behind Leonard, breathing heavily, occasionally half-groaning, half-murmuring or laughing to himself, yet never varying the distance that separated them. Then, as they reached the church immediately below the Place, he grasped Leonard's arm. He caught him more firmly by the shoulders and, almost lifting him from the ground, spun him round.

'Well? Are you satisfied?' he said, staring madly now into Leonard's face. And then, glancing back and observing Blakeley's approach, he wrenched Leonard aside. 'Come on. We'll go in here,' he said, 'away from that limping fool,' and taking a firmer grip on Leonard's shoulder, led him into the church.

20

'I didn't want to go.'

'Why did you?'

Tolson, with the weight of his body, had almost carried Leonard into the pew. He sat beside him, his tall figure scarcely revealed above the high back of the seat which concealed Leonard completely.

Beyond them, where the choir raised itself by a flight of steps above the narrow nave, the darkness was relieved by several white figures, recumbent beneath the smooth, blackened arches and the dull, ochre-eroded walls. The columns of the arches shone, as if stroked to their luminous blackness by hands, a greasy affection; the weight of the stone was lightened and the shadow of the roof suspended over rather than upheld by the stone girths. The light flowed in through five stained-glass windows on either side of the nave, the beams almost meeting in two dull waves, yet separated by a narrow band of shadow that drew a common ground round the feet of the central pillars, and around the figures of Leonard and Tolson themselves.

For a while they sat in silence, Leonard gazing fixedly into the darkness by his feet; Tolson peering, not into his face, but at a point just beyond the profile of Leonard's head. Here a blackened wooden figure struggled from the structure at the end of the pew. Its tiny face was wrenched upwards, its eyes bulbous with some inarticulate labour, its teeth crumbled, half-formed pegs set round a tongue like rope. Tolson's figure, as he gazed at it, seemed to grow out of the pew.

Leonard flinched. Tolson had stood up. Limping towards them was Blakeley. He too started with surprise as the head and then the massive shoulders rose like an uncanny edifice from the terrace of the pew.

'Oh!' Blakeley said. Then recovering, he looked round the dark interior. 'It's like a museum, wouldn't you say?' he suddenly stated. He took out a cigarette which, plainly, he had lighted just outside the door. He plucked it from his mouth, glancing quickly at Tolson, then more certainly at the several effigies and carvings that characterized this section of the church. His raincoat hung loosely, like a second, redundant skin from his bony shoulders. 'Quite a collection. All yours, I presume?' he said to Leonard who, however, scarcely raised his head. Blakeley laughed, a high, shrill sound.

Tolson had begun to pace up and down the aisle, his hands thrust into his pockets, staring at the ground, his figure passing and re-passing the columns of light that slanted down from the narrow windows. Blakeley continued to glance at him, but with an increasingly nervous expression. Nevertheless, he went on speaking in a relatively calm and reflective voice. 'Do you realize the unusual thing about the altar ornaments? I mean the silver ware, of course. It's Spanish of the seventeenth century yet made of beaten metal, and not castings. It's extremely rare. The candelabra, though, are made of brass. William Howard of Exeter. A craftsman and nothing more. The Last Judgement there, Italian, early sixteenth century, as are the carved reliefs. They're German.'

Tolson had suddenly stopped his pacing. He was staring at Blakeley with a ferocious intensity.

'It's a strange museum,' Blakeley went on, 'idolatrous for such a puritan family. That is, for people of such inward and not outward graces. Look. "Orate pro anima Thome Radcliffe militis qui hanc capellam fieri anno Domini 1477".' He gestured at the vast white effigy of a knight which, hands poised in prayer above its slenderly featured face, lay like a metal pod between adjacent columns of the central row of arches. Blakeley's Latin was fluent. 'Have you attended a service here recently?' He glanced at Leonard's bowed head. However, he gave no response. 'There were seven of us. Five women, a child and me. Oh, I'm not complaining. But imagine. This church was built to serve the spiritual needs of one family, and now it's sufficient to serve the similar needs of twenty thousand.'

He laughed again. Then coughed. He dropped his cigarette and stood on it. For a moment he seemed to rise in the air as his toe swivelled on the ground. Then he glanced up once more, desperately, at Tolson.

His eyes dropped. He looked at Leonard, licked his lips, and began to limp away. He reached the yellow cone of light that filtered through the open door and, without turning again, disappeared outside.

Tolson's head had slowly reared itself towards the vault of the ceiling. He gazed up, his mouth peculiarly open. Then he screamed: '*Bastard! Bastard!*' The sound was strangely dull, as though buried in wood.

Leonard stood up. He attempted to follow Blakeley to the door. Tolson quickly stepped into his way.

'You know the thing about Blakeley?' he said, staring at Leonard's eyes. 'Do you know? Do you realize? He wants to get rid of you, yet he wants you to save him as well. *You*. He wants you to save him! He's mad.' He laughed. 'Don't you think so?' His amused eyes continued to stare into Leonard's for some time. 'Do you know that he came and told me about you seeing Kathleen this afternoon? He told me even before he'd written the letter inviting you there. He wrote it knowing I'd be there! He wanted to get rid of you, yet he can't bear to lose Kathleen. And he hasn't any real hatred or badness inside him so he does both things. And bang! They cancel each other out. Can you believe it? He's mad!' He watched Leonard a moment longer. 'Has he ever told you about this peculiar relationship he has with Kathleen?' Leonard didn't answer. 'Do you know, he even told me to go and look in the window.'

Tolson laughed more heavily now, yet scarcely taking his eyes from Leonard.

Suddenly Leonard said quietly, 'We mustn't fight. We mustn't.'

'Fight? How do you mean? I'm not fighting.'

'Why must you always live through your gestures. Why can't you live through what you are?'

'What I am?'

'Why are you afraid of your feelings? They're not wrong. They're not wrong. They're not things to abuse, or to despise. They're you. Why must you always destroy them? Why are you always trying to destroy *me*?'

'I don't want to destroy you. . . .'

'You make these situations. It's as if you're afraid of loving. Of loving. Of any feeling at all.'

Tolson had begun to smile again.

Leonard stared at him intensely a moment. Then he half-sprang at him. He clutched Tolson to him and kissed his open mouth.

Tolson yielded. Then he flung Leonard back. 'What! . . .' He stared incoherently at him.

Leonard turned and walked slowly up the aisle. Occasionally he paused, glancing at the carvings on either side until, as he reached the choir, he looked back. Tolson hadn't moved. His huge figure stood solidly amongst the shadows of the nave.

Leonard moved on until, finally confronted by the altar, he turned round.

Tolson had mounted between the choir stalls and was gazing at him with the same fixed, uncomprehending look. His features, in the faint light, seemed rammed apart: absurd protuberances bolted disjointedly to his face.

Yet, when he reached Leonard, he stood massively over him as if completely unable to express any of his feelings. His shoulders mounted, his fists were slowly clenched, and he stood over Leonard in a shaking, helpless agitation.

'You! You understand nothing of me!'

'You're afraid!' Leonard's eyes seemed driven back into his skull.

'Afraid!'

'You're afraid of any absolute thing. You're afraid of anything that's complete. That's whole. Anything that takes the *whole* of you!'

Tolson suddenly leaned his head back. He seemed stunned. Then, with a prodigious lunge of his arm, he swept the metal ornaments across the surface of the altar beyond Leonard's head. They crashed against the wall and the floor, spattering and splaying out like shrapnel. 'You know *nothing*!'

Suddenly he grasped Leonard's wrist and, as Leonard cried out, covered his mouth with his own. The whole of Tolson's body seemed centred on the wrist, bowed, stooping towards it as his fingers forced open the skin. For a moment he withdrew, listening to Leonard's cry. Then, curving his body more leniently, he enclosed Leonard fully, pulling him between his thighs and locking him securely. Together, with Leonard's smothered cries, they swayed hip to hip, swung to and fro like a huge and single pendulum, their mouths pressed against each other's. Their shadow fled across the empty surface beyond their heads.

Tolson paused. He tightened his grip. Between his lips came a fresh suffusion of cries. He gazed into Leonard's face: mouth, eyes, nose, head were flung back in a shriek of pain and, driving home his thumb and finger against the pierced wrist, he tenderly covered with kisses the screaming face.

When he released him the full weight of Leonard's body fell into his arms. He held him there, gazing now almost abstractedly, half-dazed, into Leonard's face: it was screwed in an intent frown, the eyes closed, almost sleeping. He kissed the swollen lids. Small vibrations drew the broken body up. He released him, watching morosely, jealous it seemed of such private pain and such private consolation, as Leonard stooped over his wounded wrist, crying now, with a whimpered breath.

Then, as Leonard turned, he turned too, and together, they moved down to the aisle. Neither spoke until they had almost reached the door. Then Tolson said, 'If you're frightened of me now, what will you be like in three or even two weeks' time?' Yet Leonard only gave him a sunken look, torn, and half-appealing, and without another word Tolson hurried to the door.

Standing there, in the now diminishing shaft of light, was a figure whom clearly Tolson couldn't recognize. He paused, glancing round quickly at Leonard as though in some way betrayed. Then he approached the door very slowly, nodding his head in some uncertain gesture of introduction.

Leonard, with a similar shock, had identified the intruder, and for a while he stopped and gazed about him as though deliberately to postpone the inevitable encounter. Occasionally he glanced over to where the intruder's head moved slowly above the high backs of the pews. It possessed, isolated like this, a strange though remote sense of threat. It was his sister, Elizabeth.

After a hesitant introduction, she now stood talking to Tolson, looking round at the interior, her arm raised to indicate something of interest. She was laughing at some allusion of Tolson's. For a moment the sounds of his voice and hers were joined. It was only as they turned towards the door that they appeared to remember Leonard and, glancing round, Elizabeth called his name.

When he emerged from the church the brightness burned his eyes. A shower of torn paper fluttered round his head as he heard Blakeley's laughing voice, 'Oh, isn't he lovely! Isn't he lovely!' Then he felt someone take him roughly by the shoulder, and a voice hissed in his ear, 'There! I hope you'll live a long and happy life, and may all your troubles be little ones!' He recognized Blakeley's laughter again, beside him, and, further away, Elizabeth's and Tolson's.

He looked blindly in the direction of the row of houses which separated the church from the Place. Gradually he was able to make out various figures.

Standing by the low stone wall close to the porch was a single figure, and beyond, by the wooden gate that opened onto the estate road itself, he recognized Tolson and Elizabeth. They were still talking and, apparently, completely absorbed in one another. In the roadway several women had stopped to watch as though an event had taken place.

As Leonard stepped from the porch Blakeley moved in front of him and began to walk towards the gate. At a point roughly half-way between Leonard and Tolson he stopped and turned round.

'Have you ever actually witnessed a miracle?' he said to Leonard, who still appeared dazed by the light. 'Have you?' He waited for a reply.

Blinking his eyes as though awakening from a dream, Leonard gestured at him as if both to apologize for his inattention and to discourage any interest in his condition.

Blakeley glanced up at the church, now fiercely illuminated in the late afternoon sun and, without changing his expression, added, 'You remember that slight physical impediment I had?' He had begun to walk round Leonard without limping. 'Well, it's suddenly been cured! Don't you think it's incredible!' Yet, despite his anxiety to attract Leonard's attention, he was watching Tolson who stood disregardingly several yards away. 'No! I mustn't go giving you illusions,' Blakeley suddenly laughed, catching Leonard's arm. 'I only limp as an affectation. An important and very necessary affectation, albeit, but nevertheless, an affectation. I'm sorry, by the way, about Kathleen. I'm very bad at these sort of things.' He added the last sentence without any change of inflexion in his voice, and without even any change of expression, and went on in a slightly more cheerful tone, 'Perhaps I ought to have told you. I get *moods*. Moods when I have to do it. I *have* to! Can you understand that? The limping, I mean. It makes me look slightly pitiable, don't you think? Nothing much. Just the right touch.' He suddenly leaned forward and patted Leonard's cheek. 'Oh, what a blushing bride! How I wish I was young all over again. I'd show you!' He burst into laughter and, moving backwards, led Leonard towards the gate.

Elizabeth was evidently saying good-bye to Tolson, who now began to move off down the road at a brisk pace, calling cheerfully to Leonard and giving a loud, 'Come on, slow-coach,' to Blakeley, who immediately hurried after him.

For a moment it looked as though Leonard would follow too. He called out wildly, 'Vic! ... Vic!' but Tolson only spun round, waved, and increased his pace down the estate.

After a moment's reflection Leonard turned up the rise towards the Place. Elizabeth walked beside him. She was still excited from her recent encounter.

'What made you go inside the church? How did you know I was there?' Leonard asked as they neared the Place.

'That man. He stopped me. What's his name? He said you and Vic were in there. The funny thing was, he told me a wedding was taking place!' She laughed. 'It was that

that made me go in.' Her laughter seemed to be flung out at the hedges, the road, the houses as some sort of challenge. 'And there you were. The two of you!'

After a while Leonard said, 'What do you think to Tolson?'

'He's very charming.' She glanced at Leonard's sultry face. 'He's a kind of heavy-handed knight. It makes a change.'

'Yes!' he said, surprised, as though suddenly he had realized she was waiting for some sort of response.

'He seems to respect and admire you.'

'Yes.'

She continued to smile at his moody expression.

'You'll keep away from him, won't you?' he added.

'Away? And why?'

But Leonard didn't answer. His face burned, his eyes frowning as though resisting the temptation to cry.

Elizabeth laughed at his bewildered looks. Then she glanced round, slightly flushed. But Tolson was out of sight. The other man, however, who had followed him, was limping heavily round the furthest corner.

'But he's married, isn't he?' she said uncertainly. 'What's his wife like?'

Yet when she turned to repeat the question, she saw that Leonard had already disappeared into the grounds of the Place.

21

In the passage children crashed by and further on a second group ran screaming down the main stairs. Leonard stood at his window, looking down into the yard. Groups of people stood talking in the sunshine, waiters moving aimlessly between them with trays of drinks. The secluded square was resonant with sound and colour, the interlacing of sunlight and shade, although, since it was set against the northern flank of the Place, even in midsummer the building's shadow never quite left it. In the trees which formed the eastern side of the square, mellowing now prematurely with autumn, two blackbirds were calling in agitation.

Several heads had turned towards the kitchen door. Then, like flowers, more hats and dark crowns of hair slowly rotated in the light. Almost immediately below him Elizabeth had appeared.

Dressed in a dark blue, flared dress, she wore her black hair swept tightly back from the pale shell of her face. She seemed, in this vertical perspective, like some component of the building itself. There was a slight inclination of her head and a faint flushing of the forehead and high cheek-bones, as though she sensed herself the object of the aching curiosity of these people. She moved from group to group, only finally coming to rest in the furthest corner of the yard, by the outbuildings, where her uncles, Isabel and the Provost, a small and extremely ugly man, were talking.

It was towards this spot that his father, by a series of introductions to his guests, was gradually making his way. Having reached the group he shook hands with Thomas, then the Provost, and finally asked some question of Elizabeth. He immediately turned towards the building and, glancing up at the shadowed façade, walked quickly over towards the kitchen door.

Assuming that his father was searching for him, Leonard turned from the window and crossed slowly to his bed. He sat down, moodily waiting. Yet when some time later there was a knock on his door, he looked up in complete dismay. The voice which called out to him was not his father's but Elizabeth's.

As he stood up he glanced hastily around the room and, after a certain hesitation, picked up an object which had been lying beside him on the bed. It was Tolson's hammer. Staring distractedly about him for a moment he suddenly thrust it into the drawer by his bed and, glancing at himself in a mirror, went to the door and drew back the bolt.

Elizabeth gazed in at him with an inquiring expression, as if her sudden appearance were due to some remark about her brother which she had now taken the trouble to confirm. She shook her head meditatively.

'Well, they're all waiting for you.' Then, recognizing

something of Leonard's expression she came into the room. 'Austen's sent me up to fetch you. He insists that you come down.' She added something which was drowned by the sound of children running past the room. She closed the door suddenly. 'Or don't you intend to make an appearance? Though you must let them see you. You look tremendous.'

Leonard was dressed in a dark suit, almost black, and a white shirt. A slim red tie ran down from his throat. He was extremely pale.

He stood peering at her intently, as though he had in fact asked her a question. When she smiled at him with some curiosity he turned to the window. He glanced back suddenly at the bed, then down at the yard. 'I feel frightened,' he said. 'No, I honestly don't know why,' he added, turning round to her as though she had interrupted.

'But I feel nervous. We all do,' she said, familiar with and undiscouraged by the suddenly childish tone of his voice. 'My father especially. There are nearly thirty people here. It's such a big thing.'

'Yes.' His look returned repeatedly to the window. 'I noticed all your admirers down there.'

'Are you coming, or do you intend to hide yourself up here?'

There were shouts from downstairs. Several people strolled past the room. As Elizabeth turned to the door Leonard suddenly caught hold of her arm.

'Liz. Shall I tell you what happened this morning? Just before you got up. The tables and chairs were brought up in a lorry.' He had begun to smile at her nervously, and to guide her away from the door. 'Austen had ordered them, of course. I counted them as the men carried them up. Thirty chairs and five trestle tables. And would you believe it? He'd ordered them from Ewbank's!'

He was now escorting her round the room as though they were casually strolling round a vast arena. 'Their famous red lorry was parked at the end of the drive. And there they were. Arguing with my father because he refused to let them dig back the drive so that they could open the gates and bring the lorry all the way up.'

He had become quite excited, releasing her arm so that he could move more hurriedly about the room.

'But there's no reason to get so worked up about that.'

'Ah, but you should have seen Tolson. Standing there. Tolson! He'd come with them of course. Quite by chance! Standing there and looking up at the building. It's amazing. Amazing!' He laughed suddenly, nodding his head. 'I've seen that look before.' He glanced wildly at her while still continuing his frantic pacing of the room. 'You can just imagine how it all seemed. No, of course, I'm forgetting. You won't see anything suspicious in that. Tolson is simply a benevolent and misunderstood giant.'

He was now hurrying about the room as though searching for something and yet, by numerous smiling expressions and gestures, at the same time attempting to conceal his intentions from his visitor. He seemed to visit the opposite corners of the room alternately, yet although Elizabeth had never witnessed behaviour such as this before she appeared unperturbed, almost amused.

'You've promised, of course, never to see him. God. All these people. They make me nervous.' He paused to smile at her, and yet perhaps disappointed not to see his eccentricity reflected in surprise on her face. He added hastily, 'I was watching them all earlier on. From the window, as they came up the drive. Matthew, and that blonde hostess wife. It's terrible. There he is, all impersonal and dignified. Then his wife appears. Crash! He's naked. Do you realize why the Provost is so ugly? It's because, by some unfortunate oversight, his face has been provided with sufficient skin to cover one twice its own area. That's what gives him that importuning look, like someone struggling ineffectually against the onslaught of their own flesh. And there's Thomas. All the time like someone planted in the very core of hell and yet trying to assure you by his looks that it's really quite congenial after all. And Alex . . .'

'Alex is a tornado. Are you coming down?' Elizabeth had turned to the door. 'He insists you come down and meet him.'

'But I must tell you the last thing. It's very remarkable. About Austen.' Leonard waved his arms as though clearing an imaginary space around him. 'He was the very first to arrive. He came up the drive like this. Then he paused as he reached the terrace, took off his Homburg, inspected it a moment, then returned it to his head with that little complacent nod, a sweep of his hand which included a casual caress, a brushing of his coat; then, with an expression which suggested indulgence of any sort was somehow displeasing he turned and approached the building, bowed gravely towards it, and using his cane to hold back the branches disappeared round the side. . . .'

'But what on earth . . .'

'Then as I stepped back from the window I saw an incredible sight. I thought at first it must have been my imagination. About a dozen of the mill and factory chimneys sticking up out of the valley had more or less simultaneously grown huge black bulbs of smoke. They shot up into the sky and almost immediately disappeared.'

'Oh, Leonard!' Elizabeth had been about to open the door but a rush of children and people outside made her hesitate, her fingers on the handle. She was laughing.

'I know, it could have a reasonable explanation. . . .'

'Now come on, you *must* come down.'

Leonard was looking at her with a reconciled, perhaps even a bored expression.

'Shall I tell you why we get on so well together?' he said quietly. 'I mean, why it is that whatever we say and do together it's of no importance whatsoever?'

'All right.'

'It's because, unlike everybody else – Austen and my father for instance – you treat me openly and *sincerely* as a fool. As a simpleton. The odd thing is, if I'm treated like that, as an imbecile, I can understand perfectly what's going on, what everything means, all the nuances and subtleties of a situation, however sophisticated it may be. Don't you think that that's a very strange thing?'

'Perhaps you are a fool, then. A wise fool,' Elizabeth said, smiling still, yet increasingly impatient.

'No. The strangest thing of all is that I'm not an imbecile at all. I'm not a simpleton. It's like some perverse disguise I can't help taking on. And I *mean* I can't help it. The moment somebody starts casually talking to me about ideas

216

and abstractions, or the moment somebody makes a direct physical demand which any normal person would respond to in a minute, I immediately become a simpleton. It's as though I wished it on myself. For example, the other day in the York Room, Austen . . . You're looking incredibly beautiful, Elizabeth!'

This last remark was stated as if it were the only natural conclusion to such a rambling series of thoughts. At the same moment Leonard had started his erratic pacing of the room again, and even began to look up at Elizabeth furtively, as though suddenly suspicious. 'Tolson, you know, is an absolute monster,' he said, then a moment later he added in a reluctant voice, 'There's a kind of secrecy about me which is completely innocent, a kind of shyness, which nevertheless gives me all the appearances of a cunning and even mischievous man.'

'My God, but don't you go on! And don't you see things in yourself? I can assure you, it's far more than anybody else ever does.' His sister regarded him with not a little irritation.

'I'm so damned nervous, that's the trouble today.'

'Nervous. But aren't we all nervous? After all, this isn't an everyday occurrence for any of us.'

'I feel frightened.'

'Frightened what about?'

'I feel that Austen and my father expect something from me. But it's not that I feel frightened for myself. I feel afraid for them.'

'What is it they see . . . expect in you?' Yet Elizabeth's attention seemed to be on a conversation that was now taking place outside the door.

'But who on earth *is* the old man?' a voice said.

'But that's not the most disturbing part,' Leonard said. 'The worst thing is that they don't really understand what it is in me that attracts them.'

Elizabeth was now opening the door, and beginning to smile as if she were being mocked. 'And what is it?'

'That they're all concerned with their own consciences whereas I have no conscience at all. That's what attracts them so passionately.'

She burst out laughing, opening the door and even

turning her head as if to include in her amusement those who were standing there, and who now momentarily stared directly into the room at Leonard, then began to move uneasily away. One of them was the Provost, who glanced quickly away and blushed before moving down the landing.

'All right, then,' Elizabeth said. 'I promise.'

'Promise what?'

'I promise. I'll treat you as a simpleton. Then you won't feel so uncomfortable down there. Now, are you coming?'

There was a momentary harshness in her voice which in some way coincided with a particularly clumsy movement of Leonard's as he came out of his room. It was as if he were emerging yet at the same time determined to go back in. Elizabeth, however, closed the door quickly behind him and they went through into the main part of the building.

They joined a general movement of people down the main stairs to the hall where a strong light and the sound of excited voices streamed in from the front entrance.

'And where does Victor fit into all this?' she said as though to fulfil her promise; Leonard was lagging behind.

'It's very simple. He has a conscience. But all his actions are directed against admitting it. That's why he can't forgive me. Why he torments himself. I *insist* on him having a conscience. The whole time. It's the one thing that can save him.'

'You sound like a tyrant,' Elizabeth said without interest. She had been attracted by the sight that now greeted them through the open front doors of the Place.

A mass of people was assembling in a loose group in front of the portico. A large, red-faced man in a brown check suit, a camera suspended from his neck, was trying to arrange the crowd into two groups on either side of the pillared entrance. Already mounted on the steps between them were the members of the family, including the uncles and the aunts. They were staring suspiciously at the stranger who slowly retreated to the edge of the drive as he peered into the top of the camera. Eventually he hoisted himself onto a block of stone and began to shout at the people at the extreme fringes to move closer in to the steps.

There was now a great deal of laughter and shouting, from amongst which Elizabeth's and Leonard's names were called several times.

Elizabeth had in fact emerged into the sunshine at the back of her parents' group just as Isabel succeeded in encouraging the Provost to join her from the anonymity of one of the flanks, when at the same moment a cry went up for another name which at first was not quite discernible. An elderly figure was being helped slowly up the steps to join the family party. An extremely old man, with a mass of white hair that came forward in a limp shield as far as his eyebrows and whose face was remarkably elongated by a pointed white beard, he seemed scarcely aware either of the surroundings or of what was about to take place. For a while he stood facing the wrong way, gazing into the hallway where Leonard was standing motionless in the shadows, before being turned round to the sunlight and the desperate commands of the stranger with the camera. Although no one amongst the family appeared to recognize the old man, they parted in the middle and allowed him to stand to one side of John. Stooped forward and trembling slightly he peered round incomprehensibly at the excited crowd below.

Elizabeth's appearance had as yet gone unnoticed. She had come to stand several paces to the rear of the old man and was staring out, as though in confirmation of that elderly figure's gaze, towards the trees that faced this southern façade of the Place. Here, between the gnarled trunks and apparently unnoticed by the crowd, were several people from the estate. Even as Elizabeth watched, more were emerging from the trees to stand silently within the shadows and a moment later to spread out in the space afforded by the drive. Then she recognized Tolson.

At the same moment Austen and Isabel saw her simultaneously.

'Elizabeth!'

She was eagerly brought forward into the group and given a place to the left of the old man. He was smiling and gazing out at the trees as though he recognized there something with which at last he was familiar.

'Well, have you brought the hero?' Alex said, leaning

forward from the confusion below. The photographer had come up to the group on their left and was attempting, despite several protests, to push people into place.

'Yes. He's just here.' Elizabeth turned round with something of a dramatic gesture. The hallway, however, was deserted. 'He was with me. He came down with me,' she said, and for some reason looked over in the direction where she'd last seen Tolson. He too had disappeared.

The confusion amongst the family, not least Alex's protest at his nephew's continued absence, was further accentuated by the photographer who, his face inflamed as though he were directing his anger against John himself, was shouting, 'Could you come and resolve this matter of precedent, sir? Everyone insists on being closest to the family when the photograph is taken. And God knows, half of them aren't even distantly related.'

As her father pushed his way among the arguing group, Elizabeth suddenly saw Tolson standing now under the nearest of the trees opposite them and, from his expression, evidently enjoying the situation. His arms folded and his head bent to one side, he seemed to be smiling directly at her. He was obviously on his way home from work. Behind him and to either side the spectators, mainly women and children and a few elderly men, had begun to move forward, apparently encouraged by his confidence.

Leonard had in fact followed Elizabeth to the door only to see, the moment he stepped onto the porch, Tolson facing him under the trees. Everyone else had had their backs to him and the familiarity of that face, distant as it was and shrouded by shadow, had made him recoil as if he had been touched.

Yet it was not so much Tolson's appearance itself that had made him retreat unobtrusively into the hall, as the rather helpless attitude of his father beyond the silhouette of whose head Tolson was significantly visible. In the noise and confusion his father stood quite still as if drained of all enthusiasm for something which, modestly enough, he had looked forward to with some expectation. As though propelled by the clamour itself Leonard had turned back up the stairs.

As he did so he had the distinct impression that someone was scrambling hastily up the stairs ahead of him. When he reached the first floor, however, the only people in sight were the caterers. The York Room had now been fully arranged, the tables and chairs set out in a T-shape and laid for the meal. The food itself was in an adjoining room waiting to be served. Two men who hadn't gone downstairs for the photograph were standing at the far end of the room talking to the waiters and drinking.

One of them said, 'I didn't want to distress her, so I just did it as though nothing had happened.'

Leonard climbed to the second floor, then by a narrower staircase to the top. Again he had the impression of someone hurrying ahead of him, and when he reached the final landing he thought he detected voices in one of the rooms that led away to his right. He stood listening for some time. The noise persisted from below, its dissonant effect accompanied by the stifling smell of warm food mingled with the more permanent odour of decay.

He moved down the passage to his right. It led into the older part of the building: a long gallery which flanked the western side and was illuminated along its entire length by mullion windows. As he entered this impressive room he passed a much smaller room to his right which overlooked the rear of the house. Its single window was shuttered but sufficient light penetrated from the rooms opposite to indicate two struggling figures.

As he stepped into the doorway he saw that in fact it was two boys fighting, welded together as if they had been flung at one another by some preternatural force. They rolled together on the floor grunting and snarling and, so far as he knew, unaware that they were observed. He stood there for what seemed a considerable time, yet when he suddenly went into the gallery and looked down at the front of the house he discovered that the group below was more or less in the same confusion as before.

He was just beginning to wonder why he hadn't interfered in the peculiarly bitter struggle when his father stepped down from the porch and crossed over to the nearest group of spectators. A moment later they began to move away. The photographer had taken one photograph now, perhaps more, for he was standing with another man looking down at the camera suspended over his stomach, making some adjustments to it.

At first the guests watched his father's effort to dislodge the spectators with some amusement. The majority of them had already disappeared under the trees, but several retreated only a few paces, and one man in particular, dressed in overalls, refused to move at all. For a moment he and his father were engaged in a fierce argument. Then his father suddenly appeared to recognize someone standing close by him under the trees. He paused, hesitated, and without offering another word to the workman turned back to the porch.

Yet as he did so a figure leapt down the steps and, evidently inspired by some insult shouted by the workman, hurried up to him and smashed him violently in the face. It was done so confidently and quickly, and with such power, that the workman fell over on his side. Before he could rise he was grasped by the collar of his overalls, half-dragged to his knees, then flung towards the trees. Leonard now recognized the figure as that of his uncle, Alex.

The guests were silent. Behind him Leonard could hear the fierce sounds of the struggling boys. Below him everyone was watching Alex with fixed attention. Only the photographer had his back to his uncle, and appeared to be staring at the crowd with frustration. Half way across the terrace, and standing quietly resigned, was his father. He was staring towards the trees as Alex turned his attention from the workman to argue ferociously with someone who remained hidden under the foliage. From his father's expression Leonard knew that this could be only one person.

His uncle turned back confidently to the party, and from the activity around the porch it was obvious that this final intruder too had been dealt with effectively. People began to move into the building. Leonard gazed across at the summits of the trees below which he knew Tolson must be making his way back to the road. It was as if he expected those browning canopies to burst into flame. Behind him one of the boys cried out. The sound was followed a moment later by a rapid and bewildering succession of blows. He doubted at first whether the sounds could be those of a fist, but when the cries suddenly increased he turned round.

As he hurried to the door he had the distinct impression that the gallery was lined with paintings. This curious sensation lasted scarcely the seconds it took him to cross to the door, and was merged in what he had just witnessed outside and by the sounds which came from the next room. The next thing, he was standing at the door of the small, dimly-lit room and staring in at its confused interior. The room, however, as he confirmed when he stepped inside, was empty.

Thinking that he might have mistaken the entrance, he hurriedly looked inside the next two rooms in the passage. They too were deserted. No sound at all disturbed the upper floor. When he reached the stairs and looked down he could only hear the preliminary sounds of the party ascending to the York Room. He could distinguish his aunt's excited voice, then what he imagined to be Alex replying.

For some time he stood peering down the empty staircase until the crash of cutlery and plates, the scraping of chairs and the intrusive murmur of people became so loud that he was compelled to move away down the passage, back towards the gallery. He paced up and down in a state of extreme agitation and indecision. Then, finally, he stopped and swung round and, quite still, began to examine the pale, irregular rectangles of sunlight on the wall.

22

An argument had broken out at the top table, which was formed by the transverse section of the T. John had refused to sit at the very centre, the junction of the two rows of tables, and for a while the chair had remained empty. Then, as the result of popular appeal, it was decided that the old man should sit there.

He had in fact within a very short time of his appearance become a favourite figure, largely because he seemed the only person genuinely oblivious of the increasing abnormality of the proceedings. Something of its incongruous nature had begun to creep in from those who, on the fringes of the party, had been embarrassed by Alex's display of violence outside. The paradox of soberly dressed people celebrating in a room which to a stranger's eyes was a model of decay might at first have been amusing; but now that the occasion had been solemnized, first by Alex's gesture, then by the Provost's rueful incantation of grace, a sort of self-consciousness, an uncertain awareness of morbidity and intenseness, had reduced the initial spontaneity to a low and suspicious murmur. The old man, however, was extremely relaxed and indeed seemed almost familiar with the extraordinary environment, even provoking some amusement by his reaction to the deportment of the waiter who served him. It was rumoured that in his early youth he had been a retainer at the Place.

The murmur of conversation had now sunk to a level where it was easily dominated by the sound of cutlery and plates and the quiet orders which sent the waiters moving to and from different parts of the room. John, tense and withdrawn, sat as the focus of this subdued party, occasionally raising his head to smile at Stella or to acknowledge some casual remark from Austen, who seemed unaware of the atmosphere and chatted to those on his right and left as if all were going off as he had intended.

Then, when it seemed that some intrusion by John was inevitable, the doors, which had been closed against the draughts of the building, were pushed open, and Leonard entered.

Conversation, already considerably diminished, stopped abruptly. Those with their backs to the newcomer turned to stare over their shoulders; those facing him peered with a kind of inscrutable curiosity; the waiters stood erect in almost parodied attitudes of respect. Intensely pale, and with a ferocious look in his dark eyes, Leonard entered and walked down the length of the room. Alex, who rose to greet him with extreme and sudden affability, he acknowledged with a slight, awkward bow; once seated, he gazed down at the table with an expression which, to the surprise and the concealed amusement of some, was unmistakably one of acute embarrassment. His face slowly coloured until, raising his head slightly, he glanced up from beneath his dark brows as if to confirm that he was still the centre of attention.

Alex, however, seemed the one to be most surprised by his behaviour. He glanced at Austen as though in some way he had been deceived; then, as if such shyness were itself contagious, he sat looking at his nephew with a faint blush on his own determined features. Only when a waiter approached and asked what Leonard would like did Alex relax with some commentary on the choice of food. He watched his nephew acutely.

Conversation restarted. The red-faced photographer had suddenly reappeared and backed into a corner, peering into the top of his camera. Apparently having taken one photograph very quickly he suddenly turned to the window beside him and, after a lengthy struggle with the catch, opened it and stood breathing deeply. From some distant corner of the Place came the sound of breaking glass, like a stone penetrating a window, but although several heads turned at the noise, in the rising tide of animation that had begun to sweep the room no one gave it any real attention. Suddenly there was a burst of laughter.

As though resenting any detraction of interest from himself, the old man had risen from his place at the centre of the top table and was now making gestures in the direction of the photographer, whom he obviously had some difficulty in seeing. Reassured by sounds of amusement, he began the difficult feat of climbing onto his chair which, despite the discouragement of those on either side, he eventually accomplished. Balanced precariously above the table he now gave his gestures freer reign, increasing them in scale and variation, and bringing from his audience cries of 'Good old Arthur! . . . Come on, Arthur!'

Interspersed with demands for the photographer who was now making frantic adjustments to the lenses of his camera, the old man's gestures gradually matured into those of an unmistakable obscenity, a kind of unwitting insolence that was heightened by suggestive undulations of his emaciated body. As he gyrated precariously on the narrow pivot of his chair his gesticulations attained an almost rhythmical frenzy, until they were abruptly terminated by a loud and unnaturally prolonged emission of wind.

The photographer now found that all eyes and interest had reverted to him. It was as if he had been the real centre of curiosity all along. For a moment he occupied himself with a large attachment protruding from the front of his camera, then began to wander slowly round the tables sighting the instrument at various groups of the party. By this time the old man had returned to his chair and, considerably flushed, was grinning cheerfully at his closest neighbours and nodding his head as if in satisfaction at his recent display. A moment later John rose to his feet, banged the table erratically with his spoon, and announced that Austen would make a preliminary speech on behalf of the hosts.

His brother rose with notes in one hand, his glasses, which he seldom if ever wore in public, in the other, and a certain calm, almost mischievous expression on his face, which he turned first on John, then on his audience at large. He spoke briefly and concisely about the history of the family and the Place, tracing in its struggles the battle between on the one hand its strong puritan and republican character, and on the other certain catholic and royalist sympathies which had never quite abated. He spoke of the Civil War, and its division of the family, as if it were an event that had taken place only in recent years. It was an ambiguity that was never really resolved, so that when he eventually referred to Leonard as 'that one person whom we must now impress not only with the weight and the significance of his inheritance, but with his obligation to respect and to uphold those traditions which in a decaying world the family has struggled to maintain,' no one was quite sure whether to interpret this as an ironical comment deserving laughter or as a serious if inelegant attempt to retrieve for the party some sort of dignity and purpose.

As Leonard began to rise during the hesitant burst of applause which ended Austen's speech, his father stood very quickly and, raising his hand, began to respond to the toast of the family which Austen had proposed.

John spoke hurriedly, almost incoherently, as though activated by some kind of shock, glancing whenever he paused in Austen's direction and driven on it seemed by the open curiosity that began to centre on Leonard. Eventually, however, he was distracted by sounds which rose from the old man's direction: they might have been the mumbling of words or even a more generalized indication of boredom, a noise like a low and persistent groan. The guests refrained from acknowledging it by avoiding the spot with their eyes.

Then a loud and certainly more familiar sound came from the elderly guest. It lasted several seconds, was interrupted, then continued at a slightly higher and more penetrating pitch, wailing off into a distant moan like a faint and derisive echo of itself. Such a versatile demonstration of his powers the old man himself seemed incapable of resisting and, to suppressed murmurs from his audience, he half-rose from his seat.

Whether he was about to speak or not they never discovered, for the next moment the upward motion of his head changed to a slow, parabolic descent, and he crashed forward into a bowl of fruit and cream which lay on the table before him.

The hideous repression of amusement could no longer be restrained, and with guilty looks at their host who, strangely, was holding one hand to his eyes, they burst into loud and uproarious laughter – expressing their concern, however, by standing up and preparing to go to the old man's help. But what stimulated their laughter, driving it on to fresh peaks of hilarity, was that he persisted in keeping his head immersed. It was only when Alex, sternly immune to the mood of the room, reached across and lifted that ancient skull and peered into its whitened face, that it became apparent that things were not quite what they had seemed. Within a moment, and before the real climax of laughter had passed or the photographer, who had already taken several pictures, had had time to adjust his lenses, Alex announced that the old man was dead.

At the same moment that the murmurous shock swept through the room, Leonard stood up and, as though it had been at the back of his mind the whole time, turned and walked stiffly over to the fireplace where, peculiarly erect, he stood gazing intently at the figure carved in relief. It seemed a genuine moment of distraction as though noticing the conclusion of the meal, he had excused himself and gone over to investigate something which until now etiquette had prevented him doing. Genuine, that is, but for a certain stiffness, most conspicuous in the erectness of his head and shoulders.

Meanwhile the Provost had taken charge of the body, discouraging Isabel's more extreme attempts to confirm the absence of life, and calling on the robust photographer to supervise the clearing of the room. Alex had gone to the door, taking Matthew with him, to drive down to the nearest call-box on the estate. John and Stella stood silently to one side as the Provost laid the body on the floor and knelt beside it. They seemed absent-minded, expressionless. Yet a moment later there appeared on John's face a strange, almost strangled look of elation.

Austen had gone over to Leonard, standing behind him a moment, then suddenly touching his shoulder reflectively. Leonard swayed slightly as the tension immediately left his body in an attitude of physical exhaustion. Only as he went towards the door did he seem to notice the old man and the group collected around him and, pausing a moment as though to reassure himself that they no longer required his assistance, he left the room.

23

'It's very difficult to describe,' John said, 'but about three days ago I had an extraordinary experience. Well. . . .' He paused, waiting.

A reading lamp illuminated Leonard's head, holding it

within its red glow. He lay on his bed gazing up at the ceiling.

For a moment John looked round the room as though to discover some object that might make the incident more accessible to Leonard. Outside it was dusk. A faint murmur came from the yard below where the last group of guests stood talking on the lawn. Further away there was the roar of an engine. Then a car moved off rapidly, down through the estate.

'I was going down the drive towards the gates,' John suddenly added, 'when I just happened to look up to the right. To where the wall dips slightly beside the road. There were two people walking towards' each other. I couldn't hear them, because the sound was muffled by the wall, so I don't know what it was that actually made me look up. And I couldn't see them either. Except of course for their heads. I just saw the two heads approaching each other along the top of the wall. One was a man, the other a woman. And they were both about fifty, perhaps slightly more. Then, just when it seemed they'd crash into each other, they suddenly paused and, after a moment, kissed each other on the cheek. It was extraordinary. But do you know, for that second I was filled with absolute terror.'

Leonard scarcely moved. He gave no indication that he had even heard. Then he coughed, and his body appeared for a moment to be flung loosely against the bed.

'It's odd. I mean, at first I thought it must be something in the two people themselves, or just a bizarre impression created by the obstacle of the wall. But then yesterday I was digging in the grounds for some humus, under the beech trees at the far side, when I moved some leaves aside and uncovered a plant growing there. It was whitish-green, just a thick, bulbous shoot. I was bending over it, looking at it, when I had exactly the same sensation. It seemed ages before I could even straighten my back. I was absolutely terrified. And for no reason at all.'

He laughed rather helplessly and looked round the room. Then his gaze returned to Leonard as though it were Leonard himself who had been speaking.

'Exactly the same thing occurred this morning. I was

going past one of the rooms when I noticed that the floor at the opposite side, just beneath the window, was tilted slightly. That in fact the floor had subsided a fraction. And believe me, it froze me as though I'd seen an apparition. I don't know how to describe it really. The sensation. It's as if my skull had been peeled away and my brain exposed to a violent stream of cold air. Like being driven up off the ground, rammed up. And everything: it just seems hopeless, without any definition or purpose. I don't know, but it's like glimpsing something which you've sensed all along was there and which is only revealed in brief and particular moments.'

He began to laugh quite freely, rubbing his hands along his thighs and gazing at Leonard, but blindly as if he were some inanimate thing on the bed, or at least something from which certainly he expected no response.

'But of course it's been a terrible day,' he went on. 'And that policeman asking questions as though the old man had been poisoned. I was completely deceived by Austen. You realize that. It's quite incredible. I've even begun to think that the whole thing was a practical joke. Apparently the old man was once employed at the Place, and lived alone in one of those stone cottages at the top end of the estate. Austen, of course, pretends that he knew nothing about it.'

He stood up suddenly: so quickly that Leonard flinched.

'Are you sure you're all right, Leonard?'

Leonard's voice answered briefly out of the shadow.

'I better go down, then. There are still people I should say good night to.'

John went to the door. For a moment he waited there, chewing the inside of his cheek and staring down at his feet as though trying to recollect something: but a second later he closed the door and hurried down the landing.

Yet no sooner had he reached the stairs than he paused again, turned round, and went back to Leonard's room. He pushed open the door.

'Are you sure? Is there anything you want?'

Leonard hadn't moved. The lamp was still alight, though his eyes were now closed. The light glistened round the lids as though only a moment before he had been crying.

'Well, if there is nothing. . . .' He waited with his hand on the door, half-leaning into the room. Then, nodding as though Leonard had indeed answered, he closed the door a second time and returned down the landing. He had begun to hum a tune.

It was dark by the time the last guests left. Clouds flowed quickly across the narrow lip of the moon, roaring across the sky in nervous sheets of vapour, silently convulsed it seemed by some freakish disturbance of the air. As Eliazbeth lighted Austen and Alex down the drive with an electric torch, Austen said, 'I hope you won't let it affect you so acutely, Elizabeth. I mean, your father seems to have taken it more to heart than anyone else.'

'No.' She was subdued.

The three of them stood by the gate, Austen, herself and Alex, their feet contained within the single pool of light.

'I'm afraid your father, although he could never admit it, tends to look on these events as tokens of some sort of deterministic force,' Austen added. 'Just as he tends to turn Leonard into some sort of mirror in which he can view his imperfections and disabilities, rather like a miser counting his money and assessing his wealth.'

'That's strange,' Elizabeth said, 'for he's said much the same sort of thing about you. About the mirror, I mean, and Leonard.'

'Oh has he?'

But Alex had begun to laugh, and then Austen; they weren't sure how serious Elizabeth had intended to be.

'Well, remember what I said,' Austen added. 'Now off you go. Good night, Elizabeth.'

She turned up the drive, hearing her uncles' footsteps echoing amongst the houses. The light from the torch flowed evenly over the stone of the Place and all sounds were muffled. The pale circle assimilated twigs and leaves and stones in its enigmatic course. Yet, when it suddenly illuminated Tolson standing there, his body thrust out from a bush, her cry seemed half-expected.

As she attempted to move past him he caught hold of her, with a kind of hesitant violence; she cried out and almost fell, her face turned up to his with a look of angered disbelief. The torch dropped and its light fled indecisively amongst the dead leaves. It filtered whitely and loosely over the grass and broken twigs.

A single, loud stroke of a bell had made Leonard get up and look out of the window. By some mysterious orientation the sun was now shining directly at the northern flank of the Place and therefore straight into his window. It was a white ball of rabid intensity set against a smooth and impenetrably black sky. White drops fell from its phosphorescent interior, draining against the blackness until they touched the earth in luminous explosions.

The next moment, it seemed, the Place itself spun round, swung ponderously on some central pivot of stone, for immediately below him appeared the valley, deeper now and darker, as though the river bed had been jaggedly gouged and, like a vast, black cell, the inside of the rock exposed. Black pygmies, with frozen limbs and faces, struggled up the heavy sides of this cavernous pit, ejected it seemed by the force of their wooden frenzy, and lit from below by intermittent lights that momentarily glistened on eyes and heads, their ropy tongues and polished hands, so that it was like a huge forest stirring beneath the shuttered face of the land. Yet the only sound, the solitary sound that escaped this pit was a simple, slight, nail-like scratching, an individual finger grazing a piece of wood. So strange and so deliberate that he spun round as though suddenly threatened from behind.

He woke to find himself in complete darkness. He was turning onto his side as he came to his senses. Gradually the faint night glow of the estate was reflected in his window. He could still hear, however, the peculiar noise.

Reaching out he switched on the small lamp by his bed. For a while he saw nothing unfamiliar, then his gaze was directed downwards by a slight movement on the floor.

From a crack between two ill-fitting boards emerged an enormous beetle, so large that at first he thought it must be the gleaming surface of a shoe. Then two tendrils groped forward to hoist from the crevice the remainder of its prodigious body. The sound plainly came from the crackling of its hard shell against the rough edges of the wood.

It stopped, perfectly still, perhaps distracted by the light. Intermingled with the blackness was a rich crimson sheen. He stared at it in terror. It was quite close to the bed.

He moved slightly. There was no reaction from the insect. He glanced round to see where there might be others. But the floor was bare. He stretched out his arm and from the drawer beside his bed drew out the claw hammer.

He got out of bed and for a while stood gazing down at the close juxtaposition of the beetle and his bare feet. Now that it was vertically observed, the redness of its dark shell was more apparent.

He stooped forward and, his eyes closed, crashed the hammer down on the smooth back. He felt its brittle disintegration beneath the steel head.

When he looked down he saw that in fact the insect had crumbled into dust. It was a dead leaf. From where he was stooping he could see several more blown together beneath his bed. He heard his mother calling to Elizabeth, then her muffled answer from her room. His mother went downstairs. He heard the bolts and the locks slammed on the back door. When he went to the window he saw that above the Place a wind was blowing. The summits of the trees were bowed down against the palely illuminated sky, the clouds flowing past in a single extravagant sheet.

Below him a figure detached itself from the deep shadow of the outbuildings, then a second, and together they walked across the faint square of the lawn. At the centre, as though to confirm the exact spot where the diagonals crossed, they paused and stood looking up at the Place. Then, as the moon sank into a torn space in the clouds, the two men moved off and disappeared into the darkness beyond the fringe of trees.

A gust of wind had shuddered the house, like a sea, the spray a flung cloud of dead leaves that spattered against the windows and the roof. Doors were sucked to and fro, and the timbers creaked. He climbed back into bed and laid the hammer beside him. For a while he gazed at its steel boss cradled on the softness of his pillow and at the two claws that swept back from this metal skull like narrow, half-formed horns. Even when the lamp went out it glistened, like a metal figure hurtling through space, yet lying quite still and close to his face.

24

The bright red lorry whined up the empty roads of the estate. It had recently been cleaned and it gleamed, curiously silk-like, in the early sun. A few loose timbers and ropes bounced on its lightly springing back.

After its growling ascent of the final slope it stopped at the gates of the Place, its bonnet almost touching the eroded ironwork, and Ewbank's black figure climbed awkwardly down from the driving seat. He stood for a while looking at the closeness of the lorry to the gate as if their juxtaposition in some way resolved the dilemma in his own mind. Rooks, which had been disturbed by the intrusion of the vehicle, now returned to the summits of the overhanging trees.

Suddenly the lorry began to run backwards. There were agitated movements inside the cab, then Ewbank reached up, wrenched open the door and pulled clumsily on the brake. He could scarcely reach the lever, poised forward on the toes of his tiny shoes. The vehicle rocked. It swayed, arrested. Pilkington climbed down from the other side. Then Tolson.

The contractor immediately stepped onto the footboard, then onto the front mudguard. His arms reached up to the top of the cab from where, after a certain struggle, he flung down two shovels. Dropping to the ground, he gave the two men instructions and watched them push between the embedded gates and begin digging the drive on the other side.

They shovelled out two symmetrical quadrants in the gravel until they were able to swing back the gates within their circumference. The three of them worked first on the right hand gate, the track of which Pilkington had dug, then on the left, which was Tolson's.

The right hand gate was moved with some difficulty, its

three hinges so eroded that within the space of a few feet the centre one snapped and the cumbersome structure groaned on the remaining two. The sound of crunching metal accompanied its retreat, Tolson standing at its head and straining to support the weight between his arms. It travelled to within a foot of its full radius and, easing its weight down, Tolson released it cautiously and began to dig out a deeper trough. He discovered a rusted hook secured in the ground and, pressing the gate fully back, set it over the lowest strut. He stood up rubbing his hands and looking at the other two with a slight smile.

They moved the second gate more confidently, forcing it back through the gouged arc and allowing its weight to smooth out the remaining pebbly obstructions. Then, half way across the quadrant, and with a sudden shower of rust, the upper hinge snapped, then the second, and the gate sprang like a compacted spring from the stone pillar. Ewbank and Pilkington leapt back, and the gate was left leaning across the drive, supported at its foot by the remaining hinge and at its side by Tolson himself. It swayed hugely as he fought with the structure, then it began to fall back against the post. As its head touched the stone the final hinge broke and the gate subsided onto the ground. Lifting it between them, they propped it against the pillar and rested a heavy stone at its foot.

The shovels were flung back on top of the cab and they climbed inside. Then, with a particularly clumsy application of the clutch and a guttural roar, the vehicle suddenly sprang forward, its tyres groping at the loose gravel, sinking slightly then spinning forward more quickly. The lorry passed between the two leaning flanges of the gates; they rested there like wounded guards as it forced its way beyond them through the low foliage of the drive.

The sun slid from the banks of vegetation, casting dull waves of shadow and reflecting from the damp leaves and the windows of the Place itself. It was still; the red metal glinted between the green slips of shrubbery and the darker stooped boughs. Across the terrace came the grating percussion of the engine. The light moved on the windscreen like an introspective eye, slow, half-glazed.

The moment Ewbank dropped onto the terrace the bolts crashed back in the shadow of the porch and the left-hand door was pulled open. John stood in the porch waiting for them to enter, and scarcely seemed to notice when first Pilkington, then Tolson appeared from the other side. He turned and led the way up the stairs.

The York Room was as the caterers had left it, the chairs indifferently collapsed or thrust to one side and the tables standing at varying angles, two of them kneeling on broken trestles. When Tolson came through the door Ewbank turned quickly to him. 'We'll just have them straight out as they are.' He pushed his foot against the nearest table and, unintentionally, toppled it to the floor.

John, standing moodily at the far end of the room, glanced round. 'Do you mind doing it quietly?' he said. Then he recognized Tolson standing in the doorway.

Tolson stood gazing in at the barren interior with a kind of stifled curiosity, half-embarrassed. He seemed neither to hear nor to see John who, as though recognizing some sort of threat in Tolson's attitude, had suddenly leaned against the wall in a vague gesture of appeal.

Pilkington pushed obliviously into the room past Tolson. Picking up the nearest table, they carried it out between them. Ewbank, his eyes concealed beneath the broad brim of his hat, reflectively smoked a cheroot, glancing occasionally at the figure across the room and then, on their reappearance, at the two workmen as they took out a second table. There was, after all, only a few minutes' work altogether, and he seemed content that they should prolong it by duplicating each other's efforts. Normally this was a job he would have delegated to a foreman. As the room was gradually emptied he began to walk up and down with increasing ease, puffing out vaster clouds of smoke. Any stranger coming in at this moment would have naturally assumed that Ewbank was the proprietor of the place and John merely another employee.

He took out his glasses and balanced them briefly on his nose to glance casually at the carved relief dominating the room.

'We were sorry about Leonard leaving, you know, Mr

Radcliffe.' He swept the glasses from his face to illustrate the sincerity of his observation. 'He was a good workman. And very reliable. We lost two of them that week. He probably told you.'

He had begun to look determinedly at John who was still watching him with an absent-minded, half-wakened expression.

'The other one, Shaw, they had to commit, you know. To a mental institution. I think that's the phrase currently in favour. He had some sort of breakdown.' He nodded his head in a gesture of self-agreement. 'Yes.' Then he looked away.

Tolson had come back into the room. He threaded his arm through the struts of several chairs and swung them with him through the door.

'And what's your son doing now, Mr Radcliffe?' He pointed at the door where Tolson had just disappeared. 'I mean, has he taken another job?'

'No.'

'I see. Well . . .' He nodded again and dropped his cheroot on the floor. He trod on it, grinding it out. 'We had a bit of difficulty with the gates when we came in,' he said, watching the slow activity of his shoe. 'I had the men dig them out a bit, but when they swung them back it seems the hinges . . .'

'It's all right.'

'This has been a very nice room indeed, has this.'

'Yes.'

The early light was flung in parallel rays towards that end of the room where John was standing, immediately below the fireplace. Ewbank looked up in some irritation. He saw that John's gaze was directed to the door. Standing there was Leonard.

Pilkington came into the room at that moment, pausing as he recognized the figure beside him, then dumbly lifting a table and carrying it out. He nodded slightly as he passed through the door.

'How much longer will you be?' Leonard said as though, concealed nearby, he had been impatiently watching their progress.

'Well, we're nearly through.' Ewbank's face was still twisted in greeting.

'Hurry them up, then. Get them out of here.' He was nervously excited, his hands trembling slightly by his sides. His father had moved from the wall and was now standing only a short distance behind Ewbank himself, in the centre of the room. One table, leaning down over a broken trestle, and several overturned chairs were all that remained of the previous day's celebration.

'We'll do our best.' Ewbank, skilfully humouring this familiar abruptness, walked slowly over to his former employee. 'Well, young man. How are you keeping, then?'

'I'm fine . . . I'm fine. Very well,' Leonard said, not knowing quite what to do in the face of such an oppressive affability. He continually glanced behind him towards the head of the stairs, as though expecting some interruption from that direction.

'You'll have heard about Shaw, of course,' Ewbank went on, glancing quickly at Leonard, then up at the ceiling which surged in hopeless frenzy above their heads. 'It's an impressive room is this, and no mistake. I was saying to your father just before you came in . . .'

'Look, can you get out?' Leonard said as though despite his agitation it were something that could be amicably arranged between them. 'I don't want you in here. Do you understand? You could have sent a couple of the men who didn't know the place.'

'We were wondering, you know, if you'd be coming back to work,' Ewbank said as though such amicability were the thing he recognized most easily. 'Now that you've recovered from your accident. There's no reason why you shouldn't, as far as I'm concerned. You know that.' He glanced behind him at John. 'Poor Shaw seems to have found everything too much for him all of a sudden. I suppose Tolson's told you. We're quite short of men now. What with the season reaching its peak.' He distributed this information equally between father and son.

'There's no reason for you to stay here, Leonard,' his father said. 'They'll be finished soon and I'll see to it that it's cleared up.'

'But why have they come?'

'It was Austen's idea . . .'

'No. Why have *they* come?' He was glancing behind him the whole time, the conversation, his distress even, a formality which he impatiently maintained. It was almost with an expression of relief that he greeted Tolson's appearance.

Whether they stood regarding each other as two protagonists or two friends, it was impossible for either of the men watching their encounter to decide. They seemed in fact to peer at one another for such a length of time that Ewbank turned round and walked over to the windows from which he was able to watch Pilkington arranging the load on the back of the lorry. The vehicle now stood fully in the sunlight, a heavy shadow underlining its red sides.

'There's no reason for you to stay up here, Leonard,' his father said again.

'Ah, now, Mr Radcliffe. You can't go hiding him all the time. He's got to live like the rest of us.' Tolson stated this quite genially, yet looking at the older man as though inviting him to reveal the extent of his concern.

'No, it's all right,' Leonard said. 'I want to see him. There's something I want to tell him.' He even laid a hand on Tolson's arm as though anxious that he shouldn't be discouraged by his father and, turning this into a more decisive grip, he began to guide Tolson from the room and along the landing to the stairs.

As they reached the staircase Pilkington, his head bowed to watch his ascending feet, was coming up from the hall. Leonard immediately turned to the stairs leading to the second floor. Having reached this landing he glanced about him uncertainly, at the passage leading off on either side and at the innumerable entrances to the rooms, then turned once more to the stairs and continued up to the top floor.

He had to stand and wait here impatiently for Tolson to come up, listening first to his feet then, as he reached the turn of the stairs, watching the tight, curled knots of his hair and, a moment later, his amused, upturned face as he ascended towards him. Leonard paused, glancing in both directions, then led the way down the passage to the right.

When he reached the gallery at the far end, however, his indecisiveness momentarily returned and he stood in the centre of the long rectangular room staring at the featureless walls and then at Tolson. He had started trembling, and quite violently. Then suddenly he began to move towards Tolson.

'Oh, Vic . . .'

He put his arms round Tolson with the same delicacy with which a man might have explored an unusually shaped stone. Except that it was with a shuddering curiosity, and that the stone bore its own peculiar life.

Tolson glanced round the room with a kind of sombre surprise, heavy, purposeful. Like a retreating spider he began to draw Leonard with him towards the door. To one side of the gallery was a darkened room, and it was into this that Tolson finally withdrew with his burden. He laid Leonard down, then knelt beside him and began to loosen his clothes, stooping forward and kissing him gently.

A short while later Tolson lay back on the dusty floor. They were silent. Then Tolson said, 'What would you have done if your father had come up? Or better still, Ewbank?' And when Leonard didn't answer Tolson rolled onto his side. 'Why, I think that's the reason you came up. Isn't that it? Knowing they were there, waiting.' He leaned forward and stroked Leonard's thighs. 'Why, you're like a woman. Once you've started you're always wanting it. And showing it, too. You can't do without it.'

Leonard moved restlessly against the floor, his head sinking and turning away. 'You ruin everything. You spoil everything.'

'There's one thing I've always wished,' Tolson went on quietly. 'I wish you were built a bit bigger. I wish you were bigger. Then we could box together. God, I'd love to fight you. It makes me bloody ache.' He moved his body aimlessly against Leonard's. 'Why don't you fight!' he said wildly. He ran his hands the length of Leonard's body. 'I wish you would at times. I wish just once you'd fight.'

Tolson stood up. He began to fasten his clothes. A moment later he went to the corner of the darkened room. There was the splashing of liquid against the wall and floor. 'Do you know what Blakeley calls you?' he said above this sound. 'The reluctant messiah. I know what he means now.'

Leonard pushed himself to his knees. He stooped forward, pulling and fastening his clothes. Then he stood up.

'Listen,' Tolson said. They were silent. From deep down in the house came the crashing of chairs. Then Tolson released a huge clap of wind. He laughed. Leonard went to the door. He stood frowning in the light.

'Why do you act like this,' Leonard said, holding his hand to his face. 'Why do you make it like this? You absolute *bastard*.' He leaned against the wall.

'For Christ's sake,' Tolson said bitterly.

'If you're ashamed of it. If you feel guilty . . . why do you keep on? It's none of those things to me. If my father had come up it just wouldn't have mattered. I wanted you. I wanted you. And then you become like this.'

Tolson was silent, standing in the door of the room. He looked about him distractedly. Then he said quickly, 'Has Elizabeth said anything to you? I mean, today, this morning.'

'No.'

'She hasn't spoken to you or anything?'

'I haven't even seen her. Why?'

'It doesn't matter . . . Len.' Tolson came to stand by him. He stroked Leonard's hair a moment. Then he kissed his neck.

He stood bowed over Leonard, his face pressed against his hair. Then Leonard swung round and folded his arms round Tolson's neck. He kissed him wildly, pulling Tolson's face ferociously against his mouth.

'You shouldn't abuse it. You shouldn't!' he said as he withdrew. He rested his head on Tolson's shoulder, staring down. 'Don't you see what it does? It makes me frightened for you. You don't know what it does to me. I don't know what it might make me do.'

He looked up at Tolson's face. 'There's no need to be like this. I'll never betray you.'

Tolson didn't answer. If anything, he seemed confused. 'Why . . . Why do you think I came up here with you?

Why do you think I *brought* you here?' Still Tolson didn't answer.

'You make these situations, then you drive me into them. There's no need. There's no need! We mustn't fight!'

'You don't know. You don't understand,' Tolson said. He suddenly wrenched himself away from Leonard. Yet it was only as if the next moment to take hold of him more fiercely. It was then that he heard Ewbank's voice calling, 'Tolson! Tolson!' He swung round with a half-cry and started down the landing to the stairs.

Leonard watched him, his face torn with despair. Slowly he began to follow him. 'There's no need to feel ashamed. There's no need to be frightened,' he said to Tolson's back. 'Don't you understand? I want you. And there's nothing else. I'll never betray you. Vic. . . .'

'Hell!'

Quite unintentionally – he seemed in fact to be tormentedly and wholly preoccupied with his own thoughts – Tolson had missed his foot on the top step and, his hands clutching out unsuccessfully for the support of the banister, he began to tumble down the stairs. It happened so impulsively that at first it seemed almost a deliberate projection of his heavy body. But the next moment the awkward convolution of those massive limbs, turning slowly and ponderously in that narrow space, had gained such a momentum that by the time Tolson reached the only bend he was unable to prevent himself from being flung round it by his own prodigious weight and sent by a series of incredible leaps and bounds to the landing below.

Such a helpless display from someone who normally was so portentously co-ordinated seemed to affect Leonard more than anything that had happened that morning. He gazed tormentedly down the empty stairs as though there were still some visual evidence lingering in the dimly-illuminated space, and it was with almost paralysed gestures that he began his own descent. When he reached the landing below, Tolson was standing with his back to the wall opposite the foot of the stairs and looking at him with a sombre and hideous smile which seemed to indicate, if nothing else, a need to express some sort of extreme threat.

'And what do you expect me to be, then? Frightened of *you*? Giving in to you!' Tolson cried, referring to their previous conversation, as if by some ludicrous assertion of his personality he could continue as though the accident had never taken place. 'Is that what you're trying to say? Expecting me to be frightened! Can't you see what I am!'

'It doesn't matter now,' Leonard said quietly, watching Tolson as though he had now reached some important decision. He seemed almost in tears.

In Tolson himself there had appeared a sudden hardness. Almost the need, it seemed, to exact some sort of revenge.

They gazed at one another in silence for some time, standing so still and intent that John, emerging from the stairs below, did not see them until he almost collided with his son. He looked up at them in terror.

'Leonard! . . . Vic. Mr Ewbank's looking for you.' They seemed dazed, completely unaware of his presence. 'Mr Ewbank's looking for you.'

Tolson turned an almost hysterical look of threat on him, then more potently on Leonard. As if re-animated by Tolson's look, Leonard said incoherently to his father, 'It's all right, is it? We're coming.'

He immediately turned to the stairs.

John watched first Leonard then Tolson pass by. He seemed about to speak, his mouth opening, but he watched them in silence as they sank below him.

When they reached the first floor Ewbank came along the passage from the York Room accompanied by Pilkington.

'Ah, so you've found the two miscreants,' he said, calling to them in an unusually loud voice and expressing with this last word that tone of ridicule upon which were hinged all his remarks and gestures directed at the Radcliffes. 'I must say, they were forever off on their own when I had them working together, so I'm not so sure exactly what advantage it would be if Leonard *did* come back.'

Perhaps intended as a note of badinage, the remark emerged from Ewbank as one of specific condemnation. But even if he were aware of the ambiguity of the words he saw no suspicion of offence in any of the three faces confronting him. If anything, Leonard and Tolson appeared to be suffering from extreme shock, while John seemed lost in a private wilderness of regret and confusion.

It was only as Tolson reached the broad turn leading down into the hall that he looked back, past Pilkington and Ewbank who were close behind him to where Leonard stood on the landing with his father. 'I'll see you again, then?' he said to Leonard.

He continued to stare up at the two figures, Ewbank and Pilkington waiting beside him, until Leonard nodded his head.

'All right, then,' Tolson said.

He swung round and crashed down the stairs to the door and disappeared.

Leonard and his father walked back in silence into their inhabited part of the building, leaving open the partition door and going down to the kitchen. As they passed Elizabeth's room she called Leonard's name; but it seemed that John himself was too immersed in his thoughts to give her any attention. It was only when he entered the kitchen, and Stella told him that Elizabeth was unwell, that he realized Leonard had not followed him down.

Having already picked up his coat at Stella's suggestion that he should call the doctor, he dropped it into a chair and hurried back up the stairs.

He emerged on the landing just in time to see Leonard coming out of Elizabeth's room, and apparently excited, hurrying to his own room and closing the door. When he entered Elizabeth's room, she appeared to be fast asleep. He was unable to wake her. Her face was flushed and her forehead extremely hot. He stroked her cheek a moment, calling her name. Then, a short while later, he hurried out to telephone the doctor.

Ewbank, lean and almost child-like in his grip of the huge circumference of the steering wheel, watched the Place vibrate in the mirror. The leaves, then the branches, enveloped it until, swinging abruptly round the descending curve of the drive, he was distracted by the sight of one of the metal gates lying across the opening to the road. The heavy vehicle lurched, braking, and almost stopped.

Then, gradually urged forward by its own weight, the lorry ran onto the metal skeleton. The tyres, scarcely deflected by the gate, rode up over its narrow ribs, the wheels driven up slightly onto their springs, then released suddenly as the eroded metal snapped in several places so that, as the truck turned out into the road, it left in its wake a strung network of debris. Ewbank stopped and got down. After kicking the tyres and glancing beneath the axles of the machine, he walked back to the gate and examined the fragments.

He called the men from the truck to clear the debris to one side, and, while they worked, strolled back up the drive. When the building came into view he stopped and glanced about him as he might have examined any site which his tents had recently abandoned, and very much as a man might inspect a derelict home for the last trace of things he might wish to take with him. Except that the contractor's gaze was arrested by the building itself as if that blackened stone tent had somehow escaped dismantling and he was now considering whom to reprimand and whom to send back to load it on his red, titanic lorries. When he turned back down the drive it was in a grave and restless mood.

The two men had finished clearing the drive. The largest segment of the gate was propped against one of the posts. After examining it, Ewbank instructed them to lift it onto the truck. As they drove off he looked back at the chimneys of the Place diminishing over the roofs of the houses and said, 'It reminds me of something, does that . . .' glancing at the two figures beside him as though having to identify it in so many words would somehow obscure his meaning. Tolson, however, was gazing straight ahead through the windscreen, apparently unhearing; and Pilkington, in the cramped space, was struggling to light a cigarette.

When they reached the yard Ewbank got down from the large vehicle, lit a cheroot, and stood gazing up at the incredible emptiness of a clear sky. The sunlight fell directly into the yard. There was a light breeze. He set Tolson and several other men onto dragging out the wet tenting that had accumulated in the sheds and stretching the creased and greying canvas across the paddock. He seemed scarcely satisfied until the alleys between the sheds and the grass beyond were full of the flattened shapes, like sucked bodies, swaying and billowing with every variation of the breeze.

25

There had been a sudden change of temperature and clouds had compressed the hills beyond the city, absorbing their rocky outline so that they appeared the least substantial thing in all that landscape. The jutting crown of the city was lost in the lowering mist, and the Place, poised on the summit of the opposite escarpment, intermittently appeared through the white clouds like a constantly moving thing. It made a slow and indeterminable progress. Leonard, standing at the window of his room, observed a figure cross the lawn below in the same direction and at the same pace as the one that he had witnessed the night before. It cast a similar bleak look at the building before continuing towards the path that circuited the Place.

He left his room and went down to the front entrance. The doors were still open from Ewbank's departure and he stood there a while listening. Then he descended to the terrace. No sound came from the heavy shapes of the trees. Stooped down, moist and bulbous, they rested like plants on the bed of a lake. The mist, exhaled by the land, absorbed everything.

He stood there so silently that a man, coming up the drive and passing within a few yards, disappeared round the side of the building without noticing him. It was the doctor. Leonard heard his feet echoing on the gravel at the back of the Place, then the sound of the closing kitchen door. It was several minutes, in fact, before some instinct made him turn round and stare into the shadows on either side of the porch.

'I was hoping I'd be able to see you, you know, without having to knock or to trouble your family in any way,' a man's voice said.

A moment later Blakeley limped from the shadow to the

right of the porch, then stopped as if Leonard's physical presence were in some way disadvantageous to his real purpose. He coughed and took a cigarette from the pocket of his raincoat. Yet he didn't light it. It remained as an extremely white object in his hand.

'I was hoping to see you last night,' he added, coming one step nearer then stopping compulsively again. 'I didn't want to knock. And I couldn't see you about.'

He gazed vacantly at Leonard, then suddenly, almost impetuously, crossed the gravel towards him. Yet the sound, muffled by the mist, seemed cautious. Peering into Leonard's face, he said, 'Do you have any respect for me?' and as if such a question itself set off some fresh agitation in his mind, he limped heavily around him and went to stand a few feet away.

'Why do you ask me?'

'Tell me. Did you see me from one of the windows and come down on purpose? I mean, you came down here to see me? You didn't think it was anyone else, did you? You see, I'm not too well. The fact is, I suffer a lot from depression.'

He had stated this almost in one breath, so that when he paused tiny clouds of vapour rose from his mouth. As yet he had not moved any nearer and the intimacy of what he said contrasted strangely with the distance that separated them.

'Certainly I get very pessimistic moods,' he added as though Leonard had made some reply to this, and a moment later he began to laugh slightly, a helpless yet antagonistic sound. 'I can't very well describe it without making it sound, well, *mercenary*. That's the root of it. Because you can't communicate it, because everything in the end is so cut off, I get these feelings. You see yourself surrounded by people, yet you know that you're as far away from them as if you were on an island.'

Leonard looked about him disconcertedly, at the trees, at the shrouded pinnacles of the building. He was about to ask some question that might distract Blakeley when the older man added suddenly, 'Someone died here yesterday, didn't they? An old man wasn't it? Who came to your famous party.' But before Leonard could answer he went

247

on, 'You see, I've asked you, do you have any respect for me, but I know really that you haven't. That in fact I wouldn't have to ask the question if you had. Respect is a thing that shows as plainly as a man's face.'

'And is that what you came up here for?' Leonard was standing now with his arms clasped to his shoulders.

Blakely looked away. 'No.'

The cigarette which had been in his hand was now distributed in fragments around his feet, and he began to take out another, allowing his fingers nervously to play with it before putting it into his mouth. Almost immediately he snatched it out.

'Why did you come out to see me?' he asked.

'I don't know. I suppose I wanted to see if it was a person. That I hadn't imagined it, I mean.'

Blakeley laughed, and began rubbing his face. 'Well, so you think I'm a ghost now.' His head turned slowly and he stared round at the trees as though counting their trunks, acknowledging their presence by slight, compulsive nods of his head. Leonard continued to watch him, though still standing several feet away, and beginning to rub his arms urgently through the thinness of his shirt.

'You see,' Blakeley said in such a different pitch of voice that it seemed as though a third person he'd been expecting had now arrived. 'I've reached the point where I've got to decide . . . to decide whether it's all right to go on as I am, or to step back and make a criticism of it. That is, do something that there'll be no going back from, something that nobody will be able to deny. If a man wants to count at all in his life, he's got to come to that sort of decision, hasn't he?' He looked at Leonard darkly, nodding his head with a kind of minute vexation. 'That's what your father did. I know.'

Leonard had suddenly moved closer and for the first time appeared to recognize the expression on Blakeley's face. His eyes were discarded-looking, and swollen like bruises. He looked so sickened and ill at that moment that Leonard almost raised his arm towards him. But whether to protect himself or in a gesture of consolation he couldn't determine.

'I suppose my behaviour the other day put you off,' Blakeley went on, but now in a plainly sarcastic tone. 'I mean, what my daughter was saying, the night I took you home. About being *Spanish*.' He smiled heavily at Leonard, leaning forward slightly to gaze into his face. 'You mustn't be misled by what I said. I don't know what it is. But I get carried away when I'm with Tolson. I tell you, I don't know why. But there's nothing I regret more. Yet I can't help it. It's a terrible thing. And I drive myself mad afterwards with the thought of it.' He coughed, and lurched vaguely to one side, but continued to look at Leonard with the same tormented expression. 'I hope you'll excuse me, Leonard. Being like this, I mean. It's just that I've had something of an argument with Kathleen. But that . . . that doesn't matter any more now. What I wanted to say is . . . it's what I said in the church . . . that the same place that catered for the need of one family in the past is now sufficient to cater for the similar needs of twenty thousand... What I really meant was, *what are you going to do about it?*'

For a moment Leonard didn't answer. Then he said, 'But is that my responsibility? Am I responsible for that?' Yet without any surprise or incredulity, as if having accepted Blakeley's manner and appearance, this absurdity conflicted with neither.

'That's the trouble, isn't it? At one time you were responsible, but now no one demands it of you, no one bothers you with it, torments you with it. It isn't that God's no longer relevant, no longer real, it's simply that God's no longer interesting.'

As though the increasing violence of his words had spread to his body, he burst into another and severer fit of coughing. 'And the result is what?' he went on, his eyes streaming with tears and his face screwed into an apoplectic expression. 'Nothing! Nothing but this soot and rock and smoke, and the scuffling of workmen. And nothing, not one drop of these acres of blood can be shown to mean one mortal thing. That's what I'm asking. I've had enough of the working man, the ordinary man and his shit-stained mind. I want a king, I want dignity, and authority . . . and *certainty*. Because without it it's the death of all extremes, and it's only at the extremes that man is finest and noblest of all.'

Leonard had moved closer. Some instinct to rest his hands round the man's throat made him touch Blakeley, laying his fingers for a second on the damp lapels of his coat. So gently, however, that Blakeley interpreted it as a sign of commiseration and immediately burst into tears. It was the same soundless crying that was an indulgence of the man. That it came out of some real yet completely incoherent distress, Leonard had no doubt at all: but he only gazed at Blakeley with a profound and exhausted look and let his arms drop to his sides.

'It's not wrong,' Blakeley said. 'It's not wrong to think like this. But no one cares. The agony of it all is that no one cares, no one gives a damn. I might feel like this but it's no longer even a part of life.' The thick band of mist drifted between the two figures. It consumed Blakeley so that Leonard, who had stepped back a pace as if to answer him, stared at the moving strand of air as though his subject had suddenly been wafted away. 'All that people do nowadays,' Blakeley added out of this anonymity, 'is see to what extent they can entertain each other's sense of despair.'

He suddenly moved forward, nearer to Leonard, the mist draining from his face as though he were moving at speed. 'I'm a Catholic. And I go into all these different churches. They should be unified. They should all become the one thing. But what does it matter? Can you tell me? What does any of it matter? The fact is, we're of no more importance than if we'd never existed.'

Leonard, however, had begun to look away towards the far end of the terrace. Very faintly came the sounds of someone moving cautiously up the drive.

'Do you know, when I first came to live round here,' Blakeley said as though oblivious of where he was and to whom he was talking, 'I was still working down the pit. Kathleen had just been born, and only half of the estate had been built. The house here was still standing in a sort of park. It was winter. I used to come up here and look round the rooms. There was an old man with a dog who was supposed to look after the place. But he was as deaf as a post. Either that or he didn't mind who came in. It'd started snowing, and the builders had knocked off until it cleared. I went up in that window one morning. Everything was covered in snow. All the roads and the foundations and the causeways they'd just laid out. Curving this way and that. Just little ridges of snow. But the whole of it, the whole side of the hill, was like a giant skeleton. A giant. Just casually laid out there waiting.'

Leonard was staring anxiously through the mist at the huge shapes of the trees at the head of the drive. The crunching of feet on the gravel was much louder and seemed to be coming purposefully in their direction.

'I know lots of facts about the Place,' Blakeley added, speaking now quite calmly, with an almost insane composure, for his body was still shaken by minute sobs and intermittently his face would be screwed up as though he were frantically resisting the need to cry. 'Did you know that the first Radcliffe recorded in the family was a tutor to Richard, Duke of York and later a master of ordnance under Henry V and a Governor of France? I know all these things. And that the Radcliffes got the land around here from that forfeited by the Lancastrians. And that part of the family was Catholic and were even leaders of the Pilgrimage of Grace, while another part, those that lived here, were Protestant and joined the Parliamentarians in the Civil War. There's lots I know. The first Wesleyan chapel in town was built with Radcliffe money. The first Member of Parliament for the town in 1832 was William Radcliffe. . . .'

Blakeley had now come so close that it seemed to Leonard that those bruised eyes were touching his face. He seemed completely unaware that someone was approaching them through the mist.

'They even financed two privateers during the eighteenth century to prey on Spanish shipping from Liverpool and Cork. The "Duty" and the "Avenger". And with the money they built the first school for underprivileged children. . . . The fact is, I met Tolson last night, Vic, and he told me an extraordinary thing. He said that he'd been with your sister, Elizabeth.'

Blakeley had now grasped Leonard's arm, and so violently that Leonard had called out. The next moment, however, he had started forward in order to anticipate the arrival of the intruder. Blakeley had at last turned round, still holding Leonard, and was staring in the same direction.

At the end of the terrace, where it abutted onto the drive, a figure had appeared. It came towards them a moment, blindly, then turned towards the path at the side of the Place. Only then did some movement on Blakeley's part cause it to look up. And with something of a shock, for it stopped abruptly and even moved forward slightly as though to confirm an unpleasant impression. Then, without any further sign, it walked on, holding up a stick against the wet foliage, and disappearing round the side of the building.

'Austen. Your Uncle Austen,' Blakeley said.

'You know him?'

'Oh . . . I used to know him. Did you hear what I said? Your sister . . .'

'But how do you know him?' Leonard asked, more disconcerted by this than by anything Blakeley had yet told him.

'Can't you hear what I said!' Blakeley cried out. 'I met Tolson last night. And he told me.'

Leonard had swung away, but the movement was just as impetuously arrested by the weight of Blakeley clutching his arm. He tried to prise up the fingers, half-dragging the older man with him towards the spot where Austen had disappeared.

'Don't you care about your sister!' Blakeley demanded.

'Why should you be concerned? What does it matter to you?' Leonard suddenly cried, yet scarcely coherently. He seemed to be in a state of complete dejection, hopelessly confused, and unable to follow two consecutive words of what Blakeley, with increasing agitation, was saying.

'But your sister's the one person I admire and respect above all others. She's the one innocent party in all this. And Tolson . . . if Tolson has carried out that sort of assault . . . I'm speaking delicately, of course . . . if he's done that, then he ought to be destroyed like . . . although

252

I've only met her briefly. It seems you're quite right. There's no remorse in Tolson at all.'

Leonard, who had been rubbing his arms with an increasing rapidity, now held one hand to his forehead. He seemed completely distraught and vulnerable, almost insensible. Having reached the corner of the Place, he was suddenly uncertain in which direction he should go. He glanced about him at the misty foliage as though it were somewhere he had never seen before.

'All day . . . ever since I last saw Tolson I've been trying to think of an image that would really express what I meant,' Blakeley said, standing now decisively in the path that Leonard would have to take in order to escape. 'And it was only as I came up here that I thought of it. I was walking up through the estate, and hardly able to find my way, when I heard a sound coming from somewhere. For ages I couldn't decide what it was. Then I suddenly realized it was an aeroplane. Flying, God knows where, at God knows what speed. But don't you see? Just think of all that energy, all the years of work, the planning it. By thousands of people and at enormous cost. . . .'

Leonard appeared not to hear. His face seemed melted by the mist, his eyes glazed. Blakeley caught hold of him more firmly, with both hands, and swung him round to speak frantically into his face.

'Just think of all that energy put into something which in five, in ten years at the most, will be redundant and broken up, destroyed. But think if it had been put into something that would outlast the lives of the men who made it. Don't you see? It's *that* that's at stake.'

'Was it . . . would it be about two years ago that you knew my uncle? That you knew Austen?' Leonard said slowly, and with great difficulty. It seemed that a muscular inertia restricted his speech, his mouth scarcely opening, his lips thin and stiffened.

'Austen? Yes. Perhaps two years. Why? Do you think it gave him a shock? Him recognizing me? Maybe I ought to have acknowledged him. It's been such a long time. He might not have wanted me to.' He pulled heavily at Leonard's arm. 'What I was saying. Isn't it true? Isn't it?

253

Haven't we had enough of the working man? Of his smallness, his fawning ways, his cheapness. Above all his *cheapness*. The way he reduces everything to his narrow-minded size. These shitty little pygmies, under a compassion for whom they now hide all the old ambitions for power. Compassion! Was ever any emotion more cynically deployed!'

These phrases, said despite their apparent violence in an astonishingly controlled voice, seemed to strike some note of familiarity in Leonard. He looked at Blakeley in astonishment. It was, even to the intonation of the voice, an uncannily perfected imitation of his uncle. But not the uncle he knew, but rather that of a man speaking to himself in the privacy of his room. Blakeley, however, seemed completely unaware of any duplicity. If anything the sentiment, or the attempt at its portrayal, had left him exhausted and dazed, and he almost whispered the last remark. 'If anyone not only knew but *understood* the working class their immediate and only reaction would be to vomit.'

His words, however, were interrupted by a remarkable occurrence; one so unusual that it had the effect of distracting both men from everything that had been said.

The mist, which until now had enclosed them within an area only a few yards in diameter, concealing all but the silhouette of the nearer trees and the closest flank of the Place suddenly lifted at one side like a curtain. Immediately visible through a gap in the trees was a distant yet minutely defined view of the valley. The sun illuminated the opposite flank, and individual buildings and even vehicles, the light glinting from their windows, could be seen with an astonishing clarity. This brilliant conjugation of buildings and rock was revealed so suddenly that both men seemed bewildered by its appearance. And yet scarcely several seconds elapsed before the mist descended and enclosed them once again. For some time they continued to stare in that direction as if the momentary impression could only have been an hallucination. Yet on Leonard's face there gradually appeared an expression of intense and private rapture. His eyes had glazed and his lips parted in a half-smile.

Blakeley seemed drained of all feeling and strength, though he still clung to Leonard's arm determinedly. 'No, don't go,' he said. 'I wanted to ask you . . . if you'll come and see me . . . tonight.'

From the back of the Place came the murmur of voices, then the shutting of a door. Feet crunched on the gravel, then thudded more heavily on the earth path. Blakeley looked up in alarm.

'It's terribly important,' he said, releasing Leonard's arm and preparing to back into the bushes close by. He was already ducking his head as if to conceal himself.

Leonard was beginning to move off. He seemed now completely abstracted, his mouth still parted as though pressed back in a smile.

'I mustn't see your uncle. Not yet,' Blakeley said as Leonard left him.

'I don't want to see you again,' Leonard told him, wrenching his body as if it were still restrained by Blakeley's grip.

'Wait. Just a few seconds. It's very important.'

But Leonard had already disappeared. He could hear Blakeley's voice calling after him, then the next moment he passed the doctor, who looked up almost in terror at his sudden and silent appearance. Before he could speak Leonard had plunged on, beginning now to run as if pursued.

When he entered the kitchen, however, Austen scarcely looked round. He was sitting with his back to the door and appeared to be in the middle of some discussion with his father.

'How is Elizabeth?' Leonard asked formally. Yet he was so flushed and excited, he began to walk restlessly about the room.

'Your mother's with her now,' his father said. 'It seems it's nothing serious. Some sort of delayed hysteria. It's passed now and there's no need to worry.' He gazed at Leonard with a strangely resigned expression.

Then Austen said quite suddenly, 'Who was the man out there?'

Leonard stared at his uncle with a fixed and bitter

intensity. He now moved rather slowly about the room, touching each piece of furniture with the tips of his fingers. 'His name's Blakeley.'

'How long have you known him?'

'Not long. Only a few weeks.'

Austen sat waiting, his back still to Leonard. Eventually he said, 'How did you meet him?'

'Tolson.'

'Tolson?'

'He introduced us.' And when Austen made no response to this but continued to stare down at his feet in, for him, an unusual attitude of dejection, Leonard added, 'He says that he used to know you. About two years ago.'

'Yes,' Austen said without looking up.

'He does an incredible imitation of you,' Leonard went on, now quite red, his excitement twitching his face into a vague smile.

'An imitation?'

John had turned to watch Leonard, but as if in a reverie.

'The amazing thing,' Leonard went on, 'is that he doesn't realize it's an imitation. He carried on as if it were all his own thoughts and feelings. Don't you think that that's rather frightening? Unusual, I mean?' And when it seemed that Austen was about to reply to this, turning round in his seat to look up at his nephew with a hard and agonized expression, Leonard suddenly added to his father, 'Is that how the doctor described it? Delayed hysteria? Did he say what had caused it?'

'Well, we explained about yesterday. The circumstances of the old man's death,' John said. 'He said it was undoubtedly that.'

'And Liz? How is she?'

'She's very quiet now. He's given her a sedative.'

Leonard suddenly sat down. But only for a moment. It was as if desperately to gather together wildly dispersed energies and feelings.

He stood up almost immediately, just as Austen said, 'Isabel rang me this morning. She had some party this afternoon which she couldn't put off, otherwise she would have come with me. But she was wondering, Leonard, if you could go along and see her. It would only be for a short while.' He stood up now as if to dismiss him. 'It will mean leaving almost straight away if you're to catch her.'

'But why should she want me?'

'It's something she wants to ask you, I believe. Alex will be there too.'

Leonard went to the window. The mist drifted slowly by. Beads of dull, leaden moisture stretched across the black fringes of the stone.

'I shall have to take my raincoat,' he said, even more thoughtfully, rubbing his hand nervously against his face. 'And there's Blakeley still waiting out there. I'd better leave by the front.'

He turned and went quickly to the stairs. Then he paused as though reconsidering his decision. He glanced at his father's face a moment, swung round, and continued up the stairs as if this unexpected invitation to his aunt's had coincided with a more urgent and compelling errand.

26

A tall, ornately built church stood in a Georgian square, its stone a sooted scroll of rock sprung from the deep bed of the houses. The mist trailed in uneasy pennants from its tower, its swirled descent reflected in the swerving stone itself. Tombs hung like massive fruits amongst the stunted trees. The place was sucked down by stone, the black trunks of the trees the veins of its heavy body.

Leonard walked purposely as if, by exaggerating each mechanical movement, he could compensate for a lack of substance. It was at his raincoat – a fawn light-coloured garment folded neatly over his left arm – that his aunt stared when she opened the door. Leonard stood facing her at the top of a broad flight of steps. He was frowning slightly, and sombre-faced.

'But why haven't you put your raincoat *on*?' she said. A film of moisture had settled over his clothes and the exposed parts of his body. His eyelashes glistened with the damp.

'You'll be soaking.' She closed the door and picked up a clothes-brush from a hall stand. 'I hope you're in a good mood if you're going upstairs.' She indicated the open door on the first floor, facing the head of the stairs, from which emerged the low murmur of voices. 'There are several people who'd like to meet you. But there's no *need* for you to go up.'

She swept the moisture from his shoulders and back. A thin shower fell on the thick, dark blue carpet covering the hall floor. The furniture here was of pale, unvarnished wood. The strokes of the brush on Leonard's shoulders suggested a muted elation on the part of his aunt: they were almost absent-mindedly ferocious.

'Austen said that you wished to see me.' He stood facing the stand. In the centre was a mirror in which he was clearly reflected.

'I can't imagine why you didn't wear your raincoat. It's ridiculous. Yes. There is something. We can go in here to discuss it.' She indicated a comfortably furnished sitting-room, lined with books, which opened off to the right of the hall. Several reading lamps relieved the gloom of the afternoon.

Leonard hadn't moved. He still held his raincoat over his arm, and seemed preoccupied with the sounds that came from the top of the stairs. His head was lifted in acute attention.

'Can't we talk about it here? I hate to go into different rooms to do different things.'

His aunt brushed her small hands over her dark velvet dress. A few drops of moisture gleamed on its heavy surface. 'Do you know why Austen has gone to see your father?'

'No.'

'It's to try and persuade him into leaving the Place. It's so obviously the best thing for him to do. But now he refuses completely. Before, he was seriously considering it. But yesterday's events seem to have changed his mind. For some reason he now says he'll only go if he's forced out.'

'And what do you want me to do?'

'If you asked him, explained to him, then I'm sure he'd agree.'

258

'I can't see any reason why he should leave, though,' Leonard said, glancing again in the direction of his aunt's sitting-room above. 'In any case, where would he go now?'

'We would take care of that. If necessary he could go south. With Alex.'

'Alex?'

'He's entirely behind the idea.'

'Is he here, then?'

'He went out. Apparently he couldn't tolerate my guests.'

'Is that the Provost's voice I can hear?'

'If it's so important you can go up there in due course. All I'm asking you to do, Leonard, is to think carefully about this. Your father's not growing any younger, or happier, by staying on at the Place. The sooner he leaves the better. I can't understand why you don't want to help.'

'There's nothing I can do,' Leonard said, looking at his aunt with some surprise, and as if intrigued that she shouldn't realize it. 'If you want to drive him out, then well and good. There's probably nothing anyone can do to stop you. But I'm not going to ask him to leave. It's like asking a man to dismantle the whole of his life. And in any case, it's too late.'

'Too late? But what do you mean?'

'Shall we go up?' He moved to the foot of the stairs, stepping aside to allow his aunt to precede him.

'But aren't you concerned with what's happening to your father?'

'Concerned?' The idea seemed to bewilder Leonard.

'Or is that something you can't feel?'

'You are an extraordinary woman, Isabel! Why should I be concerned about all this?' He looked at his aunt in amazement, then suddenly burst out laughing.

She regarded him in silence, no less astonished herself. 'Don't you feel anything for him?' she said slowly.

'Feel? Yes, I feel things about him. For example, at the moment I feel I could kill him.' He was still laughing, and watching her through tear-filled eyes. 'He's a weak and feeble man. Do you want to take away his last crutch and support?'

'He's not a feeble man. He's not a weak man, either.'

'Then there's no need to worry.'

Leonard was laughing so openly at Isabel that she seemed both unable to understand or to take seriously anything he was saying.

'I've told you, it's too late. If you'd wanted to help him you should have done so when he first went there. Are we going? I'm standing here like some lousy gentleman just to give you the privilege of leading me up.' This was stated with such evident bitterness that his aunt stared at him in alarm, then suddenly stepped past him without another word and immediately began to climb the stairs.

'I'm sure I don't know how seriously to take you,' she said. 'But it's not only your father. There's your mother. And there's Elizabeth . . . And there's you.'

'The Provost is here, isn't he?' Leonard said. 'Things run through my mind and I can't remember them two minutes together. You did say that? The fact is, it's really him I was hoping to see.'

Isabel was being driven up the stairs, so closely was she pursued by Leonard. When she glanced round she saw that he still held the raincoat clutched tightly over his left arm.

'You won't discuss it then with your father?' she persisted.

'Look! Will you leave me alone!' Leonard suddenly pushed past her, violently thrusting her to one side. 'Will you leave me alone! Will you *stop*! I can't do anything about him. It's too late.'

Yet, despite his agitation, he appeared to enter the room before her quite calmly and relaxed. As he did so the shaft of a hammer momentarily protruded from the lining of his coat.

'I'd say it was a thin, round shape with grooves scored in the side so that a *hollow* shape with corresponding grooves inside would fit onto it . . . the alternate grooves binding together.'

Several people murmured to one another but the Provost's voice dominated them all. As Leonard and his aunt entered he continued his analysis although his head, and the heads of eight or nine other people, turned towards the door.

The room was high, with three tall windows overlooking the square. As Leonard was introduced, several people continued talking as if to accommodate a certain uneasiness at his entry. Placed centrally on each of the three unbroken walls of the room was an eighteenth-century Radcliffe portrait, full-length and in shape reflecting the proportions of the windows. Dark, with pale, narrowly-boned faces, they appeared in the muted light like so many reflections of Leonard himself.

His aunt took him to one side of the room where a sideboard was laden with half-full plates of food. He shook his head, gazing round at the seated figures, and beginning to play restlessly with the folds of his coat. He was becoming increasingly excited, and when his aunt tried to take the coat from him he snatched it away as though he were being attacked. She let her arms drop and looked away, turning her attention to the Provost. He was still speaking, his lips set like a navel in the belly of his face, his mouth scarcely moving as it accommodated the most cumbersome words. He was the only other man in the room. 'I wouldn't say that clearly defined it,' he said.

'Then, a cylinder with a continuous and unbroken groove along the whole of its length.'

'A circular groove.'

'And not necessarily the whole of its length surely?'

'How would this be, then? A solid, cylindrical shape with a continuous, circular groove starting from one end.'

'And ending where?'

'At any distance from its beginning. That's fair enough.'

The people laughed. Leonard had begun to nod rather eagerly.

'Definition is a marvellous thing,' the Provost said.

'But surely not one required in your trade,' Leonard said. Yet no one turned in his direction.

'And how difficult,' a woman continued.

'The most difficult and yet *apparently* the easiest. There is, of course, a certain allegory to be made there, Provost.'

'Yet the thing is, once an object has been defined, however wrongly, it's very difficult to think of it in different terms.'

'Can there be a wrong definition? Isn't it either accurate or misleading? One of the two.'

'Accurate to what?'

'Well, to our sense of it.'

'But doesn't a thing *exist* irrespective of our perception of it?' The Provost's face was so remarkably ugly when he spoke that it clearly held a certain fascination for these women. As though aware of it the Provost had turned to Leonard to ask, 'Can you tell us what it is we are trying to describe?'

'Trying to define, surely, Provost,' a woman said, smiling at Leonard.

'To define.'

They waited, relaxing, regarding Leonard with a subdued interest. His face was covered in a thin sweat and his eyes glistened as if reflecting some distant and intermittent light. He held the raincoat even more rigidly against his side. Since coming into the room he had in fact grown extremely pale, and had gradually moved away from the wall to stand some distance towards the centre of the floor, a shadowed projection it seemed of those tall portraits which flanked him on three sides.

'I imagine it's some sort of void. A spiritual vacuum,' he said eventually. They glanced up at him uneasily, though one woman had begun to laugh.

'What *thing*? What object?' his aunt said deliberately.

'Admitting, of course, that it is of no importance whatso-ever,' the Provost said as though genially attributing some humour to Leonard's remark, 'what in fact do you think it is?'

'But why aren't you outside, preaching and administering the gospel?' Leonard said with a sudden burst of anima-tion, glancing round anxious that they should recognize the ease with which he had discovered the solution.

'Ah, now,' the Provost went on, apparently unsurprised, 'you mustn't try and amuse yourself at *everyone's* expense, Leonard. One can discriminate in one's criticism of people just as I can in the way I choose to spread Our Lord's word. Do you understand what I mean?'

Leonard had begun to fumble with his coat. Draped over

his left arm, his left hand was concealed now by its folds. There was a sudden agitation beneath them; then, after a moment's hesitation, he said, 'Christ is a flame, an element of our imaginations, not a religious ornament. Tell me. How many cars have you got? What's your salary? Then tell me where you keep your vision, inside the boot or on the back seat?'

'Now, Leonard. . . .' The Provost looked round reassuringly at the women; they seemed disturbed not so much by the remark as by the disjointed and obscure manner in which it was presented. They scarcely looked at Leonard.

'I don't think this aggressiveness is directed at me personally so much, is it?' He glanced up at Isabel to see what she might advise in the face of this behaviour. 'But just to keep everything as simple as possible, what do you think it was, Leonard, that we were trying to define?'

For a while he didn't answer. He glanced behind him once at his aunt, then at the portrait directly opposite him as if he had forgotten there was anyone else in the room. The colour which during the previous moments had mounted rapidly to his cheeks, just as quickly faded and his face assumed its original pallor. Then, quite suddenly, he said, 'If I answer correctly . . . correctly mind you, and in no way else, can I ask you a question in return?'

The Provost leaned back, his small mouth depressed at its corners. 'Well, yes.' He smiled with a certain shyness.

'Exchange is no robbery,' said the woman who had laughed initially at Leonard's behaviour.

'Indeed not.'

'But it's with a provision,' Leonard added with a growing intensity, corresponding, it seemed to a suddenly resumed agitation of his raincoat. Several of the women now watched his almost feverish movements with some embarrassment. 'I want you to answer my question with the same care and attention which you used in reaching your definition.'

The Provost nodded. 'If it deserves that amount of interest, Leonard, of course we shall. Do you know what it was we were attempting to define?'

Leonard looked round at their curious faces. Several

glances cautiously avoided his slow look. 'I think it's a screw.'

'Ah. . . .'

'You see.'

'We should have someone come in each time at this point to see if they can recognize the definition.'

'Yes, it was a screw.'

'It's extremely good. It just goes to show.'

'But didn't you decide on the object before you tried to define it?' Leonard said. 'Where's the communication in that?'

His aunt said, 'It's just a game we were playing.'

It seemed that now she wanted him out of the room; for her, at least, his behaviour was not unfamiliar. It was merely a nuisance that had to be removed.

And it appeared in fact that Leonard was about to comply. He bundled his coat tightly under his arm and glanced round at the apprehensive faces with a rather apologetic look. But suddenly he moved away from the door towards the windows and began to stare down into the square. He stood there for some time, an uncomfortable murmur rising behind him. Then, as his aunt began to move decisively towards him, he appeared to recognize someone in the street below and turned back to the room with a half-frightened expression, coming almost face to face with Isabel herself.

'What I wanted to know,' he said, staring at the Provost with the same alarmed look, 'is, did Christ ever make love to a woman?'

His aunt had begun slowly to walk across the room as if she might have been moodily deliberating on subjects which had no relevance or interest here. The movement itself appeared to deflect any immediate reaction, and when someone began faintly to protest the Provost said, 'Well, I think one must assume that such a question is not posed mischievously but more out of genuine naïvety.'

'Do you *know*?' Leonard said impatiently.

He glanced once more out of the window, as if the justification for his question lay there. Gas lamps were being lit round the perimeter of the square, and their yellow glow melted faintly through the mist close to the windows. Then he moved across the room towards the door. The frightened expression had still not faded from his face.

'He never knew a woman *physically*, if that's what you mean,' the Provost said. 'And as to what is now a not uncommon rejoinder – was Christ a homosexual? – the answer is again in the negative.' He seemed familiar with this particular text, speaking with a calm vigour and confidence. 'You see, these are old and famous heresies, Leonard, and are far more frivolous than, say, trying to define correctly a natural object. Do you understand? The best work for the Kingdom of God is done from a background of either of two things, a prophetic temperament, or a contented and stable mind. And I'm afraid, Leonard, mine is one of the latter. As to your question, one cannot talk of Our Lord in these terms. Purely physical attributes may have a certain sensational significance, but I can assure you it's far more important to me to try and define a nut and bolt as a nut and bolt, and Christ as Christ, than to try and overlap the two.'

'Yet Christ *was* a man,' Leonard insisted, staring at the Provost with a peculiarly threatening expression. 'He was *flesh*, and He was *blood*.'

'Yes.'

'How then could He be a man different from other men? *Physically*, I mean. *Physically*!'

The Provost was staring at Leonard's hands. Both of them were now spread nervously over his raincoat, the garment itself rolled so tightly that he might have been holding a swab over a particularly painful wound. 'Jesus Christ was the Spirit first,' he said, 'only secondarily was He the Body. He invested, if you like, the physical apparatus of a man.'

'Ah, then you can separate a man! You can separate someone *physically* from what they are?' Leonard went on with mounting excitement.

'The Church does so to the extent that a man's soul is never irredeemable.'

'But if you say Christ invested the physical apparatus of a man, just how much of it did He invest? How much? And where did He draw the line? Did He decide to invest so much, and then no more? . . . Surely He never *suffered* as a man. As a man *condemned* to his body.'

'Christ suffered as a man. And Christ died as a man. There's no doubt of that.' The Provost's attention, however, was divided between the curious play of Leonard's hands with his raincoat, now a totally unrecognizable bundle, and his face, which had such an acute look of self-absorption that it seemed impossible that he could be speaking at the same time with such animation and energy. Their audience, by its silence, might not have existed for either of them.

'If He could bleed and sweat and be exhausted why couldn't He feel equally the natural desire for a woman, or for another man? What is it that a man wants from such love that Christ Himself had no need of? How on earth can we accept Him as an example when He was only half a man Himself?'

'A man, from human love, requires a bond and a reassurance, which, as a man, he can only approach or *fully comprehend* through his body. Christ, as the Son of God, had such communion with the Spirit that such a relationship for Him would be meaningless.' The Provost stroked his face, his fingers delving into the loose skin.

'But if Christ came to earth as a man why didn't He come as a man that we know? Why didn't He use His sex? Isn't it from sex that all our problems and confusion rise, yet He refused even to acknowledge it by His own example? What a pitiable and feeble thing He must have thought our earthly love was. Something He didn't even bother to experience, to *invest* even, though He took on, as you say, the physical apparatus of a man. What can He tell us about our lives when He didn't even bother to acquaint Himself with the half of it that oppresses and confuses us the most? What a wretched and irrelevant thing He must have thought our physical love. He had no need of it.'

But Leonard was no longer talking to the Provost, or to anyone else in the room. He had sunk down on a chair and seemed in absolute despair, bending forward and nursing the coat, tears beginning to run down his face.

'What a contemptible and putrid thing the body is,' he said in a reflective tone. 'It does nothing but destroy us, hanging on us like a sickness, devouring us until we're assimilated by it, and die with it. . . . And Christ was separate. He destroyed His body, showed His contempt for it, hung it up like a bit of canvas. He cast it in the face of men who have to live *within* their bodies, taunting them with salvation, His spiritual grace.'

He was staring at the Provost as if he had lost completely any sense of where he was and as if he were trying passionately to recollect some thought or feeling which persistently slipped his memory.

'What a trivial thing you've made of Christ. You've cut His body away from His soul, and condemned *us* to live with the body and to be ever wanting for the soul. You've condemned us to be separate things when our only salvation lies in wholeness and completeness. When the body and the soul are the *one thing*.'

'God is our vision of everything that transcends our own physical lives,' the Provost said quietly, no longer interested in the theoretical interpretation of his own beliefs but in trying to control Leonard's outburst by his own calmness and manner. 'Our physical nature is an impediment to that state of Grace, to the spiritual world which, in one form or another, we all long for. To separate the Body from the Soul was Our Lord's gift to man. He *freed* the soul from the human body and gave us the true gift of immortality.'

'His gift! It was His *damnation*! . . . His curse!' Leonard sprang up, the sweat running freely from his forehead and his eyes filmed with tears. 'To make us free of our bodies was to *despise* everything we are, to despise our only hope of salvation. And now that Christ is dead, what are we left with? What is the legacy of this magnificent corpse? We're left with His scepticism of the human body. His relegation of it to *sacrifice*! But that isn't *our* life. He never even lived our life. Our lives are committed wholly and completely to our bodies. What could He know of that if He never loved!'

He began to move hurriedly about the room disregarding

the people who watched him with embarrassment and dismay. Several of the women rose to their feet.

He reached the door and suddenly began to look around him in confusion. Then, apparently seeing his aunt coming towards him, he lurched to the stairs, the coat now being nursed at his side like a broken limb.

For some time after he had vanished, the occupants of the room sat in silence, the room itself darkening under the sombre clutch of the night and the mist.

When Leonard reached the street Blakeley was standing on the opposite side, almost hidden against the high wall of privet that surrounded the church. For a while he followed Leonard, walking abreast on the opposite side of the road until, as they reached the narrow lane that led like the neck of a noose from the square to the main road beyond, Blakeley crossed quickly towards him. Neither of them spoke. Leonard walked with a determined stride and with an expression that had none of the wildness of a few moments before. Strangely, he appeared quite composed. He gave no sign that he recognized or even noticed Blakeley. They walked side by side in silence.

Evening traffic crashed by on the main road. As they approached the noisy stream Blakeley stopped, stretching out his arm to delay Leonard, and nodding his head slightly as if in confirmation of some private opinion.

'I wanted to ask you something. I suppose you realized ... you knew that I'd followed you.' His face still held the look of heavy resignation which had been Leonard's last glimpse of him. 'I wanted to ask you if you'd come and see me tonight ... see me perform. I promise you, it's *the last thing I'll ever ask you to do*.'

He laid such peculiar stress on this phrase that Leonard, who had submitted to being waylaid, glanced at him with a sudden expression of alarm, almost as if his own thoughts had been pierced. Yet even after he had hurriedly agreed and noted the name and the address of the club where he was to appear, Blakeley continued to hold rigidly to his arm and to stare anxiously into his face. Then, without a word, he hurried off into the growing darkness.

27

A dull redness suffused the smoke and outlined the packed shapes of darkly dressed men hunched tightly together in the narrow spaces between the tables. The long, broad trough of the room was like a huge stained window, one that had crashed intact from a high wall. As one of the components of this sombre mosaic, Leonard stared up at the white pool of light over the stage where Blakeley, in his costume of genial imbecility, tapped his cigarette into the top of his pouched trousers and sang a song which, over the murmur of conversation and laughter, could scarcely be heard. His toothless mouth was held open as if sucking in the air of his audience's amusement. As he interrupted his song to recite a joke, they laughed, a dolorous, hard sound like the crushing of stone; then they watched, moodily reflective, their eyes turned dangerously onto his slight figure. He beat his fists against his thighs, stooping towards them. Their laughter withdrew, then surged forward, an impatient, temperamental tide. Waiters pushed between the groups of men, trays poised on their raised arms. Across the room Leonard saw Alex.

His uncle's bronzed face was turned up to the stage with a questioning eagerness, absorbed in the grotesque figure and the smouldering laughter around him. He talked animatedly to the men crouched at his table and they laughed, diffidently, relaxed. One of them banged his back. Then, from a quick look in his direction, Leonard realized that he too had been observed. The men at Alex's table drew back, turning towards the white figure on the stage. The lights were intensified to a crescendo of music as Blakeley stood there singing.

Some laughed still; it seemed, despite that pleading voice he had been consumed, dissolved by the light. Others stared blindly into the brightness, trying to discover some focus within it. The club had a reputation for its lighting displays; innumerable effects were obtained from expensive batteries of lamps which normally would have been sufficient to illuminate a stage several times its area. Gentler lights now sprang down like sprays and the dazzling concentration was broken, then turned off. In the sudden darkness of the stage a slight figure could be seen stumbling, slightly dazed, towards a door at the rear. Above it, a faint red neon sign outlined the word, 'Artists'. The hall was lit up.

'So you're not above coming here,' Alex said after struggling across the room. He seemed pleased to have discovered Leonard in such surroundings, and alone. 'It's the second night I've been here. I've really enjoyed myself. There's nothing quite like this, Leonard, where I come from.' He watched his nephew acutely. 'That last performer they've had both nights I've been here. He seems rather strange, though. What do you think?'

Leonard scarcely glanced at his uncle. After a short silence he said, 'When are you going back down south?'

'I've still a few more days leave yet.'

'From making cars?'

'I intend to see your father first, Leonard. Before I go back.'

His nephew was suddenly thrust forward as several men pushed between the tables.

'I was hoping to see you at Isabel's,' Alex went on. 'But apart from that Provost, I was the only male guest there, so I found some excuse to come away. He's a fool. The Provost, I mean.'

He looked at Leonard as though expecting some sort of affirmation, but Leonard continued to gaze uninterestedly at his uncle, almost bored. Men's voices suddenly roared, and a large group began to press in through the double doors at the end of the room opposite the stage. Red canvas curtaining shielded the five windows down one side.

'Have they heard any more about the old man, yesterday?' Alex said, and when Leonard shook his head with the same aloofness he added, 'You know, I haven't been above catching certain references these last two days about me and . . . what shall we say? The manufacture of cars. As though, through working in industry, I'm somehow not as complete a person as those who don't. Or at least, as those who don't have to.'

Over Leonard's shoulder he suddenly caught sight of the man who, the day before, he had expelled from the grounds of the Place. Tolson was staring at them with a moody, vaguely threatening expression, and seemed unconcerned whether he had been observed or not. Alex glanced at Leonard but he appeared completely unaware that they were being overlooked.

'What references do you mean?' Leonard said, staring down at the plastic surface of the table.

'Oh, your father's for one.'

'He probably resents your success, and ascribes it no doubt to a lack of any real conscience or feeling.'

'Why should he do that? He's scarcely in a position to criticize anyone, let alone someone who . . .'

'It's the nature of your work that antagonizes him. At least, we must assume that it is. After all, cars aren't much for a man to have as the end of his life. And he's very much like that, I'm afraid, always looking for some justifiable *end*.'

For a while Alex watched his nephew in silence. Then he gazed almost abstractedly across the room at Tolson.

'I'm not very good at arguing. Finding reasons for what I do,' he said. 'Though I am – although I say it myself – a good *negotiator*. But coming here, to a place like this, it means something to me. These men. This is something I can understand. And looking at it another way . . .' He continued to stare beyond Leonard's shoulder. 'You can't change men's nature, only the context it has to work in. It's that that makes for better things. The context of a man's life, rather than the man himself. The man himself, that's something different.'

'Oh, I agree with that,' Leonard said amicably.

'And the manufacture of cars, or of any consumer goods for that matter. I realize perfectly well that they're only a commodity, a means to an end. But simply looking at it as crudely as you can, without the manufacture and the export of cars this country would go to the dogs.'

'Yes, I understand that,' Leonard said with increasing friendliness, even beginning to smile. 'You see, I'm only trying to suggest something of the way in which my father feels.'

Alex clenched his hands and pushed them onto the edge of the table. 'I'm not so sure how to describe it,' he said, 'but I'll admit that by isolating himself, even though I don't understand the reasons, your father's found for himself some sort of authority. Or power, if you like. I mean, you tend to listen more to what he says than you would to somebody who lived a more ordinary life. But the fact is, it's made him a bit potty as well. All of you. And I don't mind. No, I mean that. People tend to be too much like one another these days. But your father even thinks, for example, that Austen organized yesterday's affair just in order to humiliate him.'

'But didn't he?'

'No . . . no. Certainly not as far as I'm aware. I don't think Austen could do that sort of thing, anyway.'

'Don't you? You don't know Austen. What a merciless and frustrated ambition for power he's got. I mean, did you know that he still believes in the divine right of kings? If you mention it to him he'll laugh, of course. But inside him, he believes it. And something as absurd as that. He's a fantasist of the strangest sort.'

Alex looked at Leonard seriously a moment. Then slowly he began to smile. He glanced quickly across the room, then said, 'No, the only power I understand is the power of men like this who, whatever their strengths and weaknesses, work and live together for their common good. Because they know that's the way they can survive, all or nothing. That's power. When you can share it in the bottom of a mug of ale after a day's work.'

'You mean the only way for *them* to survive,' Leonard said with the same friendliness of tone – one so unnatural, it seemed, that Alex began to look at him with sudden suspicion. 'But what of those who *won't* . . . No, let's just say, those who *can't* reduce themselves to the lowest common denominator? What's to become of them? And in any case, this isn't only power you're talking about. It's *force*.'

'Force? What force?' Alex said, and with a certain preparatory movement, for Tolson had risen from his seat and, despite the thick crowd separating them, was clearly intending to come over.

'Do you remember the York Room at the Place where we had the meal?' Leonard said with the same friendly tone. 'And the carved figure over the fireplace? Do you know what the figure is? Imagine this as the room. There's the double doors. Those are the five windows, and at the end, where the stage is, stands the fireplace, and in the centre that carved figure . . .'

Several things, however, happened all at once, distracting Alex from the curious parallel Leonard was tracing. Just as Tolson reached them the lights were suddenly dimmed and from the shadow of the stage, at which Leonard was gazing as though suddenly in a trance, appeared a huge and hideous face.

It was so large and misshapen, and so white, that there was no possibility that it could be human. Each feature was wildly distorted, the nose bulging forward like a corrugated trunk, and the mouth pulled back from twin rows of deformed and giant teeth. Deep crevices grooved the skin like wounds. As the spotlight retreated slightly, it glistened on a black flange of hair, almost metallic in its luminous sheen, and indicated beneath the face, like a narrow and exhausted stalk, the figure of a man. A belated roar of laughter hardly concealed the disturbing effect this apparition had had. One or two women had screamed, and a single voice called out in a kind of bated defiance.

Then, at the humility of the voice that suddenly emerged from this grotesque vision, the men laughed. It was a heavy, stinging crash, dispelling their apprehension.

'I've come. And to prove it, I'm here. You didn't think I looked like this without my make-up on, did you, love? No. But did you guess? It's what my wife calls her going-away face. Every time she sees it . . . Yes! You've got it! That's right!'

The face, completely motionless and inexpressive, reflected nothing of the feelings which lay behind it. A burnt sound of self-amusement, a metallic laugh, slid from the same swollen lips which, a few moments before, had suggested a melancholic disaffection. It was as if the face were detachedly resigned to its appearance.

'Now don't look at me like that, love. Because I'm not as

273

pretty as *you* it doesn't mean I haven't got feelings. I *feel*, I do.' Another, more relaxed kind of laughter broke out at this preposterous idea. 'I feel, I do. I might have an ugly front but I've got a lovely behind.'

The men laughed with a certain relief, staring at this absurd intruder with increasing shyness.

'I mean, to look at me you'd think I was perfectly normal. Yet when I was born my father took one look at me and said . . . Ah! What? I've heard that one before? Shall I tell you a little secret? You've heard *everything* before. Perhaps because you think I look like this I don't know. That I haven't any problems. You ought to see my girl friend. If you think I'm not very attractive, you should see her. Last week she frightened a pig into giving birth to three mutton chops. No, though, it's not everybody who's as lucky as me. I mean, don't you think really that I look just a *bit* fine? That it's not *quite* as bad as it seems? If I thought that, then I might even want to go on living. Do you know? Do you think . . . if you think it's just a *bit* better, just a *teeny weeny* fraction better than it seems, just the smallest fraction of the smallest part, do you think you could call out, "Yes!"?'

He waited a moment. 'Come on. Please, ladies and gentlemen. If you just *think* it's not quite as bad as it all seems, could you call out, "Yes!" *Please*!' He waited again, the mask turning for the first time, giving its features a simulated look of anxiety.

Then several people called out, 'No!'

There was a burst of laughter, then a louder and more confident shout. '*No*!'

'Oh, dear. What shall I do? How could you be so cruel? How could you be so wanting in the finer human senti-ments? . . . How would you like to wake up next to this on a morning love? Just your cup of tea? She thinks it's real, you know. Poor old soul. She's right. It's all solid bone under here. Good thick stuff all the way through.'

A slight tone of derision had hardened into a more petu-lant sarcasm, the mask turning from side to side as the head beneath it grew more animated. 'I'm not looking my best today. I think that's the trouble. I had one of my teeth out yesterday, you see. My first milk one. This here at the back.'

A white hand with no apparent attachment to the figure emerged from the darkness and held back the rubber lip to reveal several large and eroded stumps.

'I've suffered. You don't know how much I've suffered with it. You don't realize. There've been times when literally, I've just not known what to do with myself. You don't understand what it's like to be like this. But even then, if you think that *I* don't look too good you should be up here where I'm standing. You might laugh at me, but my God, was there ever a more pitiable and snotty herd of . . .'

A table had fallen over, scraping, then crashing with the multiple percussion of breaking glass; like a giant insect, its legs protruded in the air, rocking slightly from some object pinned underneath.

Leonard, turning from a sudden and hysterical recognition of Tolson, had bent forward to retch over the white underside of the plastic table, one hand clinging to an upturned, metal leg, the other still clutching his raincoat. For a moment he seemed completely helpless, swaying with the table, then he swung round almost in a complete circle. He seemed to see and to move towards the door in the same instant, a simultaneous impulse which gave those watching the impression that he was being ejected from the room by some invisible force. And as he hurried towards the end of the hall a larger figure detached itself violently from the surrounding crowd and followed him out.

The men stood in darkness. The light on the stage had dimmed, and for a moment there was no illumination at all. Then simultaneously several lights sprang on, and in such profusion that the men shielded their eyes, calling out, blinded.

It was some time before the correct combination reduced the brilliance, and it was only then that Alex, standing quite close to the upturned table, was actually aware for the first time of Leonard's absence. Tolson was also nowhere to be seen. As Alex hurriedly peered round the room he had a distinct impression of his brother, Austen, standing to one side of the door; then the confusion and the crowd masked everything. All around him men were looking at one another with an unaccustomed dumbness as though waiting for an event to begin.

28

The mist, swirling in thin clouds, was illuminated by still blue arcs of light. Leonard felt a new alertness, a breathlessness, his mouth open to a quick harsh breathing. His raincoat trailed beneath his arm. It swung loosely with the heavy weight of the hammer, its hem dragging along the pavement.

The street was now only marked by the diminishing blue intensities in the mist. Tolson held him by the shoulder, half-supporting him.

'What's the matter, then?'

'I don't want to see you.'

'What's the matter with you?'

'I don't want to see you.'

Yet he walked in rhythm to Tolson's own pace, his body sunk within Tolson's arm.

'I don't want to see you.'

Tolson loosened his grip, his head moving towards Leonard's with a careful, perceptive affection. 'What do you mean?' he said. His voice, though gentle, was heavy with threat.

Leonard shook his head. He was drenched in mist, his face glistening with a fine mesh of drops, beaded on the narrow fringe of his hair and across his sharp brows. He seemed dazed.

'Here.'

He pulled Leonard to a halt. He folded him in his arms and, his head bowed like a man consulting a watch in the dark, he kissed Leonard's mouth.

'Why don't we go somewhere?' he said after a while. He was rather breathless, looking up at the mist as he might have glanced at an opening door. Suddenly he released Leonard.

But only a large dog passed them, soundless on the wet pavement. The next moment he wrenched Leonard's shoulders more fiercely. 'Look, I'm not running after you all the time! What're you trying to prove? What the hell is it?'

For a moment Leonard didn't answer. Then he looked up at Tolson directly for the first time. He still seemed shocked and distracted.

'Perhaps, then, I ought to make a time to see you,' he said after a while. 'If I make a definite time then I'll have to keep it.' He stood thinking about this proposal, staring up into Tolson's face and drawing his raincoat more firmly over his arm.

'If you're worried about us being seen together,' Tolson said, 'we could go off somewhere on the bike.'

'No. No. I don't think so. I don't think so. If I see you, it has to be somewhere I *know*.'

'But what's all the bloody mystery about? I'm warning you. Don't start playing these games with me, you shit.' He glanced wildly about him for a second. 'Can't we go somewhere now? You bugger, I want you.' He was nodding his head at Leonard in a violent kind of agitation.

Leonard had backed away slightly. 'Doesn't Audrey go out on Wednesday nights?' he said hurriedly. 'To her mother's, somewhere.'

'Yes. She goes out Wednesdays.'

'Oh, God. I don't know. I don't know what it is.' He ran his hand across his face. The next moment he drew it away and stared at the beads of moisture that lay in his palm. He rubbed his hand across his forehead and looked again at the drops of liquid collected there. 'I'm terrible at arranging anything,' he said, still gazing at his palm, and even holding it towards the vaporous glow of the nearest lamp. 'I can never plan things and see all the unexpected contingencies that might arise as you're supposed to. And the worst thing – I suddenly lose all idea of what things mean.' He dropped his hand and stared down at the pavement as though moodily deliberating with himself. 'I don't know . . .'

'Look, there's something I want to tell you. About Elizabeth.'

'It doesn't matter.'

'But I want to tell you.'

'I already know. She's told me. It doesn't matter. Now will you leave me alone!'

'She's told you? Has she told you?'

'It's all right. She's told no one else.'

'But I wanted you to know. It wasn't all one-sided.'

'It doesn't matter!'

'I want you to know.'

'It doesn't matter!'

'I want you to know. I was wrong!'

'It doesn't matter! Leave me alone.'

Tolson had begun to follow Leonard down the street, one hand stretched out to his shoulder as if uncertainly trying to waylay him.

'I'm telling you. It was wrong. I'm telling you now.' He caught hold of Leonard more firmly, preventing him from walking any further. 'Now don't go cutting up like a tart! It wasn't one-sided. I've said I was wrong. I'm telling you.' Tolson was desperate.

A familiar grimace of pain had reappeared on Leonard's face, yet he seemed completely preoccupied with searching for something in the folds of his coat. Only when he had apparently found it was he still, and he began to stare intently, not at Tolson's eyes, but at some point at the top of his forehead.

'Don't go acting like a prick! I've told you! Don't act! Don't act with me! I've told you!'

Leonard made no reply. He scarcely showed that he'd even heard Tolson. He stood perfectly still, his right hand pressed awkwardly across his body and buried in the folds of his raincoat, his eyes turned up to the dark knots of Tolson's hair. He looked very much like a man about to take possession of something which for a long time he had known to be his.

'Ah, fuck you!' Tolson said, flinging Leonard from him, yet almost in tears. 'Fuck you! Fuck you!' He buried his head in his hands. 'You never let up. You never let up. You *shit*!' He wiped his wrist across his eyes and suddenly glanced round at the mist as though for the first time recognizing its confining obscurity. His eyes glistened. He looked massive, penned-in.

Still Leonard watched him, almost remotely.

'Fuck you! Fuck you! *Fuck you*!' Tolson screamed. He kicked out against a lamp-post. The metal structure shivered, rasping, and something dropped into the road. 'You stinking, shitting runt. You runt. You runt!'

Tolson seemed to reach up as though, suspended above him, were some means of hoisting himself from the ground.

Then suddenly, he dropped his face into his hands. 'Len. Len. Give us a chance, love.'

Leonard had begun to walk away, his feet echoing, a tiny, hollow sound flung out between the houses and buildings. An extraordinary silence had descended in the mist. The next moment they were consumed in a yellow ball of fluorescence as a vehicle swept by on the road.

Leonard walked stiffly, with a strange angular movement listening to Tolson's feet as he began to follow him.

'What do you want? What do you want?'

They walked like this for some distance, separated by three or four yards. Then Tolson suddenly began to laugh. For a while he appeared to be talking to himself, his eyes screwed up in a half-smile, his lips moving rapidly and soundlessly. Then suddenly he increased his pace and was soon walking alongside Leonard, stooping slightly towards him as though to look closely at his right cheek.

They walked along like this until they reached the turning which led from the main road up onto the estate, Tolson laughing to himself very quietly, his eyes never leaving Leonard's face for a moment.

Then, as they reached the sideroad, Tolson stepped into Leonard's path.

'Well, you said Wednesday, then?'

'Yes.'

'Between eight and nine.'

'Yes.'

Tolson was still laughing, yet watching Leonard intently. A moment later he slowly bent back his arm and, with a half-cry, smashed him across the face. The sound itself had seemed almost one of warning.

Leonard stumbled, then he regained his balance, his arms flung out as though invisibly supported.

Tolson didn't move. He still watched him intensely. 'Wednesday, then. You'll be there?'

Leonard made no response.

'If you're not, I'll come and find you. Wherever you are. I'll find you.' He waited. 'Is that all right, then?'

Leonard nodded. Tears had sprung to his eyes.

Tolson stared at him a moment. Then he swung round and broke into a run. Leonard, standing still, listened to his feet. They seemed to move at an unbelievable pace so that, rather than a fleeing man, they suggested far more the rapid and metallic chatter of a machine.

29

On the Wednesday afternoon John had several visitors, and as soon as they had gone he immediately set out to search the Place for Leonard. After a while he found him standing at a single unshuttered window of the York Room.

Leonard didn't turn from the window.

'You knew they were here?'

'I saw them come up the drive. And I saw them go down it.'

'They gave two unusual accounts of your behaviour, at Isabel's, and at a workman's club.'

'Yes.' Leonard was extremely pale and lifeless. He moved suddenly away from his father and walked across the room, glancing about him as though casually searching for something. 'Well, is that all they said?'

'No.' John paused indecisively by the window. 'All three now have the idea of disposing of the Place.'

For a while Leonard didn't answer. He stood by the fireplace gazing up at the relief. Eventually he said, 'Are they in a position to do that?'

'Providing they can get the majority of the family to agree with them. And that the trustees raise no objections. I don't think they'll have any real trouble.' After a while he added, 'It will probably mean the conversion of the Place . . . or even its demolition.'

'Its demolition?' Leonard turned and gazed across the width of the room at him. Then suddenly he stared upwards. 'How did that get in here?' he said.

John looked up, and saw nothing but the cellular relief of the ceiling itself. He glanced at Leonard, uncertain whether to treat this as some further eccentricity of his son, one no less peculiar than the scenes which had been described to him by Isabel and Alex a short while before. Yet as he started to speak he saw, hovering in the shadows above their heads, the shape of a large moth. Leonard continued to watch it, his head flung back with a peculiar, static violence. His eyes had rolled back in the shell of his skull with such contortion that it seemed at any moment a cry of pain would escape from his gaping mouth. To John he looked quite insane.

The moth was like a nervous element of the air itself, barely substantial, its flight created from innumerable shattered movements and flecked convulsions. For several seconds it was lost to sight, then a tiny agitation in the corner of the room brought it back once more into focus. Leonard watched it with a kind of snarled intentness, his hands and arms swinging restlessly by his side, as though he scarcely suppressed a desire to leap at the insect and snatch it from its hopeless meanderings through the room.

'Why, are you hoping to catch it, Leonard?' John said, as though in some way to divert his attention.

Leonard murmured in his throat and slowly lowered his head. His eyes, from their straining after the elusive shape, were wide as he stared at his father with a lunatic look of abstraction.

'Whatever was that scene you created at Isabel's on Sunday?' his father went on. And as Leonard's features relaxed to something more recognizable and normal, he added, 'They apparently included some sacrilegious statements about Christ intended to provoke and upset the Provost, not to mention the other people present.'

'Was Isabel upset?'

'Not at your arguments so much, it seems, as at your behaviour.'

'Are you sure it wasn't just slightly the arguments? After all, people like their arguments clean and white, and with no blood on.' Yet even as he said this he waved his hand at his father in a gesture of frustration. 'But what's it matter? No doubt she's right to turn her concern at my ideas into her concern for *me*. It's what they're always doing, isn't it, father? They're crying out for a touchstone but the moment it's there. . . . Oh, God!' He clasped his hands to his head with the same impulsiveness with which he might have snatched at the moth. 'Why do I go on talking like this? All this nonsense. All these stupid aphorisms. Worse. Far worse than Austen. And it all means absolutely nothing to me. Absolutely nothing. It's just nerves. I'm terribly nervous today.' He smiled with a sudden and insidious slyness at his father. 'Have you got the time? Do you know what time it is?'

John watched him a moment, suspecting some sort of ridicule. Then he shook his head. 'Are you no longer concerned whether we stay here or not?'

Leonard had begun to smile. 'What is it? Are you beginning to suspect that I don't understand you?'

'I don't know about understand. You don't even seem to be interested.'

'But I am interested. After all, I'm part of the thing, aren't I? All your life you've hidden here. Waiting for some sign, some revelation. Yet when it comes, are you sure you'll be able to *recognize* it? I mean, what really exhilarated you about the death of the old man was that you thought it was a sign. The moment you throw open the Place, the moment you endow it with all those shady powers of determinism you affect to despise, something terrible occurs, a sign, a message. The old man was simply putting God's mark on the event: "This is wrong!" It was something sufficient to incur a warning. Isn't that how you see it?'

Leonard had begun to pace up and down the room as if he had suddenly remembered he had somewhere to go. Only once did he glance up at his father, and then with a look of extreme distaste. The next moment, however, he added, 'It's too late for you to give up the Place now.

You've been offered one sign here, and now you can wait more confidently for the next. And if you've hidden yourself away here all your life, until your muscles are too stiff and your bones too corroded to move, why, there's always your son to rise up in your stead! What has your isolation meant if it can't be measured in *him*!'

'Don't fight me with this,' his father said. 'Don't force things onto me.' He looked distractedly about the room, then at the window through which the light was now beginning rapidly to diminish. The shadows of the trees crept into the room, deepening the dusty crevices.

'No, it's too late,' Leonard said. 'When I told Isabel, she didn't understand. There's no choice now, either for you or for me. You've made sure of that. That's *one* thing you've made absolutely sure of.' Yet as he turned violently towards the door his mother appeared in the opening. Behind her, in the passage outside, was the vague shape of another woman.

'What? Why has she come here?' Leonard said, yet so quietly that they scarcely heard. He had stopped in the centre of the room, staring down and moving restlessly from one foot to the other. Then, as the woman came through the door and his mother attempted some sort of introduction, he asked her directly, in a whining voice, 'What has *she* come up here for?' It was Kathleen.

Bowing her head awkwardly towards him she indicated that she wanted to see him alone. They stood there for a moment in silence.

John had begun to move towards the door. As he did so he was attracted by a movement above Kathleen's head, and looked up to see the moth fluttering from the ceiling. As he was introduced to the visitor he saw the insect settling down, its slooped expanse of wing suddenly still and seemingly pinioned to the wall immediately above the door. Then, for no apparent reason at all, he turned and looked at Leonard with an outright expression of alarm.

Leonard had flushed, in childish embarrassment, grinning suddenly and grotesquely at his father. Then he looked about him, his eyes averted, as if overcome with shame.

283

The moment was so inexplicable, the silent interchange between father and son, that Kathleen looked about her in confusion, glancing upwards as though she half-sensed its cause located in some object above her head.

John had reached the door. For a moment he still stared at Leonard in alarm. Then, catching his shoulder against the door itself, he swung round, took Stella by the arm, and left the room. It seemed as though he had been flung through the entrance.

'I'm sorry,' Kathleen said. 'I wouldn't have come unless it was important.'

Leonard shook his head in a mild bewilderment, looking at the empty doorway. For a moment it appeared that he would rush after his father.

'My father's ill,' Kathleen said. 'I wondered if you would come and see him?'

'What? But I can't! What have you come for?' He lifted his head, listening. His parents' voices came from a room close by.

Disturbed by their presence, Kathleen came further into the room. 'He's ill. He came home ill last Sunday night, and we can't do anything with him. He wants to see you for some reason, but we can't let him out of the house. The fact is,' she added, coming so close to Leonard that instinctively he began moving away, 'he tried to attack me last night. That's really why I've come.'

'What?' Leonard rubbed his face as though since his father's look he hadn't understood or heard anything at all. 'What? What do you mean?'

'I shouldn't tell you about this. Because I know he doesn't want you to know. But he went away for two years. I mean, in prison. And he's never really recovered from it. From the experience of it.'

She had come so close to him that she was almost touching him, yet appeared to be completely oblivious of his presence, staring at some point just past his shoulder, and talking as though she were reciting certain ideas to herself. Her voice was toneless, as if what she described was almost irrelevant.

'He's been in bed the last few days. And last night I was

bending over him, arranging the bed clothes, when he pulled a knife out from under the blankets and stuck it in my back. . . . Oh, I don't mean that literally,' she added as she saw Leonard's response. 'I mean, it would have stuck in had it been sharp. As it was, it was completely blunt. It's just an old knife we keep in a drawer for cleaning shoes. He knew it wouldn't *do* anything. In fact he hardly pushed it against me at all. Yet he was so serious about it, watching me like mad to see what I would do. My mother's frantic. We don't know what to do. She's frightened that if she tells the doctor he'll be put away or something. And that'd kill him. And all the time he's asking to see you, saying he wants to talk to you. My mother thinks if you'll just go and talk to him, at least he'll calm down. You see, it's not my idea at all. I wouldn't have come here if she hadn't got on her knees and implored me. Do you understand?'

Leonard listened without moving, staring fixedly at his feet, his hands thrust stiffly down at his sides, a certain rigidity which suggested that the words called up some sort of determination in him.

'You see, he's not a violent man at all,' Kathleen went on. 'It's always been as much as one can do to get him to smack one of the children when they've done something wrong. And whenever he has brought himself to do it he's always sat around for hours afterwards brooding about it. To think of him lying there with that thing hidden under the blankets. . . . And the strange thing is that once he'd done it he began to hold his own side and groan. Just as if he'd stabbed *himself*. He made such a din about it that my mother tore the clothes back and looked at his side, certain that he'd stuck it in himself. But there wasn't a mark. Not a scratch. The big baby. As soon as she *had* looked he started crying in that stupid way he has . . . well, not stupid. He can't help it. But ever since then he's been asking for you.' She glanced hurriedly at Leonard for the first time, then added, 'You know . . . I suppose you realize he gets these attachments for other men. I mean, that's what lies right at the root of the trouble. He's in love with Tolson, insanely in love with him. And he can't do anything about it. But with you. . . . You see, he's so jealous of you that it's killing him. No, I mean that. Because he can't do anything about it. That's why he thought if you became interested in me. But...' She suddenly burst into laughter, looking into Leonard's face very closely. 'You see,' she said sarcastically, 'he's dying of love!'

She had stepped back and taken a cigarette from her coat pocket. Leonard watched her lighting it as though, from within the confusion of events, he was trying to recollect whether he had seen her smoking before. He looked at the cigarette acutely, and most intensely of all at that point where it disappeared between her lips. Occasionally they trembled as though she were still suppressing her laughter.

'But what can I do?' Leonard said.

'And there's another thing,' she added. 'He's absolutely serious when he talks about himself as an artist. He means it. It's the only justification he finds for all his troubles and his own hellish nature. You mustn't disabuse him into thinking he's not one. All these theories he has about things. You see . . . you must see that it's just his pathetic attempt to try and fight off this obsession he has for Tolson. He's just trying to subdue it, that's all.'

Leonard had begun to watch her suspiciously. The cigarette, which trembled as she spoke, dissolved in a thin wreath of smoke, filtering upwards and towards one end of the room. He suddenly seemed quite shy. 'I can't do anything. There's nothing I can do,' he said abjectly.

'Do you know what he once told me?' Kathleen went on. 'He once told me that whenever he'd done something on which he felt he could congratulate himself, something in which he had succeeded, he heard a voice whispering in his ear the whole time, "Not enough, not enough . . . *not enough*!" That, well, that's what he's hearing now as he lies in bed.' She plucked the cigarette from her mouth and began to examine it closely. 'He's so jealous of you he can't bear not to be with you, not to share all the feelings you have, everything. It's a sort of love in reverse, isn't it?'

Leonard began to look around him as though searching for some object he knew to be concealed in the room. He hurried from wall to wall, his momentum gradually increasing and becoming almost frantic. Then, with a sudden wildness, he said, 'Have you any idea . . . I mean, do you know what time it is?' And before she could answer he had hurried to the window and, reaching up with an excessively awkward movement, had released the catch and pulled down the upper half. Immediately a chill of cold air swept through the room. 'Don't you think it's hot in here?' he said. 'Look, you go down and wait for me, will you. Let me see now . . . I won't be long. There are one or two things. I'll have to go to my room and get my coat, for one thing.' He stood watching her, rubbing his hands together with a peculiar violence. 'Is that all right, I mean?'

'You'll come, then?'

'I haven't got long. I'd better warn you. I have to go somewhere else. But I can come for a bit. It's not quite dark yet is it? I mean, it's not late.' He smiled at her, then the next moment appeared to forget her completely, striding out of the room with a sudden and extraordinary energy.

Kathleen stood in the silence for a while looking round at the darkening interior. A single and diminishing beam of light streamed through the window. She slowly crossed to it, and stared out through the double panes that now occupied the lower half of the frame.

The view seemed to intimidate her, for she suddenly stepped back. At the same moment something flew up from between her feet. It sprang to the window and beat dully against the glass like a piece of cloth. At first she scarcely recognized the object, frightened more by the agitation of the air itself, drawing her head back in a strange snarl.

Then the moth sprang upwards and was immediately plucked out through the open window. It was caught by the stream of air that swept round the building and was drawn up over the summits of the darkening trees. Glancing round in alarm, she hurried out.

A short while later, after making a brief excuse to Stella, John too left the Place, hurrying down through the estate as night fell, his coat wrapped tightly around him and his face burning with an unusual agitation.

30

As they approached the house Kathleen suddenly said in a very violent tone, 'Look. Don't go and see him!'

'But why? What is this?'

She came close to him as if, in the darkness, to detect the exact nature of his response.

'Leave him. Don't go in. It'll only be some endless talk of Tolson.'

'But why did you fetch me then? Why did you ask me?'

'It doesn't matter.'

'But isn't he ill? I mean, isn't any of it true, what you've told me?'

'Oh, *that*'s true,' she said as though now it was of no importance at all. Leonard seemed completely overwhelmed by the change in her; almost a change of character. He thrust his hand deep into his raincoat pocket and for a moment seemed preoccupied with what he had hidden there.

'Why don't we go away?' she added, staring into his face. 'Somewhere in the open. We could go to the park. It'd be completely empty now. We could go there. And later we could go away together. Don't you think so?' She pulled his arm to rouse his attention. They had now stopped outside the house and Leonard was gazing up at the lighted windows. When it seemed he wouldn't answer, she suddenly said, 'I mean, can't you leave Tolson? To my father.'

Leonard had moved back slightly. He was still staring up at the house. Slowly his head turned towards her. His expression was concealed by the dark.

'You want to go off with me? Go away with me?'

'Yes.'

'And leave . . . you know, your children and everything?'

'Yes.' Yet her voice sounded drained of all enthusiasm, the thing which a moment before had peculiarly enlivened her. 'Look. I've even got the money. There's no need for me to go back in the house. We can go now.' She held something out in her hands to which, however, he gave no attention.

'And what would all this be for? A sacrifice!' His voice had mounted with tension. He was trembling.

'No. . . .'

'Is that all you're doing? Buying me off?'

'No.'

'Is this what your father asked you to do?'

'No. It's not. It's just something I've thought of now. The money was already in my pocket. . . .' Suddenly she swung completely round. It was as if she had sensed someone approaching in the dark. But through the pools of lamplight there was no sign of movement.

'Can't you see, my father's obsessed . . . with you *and* Tolson. He'd do anything for both of you.' Yet she had begun to walk towards the house as though there was now no further purpose in their arguing.

Leonard followed her more slowly. She pushed open the gate and walked up the path. Then, when she reached the door, she turned. 'Remember, then,' she said, 'it's your decision.'

'But you shouldn't force these things on me! You know I couldn't possibly go away with you. The whole thing's mad and absurd.'

'Remember, you've decided that we'll both *go in*,' she added as if she hadn't heard his protest.

It seemed then that Leonard was about to turn and go. He was standing on the steps and, in the darkness, he had turned clumsily. At that moment the door was pulled open from the inside and Blakeley stood there.

'Oh! It is you,' he said. 'I thought I heard your voices.' And before Leonard could move either way he was almost pulled into the house.

Blakeley was dressed in a neat suit. As Leonard stood blinking in the strong light he noticed first the suit, which he had never seen before, then the blankness of the walls of the living-room. All the photographs had been removed with one exception, that of Blakeley and Kathleen together.

'He got up half an hour ago,' Blakeley's wife said. 'He reckons that he feels better already.' And although Blakeley was very much alive, shaking Leonard's hand and leading him by the arm as though to confirm an intimate friendship, his family was completely subdued. Kathleen, still dressed in her unusually long coat, stood sadly watching Leonard.

The three children had obviously been dressed specially for the occasion and stood shyly in the centre of the room as Leonard was brought in. Even his wife had prepared herself in a bright red dress.

'Well, how are you?' Blakeley said, leading Leonard to the nearest of the three children. 'This is young Mark, here. . . . Say hello, Mark.'

'Hello,' the boy said, then blushed as he held out his hand rather stiffly for Leonard to shake. It was such a small hand that, as it lay in his own for a second, Leonard appeared to stare at it in dismay. The next moment Blakeley said, 'There, you see what little gentlemen they can be when they try. And this is Colin, the youngest imp. Though he has a very beautiful voice. Say how d'you do, Colin.'

'How d'you do, Mr Radcliffe,' the younger boy said, nodding his head as if he were about to bow.

'You see, I've told them all about you while we were waiting. Though of course, I ought to have introduced the little lady first. This is Ruth.'

'Good night, Mr Radcliffe,' the girl said, staring rigidly at the floor, that part of her forehead which was visible a bright crimson.

'Oh, we've all met before,' Leonard said, acutely embarrassed in his turn.

'Did you hear that? Good night, and he's only just come!' Blakeley was more than pleased with his young performers. 'Here you are, you little rabbits. What did I say I'd give you all if you behaved like I said?' He winked heavily, with a certain grotesqueness at Leonard.

None of them answered, however, but began to look at Leonard with a more open curiosity. 'Well, what do you think, Mr Radcliffe?' Blakeley said. 'Do you think they *deserve* anything?'

The children's expressions turned to looks of appeal, though still slightly intimidated by this elaborate ritual.

'Well? Do they deserve anything?' Blakeley repeated, staring still at Leonard.

'Why . . . yes!' Leonard half-smiled, looking down.

'You're sure?'

'Yes!' Leonard was completely confused.

Blakeley stooped over them, turning his head momentarily to laugh at Leonard, then kissing the faces of the two boys and the girl with some ceremony. When they laughed, he stood watching them with a kind of mock surprise. Then he took several sweets from his pocket which he distributed equally among them. He kissed them all again, laughing, as if both pleased yet saddened by the little game.

Suddenly he broke off and almost with a premeditated gesture came to take hold of Leonard's coat. 'You must take your coat off,' he said. 'We've got this fire laid just for your benefit. *She's* been grumbling at the amount of coal I've been stuffing on.'

But as Leonard pulled his raincoat off he twisted awkwardly out of Blakeley's grasp and, hastily folding the garment, laid it over the arm of the chair where he sat down. After touching the coat a moment he glanced up at Blakeley as though to apologize for his impoliteness.

At first, uncertain how to react, Blakeley stared down rather emptily at his guest, then turned quickly to the children who were beginning to scamper about the room.

'Now, I'll have those sweets off you if you're going to make all that row,' he said, almost viciously, yet going over to the youngest boy and lifting him down gently from a chair. He smacked him lightly and ruffled his hair, then kissed him on the top of his head. It was done in such a contradictory and vaguely absurd way that Leonard, still watching in some confusion, began to smile. For a brief moment, scarcely a matter of seconds, Blakeley had begun silently to cry, holding the boy's head gently against his chest.

Then suddenly his wife said, 'Come on, you lot. Into the scullery if you're going to play about. We want no noise in here.' And immediately she began to half-push, half-pull them through the door.

Blakeley watched them go with the same sad reluctance. Then he glanced at the two women.

'Do you think you could leave us two men alone? I want to talk over a few things with Leonard, and the presence of the opposite sex . . . well, it makes things a little difficult.' Despite his calm tone there was an almost hysterical inflexion in his voice, and his wife glanced quickly at Leonard with a mixture of reproach and concern.

'You mustn't keep him long,' she said. 'Nor get him excited. Whatever he says, he's just out of bed, and he's not half as well as he thinks. We'll be just in the scullery.'

'Oh, now, get out woman,' Blakeley said with the same strangled humour. His face was beaded with sweat. 'Take no notice of them,' he said to Leonard as they shut the door.

A moment later their voices could be heard over the excited cries of the children.

'They'll be all right in there,' Blakeley went on. 'There's a good fire, and that's where they spend most of their time. We usually keep this room for when we have company.' He pushed his hands into his trouser-pockets and stood with his back to the fire gazing down paternally at Leonard.

'They're a grand lot. A man couldn't wish for a finer family. I only wish myself that I could do better by them. But there it is.' He smiled down at him so grotesquely that Leonard looked away. It was as if Blakeley wanted him to recognize this as a performance, and one particularly moving and full of appeal. As he turned his head to find some other focus for his attention, he saw, lying in the corner of the room behind an easy chair, the mask which a few days before he had seen eerily lit on the stage of the working men's club.

The shock that this gave him was almost immediately followed by a second and more disconcerting discovery. All the time that he'd been sitting in the chair he'd been fingering the object that lay heavily in the pocket of his coat. Looking down now, he saw that he'd pressed the cloth so tightly around the hidden shape that it stood out in clear relief, emphasized by the stained sweat of his hand.

He saw Blakeley change his position several times as he continued talking to him with the same absurd affability. And when, some moments later, he heard Blakeley say, 'Of course, Kathleen will have told you about the unfortunate incident last night,' he suddenly realized that throughout these preoccupied and numbed moments he had been answering Blakeley and even asking him questions. It was only then, in fact, that he became alarmed as to whether Blakeley had seen the shape unmistakably outlined within the smooth texture of the coat.

'I don't really understand it myself,' Blakeley went on, looking thoughtfully over Leonard's head. 'What did you think to the show last Sunday? They said somebody had been overcome by the heat. The next thing I discover, it was you! Your uncle Austen came to see me afterwards. It was he who told me . . . and said that you'd gone. He'd come to watch me apparently. Fancy that! After all this time!'

Leonard's gaze had returned to the mask. Turned on its side, its features had a heavy look of defeat, even of death; apart from the chair there was nothing else close to the mask. From this angle he could see something of its blank interior, and several tapes that were evidently used to secure it to Blakeley's head.

'Did you *send* Kathleen to fetch me?' Leonard suddenly asked.

Blakeley moved away from the fire. He was sweating now as though he had deliberately exposed himself to the heat. He sat down in the chair facing Leonard, so that they were separated by the length of the hearth.

'You're going to see Tolson tonight,' he said with such a peculiar inflexion it was impossible to decide whether it were a question, a statement or a command.

Leonard had lifted his raincoat and, somewhat clumsily, refolded it more loosely over the arm of the chair.

'Did he tell you that? He said he'd tell no one,' he replied; though with no sense of alarm, but rather a perturbed expression as though the significance of his remark somehow eluded him.

'Oh, he told me all right. Me, and no one else, I should imagine.' Blakeley, with a certain nervousness, yawned, then swept his arm round as if to dismiss the whole subject now that he'd introduced it.

'But what has it to do with my coming here?' Leonard seemed unable to concentrate, or even to follow what had been said. The children were suddenly quiet in the next room.

'As I told you when I saw you a few days ago,' Blakeley said, crossing his legs as though he were about to introduce a business proposition, 'I've come to the point where I've got to make an absolute decision about something.' Yet despite the formality of tone he watched Leonard with an almost hysterical pleading of his eyes, staring at him as if only by this fixity of vision could he keep any control over his feelings.

'A decision about what?'

'Have you ever thought if everyone at some point in their lives, either out of their own volition as it were, or at the insistence of something from outside, had to make a decision about the actual value that their individual life had . . . at some point they had *actually* to decide whether their life was worth all the expense, emotional, material, and otherwise . . . all the expense not only of their own suffering and enjoyments but of what they put other people to in order to stay alive – how many of them would answer "Yes"? And how many of them would answer "No" simply out of fear of the consequences?'

He obviously expected no answer to such a hypothetical proposition. It seemed, in fact, that he had prepared this speech beforehand, even to the careful enunciation of the words, so that he paused occasionally as though trying to recollect what came next. It wasn't the exact, practical thing he wanted to ask Leonard and he continued to stare at him with the same demanding expression.

'Of course,' he said, 'most people aren't capable of asking the question, or even of formulating it, let alone honestly deciding.'

'But why d'you ask such an absurd thing?' Leonard said, looking about him distractedly, yet his gaze persistently reverting to the mask facing him in the corner of the room. 'And what's the use of that sort of decision, even if you make it?' He looked swiftly from Blakeley himself to the discarded object as though suspecting it had been left in that position on purpose.

'You mean if *I* make it? For me? Well, it's purely a

294

question of honesty. Isn't that it? The majority of people might go on living their lives because they have neither the courage nor the means to measure its significance or its meaning, but for me such a thing has become intolerable. No. That's too pompous, isn't it? I should say, a life which doesn't involve that sort of decision is completely and absolutely meaningless to me.'

Leonard was silent. Throughout this speech he had been glancing repeatedly at the clock which stood on the mantelpiece over the fire. He seemed in fact only gradually to become aware that Blakeley had stopped speaking at all. He looked up at him slowly.

'What is it you want me to say?' he asked, leaning nervously forward in his chair, his right hand spread over the coat beside him. 'You can't possibly expect me to answer something like this. So why do you ask me?'

'But what sort of responsibility do you think a man owes to his family? I mean, how much are they *his*, and how much are they something separate from him?' Blakeley continued.

'But you don't want me to answer these questions at all, do you?' Leonard said in a sudden agony of frustration and contempt, and for a moment seemed about to get up, glancing at the clock and laying both hands on the arms either side of him.

'I do. I need to know. But I realize that this manner of mine puts you off. My self-consciousness. Perhaps you should be a bit more generous. Perhaps you're forgetting I was once a workman. All this questioning, this talking about what I feel, well all that's something I've had to learn about. I know I express it poorly. But I've had to teach myself how to put these things into words that somebody like you might understand.' He looked accusingly at Leonard, his head swaying slightly from side to side as he insisted on his intentions. 'You see, all this questioning, this self-doubt, if you can call it that. It comes from me having such acute feelings about life, knowing and feeling things that don't bother most people at all. Or perhaps they do. I don't know. . . . But what I'm trying to say is that, however depressed or upset I get, there's a part of me that

295

remains separate. A part that just watches me being depressed. It's as if I don't really *take part in* my depression. As though, because I can watch my feelings, that somehow, they're valueless ... synthetic, put on. Though I know they're not. ... It's hellish. Hellish ... watching your own suffering to such an extent that you begin to suspect that it's not really suffering at all.'

He was now sweating profusely, and even leaning towards the fire as if deliberately aggravating his discomfort. Yet all the while his eyes never left Leonard's own increasingly distracted face.

'I mean, it was a blunt knife last night,' he went on, drinking in the heat it seemed as he spoke. 'Perhaps I knew it was blunt. But recently I've been feeling an overwhelming desire to see whether the separate, detached part of me would still be there even if I did the most terrible thing I could imagine.'

He watched now with raised eyebrows as though inquiring of Leonard the significance of what he was saying. Then he added, 'But even when I struck her with the knife – and I didn't know whether it would go in her, blunt as it was – there was still this *separate* feeling. As if I were only watching myself do it. That wasn't really *me* at all. It's incredible. There's a part of me that's completely unaffected by what I am or what I do. And it's that part of me I think that makes me an artist.'

Leonard had fallen back in the chair, stifled and exhausted by Blakeley's persistence. It was as if, out of Leonard's own distress, he were describing an incident which hadn't yet taken place. A strange feeling of inevitability compressed the room itself so that it seemed a tiny cube occupied hugely by their two figures.

'It leads to another thing as well,' Blakeley went on as though Leonard's exhaustion were something that had to be pursued ruthlessly, for its own sake. 'I mean, could this separate thing watch *itself* being destroyed, do you think? Suppose I'd turned the knife on myself, would that part of me which watches *still* go on watching or would something unusual, something *unique* happen? Would that part of me actually step in and *do* something? Commit itself?'

His eyes followed every stress and movement of Leonard's face, and greedily, with a voracious intentness. 'Is it that part of you that's called the soul? And when you die, or when you're dead, is it still separate, and can even leave you? Or leave its *body*. Do you think that's what Christ meant by the spirit, by his ascension?'

'What do you mean when you say this "thing" may step in and do something unusual?' Leonard said. The question itself caused him to strain forward in the chair, yet with an expression of bewilderment, of despair.

'But did I say that?' Blakeley asked with an even greater eagerness. 'Are you sure I said that? I think you're twisting my words . . . or shaping them to some intention you have in your own mind.'

It was a look of triumph with which he devoured Leonard. He watched him with a kind of passionate ferocity for a short while, then added, 'Perhaps, then, you think that there's a point at which this separate thing can be made to *act*?'

He seemed completely fascinated by the effect this had upon Leonard: in some way it seemed to mark the success of all his efforts to express something of his sensations. His head still swayed slightly from side to side. Leonard seemed mesmerized by the motion, his eyes following Blakeley's with a look of helpless appeal.

'Can it be forced to act, this uncommitted, this separate thing?' Blakeley insisted.

'Oh, but it's an artificial separation,' Leonard said, talking more as though to himself, Blakeley leaning forward suddenly to catch his words. 'It shouldn't be apart. It shouldn't be separate. It's what you've forced yourself into feeling. Why should it be separate? Just think, if it were as much a part of the body as anything else, as the *muscle* itself, and acted with the body, with the muscle, and was indivisible from it. What if they were so close, so intimate, so much the one thing that they could never be separated?'

Leonard had stood up, and almost immediately he bent down and picked up his coat and began hastily to pull it on. It swayed heavily behind him. 'But that isn't the way the world's organized itself, is it? That's not the way things really happen. . . . But just think what if this *separate thing* were in one man, and the body, the acting part in another? What if these two qualities were typified ideally in two separate men? Then, just imagine . . . just imagine the unholy encounter of two such people!'

Yet having expressed this idea he seemed as confused and as bewildered as ever, glancing round the room suddenly as if uncertain of where he actually was.

'I don't know why I agreed to come . . . here,' he said, speaking now with the same formality as Blakeley himself, and frowning as if the light pained his eyes. He began to rub his arms as though cold, but his face was flushed and sweaty with the heat of the room.

Within himself an even stranger confusion had arisen. As he began to move towards the door he suffered the momentary sensation that he and Blakeley were pressed into the shape of one man. Then, almost immediately he had the impression that Blakeley was standing there with his face pulled open by that peculiar soundless crying, and that his body was swaying as though he were trying to speak. But when, with his hand on the door, he glanced back into the room he saw that Blakeley was in fact still seated in his chair and was looking at him with an expression he couldn't interpret. The moment passed extremely slowly. Although there was no movement of Blakeley's face, its look seemed to change from second to second, one emotion fading rapidly into another, his eyes dark with condemnation and anger, then luminously alive with some sort of happiness and relief. Leonard felt himself to be in a state of unusual detachment, as if he'd been absorbed by the air and, in this suspended awareness, was walking over to Blakeley and exchanging positions with him, even passing him as he in turn walked over to the door.

In this extraordinary confusion of his senses it seemed that he was trying to overlook something which, at that moment, he felt unable to face. It was like pressing down on a stone which he knew at any moment he would have to lift in order to extract whatever was underneath. It was from within this confused struggle that he endured the sensation of passing and re-passing Blakeley in the centre of the room, as though they performed a stiff and angular dance like two dolls along a single and unvarying line of movement. Yet he was still able to reach out his hand and touch the door. The sole spectator of this extraordinary display was the mask lying in the corner, its massive and inarticulate features lit with a desolate and helpless smile. Even as he saw it he was aware of Blakeley talking, the word 'Tolson' repeated several times then, like a voice breaking through an awakening '. . . the *right* thing to do. I don't know.' He saw the fading stream of Blakeley's histrionic gestures, and then his voice again, '. . . *can* be only two sorts of people: the divine idiot and the professional clown.'

'Ah, and which are *you*?' Blakeley said so sharply that Leonard was disconcerted to discover that it was his own voice he had been listening to.

By various gestures and a more relaxed manner Blakeley was now trying to make light of everything that had happened, as if to insist that, after all, it had only been a performance on both their parts. Smiling, and with the same affability with which he had greeted Leonard on entering the room, he now began to follow him to the door.

'I'm glad you came, Leonard. I'm glad you were able to come. When I knew you were going to see Tolson tonight I just had to see you first. Do you understand? Just to *see* you. I suppose Kathleen made up some cock-and-bull story. But the fact is I just wanted to see you.' He ran his hand across Leonard's shoulder and, momentarily, down his side. 'I'm glad I've seen you. I feel, well, you know, that we're sharing things. We're closer together. Don't you think so? If you hadn't have come, God, it would have been terrible. Now, of course . . . Now, of course, everything's resolved. It's all very clear.'

He seemed very pleased and, in response to such sociable gestures, Leonard said with a sudden laugh, 'Do you know, I've suddenly got an insatiable desire to write something, or to *draw*!' He laughed more loudly, and thrust his right hand down into his raincoat pocket. With his other hand he opened the door. 'To draw something!' he laughed.

Standing in the narrow hallway was Kathleen and,

behind her, Blakeley's family. They regarded Leonard with serious, mildly surprised, expressions. The next moment he swung away unsmiling, and as though embarrassed.

It was only after hurrying down to the gate and out onto the road that he called out any sort of farewell.

31

'Your father was here earlier on,' Tolson said as he watched Leonard moving about the room and taking off his coat. He did it clumsily, hurrying through the narrow spaces between the chairs as if about to go out again, and smiling to himself the whole time.

'What did he want?' Leonard said.

'He started talking about a moth.' Tolson was very still.

'A what?'

'A moth.'

'But what for? Why was that?'

'I don't know.'

For a moment Leonard stood perfectly still, his coat folded neatly over his arm, gazing intently at Tolson's head. He seemed to become increasingly lost in his thoughts. Then he said hesitantly, 'But didn't he mention anything else?'

'He told me to keep away from you.'

'What did you say?'

'Nothing.'

'You told Blakeley about me coming here tonight,' Leonard said, growing intenser.

'It doesn't matter.'

'Kathleen told me a remarkable thing tonight. She said her father was in love with you.'

'Is that it?'

There was now a kind of surly frustration in Tolson's attitude.

Leonard had begun another elaborate circuit of the room, moving clumsily between the furniture strewn like boulders in the narrow interior, and glancing quickly at Tolson whenever he turned.

'Yet it seems to explain everything,' Leonard went on. 'I mean, about Blakeley. If he feels like that about you. And the way he tries to rationalize it all. All these theories . . . God. You must have given him hell. You must have made it absolute hell.'

Tolson gave no answer. He didn't even move. After a moment Leonard began to smile, faintly and remotely, an awkward tension of his face.

'I'm sorry,' he said. 'I'm sorry. It's just my nerves. I'm so nervous.' He shook himself as though to free his body from some invisible restriction. 'My father shouldn't have come here. It confuses everything. I mean, has Elizabeth told him something? Did he say anything about her?'

'No.'

'I'll have to find out.' Leonard suddenly peered round the room, looking for a clock. 'It won't take long will it? I'll have to find out if she's told him. If she hasn't then it won't make any difference. What I mean is, I don't want people to think that I've behaved as I have because of her.'

'Oh, but then . . .' Tolson said, beginning now to edge slowly towards the door. 'Are you sure?'

'I shall have to go and see her. I can't have it hanging over my head like this.'

Tolson watched him carefully. 'But what makes you think I'll let you out, Len, now I've got you here? I can assure you it wasn't about Elizabeth that your father came down. He knows nothing about it.'

'But you'd better let me out. How can we discuss any-thing . . . how can anything *happen* with this hanging over everything?'

Leonard seemed completely confused, wandering aim-lessly up and down between the furniture, glancing in every direction as though he expected to find an indication of the time everywhere he looked. He clutched his coat to him with a familiar, wounded gesture.

'But I'll come back,' he said after a while.

'I'm not bothered whether you will or you won't. I'm not letting you out. There's nobody else in the house. Except us. And the kids asleep in the next room. You can see. I've organized it, Leonard.'

'I'd like to ask one question about this,' Leonard said quietly, with a sudden calmness, as though he'd been anticipating such a threat. 'If I did submit to you, how exactly do you see me doing it? I mean, physically, what do you imagine I'd do the very moment I gave in?'

Tolson didn't answer. If anything, he stood more patiently, more firmly, in the doorway.

'Do you see me lying on the floor, or kneeling down praying to you? I suppose in a way you'd like that. Me kneeling to you, even if it's only to be like Blakeley, committing some absurd action simply because I'd been told to by you.'

Tolson was moving slowly towards him. Leonard watched him, his right hand buried in the coat which lay neatly over his left arm.

Tolson looked at the coat, then said, 'Do you still think you're going, then?'

'I suppose in your imagination you've seen yourself beating me a score of times,' Leonard went on. 'Haven't you gone around the room when you've been alone, shadow-boxing? Imagining me as your *shadow*? Just like Blakeley. Beating me senseless until I realize, I see and I feel who is the stronger. Or am I wrong? Is there some other action I haven't imagined? Is there an even worse, a grotesquer humiliation that you've thought up for me? After all, it isn't that you want to see me weak *within* myself, is it? But that you merely want me to acknowledge you. What would be the worst humiliation for me that would acknowledge that?'

'Go on,' Tolson said.

'But just think, Vic. Think. If you told me what particular action you'd imagined. . . .' Leonard's voice had been gradually mounting in excitement and he now seemed momentarily to lose track of his words. 'If you imagined what action . . . I was committing at the *very moment* I submitted I might even begin to wonder whether I could actually do it.'

Suddenly, he felt a sharp pain in his side, so intense that he leaned over it, to his left. At first he thought Tolson had struck him, for it coincided with a sudden movement of

Tolson's arms, and he flinched, turning quickly away. Then, as though imagining it might have been self-induced, he stood upright with a thoughtful expression. As he straightened his body he saw that Tolson had removed his shirt and was facing him, stripped to the waist.

Only then did he seem to recognize the extreme state of excitement Tolson had been in since he'd come into the room. A wave of horror and surprise swept over his face. He seemed dazed by the sight of Tolson's body. Tolson was flushed, the redness spreading from his strained face to the thick column of his chest, and he held out his arms as though curving them to contain something he already sensed between them.

'You can't get out, Len.'

The coat swung loosely from Leonard's arm. He rubbed his hand over his face as if agonized at finding his own powerful feelings overhung by an emotion that not only transcended them but which, through his habitual self-absorption, he had completely ignored. It was Tolson now who seemed possessed of every sign of insanity, unfastening the thick belt at his waist and, bowed like some huge segment of bone, tearing off the remainder of his clothes. Leonard gazed at him with a sunken expression of despair.

Tolson stood firmly against the closed door, breathless as though at the climax of a massive physical event. Yet he went on slowly declaring, in a peculiar frustration of his own, 'You see. You see. You see . . .' calming a moment as if to judge the effect on Leonard, then adding, 'How are you going to get out now?'

He seemed half-frightened by his emotion, looking at Leonard for some sort of relief or explanation, or help.

'Tell me . . . why don't you start crying?' he said with strange apprehension. 'Shall I tell you what I want you to do? What I want you to do the very moment you give in? That question you were so keen to play around with.'

He was peering at Leonard with a hopeless violence, leaning forward slightly as though at any moment he might fall under the single pressure of his feelings. His voice was choked.

'No,' Leonard said in a hardly audible voice.

Tolson's hand fell to that part of his body which seemed to torment and mesmerize Leonard the most. 'Well? What theory are you going to make up about that?'

He had begun to move forward, still remaining, however, in the path of the door.

'Look. Look! Don't be frightened. If you want to know what famous action you'll be doing at the very moment you submit . . . here, this is it. This!'

Yet despite the threat of his body he looked at Leonard despairingly. It was an anxious, pleading gesture with which he caught hold of him, tearing the raincoat from his arm and pressing him backwards. He pinioned his arms, staring at him with a harrowed fascination.

'Why! Aren't you going to fight?' he said with the same frozen look of demand. Suddenly he thrust a leg behind Leonard and forced him over. 'Do you think if I let you go *now* you'd keep your promise and come back?'

Leonard had begun to struggle. The immediate effect was to encourage Tolson into forcing him down on his back. Then he dropped onto Leonard, sitting astride his chest. With his knees he fastened Leonard's arms to the floor.

'It'd be better if you *did* fight,' Tolson said despairingly. 'Don't think. . . . Don't think I'm playing with you.'

He fitted a hand round Leonard's neck, almost carelessly, lifting his head up a moment and peering madly into his face, then suddenly he crashed it down on the floor.

Leonard turned white as the blood shrank from his face, his head twisting as though trying to escape the smell of Tolson's body. Tolson had now pulled himself onto his chest, his thighs cushioning Leonard's chin. He leaned hard down on the body beneath him; then, clasping Leonard's hair in one hand, he took hold of his nose with the other so that Leonard's mouth slowly opened for breath. Between his lips he pressed the swollen mound of flesh.

The muscles round Tolson's neck and shoulders burst out from their bony supports, his arms curved down to hold the nose and the lever of the lower jaw. He was a contained muscle of maddened energy, almost insensible it seemed, his body raised then pressing forward like some prodigious growth unfolding from the floor of the room. He bowed forward, stooped, in an epileptic gesture of benediction, holding beneath him his frantic sacrifice.

Suddenly, he flung Leonard's head from him, banging it back against the floor to hold it like a ball between his thighs. Slowly he drew his body upright, his head upraised and turning slightly to one side, his eyes closed. Then, as though succumbing to some final assault, he drew himself back and slowly, staggering for a moment, pushed himself up to his feet. He leaned heavily against a chair.

Leonard had turned and was staring up at the red figure, a giant flame in this perspective flung up from the floor. His hands, numbed and indecisive, moved slowly. They rose clumsily, searching his face until they came to rest either side, holding his cheeks. His mouth, still open, glistening, appeared to be soundlessly screaming. Then he rolled on his side, coughed and vomited a small pool onto the carpet.

Tolson stood watching him with a dazed expression, frowning. He rubbed a hand over his eyes, stooping slightly at the same time as though to examine something caught between his fingers. As Leonard rose to his knees, he watched his laborious struggle to regain his balance.

'What is it?' Tolson said. 'What is it?' Then crying out, 'What is it!' He had caught Leonard by his jacket, half-turning him, and gripping his arms.

Leonard stumbled, falling against the wall. Then he stood upright. His face was distorted, and yet he was peculiarly calm. When eventually he looked at Tolson, seeing him across the room like someone for whom unsuccessfully he had been searching for a long time, it was with a broken smile, shy and vaguely beseeching. He seemed completely helpless.

Confronted by such a vulnerable expression, Tolson turned abjectly away. As if broken in every limb he began slowly to pull on his clothes. Occasionally he glanced up at Leonard who still watched him with such a simplicity of expression that Tolson turned away with a sound of despair.

Leonard went over to his coat where Tolson had previously flung it and, stooping to relieve a prolonged bout of coughing, eventually picked it up. He allowed it to sway a moment before slowly arranging it over his arm.

After a while Tolson said, 'What are you going to do?'

'I shall have to go and see. I shall have to see Elizabeth. You don't understand.'

He spoke so harshly, with such a grotesque deepening of his voice, that Tolson looked at him in surprise. It seemed like some monstrous imitation of a voice projected from a body substantially larger than Leonard's. As he saw the alarming intensity of Leonard's face Tolson blushed and, very slowly, began to smile.

'You don't understand,' Leonard went on. 'If my father thought I'd acted out of revenge, something that *he'd* understand, then I'd never have any peace. The whole thing . . . there mustn't be any confusion.' Yet Leonard had begun to look about him with increasing bewilderment.

'But what are you talking about? What act?' Tolson said, his looks changing with a kind of ponderous relief. It was as if nothing had occurred.

'I shall have to go,' Leonard said despairingly.

The next moment, with a cry of vexation, he swung round and flung himself at the door. He wrenched it open and hurried out, his limbs wildly uncoordinated, so that he stumbled heavily down the stairs. Several times he glanced back, as though under the impression that he was being followed.

32

A large moon, magnified by a low mist, was rising over the head of the escarpment as Leonard walked hurriedly up through the estate. Apart from a dog crossing one of the avenues in the distance he saw no other sign of life.

When he reached the Place he made his way across the terrace to the porch. He seemed disconcerted to find the doors locked and bolted, and after walking up and down he began to wander round the building, trying windows and becoming increasingly frustrated. Eventually he approached the kitchen and after some hesitation looked in at one of the lighted windows.

His father was sitting with his back to him. Just beyond, and almost directly facing him, was his mother. She was crying. It was a heavy, muscular self-preoccupation, as slow, intermittent shudders of distress were drawn up through her body. She made no attempt to conceal the fact, and his father continued talking as though unaware of it. From behind, the movements of his head and shoulders appeared to be those of a casual affability.

How long Leonard stopped there peering in he had no idea. When suddenly he went to the door, lifted the latch and entered, it seemed that he was in a fever of impatience. His mother and father looked up at him with an un-accustomed alarm.

'Why, whatever have you done to your face?' his mother said, making no attempt to conceal her tears.

He glanced round, frowning with the light. Then, staring suspiciously at them both he immediately went to the stairs, bowing slightly towards them in a vague and absurd salute.

'What did the girl want?' his mother said.

'For me to see her father. He's ill.'

'And how was he?'

'He was fine when I left.' Leonard touched his mouth, tracing his fingers round his lips. 'You can tell. They seemed quite pleased at me going.' He glanced once more at his father, then began to climb the stairs.

'Are you going to bed?' his mother said.

'Yes.'

His father hadn't spoken. He had not, apart from the initial look of alarm, even glanced at Leonard.

When he reached the top of the stairs he paused, listened a moment to the continued murmur of their voices, then immediately crossed the landing to Elizabeth's room. Pausing and listening again, he very quietly opened the door.

The room was in darkness. Moonlight filtered through the lace curtain identifying Elizabeth's vague form on the bed. Through the lower half of the window, like the dome of a giant skull, the moon had begun to rise.

Leonard closed the door and, looking hesitantly about him, crossed over to the bed. Elizabeth was breathing very calmly; her features, thrust forward from the pillow, were illuminated by the soft light.

'Liz.'

She didn't move. The light waned on her face a moment, drained over the bed, then sprang out with renewed strength. One side of her head was brilliantly lit, a carved relief against the anonymity of the shadow beyond. Leonard took the hammer from the folds of his coat.

'Liz.' He waited. 'Elizabeth.'

The body stirred, then settled back into the momentum of its breathing. Leonard stood quite still, the hammer hanging loosely by his side. From below came the faint murmur of his father's voice; then, suddenly, the strange sound of his laughter. It was a harsh self-derogatory sound.

Leonard stooped forward, peering intently at Elizabeth's head. It was a fragile shell in the moonlight, scarcely more substantial than the light itself. He examined the shoots of hair that swept back from the white dome of her forehead. Then, very carefully, he laid his finger on the closed lid of the eye. It trembled. The head, however, scarcely stirred. The nose ran as a slender ridge from the curve of her brows, the nostrils' slim crevices falling in shadow to the soft protrusion of her mouth. Her lips pouted slightly, drawn out, and between them gleamed the white of her teeth.

Leaning forward, the hammer clenched in his hand, Leonard heard his father's laugh again. It was a heavy, incomprehensible sound. He stood up, gazing still at the narrow shell on the pillow. And again, a moment later, his father laughed.

It seemed, then, that Leonard was on the point of flinging himself on the bed. But at the same moment he gave an agitated cry and immediately spun round and went to the door. Without glancing back or even closing the door, he hurried out to the landing. A second later Elizabeth rose up from the bed, too terrified, it seemed, to call out.

The front of the Place was bathed in moonlight. As

Leonard opened the front doors an animal emerged from the shrubberies and disappeared under the trees. He stood listening, then closed the doors quietly behind him. Heavy shadows slid from the trunks of the trees, running thickly across the terrace to rise up and embrace the structure. Between them the light glinted on shuttered windows.

For a while he paced up and down the shadowed terrace, walking through the alternating bands of light and shade. He seemed like something produced by the light itself. Periodically he would begin to pull on his raincoat, driving one arm down a sleeve only to drag it out a moment later. Eventually, however, as though exhausted by his restless patrol, he suddenly pulled on the coat, bowing slightly as he fastened the buttons, and set off along the drive.

He hurried down through the estate, walking on the grass verges and constantly glancing about him as though pursued. When he reached Tolson's house, he began to walk more slowly and, once at the gate, stopped altogether, staring round as though uncertain in which direction to move.

A moment later he started off determinedly down the road, walking a distance of some yards, then swung round and, without looking up, entered the gate and hurried down the path at the side of the house. A few seconds later he reappeared, closed the gate very carefully, glanced up and down the street, then turned once more down the path.

He opened the kitchen door with a certain amount of noise, clumsily, and for a while stood listening in the darkness. There were no sounds at all. He began to climb the stairs. A thin beam of light shone across the landing.

It was then that for several seconds he appeared to be seized by a fit of terror. He flung his hands around his body as if something were missing. Only gradually, and with frequent reassuring touches, delicate and oddly poised, did he return to some sort of composure, eventually drawing from the numerous folds and creases of his coat the hammer head. It seemed bound to his pocket. He tugged at it several times, twisting it in various directions, before the handle came free.

He leaned forward slightly, running the cold boss of the

hammer head across his face, tracing his forehead, his cheeks, then his mouth, as though cooling his skin. Hearing a sound from the room above he suddenly looked up. For a while he stood perfectly still, the hammer held to his mouth, staring into the darkness at the head of the stairs.

He moved very slowly, almost imperceptibly, so that for a time his feet remained on a stair while his body crept forward, his shoulder holding to the wall. Then, leaning heavily for support, he began his final ascent. It was as if in some peculiar way his feet obstructed his progress, so that when he reached the top of the stairs he stood for several seconds dizzily overcome by the effort.

Opposite him was the door to Tolson's living-room, slightly ajar and sending out a thin strip of light. It fell like a luminous rope over his shoes.

It was at this strip of light that he was staring when, like some perverse echo of his own agitation, the sudden sound of an alarm bell rang in the air all around him. He was thrust forward by the sound, stepping across the landing as though flung at the door. When he entered the room, Tolson was sitting in an armchair with his eldest son dressed in pyjamas between his knees. They were examining an alarm clock in Tolson's hand, and even as he paused in the doorway a second ringing echoed through the building. Gradually it died to a slow thudding.

'You see,' Tolson said in a peculiarly grieved voice, 'it's time to go to sleep.'

As Leonard stepped back, Tolson suddenly glanced up. He recognized him with a look of complete dismay, and started to rise. The boy, half-asleep, his eyes almost closed over a glass of milk between his hands, turned his head briefly at his father's movement. For a moment Leonard stood gazing emptily at Tolson, then, with his right hand concealed behind his back, he retreated onto the landing.

He stood waiting. A moment later Tolson came out with his arm round the boy and, without looking up, led him into the bedroom at the end of the landing. Leonard could hear him talking to the boy as he tucked him into bed, and when he'd closed the door and returned along the landing Leonard followed him into the room.

'Why have you come back?' Tolson said bitterly.

He went straight to the chair he had just vacated and sat down. He seemed overwhelmed, leaning forward, cradling his forehead in his hand. By his feet was the half-emptied glass of milk.

'The whole thing ... I don't know.' It sounded as though he were in tears as Leonard strode over to where he was sitting. 'Why do we go on like this? The whole thing, if we just treated each other gently. I know that's it.'

He looked up, his expression swiftly changing to astonishment as he saw the raised arm above his head. He bowed forward slightly, his eyes closed, as the hammer descended. Almost, it seemed, as if he were confident that his skull could withstand the blow. His head shuddered as the hammer struck.

He opened his eyes and frowned. He looked round, frowning. Then he tried to get up.

Leonard lifted the hammer again, twisting the handle, and brought the head down with all his strength. The claws on the reverse side bit through Tolson's hair. He gave a low, private cry, and continued to pull himself to his feet. He rose so slowly that Leonard had time to drag the hammer free and bring it down again on the same spot.

The bone crumbled and a fountain of blood spurted through the dark knots of Tolson's hair. He stood up with great alacrity, the hammer embedded in his head, and began to fling himself about the room, uprooting the furniture. He turned blindly to Leonard, his arms outstretched, and caught hold of his coat, pulling him towards him. Blood sprang up the hammer shaft as though accelerated by the action itself; it poured down through his hair, seeping more slowly across his nose and his eyes. His head was ribboned with violet streams, his eyes reddened crevices, brimming over. 'What have you done? ... What have you done?' he called out, half-astonished, clutching Leonard's arm between his hands so that for a moment Leonard was flung about with Tolson's own convulsions. 'What have you done?'

Someone was running up the stairs. Immediately Tolson released him and stumbled, searching for the door. He crashed against the wall, his hands groping wildly across the flower-patterned surface before he found the entrance and dragged himself towards it. The hammer fell from his head, releasing a fuller stream of blood.

'Audrey! . . . Audrey! Look what they've done to me!' he shouted. 'Look what they've done!'

Leonard had retrieved the hammer. It seemed that he was about to strike Tolson again, but he stopped, confused, staring at the head of the stairs.

'Audrey. . . . Look what they've done to me,' Tolson said. He began to fall to his knees, crying, his hands groping uncertainly to his head. His figure, in the half-darkness, was huge.

It was Blakeley who stepped out of the shadows and stooped over him, and Blakeley who was now crying, 'Vic . . . Vic. . . . Oh, Vic.'

It seemed a decisive moment. Leonard leaned towards Blakeley, peering into his face, then he hastily stepped back. For a second the hammer was half-raised in the air. Then, before Blakeley could move, he brought it down with all his strength on Tolson's head.

Tolson made a final effort to stand, to see and to clear his eyes. He crouched in the narrow landing murmuring to himself, his figure burdened by his huge ambition to rise. Then he sat down, slowly, leaning on his thigh and his arm as if, negligently, he were resting. Within a few seconds his arm began to bend, folding slightly, and he lay down with a peculiar care on the floor. Thick gouts of blood oozed from the crown of his head with a rhythmical impulse. For a while he lay without moving. Then, with an immense effort, he tried to rise again as a crescendo of hammer blows struck this time on the side of his head.

With a massive muscular contraction he heaved himself to his knees, his face upturned for a moment, speaking, its bloodied features turning like a bizarre flower. Then it seemed to disintegrate as the hammer descended on his forehead. He shuddered, absorbing the sudden force, his shoulders shaking and his arms rising until, under a succession of blows, he pitched forward like someone leaping but whose feet are securely embedded in the ground.

Leonard rushed to the stairs. He glanced back to see Blakeley standing over the low silhouette. Their two figures made a single shape against the lighted room beyond, as if Blakeley were touching the lower mound with his face. Then Leonard dropped down the stairs and hurried out.

It was a misty autumn night and the moon was now massive, orange and complete above the summit of the estate. Immediately above his head was a faint penetration of stars. He was still carrying the hammer quite openly in his hand.

His attention was initially caught by a light burning in the church, which loomed up in the mist beyond its hedged perimeter of grass. A frieze of colours, swirling and convoluting, glowed from the darkness. Contained by the slim tracery of the windows, they whirled beneath the massive spindle of the moon, an oval stain magnified by its proximity to the earth.

Leonard was immediately arrested by this extraordinary juxtaposition of light. At first he seemed about to pass the church. Then as he paused, something emerged from the open porch of the building. It seemed, at first, some secretion of the building itself, a dark and nervous ejaculation. The next moment he recognized it as a large dog.

It stood a short distance away, braced forward on its legs, its head pointed acutely towards him, scenting the fringe of his coat. It was extremely large, its upper lip curled back slightly from its teeth. A low growl periodically escaped from its throat. Only when he turned up towards the Place did he glance back. The dog had disappeared.

Walking hurriedly, he set off up the last slope of the rise. The moon slid behind a thin bank of cloud, giving a sulphurous glow to the Place, drawing it out from its stranglehold of trees. He bolted the main doors behind him, listening, then moved quietly up the stairs to the first floor.

A stream of cool and invigorating air entered the York Room through the still-opened window. When he bent down into the fireplace and looked up, the sky was visible as a comparatively bright illumination at the end of the long, winding funnel. A vague, white movement of cloud animated the aperture. He reached up with his fingers and after a while discovered a suitable crevice. Into it he pushed the hammer.

When he reached his own room he undressed and, very quickly, like someone preparing excitedly for a journey, dropped onto the bed and almost immediately fell asleep.

33

Several hours later John was woken by a strange sound. At first he thought it was the murmur of an engine hauling through the tunnel beneath the escarpment. Then he had the impression that someone was in his room. As he rose from the bed, however, it became apparent that the noise came from the door. There was someone standing there, waiting. The sound was that of breathing, but so heavy and deliberate that it could scarcely be human. It was more like an animal scenting. As he peered across the darkened room he gradually distinguished the door set in faint relief by the illumination on the landing. It was across the tiny cracks of light that a shadow periodically moved.

He watched and listened for some time, transfixed first by a sense of terror, then more certainly by the idea that what he was watching could not be real. Then, as he moved towards the door, the movements abruptly ceased and a second later the shadow disappeared altogether. He paused, then opened the door very slowly.

The landing itself was deserted although he could see now that the illumination came from a light in the kitchen reflected up the stairs to his right. Further along, at the darkened end of the landing, it seemed that the door leading into the main part of the Place was slightly ajar.

Certain unrecognizable sounds came from the kitchen and John went to the head of the stairs. As he did so he noticed that Elizabeth's door was also open; suddenly filled with the worst apprehensions, he rapidly descended the stairs.

As he reached the kitchen he saw Elizabeth at the

opposite end of the room. She was standing perfectly still and appeared to be completely absorbed by a voice which filled the room. At the same moment he realized that the greater part of the illumination of the room came, not from the solitary bulb above Elizabeth's head, but from the fire. An unnatural and extravagant brightness flickered continuously across her bewitched face. A moment later she looked up and stood silently regarding him across the length of the room. The voice had grown louder and more excited.

Then there was a huge and terrifying cry, as Leonard's figure leapt from a chair at the side of the room directly towards the fire. With a second cry he plunged both arms into an inferno of flames and pulled out a single blazing mass which, as he tried to carry it across the room, disintegrated in his hands.

John instantly moved forward, flinging the burning debris aside so wildly that Leonard himself was knocked to the floor. He lay on his side unmoving as John stamped out the flames.

'But why didn't you call me? Why didn't you call me?' he said to Elizabeth as he lifted Leonard into a chair. 'Why didn't you call me, love?' He seemed scarcely able to control his agitation. 'You'd better fetch your mother. . . . Are you all right? Do you feel all right?'

Elizabeth hurried out. John pulled Leonard more comfortably into the chair and took a piece of soap from the sink in the corner and began to rub it over Leonard's hands. He was completely preoccupied with this task, almost massaging the hands, when Stella came down followed at some distance by Elizabeth.

'He'll be all right now,' John said to her. 'If you can just take care of Elizabeth. She shouldn't have come down. She shouldn't have come down with him.'

Leonard, pale and staring abstractedly at the ceiling, had suddenly turned in the chair. 'No, don't go, Elizabeth . . . Elizabeth is so silent, father. She frightens me. She says so little. Why did he touch her? Why did he ? Why did he? Wasn't it enough that he had me?'

As they tried to distract him he turned away in frustration, looking at none of them, more at the walls and the ceiling. 'What can a *woman* say? A woman does. A woman says nothing. Women are preachers in their silences, men in their actions. All the time. Then there are castles.'

Neither John nor Stella interrupted him; he was sinking back, looking round at them calmly.

'If I could have lived in a castle. Surrounded by moorland ... how *complete* that would have been. Or in a tent. ...' He laid his head against the arm of the chair and almost immediately fell asleep.

After a while John said, 'I'll carry him up.'

He stooped forward, listening to his regular and undisturbed breathing; then he lifted him quickly and lightly and took him up to his room.

As he laid him down on his bed and removed his jacket, some weight in the pockets attracted his attention. From the side pocket of the jacket Leonard had been wearing John took out first the metal clasp of a belt, then several large buttons. He took them down with him to the kitchen.

'But what was he burning?' he asked Elizabeth, laying these objects on the table.

'His raincoat.' She seemed distracted still, gazing about the room as though Leonard were still there.

'His coat?'

'I heard some sort of noise. And when I came down, he was crouched in front of the fire with my sewing scissors, cutting the buttons and the buckle from his raincoat. He just cut them off. I couldn't do anything.'

'But what was he doing with the coat?' her mother asked.

'I don't know ... I don't know.'

'Didn't he say anything?' John said.

'I think he'd had the coat in the fire already. There were holes burned in it. When he saw me he finished cutting the buttons off and pushed the coat back in the fire. He kept asking me, "What will they think? What will they think?"'

John stood at the table fingering the buttons, turning them over in his hand. 'But why was he burning it?' he said, then suddenly stood back from the table as though forewarned before a prodigious crash echoed through the Place.

All three cried out. It seemed to shake the walls of the

building as though a weight had been hurled against them; and scarcely had its echo disappeared than a second and louder crash, a massive percussion, shook the entire room. As John moved instinctively towards the outside door, taking Stella and Elizabeth with him, a third and even heavier blow fell against the walls followed almost immediately by a loud cry.

Leaving the two women to escape by the kitchen door, John ran back up the stairs to the landing. Leonard's door was open and his room deserted. Numerous drawings lay scattered over the bed and across the floor as though flung there in rage. As he re-emerged onto the landing he saw that the door into the Place was now fully open. Hurrying to his room for a torch, he entered the main part of the building.

He went from room to room, briefly exposing each to the beam of light, working his way quickly along the first floor. There was a strange smell of decomposition, though nowhere any sign of damage. Only when he reached the York Room did any sort of hysteria overtake him. As his torch swept erratically around the shuttered interior Leonard was suddenly revealed lying on the floor at the opposite end, immediately beneath the fireplace.

He lay in fact within the stone base of the fireplace, his right arm extended as though he had fallen in the act of reaching up. As John hurried into the room he was suddenly aware of an unnatural warmth of the air, and the now almost stifling smell of decomposition. He bent down over his son's body and at the same moment heard behind him a hoarse and deliberate breathing, and the movement it seemed of some heavy and resilient weight.

For a moment the torch swung weirdly across the room illuminating first the shuttered features of the windows, then the wild vortex of mouldings that composed the ceiling. Then it shone on a massive creature pinioned to the wall. It was like a slug, struggling out from the smooth surface, its bulbous features glistening in the light. Even as John recognized the relief, wildly animated now in the agitated beam of light, he was lifting Leonard and hurrying with him to the door.

Once in the passage, however, he was compelled to lay

317

him down. For a while he knelt over his son, panting and scarcely able to regain his breath. It was as though some peculiar weight had entered Leonard's body, for when he lifted him again it was as if he were carrying a muscular and heavy man. When he looked at him more closely he saw that, in fact, Leonard was breathing quite deeply and seemed perfectly relaxed.

He laid him on his bed, went back and secured the partition door. Then he called Stella and Elizabeth from below. They stayed together in Leonard's room for some time, scarcely speaking, watching his calmly sleeping figure and occasionally glancing at one another like people waiting impatiently for some event to begin.

34

A remarkable state of affairs developed during the following day. An anonymous telephone call late the previous evening had summoned the police who arrived at Tolson's house several minutes after Audrey's own return home. They discovered her in an extreme state of shock, neither speaking nor, it seemed, able to understand any of their inquiries. Tolson lay just outside the wrecked living-room, his two children standing dumbly beside him.

Preliminary inquiries were begun amongst Tolson's neighbours; Sugdeon was questioned the closest. He had in fact returned home with his wife some time after Tolson's body had been removed from the house and, although his account of a visit to relatives was readily confirmed, the fact that there was no evidence of theft or any other obvious motive made him the one on whom initially suspicion centred. The pathologist's first report indicated that death had been caused more by the persistence rather than the strength of the blows, and this led to the suggestion that the assault might have involved a woman. The utter prostration of Tolson's wife consequently came to be viewed with some suspicion.

Throughout the day inquiries were pursued with a gradually increasing intensity, night falling with police searches of the neighbouring gardens for the murder weapon and the beginning of house-to-house questioning. Then, the following morning, all official activities suddenly ceased. The estate, already a hubbub of speculation, seemed about to explode. The immediate evidence, the continuous passage of police vehicles, the coming and going of numerous uniformed and plain-clothes strangers, were suddenly discontinued. An unnatural silence fell over the affair. It was in such an atmosphere that the family began to arrive at the Place.

They were, apart from Austen, unaware of Tolson's death, and they accepted John's subdued mood as a serious token of their meeting. They talked amicably amongst themselves until the arrival of Cubbitt, the trustees' solicitor, when they decided that for the purpose of their discussion they would go up to the York Room. Overcoming John's protests, Austen led the way, leaving only Isabel behind who, immediately on her arrival, had taken Elizabeth to one side and engaged her in intense conversation. It appeared that Austen had not kept his news completely to himself.

As he entered the York Room at Cubbitt's side, John saw Austen moving swiftly across the darkened interior to swing back the shutters of the central window. The next moment he stepped back to watch Alex on one side, and Matthew and Thomas on the other, remove the remainder. The room was flooded with light. Having introduced Cubbitt, John stood to one side of the room, gazing round it as though pondering within himself some essential though now unimportant provision for its future.

The solicitor, a tall, silver-haired man with a flushed, distinguished face, looked round to see where he could place his packed brief-case. After a moment's hesitation, and saluting Isabel who at that moment entered the room, he walked over to the fireplace and, glancing absent-mindedly at the carved figure above the hearth, he leaned it against the foot of one of the columns. At the same moment Alex crossed over and closed the double doors.

The family dispersed slowly across the room, each to stand quite alone as though isolation could itself lend force to their projected arguments. Austen, however, remained by the window and, long after the others had retreated, stood with his back to the room watching something that had caught his interest in the grounds below.

'Any decision you may come to,' Cubbitt said, 'will naturally have to be confirmed at a subsequent meeting with the trustees. Perhaps you wouldn't mind if I state the conditions of trusteeship and our mutual responsibilities regarding the Place and its annexed properties so that the whole thing doesn't sound too formidable a mystery?'

He asked this question of Matthew, the only member of the family with whom he maintained any close acquaintance, and he nodded back in dogmatic agreement.

Austen still stood by the window, his interest divided between the room itself and something that was apparently taking place outside. Alex and John stood on either side of the closed doors like two ironically contrasted guards.

'The sale of the Place can be effected in two ways,' Cubbitt went on. 'Either through a unanimous decision by the family, in which case the trustees, if so inclined, are entitled to withhold their final consent to such a sale or disposal for a period of no more than twelve months; or, if there are two or more who cannot agree with the majority, and providing of course that they themselves *are* a minority, then the trustees are the sole adjudicators of the decision and can either dispose of or retain the Place according to their discretion.'

He looked at them in turn and with some care as though he had not only clarified their situation but had also begun to disperse the disturbing atmosphere of the room itself. He had spoken in a low, conversational tone so that gradually they began to move towards him, their convergence curiously absent-minded and instinctive.

'The disposal of a property of this nature is, of course, one of some legal complexity,' he added. 'Certain deeds go as far back as the sixteenth century. I think it is fair to say that few of you, apart from Mr John Radcliffe, have had until now any call to be concerned with the Place, and that in the past, although opportunities have arisen to dispose of the building, the trustees have on each occasion felt it their duty to maintain and preserve the Place as far as was humanly possible. However, you have the power if you so wish to reverse such a decision, and I would ask you, therefore, to use it wisely and only after careful consideration, and to try in your minds to realize what it is you are disposing of.'

For a while they were silent, startled and perhaps even incensed by his tone of appeal. From outside came the faint voice of a man calling rather excitedly, 'Peter! . . . Peter, this way!' Then a sound like the tyres of a silently running vehicle braking on the gravel of the terrace.

Cubbitt had suddenly started to sneeze. He gave three violent exclamations, extracting the handkerchief which protruded from his top pocket and concealing his face. At each sneeze his figure was flung forward, bowing in a kind of devastated apology.

As though to conceal, or perhaps to take advantage of any embarrassment, Alex said, 'What we are here to do is to decide whether the Place can be put to any use, and if it can't, then to discuss how we should dispose of it. It's very simple. Will the benefits we gain from its sale be greater than if we continue to maintain it?'

'There are really two arguments, aren't there?' Austen said, moving forward slightly, but determined to keep his observation post by the window. 'I mean, should we keep the Place on because of certain intrinsic values, historical, aesthetic or otherwise: or should we try and decide whether these are things which have now given way to practical difficulties? For example, should we go on encouraging John to spend his life here . . .?'

'Are you suggesting, then, that it only requires a different *caretaker*?' Matthew said, then turned to John to add, 'Of course, *I* use the word in inverted commas.'

'But don't you think it strange . . .' John began, moving into the room and ignoring this remark, his face pale as he gazed almost frenziedly at Austen. To those watching, however, it seemed that he was speaking to Isabel who stood directly in line with Austen. 'Don't you think it strange that a man whose entire life has been concerned with what he lightly calls "certain intrinsic values, historical, aesthetic or otherwise" – isn't it rather remarkable that when he has to make a choice in a problem like this, he goes against those very things which ostensibly he's supported so long?'

'I wonder if we could open a window? Get a window open?' Cubbitt said, beginning to move away from the fireplace. Towards the end of John's remarks he had begun to sneeze again. 'I'm afraid this is the tail-end of my hay fever. But I wonder if anyone else notices a pungent sort of *smell*? Could we get a window open? Rather like something burning, perhaps.'

Alex had immediately crossed the room and begun to open one of the windows. A moment later Matthew attempted to open another. Cubbitt stood behind them both, alternately watching the efforts of each, his handkerchief held to his nose.

'No, no,' he continued to John, 'go on with what you were saying. At least if we can't clear the air literally we can do so metaphorically.' This ponderous joke he made quite seriously, turning back just as Matthew breathlessly reached down from his unsuccessful attempt to release the rusty catch.

John was silent. For a moment longer Austen continued to stare at him, then he slowly turned once more to the window. Both Matthew and Alex had also been attracted by something that was occurring on the terrace below.

Almost immediately they were distracted by a sound in the room itself, and looked up with expressions of alarm as Thomas, a small raincoated figure, began to speak in an excessively loud and excited voice. 'Do you realize that every stone of this building bears an individual mark? Do you realize that? A mark put there by the man who carved the stone, several hundred years ago. Every tiny fragment of this building has been created with love and care . . . and even now . . . I vote with John. I oppose any disposal of the Place, and the decision will have to go to the trustees, whom God trust. . . .'

From outside, amplified now by the open window, came

the sounds of several voices and of a vehicle stopping abruptly. The next moment the doors were pushed open and Elizabeth, glancing frantically around the room, called out to her father, 'Can you come? Can you come? . . . Something terrible's happened!'

One moment John was looking round at the startled faces in the room, the next he was running down the landing towards the inhabited part of the building. As he reached the head of the stairs, a wailing sound rose from the room below. He paused, overcome by some peculiar confusion, and stumbled down the stairs in a slow spinning movement which at one moment brought him facing the point from which he was descending. To those watching above, it seemed deliberate, scarcely the action of someone who had merely lost his balance. When he reached the foot of the stairs he stopped to peer into the kitchen like someone who had inadvertently opened a wrong door.

The room appeared to be full of people, although in fact there were only six or seven. Leonard lay stiffly in a chair, his head flung back in a curious, distorted foreshortening, his mouth held open as though to accommodate some huge and preposterous shape. From it emerged a hoarse and strangulated wail.

It seemed to John that he was invisibly transported to his son's side, for immediately he found himself staring down at that racked face and into rigid and unseeing eyes. John could extract nothing from the sounds around him except that single and hideously prolonged wail. He saw his own hand as it gripped Leonard's arm, then Leonard's dark suit, then Stella mopping his face with a pinkish cloth. A moment later the body rose under a painful and sustained impulse. It seemed to expand for minutes on end, the air exploding in the throat. It was like a brittle thing about to be broken. Any second John expected it to snap.

Someone was instructing people to stand aside. A stretcher was lifted in at the doorway. Outside were several people apparently arguing. One man, flushed and carrying a camera, was even shouting. The phrase, 'A friend of the family,' floated like a repeated commentary through the room.

Two uniformed attendants bent over Leonard, and John, after trying to maintain his grip on his son's arm, was suddenly forced back.

Standing on the table in front of him were seven cups of coffee, steaming, four of them already loaded on a wooden tray as though about to be carried away. Just beyond them was Cubbitt. Again he was sneezing. His face was the deepest crimson, an inflammation of his features exaggerated by the white handkerchief which periodically he held to his streaming eyes.

'Are you the boy's father?' a man said to him. But without waiting for an answer he turned away and spoke with someone standing a short distance behind him. Then he said again, 'Are you the boy's father, sir?' He swung round once more and spoke with the person to his rear, then confronted John again, 'Are you the young man's father, sir?'

'But what's happened?' John said. 'What has happened?'

'You are the young man's father, sir? This is your son?'

'Yes. . . .'

'Mr Radcliffe?'

At the same time the man conducted a vituperative discussion with the person behind him. As he turned to face John again there was a blinding flash. The room faded for a moment. John felt himself pushed back, then held in a certain position. There was a second flash as a voice said, 'Yes, this's his father.'

A man's face emerged from the whiteness. 'I'm afraid we may be partly to blame for this, Mr Radcliffe. We never realized the distress it might cause. Everything has been taken care of, of course.'

'But what's happened?' John said. The light was now alternating with a consistent and regular pulse. He was staring down at the cups of coffee steaming on the table.

'Yes, he *is* the *father*!'

Several cups had been overturned, and a dark pool lay across the wooden surface.

'What's happened?'

'I'm afraid there's been a tragic accident, sir. Apparently to someone your son knew quite well. So it seems. That's what it appears.'

The man had turned away again. John suddenly recognized the person with whom he had been arguing. It was Thomas. Beyond him in the corner of the room Austen was stooping over Isabel. On the floor, Alex was kneeling and making some adjustment to the stretcher which had obstinately folded at one end. It appeared to John that he had a spanner in his hand. Suspended over it, in the arms of two men, was Leonard. His head was flung back, his body rigid. Stella still wiped his face and neck from which ran two strands of blood. It was only as they laid him on the stretcher that John realized these were in fact the disconnected ends of his tie.

Elizabeth had reappeared by his side and he said to her distractedly, 'I'm his father. Shouldn't I know what's happened?'

'It's Blakeley,' she said with all the signs of impatience. 'These men came to the door ... these newspaper-men came to the door and Leonard answered it. When they told him about Blakeley he fell back in this sort of fit.'

'Would you like to go in the ambulance with your son, Mr Radcliffe?'

John saw that Alex was helping to carry the stretcher through the door. Preceding them was Cubbitt; he appeared to spring into the yard only to be halted by another outburst of sneezing. He bowed vigorously towards the stretcher as it emerged. As they crossed the yard towards the path that ran round the side of the Place it was this distraught figure that absorbed all John's attention.

They rounded the front of the Place to be confronted by a small crowd which had collected round the rear doors of an ambulance. John noticed that in fact Cubbitt had followed them, and as Leonard was inserted into the vehicle's white interior he approached John, bowing still with the force of each sneeze, yet making unmistakable if discordant gestures of condolence. His eyes gazed tormentedly from his crimson face.

The next moment, as John followed Stella and Elizabeth into the ambulance he thought that he glimpsed, standing quite close to the shadowed corner of the Place, as though half-determined not to be observed, the composed figure of

Austen. Then the doors of the vehicle were shut and he was staring down at Leonard's pale face. A red rubber ring protruded from his mouth.

Shortly after the ambulance's departure a hideous rumour swept the estate. Started originally several hours previously by a workman who, in the early hours of the morning, had seen a number of stretchers carried out of one of the houses he was passing, it suggested that a well-known club singer only recently released from jail had, in a fit of depression, killed his entire family and finally himself. The tragedy had been discovered by the police themselves who had gone to the house to further their inquiries into the death of Victor Tolson.

By midday other details had been added to this account, relating it to the event that had occurred that morning at the Place. It was rumoured that Blakeley had written a confession to Tolson's murder, and it had been with the intention of making an arrest that the police had gone to Blakeley's house at such an early hour of the morning.

The public was compelled, however, to wait several days before any of these suppositions could be confirmed, giving ample time for numerous variations to spring up and be discussed. At the inquest, due, it was reported, to the intervention of Cubbitt, Leonard's name had not been mentioned.

Blakeley's confession, extremely long and largely unintelligible, made several points very clearly. One of these was that he had been driven to attack Tolson as a result of that person's oppressive and destructive personality; and that his family's misfortunes, his daughter's as well as his own, had sprung from Tolson's peculiar mania for domination. Details of the attack on Tolson, descriptions of the room and the landing where the assault had taken place, a statement of the time and the content of the telephone call which had summoned the police, all corresponded to the information already possessed, including Blakeley's fingerprints which were found everywhere about the room. No reason could be suggested why the confession contained anything other than the truth.

Blakeley's motives for killing his family were much more

obscure. There was some ambiguity over the parentage of the three children to whom Blakeley had acted as grand-parent, and it was finally established beyond doubt that these were his own children conceived by his daughter Kathleen, who had herself never married. This incestuous relationship caused scarcely less of a sensation than the description of the killings for which it provided some sort of motive. It appeared that a knife had been specially sharpened by Blakeley, for a whetstone was discovered in the hearth at his house. The throats of the three children had been cut while they were sleeping, his wife's while she was rising from the bed; Kathleen herself had apparently been caught as she was about to escape through the front door. Her body was the first to be discovered by the police when they forced an entry. It was covered with such a profusion of knife wounds as to be at first unrecognizable.

Blakeley himself, it was assumed, had spent some time after this writing his confession, one which was terminated by a simple but extremely articulate appeal for the strengthening and preservation of the monarchy, and for greater support for the unification of the churches. He had then made several attempts to kill himself with the knife and, having failed, had seemingly walked aimlessly about the house for the rest of the night. Bloodied footmarks led repetitively through every room and up and down the stairs. He had finally succeeded in killing himself, it appeared, as the police knocked on the front door, and had done so by facing a mirror and cutting his throat. The mirror, for some absurd reason, was displayed in court, its surface almost completely concealed beneath a dark tracery of stains.

35

It seemed to Leonard that his brain had unfolded. It broke violently apart. He was shocked at first because he could see no cause for it. One moment he was listening to some-one speaking at the door and the next he was retreating with awkward, staggering movements of his legs. He couldn't understand it. Extraordinary pains swept through his body and he was overwhelmed by a deeper sense of shock at his increasingly helpless behaviour. His brain was surrounded by a thicket of flame, separating him from all the things he could now only imagine, his composure, his control, his ease of expression. He saw all that he wanted most to retrieve disappearing beyond that barricade of fire. He was acutely embarrassed, for he was filled at the same time with a great desire to apologize to all those around him: the men who came through the door, his mother, and to Elizabeth making the coffee on the table. He saw this quite clearly, even to the individual and varying expressions of alarm. Several faces seemed to peer down and pursue him into this heatless blaze. He tried to reason and to show his shame. Then with a mixed sensation of relief and alarm, a black film like a helmet was drawn slowly down from the crown of his head, over his eyes, then his nose, and finally over his mouth so that he could no longer see, breathe, nor cry out. It enclosed him in a tightening black shell. A single white circle receded into the distance. Then he woke. He was lying in a bed of stiff sheets and felt sore and utterly tired.

For a while he could remember little. He accepted people with the same lack of sensation with which he received injections or other medicinal treatment. He saw his parents and Elizabeth quite frequently but once they'd gone could recollect little of what they had said. Whenever he looked round from his bed at the other people in the ward it was with a half-formed expression of apology, a disjointed look of commiseration. Only during one of his father's early visits, when he suggested that Leonard should be moved to a room of his own where he could read or draw in private, did any strong feeling rise up in him, briefly yet so intensely, that it was agreed he should remain in the public ward until he himself should demand a change.

When he was relaxed he tended to watch the people around him with an exhausted and defeated air, as though any activity in itself bewildered him. He appeared to have little impression of time, one mood of feeling separated from the next by sleep. He was also left with a certain deafness, the delayed effect, it was suggested, of the hammer blow a few weeks previously.

He was encouraged to walk. He moved amongst the other patients silently at first and with heavy, deliberate gestures. Then, when he began to take notice of the various conversations around him, he would stand listening with a slight though intent inclination of his head, occasionally nodding reflectively and gazing at some distant object in the room. When asked something directly he would look at his questioner with a half-curious, almost imperious look, then walk away without answering.

Frequently he would go to one particular window at the end of the ward and stand looking out at the top half of a lime tree directly facing him. Sometimes, usually in the early morning or the late evening, the sunlight caught its spindly arrangement of twigs and he would stand watching the elaborate network of glowing filaments as though within its luminous tracery he detected the contours and perhaps even the shape of the thing which eluded him.

He showed no overt curiosity either in the people around him or in himself, though he gave all his attention to whatever was demanded of him; whenever he asked any questions it was as if to reassure himself of some opinion he had already formed.

Yet there was a curious, enigmatic attractiveness about him extending far beyond his moodiness that affected those who came directly into contact with him. In the ward itself it was identified as a certain patience and generosity of manner, almost an attribute of breeding and refinement.

Austen, who surprisingly showed little interest in seeing Leonard, made several regular though well-spaced visits to the hospital, staying considerably less than the permitted time and scarcely concealing behind his urbane exterior a certain impatience. He was like a man determinedly waiting for a climax which others assumed had already taken place. Leonard's mother and, curiously, Isabel saw in Leonard's condition the result of that solitariness and isolation which in the past they themselves had tried unsuccessfully to breach. Leonard had in this sense passed beyond them, and both found it difficult and excessively wearying to speak to him.

Only one person seemed detached. Having returned to his work in the South, Alex came back one week-end to stay with Isabel and, after a long meeting with Cubbitt, went to visit Leonard. Having seen and spoken with him for some time, and been to some extent irritated by his slight deafness, Alex was reluctant to admit to Isabel what his real reactions were. It was only several days later, in the taxi on the way to the station, that he confessed that he now found Leonard a pathetic though quite harmless imbecile.

Nevertheless, it was only a short while after this that Leonard was allowed to return home.

He returned to the Place with the lack of curiosity of someone making his daily return from work. And he had been there scarcely an hour before the family began to think of his absence as the least curious episode of the previous few weeks. For several days in fact they saw little of him. Unobtrusive and very quiet, he went out alone walking a great deal, chiefly across the upper ridges of moorland which fringed the vast area of collieries and mills to the north. From the summits of these remote escarpments the Place could occasionally be glimpsed like some tiny black shell laid on a flank of rock. Late in the day, when the sun hung low in the sky, a dull red flash of light frequently shot from its windows, a momentary beam splaying across miles of undulating countryside. His mother traced these journeys by inspecting his coat pockets and examining the different colours of the bus tickets she extracted. This was the only way they could keep track not only of his daily pilgrimages but, it seemed, of his recovery as well.

The weather was cold and sunny with the clear skies of early winter, the sun low and heavy, a cumbersome thing. Each evening Leonard returned with drawings. They intimidated his father. There was something familiar now in these sheets of contained violence, hard and stark and black. Neither Austen's enthusiasm nor his mother's hatred of what he was doing seemed to impinge in any way on his preoccupation. He drew continuously; large complex constructions of the landscape, and small, almost engraved miniatures of Elizabeth, of her face, her hair, and her hands. He drew with people around him, either in the kitchen or outside, as though it were a conversation he held. Elizabeth he returned to continuously, tracing out her slender face with its oval and precise features again and again as though it were not something he examined but something he chose to confirm. Occasionally as he looked at her his expressionless features would suddenly be charged with a smile. 'Why are you so serious?' he said whenever he saw no change in the intent way she submitted to him. But she never replied.

Late one afternoon as he was returning up the drive he heard a violent activity in the shrubbery on his left-hand side. It was now almost completely dark. Then, a short distance ahead, where the drive ran onto the terrace, a large black dog emerged from the bushes and, after pausing a second, its head drooping towards the ground, it moved on and disappeared under the trees on the opposite side.

Later that evening, after he had been drawing Elizabeth for some time in the kitchen, his father and Austen sitting silently by the fire, his mother working, Leonard suddenly looked up at her and said, 'Are you pregnant, Liz?'

She gazed back at him, surprised that he should ask about something which had become increasingly obvious since his return home.

'Yes.'

He went on drawing for a short while, the eyes of the family upon him. Eventually he looked up at Austen and said with a half-amused expression, 'Well, Austen, do you think I *am* the avenging angel?' And when Austen offered no answer, he added, 'Why does my father allow you to go on coming here when he thinks of you as the perpetrator of a plot . . . one of which I'm alleged to be the victim?'

'If you don't want Austen to be here,' his father said, 'you've only to say so.'

'But why are you so acquiescent? Doesn't it matter? I mean, have you, for example, decided to sell the Place?'

'Yes.'

Leonard looked briefly at Austen, then added, 'How long shall we go on living here?'

'Perhaps a year,' said his father. 'It could be less.'

Leonard allowed his gaze to remain on his uncle. 'Do you still think of this place as a castle, Austen, and see me striding through these northern lands like the Lord Protector, striking down the enemies of God? In this particular instance such enemies being made to include the lower and middle classes.'

Austen seemed heavily amused. 'Cromwell's war wasn't a war of class, Leonard. His was a war of feeling. A war of sensibility.'

'Well, then, which of us has won!' Leonard turned triumphantly to his father. 'Perhaps you haven't understood Austen at all, father, his Caroline temperament.'

'And what does that mean?' John said, looking at his son with an unusual intensity.

Leonard laughed at his father's confusion: it seemed that he was anticipating another fit.

'You've understood absolutely nothing at all! Didn't you realize that Austen has fought out the fate of our heritage under your very nose, and that even now he's congratulating himself on his complete and undisputed victory? One army has fought against the other, and both have been destroyed. Austen is about to step up once more to the throne and take his place.'

He laughed more loudly, amused more than ever by his father's bewilderment. 'Why! . . . Why, when you sell the Place as Austen has planned you should all along, you'll wake up next morning and find the anonymous bidder was in fact representing your own *brother*! Here! Here! This is where Austen wishes he had spent his life like you!'

He looked at his uncle with a wild expression of triumph. 'Even now . . . even now he'll have all the money raised from various sources just in case the sale goes through earlier than expected!'

Leonard did not stay to see the effect of these words. Yet the next day as he went off down the drive, setting out on his day's drawing, his father came after him, prepared, it seemed, to accompany him wherever he went. As they passed the church he took Leonard's arm and suggested they should go inside.

He pushed open the gate and allowed Leonard to go in before him. The interior was dark and very cold. Once inside he led the way to the nearest pew and sat down, moving along from the carved boss at the end to allow Leonard to sit beside him. At the far end of the building rose the successive tiers of Radcliffe effigies.

'I used to come in here a great deal while you were away, in hospital,' he said. 'Oh, not for the reason you're thinking. No, it's very simple. I came in here because for the first time I felt at home.'

He glanced sideways at Leonard, who sat clutching his drawing paper under his arm, gazing up at the ceiling. Then he moved his head closer as though determined that, despite Leonard's deafness, he would not have to repeat anything.

He sat silently a moment longer, then added, 'I've never mentioned my father to you, have I? And there's no point, of course, in starting now. But he was quite an elderly man by the time I got to know him, and used to a life I suppose which had its viciousness like ours but which also had its certain leisure and grace. It seems to me, Leonard, that we've retained the cruelties and the viciousness and dispensed with the rest. At least we've done one thing. We've made the descent into Hell more democratic.'

Leonard watched his father while he spoke, but absent-mindedly, a familiar expression of detachment, though now perhaps touched with pity.

'I was brought up, Leonard, to believe that the right political and economic institutions could bring happiness and uplift to the majority of mankind. Even transform the very character of human beings. But now, in these days, those are only the sentiments of the very young.'

Leonard had moved suddenly in his seat as though he had observed something in the shadows at the opposite end of the church, close to the altar. It was a momentary sensation of alarm. Then he stared down into the pitch blackness between his feet.

'When I was younger, your age in fact,' his father added, 'I suddenly made what I thought was a discovery: that you have only two choices, either to live in isolation or to be absorbed. Well, I made my choice. And it was the wrong one. I never realized that you *must* be absorbed. That you must take your part, and that *then* you must fight. But subversively, with all the cunning, the mischievousness, the intelligence, the perverseness, the deception, the duplicity, with every essence and every sense in your body. I never realized. I never realized. We are all partisans now. We are all saboteurs. Every one.'

For a while his voice continued to echo in the place, as if the stone whispered. It came out of the darkness, fading. John leaned back. He was sweating profusely. Leonard stared down to the far end of the church, to where the effigies glistened. Then he said, 'Why should you tell me this?' And when his father made no answer, he added, 'Is that the sum total of your experience? Shall I tell you what your disease really is? You've spent your life making a virtue of feeling, yet in all that time you've never actually *felt* one tiny thing.'

'Leonard, this is wrong. . . .'

'Is it? Is it? You never even realized how much I loved Tolson. You can't begin even to imagine what he meant to me!'

His father gazed at him bitterly. 'I think I do know, Leonard.'

But Leonard interrupted him with a growing wildness. 'How could you know? Don't talk to me! Don't talk to me about choices and your intellectual saboteurs!'

He suddenly looked closely at his father, peering it seemed into the texture of his skin. 'Austen knew,' he whispered, 'and he used his knowledge to his own ends.'

He had begun to move away, towards the door. Then he swayed as though physically waylaid. 'You've never realized. You never have! The only real politics is art. Art is the only real politics. And the rest. The rest is just sentiment!' He called in a loud voice, 'You are a fool! A fool! A maggot crawling in a carcase! And you bred a maggot for a son!'

His father sprang forward to take his arm.

'Do you think I don't know?' Leonard shouted. 'Don't you think I realized? Everything! *Everything*!' He pulled his arm free with a cry of pain, as though his father's fingers had closed over a wound. He hurried out to the gate and onto the road leading down through the estate. As John watched him he was shocked to see that quite suddenly it had started to snow.

It fell for several days. Clouds lay like vast ribs against the sky, suspended over that whitened cage where the snow followed the latticed intricacies of streets and buildings. Across the jagged ridges it brought out strange faces and the long, crushing delineation of huge bodies, black giants dormant within the bony contours of the rock. The snow seemed to confirm an unnatural silence about the land.

Each morning Leonard went out to draw. In the afternoons he had started to paint in the York Room. The whiteness emphasized the heavy declivities of the rock and stone, whether it was a small knoll seen from many miles away or a weathered protuberance on the church or the Place: it gave a strange, strutting power to the figures that moved between these black and massive blocks.

There were periods now, usually when he was painting, when he could hear nothing at all, and others when his hearing was apparently unimpaired. If his family detected a certain perverseness in this they never allowed it to anger them as they might have done when Leonard was younger. To the people on the estate, now that the immediate storm of gossip had died down, his behaviour, his paint-stained hands and clothes, his air of absorption, confirmed a reputation which had begun to grow many years before.

The snow thickened. It drifted from low, grey bulks of cloud during the day, and at night the sky cleared and a heavy frost sprang down, tightening its white hold on the land. Then, gradually, the clouds began to fall away, and throughout most of the day a red flushed sun lowered hugely between the trees, tracing a course close to the horizon and safely away from this cold centre.

Some time later Leonard stopped drawing. He began to spend all his time painting. At night the York Room was garishly lit by an eccentric arrangement of lamps, their long flexes held in place by a network of string. One end of the room by the fireplace was illuminated like a stage, the rest merging virtually into darkness. It was in this bright pool of light that he painted.

He worked very quickly. Stacks of paintings began to

mount against the walls. The two largest were laid on the floor and he stood over them to work, stooping down in swift, darting actions as if painting itself involved some intense, personal antagonism. One of them was a landscape from the windows of the York Room, looking out over the broad, descending sweep of the estate to the flattened valley bottom. Beyond, it rose to the ragged crust of rock that curved like an arm over the rim of the city. A dark shape like a crown forced its way above the jagged silhouette and penetrated a clouded sky. It was like a body moving frustratedly within its confines of muscle.

The second large painting had been incoherent for a long time: the paint was massed thickly, with the same vicious massivity as in the landscape. It was only gradually that a figure began to emerge from the cyclopean contours above its head. Beyond it was the strained, stony relief of the fireplace. Five shafts of sunlight fell into the room, huge falling pillars, whitish-yellow springing out determinedly from under the sombre passivity of the darkened ceiling. This interior of the York Room was carved out of the paint itself, a ravaged hollow, the figure pinioned by the violent columns of light. Austen, who periodically came up to examine the paintings and drawings in Leonard's absence, had identified the single figure from the beginning as himself.

One night as he was working, Leonard saw a dog standing at the darkened end of the room. It moved amongst the clutter of paintings and drawings as though unaware of his presence, only halting when it approached the pool of light.

For a while he continued working, perhaps for an hour, but the dog, apart from relieving itself over some of his work, showed no disinclination to vary its constant, circular inspection of the room. It was a large, black animal, and after a time a pungent smell began to fill the air. Leonard was compelled to stop working. He seemed stifled. Only now, in his stillness, did the animal show any awareness of his presence. It had paused, its eyes glinting redly in the light, to stare at him from the opposite end of the room.

He seemed increasingly tormented by the dog, by its

stillness and by the odour that permeated the room. Suddenly he turned round and went to the door and, after some hesitation, continued down the landing and started climbing the main stairs.

He climbed without pause to the top. It was completely dark within this shuttered section, yet he moved familiarly about the interior, hurrying along the upper landing to the gallery where the mullioned windows admitted a feeble light. Here, several parallel beams of moonlight fell on the blank gallery wall. He stood listening for a while. Then, hearing a soft movement and the heavy sound of breathing further down the landing, he stepped into the doorway of the next room.

He waited, panting from his recent exertion. The entrance to the tiny room was faintly illuminated by the light reflected from the gallery. The dog growled a short distance away down the landing.

The animal came in very quickly, as though suspecting he had escaped. For a moment it wheeled round the black interior, its head brushing damply against his hand before he rushed into the passage and pulled the door to after him. A second later the dog hurled itself against the door. Then a second and a third time, the air roaring through its throat as it struck the thick panelling. Leonard listened to its efforts for some time, then, confirming that the door was securely fastened, he returned through the darkened building to the York Room.

For a while he walked indecisively about the room until, drawn by the brightness of the moon, he went to the windows and looked down. A vast tracery of trees stretched across the moonlit snow, a black intaglioed relief. Then, as he drew away, he saw a figure emerge from the shadows of the nearest trunks and walk across the unbroken snow on the terrace. It had evidently been standing there for some time, for it now moved as though determined to restore the circulation of its frozen blood, stamping its feet and flinging its arms. He only had time to identify it as an elderly man before it disappeared in the deeply etched shadows that sprawled across the drive. He turned towards the door, surprised rather than alarmed, as though vaguely he might have recognized someone. The next day he cleared up the paintings and the drawings in the room.

He stacked them neatly at the opposite end and brought up a mirror from the kitchen. For the rest of the day, and far into the night, he sat painting himself. He worked more quickly than before, occasionally going to the door or onto the stairs from where, faintly, he could hear an intermittent barking. He painted several small heads at first in bright colours then, the following day, started on a painting sufficiently large to absorb him completely for several days. He alternated his visits to the stairs and, later, to the top landing, with brief vigils at the window. It was as though he were expecting someone.

The figure in the painting was crouched forward, urgent, buried under the weight of paint that he forced onto the surface. The head, turned slightly from the narrow pivot of the body, grew out of the heavy green of its background, a whitish, faded pink face expanding centrifugally around the blackened shells of its eyes. The hair was scattered round the head in a virulent red. It grew there like horns.

Shortly after this, in a newspaper brought to the Place by Austen, John read a report that, partly due to information provided by a man recently released from a mental institution and who had previously been employed at Ewbank's, various aspects of Tolson's death were to be re-examined.

The following day Leonard stopped painting, so suddenly that it was as if he had completely forgotten the one thing that had occupied him so intensely for the past few months.

He spent the greater part of each day in his room, occasionally emerging to wander about the building, though most frequently on the top floor. The barking, which John, whenever he had heard its faint echoes, had put down to his imagination, had now ceased. No sound at all came from the small room.

Several nights later, towards dawn, John was woken by an appalling stench and by the sounds of burning. He rushed through into the main part of the building to find the floor of the York Room already well alight. At the centre of the fire was a tightly-packed pile of Leonard's drawings and paintings, from the top of which protruded the huge head of a dog. Already encased in flames which sprouted from its skull like curls of hair, it seemed curiously alive, its eyes open, its jaws hanging fully apart, its teeth gleaming. It seemed poised there in the very act of springing. Periodically its body twisted as one by one the flames consumed its painted supports.

As morning broke the fire was brought under control. It had, surprisingly, done relatively little damage, penetrating only to one other room, Austen's so-named Braganza Room beneath. Its ceiling was damaged beyond repair. The Jezebel Mantelpiece, its wooden supports consumed, had crashed to the floor and disintegrated.

Sections of burning shutter had fallen from the windows into the snow, leaving isolated pools of water on the terrace. The five gutted windows of the York Room gave the Place a sudden and final look of dereliction.

Leonard himself was missing, but by the time he might have begun to worry seriously about his absence, John had already been informed that he had gone to the city's police station several hours before and volunteered a statement concerning the death of Tolson that contained information which could not easily be ignored.

36

Leonard appeared before the magistrates court the same morning and was remanded in custody for a week charged with the murder of Tolson.

The most impressive and convincing part of his confession was that which described the interior of Tolson's room at the time of the attack, accounting for details which Blakeley had not included, amongst them a broken glass of milk, an alarm clock and Tolson's belt which had all been concealed beneath the upturned furniture. It was as if, in its clarity, he described a particular drawing for which he had had a long affection. In addition he had explained Blakeley's presence at the scene and had produced, finally, the weapon itself. Between its claws were embedded the remains of hair and tissue which, several days later, were confirmed as having been torn from Tolson's skull. This corroborated the evidence provided by Shaw who, at the initial hearing, stated that he had seen Leonard steal the hammer while it was still in Tolson's use at Ewbank's. The contractor's name was stencilled on the shaft. Shaw also described in some detail the nature of the relationship that had existed between the accused and the victim, and a week later, when this latter evidence had been confirmed by several others, including Audrey and Ewbank himself, Leonard was sent for trial to the local Assizes.

Now that he was alone for the greater part of each day, his solitude only interrupted at predetermined times, Leonard found that he was less obsessed by thoughts and ideas that normally preoccupied him and more absorbed by certain images and visions. Even when his parents visited him he would turn aside their inquiries to describe to them the large figures hurtling through space by which he was now surrounded. His descriptions of these giants, white and black and trailing red flanges of cloud, and of massive shapes of flame and metal plunging from the sky, were interrupted with demands from his father to explain the circumstances of the confession and the delay between it and Tolson's death. For John still believed in Leonard's innocence, and saw his predicament as some hellish aberration of that plot fomented originally by Austen. Yet Leonard persisted in his descriptions, as though he were somehow instructing, advising them.

Then, one morning shortly before the trial, John visited him alone, making such demands for an explanation that Leonard, who had been absorbed in his heated description, looked up and said quietly, 'You don't realize at all, do you, how much I am on my own. . . . You don't realize . . . and not just now but always. How I've always been so much on my own.'

'But there's been no need. It isn't as if you've gone without love or affection,' John said, more wretched himself as he saw that Leonard was almost in tears. 'All these things have been available to you.'

'I don't know what it is. I think there's something in me which, however sympathetic people might be at the beginning, eventually alienates them. Even frightens them. As if the more I need their affection and spontaneous interest the more sombre and menacing, the more threatening I become. It's terrible. It's a terrible thing. It's like being damned before you've even been given a choice. Or like being shown what salvation is the moment after you've been told it's no longer yours.'

For a while they sat in silence, Leonard looking at his father directly. Then he added, 'I think there's an element in us which refutes and condemns our understanding of ourselves, as if perversely we're determined to be damned. I think that's the key to everything.'

Such an outright rejection struck so deeply into John that he turned away, his face averted as though he had been physically assaulted.

'It isn't something for you to reproach yourself with,' Leonard said. 'I think all my ambition, what *I*'ve had, has been for something huge and impassive. Perhaps to that extent I've inherited it from you. I've always looked for something like that, *something* cold and northern and precise.'

Despite his distress, John was profoundly moved. For the first time he had come so close to Leonard that he felt he could now touch him. Even feel through him. When he asked him about the trial, Leonard said, 'I don't want you to worry on account of my loneliness. The strange thing is I've found something through it which is irreplaceable and couldn't have been discovered in any other way. When I was younger, before I met Vic, I can't tell you what it was like. The absolute loneliness, so that even the houses, the buildings I passed seemed to exude something that contaminated you and made you lonely. So sombre and remorseless. It terrifies me. At times I still can't bear to look at certain things because they're so *black*. As if they're drained of life. And not just drained, but as if everything that appears to live, that attempts *any* sort of life is simply imitating some distant and incoherent ideal. Imitating. And it's the sense of imitation that's so forbidding. The whole impression of people *playing*. As though it's all a deception, and the only person it doesn't deceive is me.

341

That's what it is. The feeling that you're isolated simply because you can't be deceived.'

'But I don't understand. How can any compensation arise out of that?'

'I don't know. I think it must be the security of suffering. Despair breeds a kind of warmth which is intolerable yet a confirmation of something absolute, something final and secure. Beyond it you can see clearly where the end lies. It's all blackness to me. Everything. But there are points of blackness so intense and absolute that it's there I can feel a kind of joyless reassurance.'

He watched his father carefully a moment, then added, 'I don't think you realize what it was I found in Vic. What I *almost* found. But it was the separateness, the separateness of everything that lay between us. It wasn't that one of us was good and the other bad, but that we were both these things because we were separate. Vic was my body, and I was his soul. We were one. Or could have been. . . . It's the division that separates everything in life now, *everything*.'

Although such incoherence frightened John, he asked, 'If you did kill Tolson . . . why have you waited so long to confess?' He was now more than ever convinced of Leonard's innocence, of the perversion of his son's mind, through having witnessed the event; that it was, in fact, Blakeley's crime.

'Why have I waited? It was because I wanted a long, slow pain which I could control.'

'But what do you mean?' John said.

'I couldn't have tolerated a sharp pain. *Tolson*'s pain. One that overwhelmed all the senses. I wanted a slow pain, however intense, so that I could *think* while I had to endure it. So that I would *know*. That's why Christ had to die slowly.'

John left in distress, though knowing that he would see Leonard immediately before the trial in the cells under the court room.

When he returned to the Place, Stella, after watching his wretchedness for longer than she could bear, said wildly, 'Why do you torment yourself so much with him?'

'But can you cut yourself off so completely?'

'How can I cut myself off?' she said. 'How can I? He's the only person I've ever known who has gone through the whole of life without forming one single human relationship. You can't cut yourself off from that. How can you separate yourself from something that doesn't exist?' And recognizing the despair of her logic John could find no way of answering.

The trial created intense interest. Each morning large crowds of women surrounded the entrance to the court building, and on the fourth day, due to a mistake over the allocation of seats, there were angry scenes in the forecourt. Several women were injured, others arrested, and the hearing postponed for an hour until some who had managed to get into the building were rounded up and expelled.

The prisoner's awareness during the trial appeared to fluctuate enormously. At one moment he would follow the proceedings with concentration, and at the next he would gaze up abstractedly at the glass dome of the ceiling as though the room were deserted. When matter-of-fact details were being given to the court he would unexpectedly blush and look utterly confused, whereas when accounts of the intensity of his relationship with Tolson were being provided he would look down on witness and officials alike with a scornful composure. This was particularly obvious when evidence was provided by Colonel Wetherby and the girl Enid who described between them what they had observed of the five days he and Tolson had spent alone looking after the marquees. When several drawings and paintings, provided by Austen, were submitted to the court, he listened blushing to his counsel's description of them as unmistakable indications of mental derangement. He bowed his head, his hands clutched tightly between his knees.

The medical report submitted by the defence stated that Radcliffe was a psychotic who under duress became insane: there was an egotism, a concealed obsessive sexuality, and a mania for detail which were only associated with the insane, even an ability to explain all his own vagaries of feeling and action in terms of an irreducible and terrifying logic.

The report submitted by the prosecution stressed his rationality and intelligence, his strongly defined sense of independence, a thoughtful and careful attention to detail, and a sense of reasoning and argument that was both highly articulate and persuasive. Duress acted as a stimulus to these qualities, sharpening his perceptiveness and self-awareness to a point where it might reasonably be assumed that he could deceive most people. There was no physical evidence of homosexual practices.

The last witness to appear was Leonard himself. Until now he had shown no signs of real fear, even when listening to the evidence of Ewbank, Shaw, Pilkington and Audrey. Yet as he was led across the court to the witness box he seemed suddenly to become aware of sounds above his head; in the balcony, below which he had been seated throughout the hearing, was a solid crowd of women. They seemed to cling like a huge corporeal emblem to the wall of the room, a giant, prostrated bat. For a moment he faltered, filled with genuine dismay, even turning to one side as if he would go back. Then, flushed and responding to the pressure of the warder at his side, he crossed the room and climbed slowly into the stand. In the illumination that fell directly into the room from the glassed dome in the ceiling he appeared absurdly small and emaciated.

He answered his counsel's questions with a curious lifelessness, as if he were either too embarrassed or too uninterested to speak. His expression alternated between boredom and momentary bouts of confusion. Occasionally when the barrister could not make himself heard, questions were written on a piece of paper and passed up to Leonard to read. At other times when, quite factually and in a toneless voice, he recounted incidents between Tolson and himself that had led up to the murder, and particularly one that had taken place immediately before the killing, and he witnessed the sensation they caused both in the gallery and in the court around him, he appeared quite dazed. And when asked to clarify what he had just said, he stared round the courtroom as though he had lost all sense of his situation and was privately speculating on some other problem. Such pauses became more frequent as the hearing progressed, but in no way discouraged his counsel who, if anything, took advantage of the laborious and repetitious method necessary to communicate with his client.

Only under cross-examination did he suddenly reveal any emotion, when the prosecutor questioned his description of Blakeley as a man suffering from intermittent fits of 'histrionic schizophrenia'. Then he cried out, 'I've read books! I know how to diagnose things of this sort. He was an evangelist. And like all evangelists he was incapable of distinguishing between destruction and sacrifice.'

Then later, when he was trying to describe the relationship that had existed between Tolson and himself, he said, almost in tears, 'The battle was so intense between us because we could see something beyond it. It was the split between us that tormented us; the split in the whole of Western society.'

When it was suggested that he was trying to obscure something which was intensely personal and distasteful to him by giving it an air of objectivity, by disguising it in terms of some general theory, he stated vehemently, 'You've got to *accept* that there is a love that exists between men which is neither obscene nor degrading, but is as powerful and as profound, and as fruitful, as that love which bears children. The love that men have for other men, as *men*, may be beyond some people's powers of comprehension. But it has a subtlety and a flexibility, a power that creates order. Politics, art, religion: these things are the products of men's loving. And by that I mean their hatred, their antagonism, their affection, as *men*, and their curiosity in one another as men. It isn't that women have been deprived of these things, but simply that they can't love *in this way*. They have been given something less abstract, more physical, something more easily understood. Law, art, politics, religion: these are the creation of men as *men*.'

After a considerable silence following this outburst, the prosecutor said quietly, 'Do you think it's unusual, or exceptional for men to kiss one another?'

'This is wrong,' Leonard said, incensed. 'It wasn't physical satisfaction I looked for, and it wasn't something

345

personal either. I've tried to explain. It was something almost communal and *impersonal*. You're deliberately trying to misunderstand me.'

'But don't you feel that you're obscuring something which *is* personal by giving it this cloak of objectivity, by theorizing? And that you've done this consistently in all the behaviour you've described with Tolson? That, in fact, you are so aware of what occurred that you can only overcome your sense of distaste and guilt by explaining it in terms of the general corruption of society?'

'No! No, it was the other way around!'

'Why then did you *kill* him?'

'Because I had to! . . . Whatever we did we destroyed. Everybody! Everything!'

'What does that mean?'

Leonard had turned away. He seemed senseless. 'Oh, God!' he cried, shaking his fists at the court. 'I wanted something huge and *absolute*! I wanted an absolute! I wanted an ideal! I wanted an order for things!'

'But what does that mean?' the prosecutor said, singularly unmoved by this display.

'I wanted to love him. Everything: it was to love him. And as a man, as a *human being*.'

'Not just as a man, physically?'

'No . . . no. It was for everyone. I wanted to love him for everyone.'

Shortly after this the court was recessed and the Judge called the two opposing counsel to his chambers.

It seemed to Leonard, afterwards, that the trial had only been incidental. The hugeness by which he was now surrounded enveloped everything that had preceded it, so that even Tolson's death was only a detail of the vast structure by which he was enclosed. It had a completeness, a wholeness, that dazed him, making him so exultant he could scarcely breathe. It contained everyone and everything. It was complete.

As he listened to the closing speeches of the trial he appeared calm and reflective, only turning his head slightly at certain phrases as though he caught some fragment of their implication. '. . . A guilt so monstrous that, like all the other emotions his puritanical mind finds intolerable, it is manufactured into some heartless theory about the destiny of men in general. . . . He has asked us to look at his crime as if it were the simple illustration of an elaborate theory which he is holding up for our *approval*. . . . Asking us to approve of *his* sensations: sensations he has twisted into a logic that would not only explain with indifference the death of seven people, but seventy, seven thousand, seven million. Every action that this man has ever committed has been a blind attempt to deny his own intolerable con- ·science.'

After a while, he seemed quite impervious to the voices and sat with hunched shoulders, slightly bored, gazing down at his feet. Only when a verdict of diminished responsibility had been returned and he was asked if he had anything to say before sentence was passed did he stand up and look uncertainly around him, like someone waking from a dream.

He gazed at the wall opposite him for a while, then started speaking slowly, as though repeating something he had carefully rehearsed.

'Whatever my limitations or my weaknesses,' he said, his eyes moodily fixed on the insignia above the Judge's head, 'whatever they are and however misunderstood *I* have been, I'm absolutely sure that men desire above all things a moral authority. And that it was from a will for moral authority that I acted, and with a sense of moral authority that *I* saw *everything*. You've tried to judge my actions as though they were subject to the Common Law of the land, whereas the moral ground on which my struggle with Tolson took place was at a level outside that of Common Law. And this is its vulnerability, that the Common Law is separate from and only coincidental with *morality*. Its single quality is its expediency and not its justice. It is only by chance that what is morally right coincides with what is judicially expedient. What happens when a moral man has to act politically. . . .'

As the Judge attempted to intervene, Leonard added more vehemently, even drowning his voice, 'This has been a trial before men when it should and could have been a trial before God. To have found me insane is insanity itself, for you should have tried to determine whether I acted in accordance with a corrupt world, or against the principles of an uncorrupt world. I'm condemned not because of what I am but because of what you are. My crime is clear. It is that *you* have been content!'

He was suddenly so overcome with a fit of coughing, one in which his face turned a bright crimson, that he had to be helped into a chair.

A short while after his trial, Leonard began to feel that he'd been released. Something now was so complete and whole as to be unbreakable. He was surrounded by solidity, by the heaviness of things. Even the thick, featureless walls of the prison confirmed it. Clouds roared intermittently across the sky, great nervous sheets of vapour, convulsed by freakish disturbances of the air; then periods of stillness, so that all the human sounds that came to his ears, of voices, of feet shuffling, completely enraptured him. Whenever he saw people, particularly someone he had not met before, a new warder, a new doctor, a new minister, he was frequently overcome with breathlessness, as though he could scarcely contain his sense of them, his feeling for them. He touched them, smiling at them reconcilingly. He could tough everything.

Some while later he was transferred to a mental institution for criminal defectives. His behaviour had become so eccentric that it amounted to the continual and open soliciting of other prisoners and to fits of incoherent moralizing whenever he was confined for his behaviour.

In this new institution he was carefully segregated from the other inmates and only allowed to mix with them under supervision for short periods of each week. He became thinner, and increasingly intense, didactic and apologetic by turn in conversation; and frequently, when alone in his cell, given to long bouts of preaching in which he confirmed his discovery of the brotherhood of man.

His behaviour became even more extreme. Unless restrained, he tended to rush at people, flinging himself upon them in violent attempts to embrace them. He would hurl himself against the walls and the door of his cell, and had often to be secured to his bed before any attempt could be made to console him. Here, while waiting for the injection, he would lie straining and crying at his bonds, and shouting the word 'Love!' until he was finally subdued.

One night, when it seemed his fragile and emaciated body could no longer contain the violence which possessed it, he suffered a haemorrhage of the brain and, shortly after his parents reached him the following morning, he died.

He was thin and barely recognizable. The bone had almost penetrated the skin and even in death his body seemed contorted by some incredible power. He had a beard and his hair was long, almost white, the face itself so narrow and pale that it was like some deeply-carved piece of stone. The resemblance to their son was so remote that his parents appeared to suffer little remorse or pain at seeing him; more, a sense of distaste.

The combination of horror and shock had the effect of turning his father aside from normal life. He became silent, self-absorbed and unapproachable. He scarcely slept and was haunted by such strange visions that whenever someone spoke to him he was apt to stare at them with an expression of naked terror. Finally, at Alex's suggestion, Stella was encouraged to take the old man away to the South.

Elizabeth, at her own insistence, was left with Austen and Isabel. She had become a determined and confident woman. In the summer her child was born. It was a boy, with a physique peculiar for a Radcliffe in its size and strength. It had, however, unmistakable Radcliffe eyes, dark and enigmatic. Occasionally, as she watched it, Elizabeth saw in its face the gaze of her brother, quiet and uncompromising. But then some energetic movement of its body would dispel the brief impression and, as it grew, its look of confidence, its peculiar independence, became a source of consolation to her.

There had been some suggestion that Austen should take over John's place at Beaumont, but after considering various municipal schemes, it was eventually agreed that it should be pulled down.

349

Elizabeth, Austen and Isabel moved to the South, and were never heard of in the district again.

For a year the Place stood empty, crumbling under the fingers of vandals by day, and by night under its own aged momentum. It grew more derelict and forbidding, its blackness no longer relieved by occasional lights and gleams from its windows, its grounds no longer maintained by patient and persistent hands. Beyond its fringe of trees and shrubs it seemed to be waiting, crouched, its stone shielded by those dark trunks that grew about it like limbs. Sometimes at night the inhabitants of the nearer houses heard crashes echoing from its empty rooms. But each morning it still stood there whole and complete. It was almost as if it were struggling unseen within itself.

When the workmen came, tractors tore effortlessly at the old stonework. Steel hawsers were clamped round the walls and pillars, and within a few days the building that, in its older parts, had stood for nearly five hundred years was levelled to the ground.

The church too was demolished, its foundations pronounced to be dangerous from subsidence due to the mining beneath; the cost of renovation was too high. Its various treasures were distributed amongst local museums, though the sculptured effigies themselves were broken up. A more serviceable church of brick was constructed and, although equally deserted, it was larger, cleaner and uncluttered by decoration.

The housing estate that had previously enclosed the Place on all sides seized quickly on this last piece of ground; a crescent was laid out where it had stood, and council houses, erected on either side, finally linked the two avenues that had flanked it and its denuded grounds for two decades. All this happened within two years, so that now there is no evidence, except for a slight undulation of the ground, that the Place stood on this particular spot, or that a family, whose history extended over six centuries, had ever made its mark on this hard and indomitable landscape. Occasionally, as men dig in the gardens of the new houses, they unearth fragments of carved stone. These they stack to one side against the low fences, or use to decorate their rockeries.

More about Penguins
and Pelicans

Penguinews, which appears every month, contains
details of all the new books issued by Penguins as
they are published. From time to time it is
supplemented by the *Penguin Stock List*, which is
our complete list of almost 5,000 titles.
A specimen copy of *Penguinews* will be sent to you
free on request. Please write to Dept EP, Penguin
Books Ltd, Harmondsworth, Middlesex, for your
copy.

In the U.S.A.: For a complete list of books
available from Penguins in the United States write
to Dept CS, Penguin Books, 625 Madison Avenue,
New York, New York 10022.

In Canada: For a complete list of books available
from Penguins in Canada write to Penguin Books
Canada Ltd, 2801 John Street, Markham, Ontario
L3R 1B4.

Other Penguins by David Storey

THIS SPORTING LIFE

This is an exceptional first novel in these days, because the characters are concerned with expressing themselves in physical, not emotional or intellectual, terms.

The world in which the story is set is that of professional Rugby League football in an industrial northern city. It covers several years in the life of the narrator, Arthur Machin, from the day of his inclusion in the local team to the match when he begins to feel age creeping up on him and his feet failing. David Storey recounts the fortunes of his gladiator hero with little sentimentality and with all the harsh reality of grime, mud, sweat, intrigue, and naked ambition.

FLIGHT INTO CAMDEN

Acclaimed as a remarkable young writer for his first novel, *This Sporting Life*, David Storey was awarded the 1961 John Llewellyn Rhys Memorial Prize for *Flight into Camden*.

This moving story is recounted by Margaret, the daughter of a Yorkshire miner, who falls in love with a married teacher and goes to live with him in a room in Camden Town, London.

'A love story written with seriousness, sensibility, and intensity' – *Observer*